Anointed

WE WILL BURN FOR THIS

CHARITY B

Editor: Joanne LaRe Thompson
Proofreader: Kim BookJunkie
Formatting: Champagne Book Design
Cover Design: Jay Aheer, Simply Defined Art

AUTHOR'S NOTE

As an independent author, your ratings and especially reviews mean more to me than you realize. If you enjoy the book, please consider lending your supports by leaving your thoughts in a review.

I can't begin to tell you how much it means to me that you have chosen to read this book. This is a full-length, standalone novel. The religious group in this book is not based on any real religion or church and is completely fictional. Your support means everything to me. This book is very personal, and I adored writing it. I hope you love this story as much as I do.

Trigger Warning
This novel contains disturbing scenes and sensitive subject matter that may be triggering to some readers.

Dedication

For Oliver.
May you always follow your heart.
I love you more than anything else on this earth.

Where there is love there is no sin.

—Unknown

1

BLOOD OF INNOCENCE

Laurel Ann

"**V**ERY GOOD, CLASS! CAN ANYONE TELL ME WHAT YEAR AND in what form Zaaron appeared to the human vessel?"

Locks of blonde curls are poking out of the back of Sister Madeline Adams' bonnet, sticking to her neck from sweat. Looking at it intensifies the feeling of my own wet forehead, so I wipe it with the ruffle-trimmed cuff on my sleeve. Philistines may have to suffer a pain more terrible than our human minds can process, but at least they're allowed to show their arms in the summer time.

Since we older kids can answer most of these questions in our sleep, we don't usually participate in the closing lesson which, in truth, is just a recap of things we've heard endless times. I look over at Zebadiah Fitch who's about to fall asleep. He's slouched down at his desk, his chin nearly touching his chest. His hair, the color of warm caramel, is messy from him ruffling it and sticks out from the back of his head. I know Sister Madeline sees him, so I try to find something to throw at him.

While I've known Zeb my entire life, it wasn't until my Pa's binding to his fourth wife, Sister Mary, four years ago that he became my closest friend. I was picking wildflowers for my crown with my older sister Clary. He walked over to me with a shy smile as he held out a bouquet of yellow and white flowers.

"I thought they would look pretty in your hair," he had said.

The memory still pulls my lips into a smile. My little sister raises her hand, her long braids hanging down the back of her dress. Sister Madeline smiles at her. "Mia Henderson?"

Although her voice is kind, it's extremely loud, startling Zebadiah and causing him to jump in surprise. I snicker at him. Everything he does is so...adorable. When he looks up to find me staring at him, he grins. My heart beats fast in my chest, and it makes my stomach feel kind of twisted in a good way.

"In 1906, Zaaron appeared to the human vessel as an ox," Mia confidently answers without hesitation. I'm really proud of her. She's a lot smarter than I was at six.

"Correct. Very good!" Sister Madeline scrapes the blackboard with chalk, writing Mia's response. "In the thirty-sixth chapter of *The True Testament*, Zaaron prepares us for the Abolition. Does anyone know what this is and when it will take place?"

Serah Johnson, one of Mia's best friends, reaches her hand high in the air, using the other one to push it up as if it will lift it higher. Sister Madeline smirks, gesturing for her to answer. "Serah Johnson?"

"On May 5, 2055, Zaaron will set the world on fire, bringing us home to the Paradise Star and sending the Philistines to the abyss to suffer for eternity," Serah responds quickly in her cute, squeaky voice.

With a kind smile, Sister Madeline turns to the blackboard.

"That's exactly right."

The large, iron bell rings, sending vibrations down my arm to my fingers holding the pencil. My stomach lurches with excitement as every kid in the large classroom scurries to gather their books and papers. Everyone is more than ready to be out of this hot, stuffy schoolhouse.

"Don't forget, you must memorize 12:7 and 8 of *The True Testament!*" Sister Madeline calls, "Everyone have a blessed evening. May the holy fire of Zaaron cleanse you!"

"MAY THE HOLY FIRE OF ZAARON CLEANSE YOU, SISTER MADELINE."

We all say it, though half the kids have one foot out the door. I shove the books I need under my arm and toss the rest into my desk. I look around for Zebadiah, finding him waving at me impatiently by the open door.

Running between the desks, I rush outside to join him, where the fresh Oklahoma air fills my chest. Even with the sun burning down on us, it cools my skin from being inside for the last four hours.

Jogging backward, he hollers, "Hurry up, Laur! Last one there is leech bait!"

I laugh and chase the dirt cloud he kicks up as he runs past the tabernacle. I want to yell at him to slow down, but it will take too much of my breath if I want to catch up. He's already faster than I am, plus he got a head start. He turns right, and I'm still far behind, chasing him past the various homes of the followers. We reach the tree line, and he disappears. Since I know the way, I won't get lost, I'm just not going to beat him to the creek. I don't see him again until I break through the trees.

He turns and sees me. "Come on! I still have a ton of chores I have to do before my father gets home!"

His light brown hair disappears over the hill as I clutch my books in one hand and the floral printed fabric of my dress in the other to keep from tripping.

"Easy for you to say! You don't have to run in this dumb, heavy dress."

The wind is loud and strong, whipping the strings of my bonnet against my face, so I don't know if he hears me. Besides, it's his own fault he didn't finish his chores this morning. I was able to get mine done, and he has way more brothers and sisters to help.

When I finally reach him, he's yanking down his suspenders. He discards his boots in the sand and grins at me.

"The water is going to feel amazing. I bet it's over a hundred degrees out today."

He's not exaggerating. I was sweating into the washing bucket this morning, and that was at sunrise. I untie my bonnet and yank the strings loose on my shoes.

"Yeah, Sister Mary has been complaining about it all week."

Sister Mary is due any day now to have my new brother or sister. The heat has made her even more difficult to get along with than normal, and believe me, that's saying something.

He pushes off his trousers, tossing them next to his shoes. Standing there in only his short-sleeved union suit, he waits for me.

Although we have done this very thing a ton of times, it's still a sin to see each other like this.

"Turn around. I'm going to take off my dress."

He snorts, running toward the water. "Just hurry, I only have an hour."

My fingers pop open enough of the buttons to slip my dress over my head before I push my petticoat down, leaving me only in my bloomers and corset cover. Zebadiah is already swimming when I run down the bank. The cool water instantly gives me relief as it climbs higher up my body the further I walk.

"Are you going to Benji Johnson's soul cleansing tonight?" I ask him.

While My pa has always preferred that I go, he's never forced me, until now. Last night the Prophet's Apostle, Keaton Fitch, came by to announce that Benji's cleansing would be tonight. Once he left, my pa told me my attendance would be mandatory.

I despise going to soul cleansings, though my feelings on the matter are irrelevant. He is my father, and it's my duty to honor and obey him. I've just always thought it was cruel to gawk at someone getting publicly beaten. It may be what Zaaron requires for their soul, but He doesn't require us to watch.

"When your father is the Prophet, you don't get much choice," he scoffs.

He's been struggling with Hiram becoming the Prophet. Zeb's grandfather, Josiah Fitch, died a year ago, and *The True Testament* states the eldest son in the holy bloodline is to be the next Prophet. That's Hiram.

"Will you stand with me?" I ask.

He splashes me, and he laughs at my insincere glare. "Of course. I thought that was obvious."

I smile at him, and his eyes flip to my chest before smirking back at me. My face gets hot, so I wipe my wet hands across my cheeks.

"How did Benji even get a Devil's box, anyway?"

"Heck if I know. He's always sneaking out to explore around the edge of the compound. I'm surprised he wasn't caught sooner." He shrugs. "A Philistine must have dropped it and he found it."

The world outside the protection of the Anointed Land

is full of evil and sinners. They pray to their science and technology instead of to Zaaron. The Devil resides inside of them and their trinkets, numbing their sense of morality and humanity. They are driven by violence, greed, and pride. There's only one thing to do when coming across a Philistine, and that's run.

"I just don't understand what would make him touch that thing, let alone bring it home with him."

He raises an eyebrow. "Are you really surprised? His own mother *chose* to leave and live with those perverse demons."

Since Zeb is two years older than me, he remembers it better than I do, though I've heard the story about how Benji's mother was possessed by the Devil. She refused the tomb of abolishment, choosing to spend the remainder of her days with the heathens in the secular world.

"Do you think Benji can get possessed by the Devil's box?"

His hair is dripping water down his face and he shakes his head to clear it away. "I don't know. My father won't talk to me about it."

Benji knew what he was doing was wrong, so I suppose he deserves the lashings. He's still my friend. I don't want to watch it.

At least Zeb will be there.

We skip rocks as we lie on the bank to dry our underclothes. Eventually, he sighs and looks to the blackbirds flying across the sky.

"I need to go. If anyone needs to use the oven I'll be in big trouble. I never chopped wood this morning."

We stand, and I brush the sand off the back of my bloomers, turning to put on my dress.

"If you would have gotten up earlier and chopped the wood before school, you wouldn't have to worry about it." His face falls and his eyebrows scrunch up. I can't tell if he's mad or I hurt his feelings. He's not usually so sensitive. "I'm just joking with you, you know."

Is he going to cry?

"Laurel Ann…you're…" He points to my hand. "The blood of innocence."

I know what he means, yet it isn't until I see the red on my hand that I realize it's happening to me.

No…

Terror wraps around me like a wool blanket, making the heat unbearable. I want to cry. I can't breathe! Why am I feeling this? This is a blessing from my God. This is my purpose. I should be excited, not petrified.

This is the end of my childhood, my life as I know it. Now, I will be placed and bound. Tears burn my eyes when I think of how I will be expected to bear my future husband's many children. Who will that be? I'm meant to find companionship and friendship with my sister-wives while finding fulfillment in the family we prepare for the Paradise Star. It's supposed to be a pivotal, righteous point in my life, so why do I want to drop to my knees and purge the contents of my stomach? This is what Zaaron prophesied for us. This is what He wants. It's a sin to simply be thinking these ungrateful thoughts. I should want to run home and tell my family of this joyous news, yet all I want to do is figure out how to make it stop.

I'm not ready.

Zebadiah's chest is lifting and dropping fast, and his breaths are short and clipped. Suddenly, he walks past me to the pile of my clothes. Lifting my petticoat, he curses at the apparent scarlet spot on the back. "Damn it." He drops it on the bank to pick up my dress, turning it inside out to inspect it.

My voice is as shaky as I am. "Wh-what are you doing?"

"Your dress is still clean. We just need to get rid of everything else with blood on it. You have to keep this a secret."

"That's a sin."

His jaw twitches, his fist clenching the fabric of my dress. "So, you're ready for this, Laur? To lay with a man as his wife? To obey him in all things and bear him as many children as Zaaron will bless you with?" My eyes burn. His voice holds the fear that I feel. "You always talk about it like it's some far away life, but it's here, now. It's happening. Are you prepared for it?" I am shaking my head before I realize it, and my heart is crying in relief for his understanding in this. He reaches down for his socks, handing them to me. "Here, use these until you can get home and figure something else out."

I take them, along with my dress, and hide behind a bush to take off my bloomers. Tying one sock around my waist, I place the other one between my legs, tying both ends to the first. I bundle up the bloody linens, put on my dress, and meet him back at the bank.

This is really embarrassing, but the alternative has come too soon. He takes the soiled underclothes, bunching them up with my petticoat. Handing me my books, he says, "Go home and act normal. I'll get rid of these. Ride it out for a couple of days, and then we'll have more time to figure this out."

A jolt of fear runs up my body, forcing the tears to rim my eyes. I put my bonnet over my damp hair. "What if…what if we don't make it to the Paradise Star because of this?"

He frowns and shakes his head. "We can't think about that right now. Just get home before you bleed through the socks."

He's risking his very soul to protect me. While he's done some amazing things for me these last few years, he has never broken spiritual law for me.

He's taller than I am, so I have to stand on the tips of my toes to hug his neck.

"Thank you, Zeb," I whisper.

I quickly kiss his cheek before I turn to run home.

2

SOUL CLEANSING RITUAL

Laurel Ann

WHEN LIVING WITH FIVE MOTHERS, A FATHER, AND EIGHTEEN siblings, privacy is a myth. At least it's still early in the day, so my father, my uncles, and my brother, Benjamin Jr., will still be working the fields. My family runs the largest farm on the compound. We're primarily responsible for making sure there's enough food to eat and sell. My father and uncles are in charge, and one day, my brothers will be.

Sister Mary will be resting. For the last month of pregnancy, women are only required to do their chores in the morning. It's unnecessary to add extra strain to the wonderful gift Zaaron is bestowing upon us.

Everyone else in my family should still be working outside, save Sister Esther, my father's most recent wife. She's one year older than me and will likely be in the house with my youngest siblings.

My uncles have fifty-four wives between them. Many of them help my mothers on the farm, and the rest remain at their own homes to care for children and make sure their houses stay pure and clean.

As I run down the dirt road that leads to our farm, I wave to the dark forms in the distance, though from this far, I can't tell who they are.

"Hello, Laurel Ann! Did you have a good day at your lessons?"

I turn to see my Aunt Ethel carrying a large basket of grains. I have no idea if Zeb's socks are doing the trick, and I really need to get inside. Usually I enjoy the conversation of my family, so if I show my urgency I may raise suspicion, but if she sees the blood of innocence, it won't matter anyway.

I tap my books. "I did, although Sister Madeline gave us a lot of homework. I must get studying."

It's a lie, and everyone knows lying is a sin, however, it's a very small lie compared to the one I'm attempting to cover.

"Aren't you such a good girl? I wish I could get my Lana to be so eager to do her studies!"

Guilt crushes my lungs. I smile and stand there for as long as seems polite before I turn to run up the wooden steps leading to our white farmhouse. I stay quiet as I open the screen door and push against the wooden one. Poking my head inside, I check to see if anyone is in the kitchen.

Darn it! My brothers, Robert and Samuel, are drinking milk at the table. I try to look behind me, pulling my dress out to see if I can spot any blood. There is none from what I can tell. Sliding inside, I grab an apple from the bowl while Robert raises his eyebrows at me.

"Sister Mary was looking for you."

I attempt to hide my irritation by taking a bite of the apple, but his chuckle tells me I didn't succeed. I'm not the only one she drives crazy.

"All right, I'll go find her, just don't tell her I'm home yet if you see her first."

Sam grins at me and signs, *Why? Where have you been? I*

bet Robert and Doyle tomorrow morning's chores that you were with Zebadiah Fitch.

Samuel is mute. He has never spoken a single word. I don't know why because he can hear fine. Doc Kilmer has no explanation for it, and Zaaron hasn't felt it necessary to inform the Prophet.

I roll my eyes at him. "So? What if I was? He's my friend."

Robert groans, "Ah, man! You know it's not right, you spending that much time with a boy. Your friends should be girls. Now I have to get up extra early tomorrow."

He is my elder brother, and I know I must respect him. Regardless, my friends can be whoever I choose them to be.

I am about to tell him as much when Sam signs to me, obviously proud of himself. *He's just mad because now he has to clean the stables again.*

I love that he never ceases to make me smile, even when I'm feeling as anxious as I am right now.

"Zaaron never said it was a sin to be friends with a boy as long as our thoughts and actions remain pure. And they have" —for the most part— "so I don't feel sorry for you because do you know what *is* a sin? Gambling."

I take another bite of my apple before spinning on my heel to push open the kitchen door and march out when Robert adds, "Mother told me to tell you that your dress for the soul cleansing is in her bedroom."

"Thank you," I snap at him. It's none of his business who I am friends with. He is not my Prophet, my husband, or my father.

Walking past the living room and down the right hall, I head to the bedroom I share with Mia. There are twenty-four of us and only fifteen rooms, requiring us all to share besides my mothers.

I breathe a relieved sigh to find my room empty, the sound of the children playing outside floating through the open window. I walk across the wooden floor to look out the space between the billowing curtains. Sister Esther pushes little Phillip on the rope swing, while she bounces baby Paul on her hip. She seems much older than her fourteen years, and her maturity must be attractive to my father because he spends a large amount of nights with her. I smile as I finish my apple. I'm pleased Zaaron wanted her in my family. She was always nice to me at school and has been even kinder since becoming my fifth mother. Not to mention, she's great with the small children, which is also a blessing, because Sister Mary seems to always be yelling when she watches them.

I need to get changed before it's time to start making dinner and I run into anyone else. I throw my apple core in the wastebasket as I take a clean dress and petticoat from the closet. Opening my drawers, I remove a fresh pair of bloomers. I realize I don't know what I should use to stop the blood, so I pick out the thickest pair of stockings I have.

I hurry down the hall, luck allowing me to slide into the washroom unseen. As soon as I close the door, I fall against it and breathe. I made it.

We aren't allowed to lock doors though no one will bother me with it closed. The dress still doesn't have blood on it which leaves Zebadiah's socks to get rid of. I pump the handle up and down, retrieving just enough water to clean myself before I tie the first stocking around my waist. Taking the toilet paper, I wrap it around the second stocking many times. This is being wasteful—another sin. Once I feel I have enough to protect me, I fasten the stocking to the first one, like I did with Zeb's socks.

One day, I will beg Zaaron's forgiveness, and I promise I'll tell the Prophet what I did, but I'm not prepared to be bound. I want to stay with my family, keep going to school, and continue having fun with Zebadiah. I don't want to have a baby yet.

I've seen a ton of babies being born, and each time it's a little different besides one thing: the pain. It looks to me like it hurts something awful. Really, how could it not? Imagine trying to push a pea through the eye of a needle.

I secure my clean dress over my fresh petticoat and look at Zeb's bloody socks. What to do... Hmm... I could hide them in my room and try to scrub out the stain the next time it's my turn to do the washing. However, if I can't get the stain out, I will be in the same position I am now. I could hide them under my dress and take them to the waste site tomorrow before school...

Yes. That's what I'll do. Once they are there, even if someone finds them, they won't know who they belong to.

I add some water to the bottom of my shoes, turning the dirt into mud, and wipe them on my other dress. Wrapping it around the bloodied socks to conceal them, I rush back into the hall, and just as I am about to be safe inside my room, I hear Sister Mary's cringe-inducing, high pitched voice.

"Laurel Ann, I've been looking for you."

I blow the air out of my nose and plaster on a respectful smile before turning to her. "Hello, Sister Mary. How are you feeling?" If it's anything like the way she looks, then I'm guessing she feels about to fall over.

"I would be a lot better if you would get Bridget's spit up out of my dresses. The washing was one of your chores this morning."

I refrain from huffing. I scrubbed the heck out of those stains. "Yes, ma'am, I apologize. I will pay more attention from now on."

She squints as she looks at my hands. "Isn't that the dress you had on this morning? Why are you wearing two dresses in the same day?"

Pleased with myself for thinking of it, I show her the mud stain from my shoe. "I tripped and got it muddy."

Lies beget lies.

I swallow as her attention is swept back to herself and she fans her face. "If you continue to be careless, then you can count on double washing duty."

"Yes, ma'am."

She turns on her heel and wobbles down the hall. I just want to get these socks hidden. Tomorrow cannot come fast enough.

I open my bedroom door, almost crying when I see Mia sitting on her bed reading *The True Testament*.

"Hey, Mia. You were really good in class today."

Her face brightens every time I compliment her. It almost makes me feel guilty for having an ulterior motive for it today.

"Thank you. I've been studying really hard."

"I know you have. I'm proud of you."

I try to be casual as I set the bundle of clothes on the bed and look in the closet for somewhere to conceal Zeb's socks.

"What are you looking for?"

"Um…a box or something."

She holds up her pointer finger, jumping on her knees, before she flips over the edge of her bed to look under it. "I might have something."

Rustling and clanging noises come from where she searches, and it sounds like a pig sty down there. It's not my problem. My responsibility is my side of the room.

"Here. Kelsey Garret, Serah Johnson, and I use this to carry the wildflowers for our crowns. I can carry them in my apron until I find something else."

She holds out a blue box while I smile at her. She's a good sister. It's always been in her nature to be kind, generous, and compassionate.

"Thank you. This is perfect. I'll return it to you as soon as I can, okay?"

She grins and nods before plopping down on her bed. Putting

my back to her, I try to hide my tucking the socks inside the box when her voice squeaks out, "What are you doing?"

I sigh and turn to her. "I can't tell you. It's a secret."

She scrunches her face like she does when she thinks really hard. "Isn't a secret like lying?"

She's absolutely right, a secret is the same as lying. I just don't want to pull her into this too. "I'm sorry, Mia...I can't tell you."

Her face is so heartbreaking. Her eyes get watery, and her lip quivers as she tries to keep from crying. "Oh...okay."

I groan. I have no idea how she's going to react to this. "All right, fine. Are you sure you want to know? Because you can't tell anyone."

She nods, scooting to the edge of the bed. "Uh-huh. I won't tell. I promise."

Lying down next to her, I look at the cracked ceiling. "The blood of innocence came to me today."

She gasps, jumping up on all fours, her oak colored braids dangling as she leans over me. "Really?! Who do you think you will be placed with? Oh, I hope your first baby is a girl!" Her excitement is what I should be feeling, and I am envious of her for it. Her face falls into a frown as she suddenly remembers this is a secret. "Wait...you aren't going to tell?! Laurel Ann, that's a sin! A big one!"

"And that's why I didn't want to tell you. I don't know why I'm not overcome with joy, but I'm not. I'm scared. I'm not ready to be placed. I know you probably don't understand and think I am being selfish, because I am...I just can't do it yet."

She chews on her lip, thinking for a moment before she lies down next to me to rest her head on my chest. "I won't tell anyone. I promise."

"Thank you, Mia." I kiss her and get up to finish hiding the box under my bed. "I need to go get my dress."

She smiles as I leave to walk down the hall to my mother's

room. I knock on her door and push it open. She's sitting at her vanity pinning up her light, strawberry hair, which is the exact same color as mine, into a bun.

She looks into the mirror, her beautiful smile lighting up when she sees me. "Hello, sweetheart. Did you have a blessed day?"

Well, it really depends on how you look at it... "I did, Mother, thank you. Robert said my dress was in here?"

Securing the last tendril, she stands and says, "Oh, yes. Here you are." The dress is pale green with lace along the hem. "Wear your best shoes tonight, all right?"

I nod, and she sighs while her thumb rubs my cheek. "I know you and Benji are close, but he has endangered us all by bringing evil into the Anointed Land. You understand he needs to atone, don't you?"

"Yes, Mother."

She softly smiles. "Good girl, now go help your mothers start supper. I'll be there shortly."

I take my dress to my room to see Mia is gone. She must already be in the kitchen. Making my way back to the front of the house, I find Sister Lydia peeling potatoes.

"Hello, Laurel Ann. Have you seen Hope and Faith?"

I pump some water in the basin to wash my hands. Like anyone can keep track of those two. "No, ma'am, not since school let out."

She points to the porch. "All right then, there's a bucket of corn needing to be shucked."

"Yes, ma'am."

Once the corn is finished, I bring it inside to see the twins, Hope and Faith, setting the large table. I hand the basket to Sister Julia.

"Thank you, Laurel Ann. The girls are nearly finished, and Mia is getting the vegetables from the garden, so why don't you start boiling water."

Just then, my elder sister, Clary, walks in. While she's lived in the placing dorms since receiving the blood of innocence four months ago, she still joins the family at dinners and community events until she gets placed.

"Clary!" The twins squeal as they run to hug her.

She laughs and pulls an apron over her head. "I've missed you too."

Eventually, all my mothers and sisters are bustling around the large kitchen and dining room, getting dinner ready. My father and brothers barrel inside as the room gets instantly louder.

I love my family. I'm grateful I had the blessing of being raised in the Anointed Land. I am very fortunate to have not been born to Philistines. I often feel bad for the kids who are living around all that evil, hate, and cruelty.

We all hold hands and bow our heads.

Father's strong voice is loud as it fills the kitchen. "Thank you, Zaaron, for the sacrifices you have made for us. We pray our thanks for your time on Earth, teaching us what you desire. We are grateful that when you bring about the Abolition and set this world aflame, we can join you in the Paradise Star. Thank you for blessing us with our Prophet to guide us. May your holy fire cleanse us."

"Truth and purity, Amen," we all say.

My plate is halfway empty when my father raises his hand to quiet the room. We fall silent as he stands.

"Today is a day made by Zaaron, and He has bestowed yet another blessing upon us." He gestures to Sister Esther, taking her hand. "We will be bringing another child into our family and another soul to live with us for eternity."

Everyone claps while they speculate over whether they hope it's a boy or a girl. Not that it matters, we won't know until the birth anyway. I look at Sister Esther. Her cheeks are pushing up against her eyes to trap the tears with her forced smile. I was there when she gave birth to Paul three months ago. It was terrible. She was in labor for almost twenty hours, and there was so much blood. The midwife got nervous and made everyone besides my mothers leave the room.

I doubt she's jumping up and down to do that again. Still, she should feel pride in the price she paid in pain. Without it, we wouldn't have Paul. Yesterday, I would have thought she was being selfish, feeling sorry for herself when she should be rejoicing. That was yesterday. Today, I understand her tears and her fear.

After helping my mothers and sisters clean up, we all go to our rooms to prepare for the soul cleansing. I make sure I change the toilet paper and freshen up my hair before putting on the lovely dress my mother got for me.

Mia watches me get ready. "You look pretty."

She's trying to make me feel better because she knows I don't want to go. When Father starts making her attend, she will hate it just as much as I do.

"Thanks, Mia." I tie the ribbon on my best bonnet and kiss her cheek. "I'll see you tomorrow."

I'm the youngest of my siblings to attend. The twins and my sister, Elizabeth, will stay back to watch the younger children to allow all my mothers to go.

We all walk in our order: Pa, Sister Julia, and my brothers Benjamin Jr., Doyle, and Samuel. Then Sister Lydia, Clary, my mother, Robert, me, Sister Mary, and then lastly, Sister Esther. As we get closer to the tabernacle, we walk through the common ground, and I see Benji Johnson's family. This must be horrible for them. When I was younger, my eldest brothers, Benjamin Jr. and Doyle, both had soul cleansing rituals after they got caught skipping a holy service to play. I don't really remember it, and for that I am grateful.

We all pile into the tabernacle; most of the compound is in attendance. I keep my eyes peeled for Zebadiah when instead, I find Benji bearing the ox yoke. His arms are held up, trapped in the bows, and I cringe at how the wooden beam presses against the base of his neck, forcing him to hunch over.

I finally see Zeb's family walk in, taking their seats at the front as our Prophet, Hiram Fitch, stands at the pulpit. The golden sigil pendant shines from his neck, and his black hat casts a shadow across his face before he takes it off. My father and mothers say they can physically feel the presence of Zaaron coming from him. I think maybe I can too. He's so holy. I love him, and I'm thankful that we have such a wonderful man to lead us as we await the destruction of the planet. The big wooden doors close, and when he holds up his arms, the room falls silent.

"Children of Zaaron, this is not a joyous occasion. We are here because one of us has lost his way." He always pauses at every sentence or two when he speaks, so half the time I find myself wondering if he's finished talking. "He has tainted his soul with evil and must be cleansed of it. Benji Johnson, please come forward."

Benji stands from a pew against the side of the stage, struggling to move with his arms trapped. Ropes fall from the chain rings and drag against the floor on either side of him as he walks with bare feet to the Prophet. His eyes are filled with fear when he turns toward the followers. He should be scared. The soul cleansing ritual is brutal for a reason. Sinning tarnishes our internal light. That's not something easily removed.

The Prophet continues, "You were found in possession of a Devil's box, is that true?"

Benji holds his head up as much as he is able. "Yes, Prophet."

"And you are aware that is a direct violation of spiritual law, given to us by our God?"

"I do."

"Do you desire to have the holy fire of Zaaron cleanse you of this transgression?"

I can see him swallow from here. "Yes, I do."

We all clap because he's making a brave and righteous decision. He has recognized his failure to remain pure in the eyes of Zaaron.

The Prophet places his hat back on his head and lifts the ropes tied to the chain rings, using them to lead Benji like cattle down the aisle between the pews, and back outside.

Filing out of the tabernacle, we gather around the cleansing station at the edge of the common ground. The cleansing station is simply two large, wooden pillars mounted into the dirt, placed roughly five feet apart. There are grooves at the top of each pillar for the ropes to slide through. The small stone altar sits next to the north-facing pillar, holding the flame previously blessed by the Prophet.

I stare into the ember tendrils. It's incredibly beautiful and powerful. It's not just a regular, plain fire. Zaaron and the Prophet are tied together in a sacred bond. The Prophet is not only His direct descendant, but He flows through him, allowing the fire to be blessed, possessing the ability to purify our souls.

I look beyond the flame to see Zeb standing next to his mother. I try to get his attention to make him stand by me like he promised. Finally, he looks up and our eyes meet. I smile at him, yet he turns away. My stomach sinks, feeling hallowed out and empty. What's wrong? Is he angry with me about this afternoon?

The Prophet leads Benji between the pillars, giving the rope on the right to Apostle Keaton and the one on the left to Zeb's uncle, Counselor Cyrus. Both men throw the ropes over each pillar, and pull them tight, lifting Benji's body as high as they can until his feet nearly leave the earth. The Prophet stands behind him, using a blade to cut his shirt open.

"Benji Johnson. Five lashes with the holy fire, and twenty-nine hours in the box of repentance is the price to free your soul from the bonds of the Devil. I ask you again, do you accept this penance?"

Benji lifts his head to look at the crowd. "Yes, I do."

I shift my gaze to the left, glancing at the box of repentance. It's well outside the circle of the common ground and not something I ever want to experience.

The Prophet removes his jacket to hand it to one of his nephews, rolling the sleeves of his shirt to his elbows. He takes down the locust tree whip, named because the thorns from a honey locust tree are burrowed within the leather, and takes his place behind Benji. Our earthly flesh must be broken if it is to be cleansed.

Apostle Keaton dowses the whip in kerosene before the Prophet dips it into the blessed fire. The purpose of the fire is not only to cleanse Benji's soul, but to remind his flesh of the Hellfire that resides in the abyss. Apostle Keaton backs up with the rest of the followers, allowing plenty of room for the strike. The Prophet's shoulders rise with a breath as he swings his arm behind him, landing the flaming whip across Benji's back.

With the impact, his body arches, and he releases a loud cry. The sound blends in with the whole compound praying, "BE CLEANSED OF THIS EVIL!"

I look back at Zebadiah to see his face harden, as he watches his father bring down the whip a second time. My eyes move to Benji's family. Although his father remains unfazed, his mothers look as if they're struggling for strength.

"BE CLEANSED OF THIS SIN!"

Tears roll down Benji's cheeks, glistening in the fire light. Though I can't see, I know the damage the burning whip can do. I'm sure he's bleeding already.

My attention is back on Zeb, and I fight the tears attempting to appear. Why won't he look at me? What's going on?

Three more times the Prophet hits Benji. With the last assault, his wails can easily be heard over the praying.

"THE SPIRIT OF ZAARON WILL BURN FROM WITHIN!"

His head droops and his body sags while Apostle Keaton pours water on the whip, extinguishing the fire. As the fire sizzles, the smoke snakes beneath my nose. The smell of burning has always given me a sense of comfort. Knowing my mistakes can be forgiven through His grace makes me feel secure in my mortality.

The Prophet hands the whip to his nephew. Since it can't be used again, it will now be destroyed. Apostle Keaton and Counselor Cyrus release the ropes, dropping Benji's body to the dirt, his shoulders shaking as he sobs.

Benji is a bit of an odd boy, and that's part of why I've always liked him. I consider him one of my closest friends. Even if he does seem to have an unhealthy curiosity about the Philistines, he's nice to everyone, and he's pretty funny too. I wish I could go lie next to him, tell him it will be okay, and that the worst part is over.

The Prophet pulls him to his feet, leading him, along with the rest of us, to the box of repentance. Besides the occasional whispers, everyone is mostly quiet as we reach the place of Benji's confinement. He groans when the Prophet releases him from the ox yoke.

"You will spend the next twenty-nine hours praying. This time is meant for repenting to Zaaron and thinking on why you broke His spiritual law. Do you have anything you would like to say before we proceed?"

While Benji's voice has a nasally sound, it's still loud enough so everyone can hear. "I made unholy choices. I am sorrowful I let down my family, my community, my Prophet, and my God... I am unworthy of His mercy."

The Prophet climbs the wooden plank, opening the door of the four-by-five-foot wooden shed with no windows, nudging Benji inside. Once the door is securely locked, he holds his hands up again.

"We have not lost a child of Zaaron this night. Benji Johnson has been washed of his sins and transgressions. Let us rejoice in Zaaron's gift of forgiveness. Have a blessed evening, and may the holy fire of Zaaron cleanse you!"

"MAY THE HOLY FIRE OF ZAARON CLEANSE YOU, PROPHET."

Everyone begins to disperse, making their way back to their homes, but I really need to see what's wrong with Zeb. I scan the crowd, finally finding him standing next to his father. I raise my hand to wave though when I do, I realize they are making their way toward me.

My heart beats rapidly against my chest, so I inhale a calming breath. I'm being silly. I'm sure this has nothing to do with this afternoon.

"Prophet." My father shakes his hand. "Zaaron has once again shown His compassion and grace through you."

He nods and removes his hat. "May I have a word, Brother Benjamin?"

"Of course." Pa glances at Sister Julia while I keep my eyes on Zebadiah. I'm starting to really worry now. He won't even look at me.

Pa, the Prophet, and Zebadiah all walk far enough away that I can't hear anything they're saying. After a moment, Pa's head whips toward me, his scowl making a lump grow in my throat. I attempt to swallow it down as they shake hands, and he glares his way back to us.

"Back home. Now. All of you."

He speaks low and angry, making my skin clammy. We hurry back in our order as we try to keep up with him. The closer we get to the farm, the more ill I feel.

We shuffle into the kitchen, and when the door slams behind us, I jump around to see my father stalking toward me.

He points to a chair at the table. "Sit!"

I automatically lower to obey as he towers over me. "You get one chance to answer. Have you received the blood of innocence?"

My tongue folds in my mouth, making it impossible to speak. The dread of what will come of this has me shaking my head in a lie. His nostrils flare as he scratches angrily at his graying mustache, looking at me with a disappointment I have never seen.

"You have disgraced this family in the eyes of our God, our Prophet, and me."

My mother takes his arm. "Benjamin, please. Why would you think she would keep that from us?'

"Are you questioning our Prophet, Grace?"

Her head shakes hard enough that her bonnet strings whip around. "N-no, of course not."

At that moment, there is a *rap, rap, rap* at the door.

I think I might throw up when my father answers and says, "I apologize that this incident requires your assistance this evening, Prophet."

I look up, not knowing if I can stop the tears, when I see Zebadiah holding my stained bloomers and petticoat.

He...told.

He told on *me*.

3

A BLESSED GIFT

Laurel Ann

MY MOTHER BOWS HER HEAD BEFORE SHAKING THE Prophet's hand. "Blessed evening, Prophet."

He clicks his tongue as he removes his hat. "I do wish it was a better one, Sister Grace. It does not give me joy to punish," he turns to me, "but it is the task bestowed upon me by our God, Zaaron."

My mother nods, backing away to give him room. Everyone is watching, and I'm sure at least a few of my younger siblings have snuck out of bed to hear what's happening.

The Prophet walks over to me to take my hand. "Stand, my child." Even with my legs feeling too weak to support me, I wouldn't dream of disobeying. He reaches behind him with his free hand. "Come over here, Zebadiah. Show Brother Benjamin what you were attempting to dispose of this afternoon." Zeb still won't look at me as he hands my bloomers and petticoat to my father. The Prophet asks, "Are these Laurel Ann's?"

I don't think my father really knows if they are mine because he looks at my mothers. Sister Mary and my mother both nod in answer.

I close my eyes as if it will hold off what's coming, yet the Prophet's voice forces them back open. He takes my garments back from Pa and holds them out to me. Everyone handling them is humiliating. I want nothing more than to flee this room.

"Are these yours, Laurel Ann?"

I can't make myself say yes. I want to, I just can't. I don't want to lie, especially to the Prophet! My heart hammers against my chest as I take a deep breath.

"No, Prophet."

His lips thin out with his glare. "I will ask you once more. Are these yours?"

I pray for strength to do what is right. To be honest.

Please Zaaron, I want to be pure, I want to be good. Help me be a holy example of your truth.

I wait, and I still can't say the words.

The *N* is on my lips as Mia bursts into the kitchen. Every wisp of air is sucked out of my lungs when I see her holding the box she gave me earlier.

"Just tell them the truth, Laurel Ann…please?"

I know she thinks she's doing the right thing. In fact, she is. That still doesn't change how angry I am with her in this moment. I want to scream and yell at her, tell her I won't ever trust her again! She has never betrayed me before, and I have never felt this fury toward her.

The Prophet crouches down to one knee, holding his hand out to her. "Bring me the box, my child."

Her eyes flash to Pa then to me before she slowly walks across the kitchen. I can't look at their faces, so I watch the hem of her nightgown swing around her ankles as her bare feet walk across the floorboards. The Prophet opens the box, his eyes searing into me after he shoves my bloomers and petticoat inside.

I quickly flip my eyes to Zebadiah. He's finally looking at me too. His eyes are deeply sad and wet with tears. He's either trying to tell me that he's sorry or to forgive him. Maybe both. He just got caught…like I'm getting caught right now. He didn't tell, not like Mia. I give him the slightest nod I can.

"Laurel Ann." I snap my attention back to the Prophet to see him holding the box under his arm. "These are serious transgressions against Zaaron." His face becomes stone, and I think his eyes darken as he seethes, "He has bestowed upon you a gift! Why do you repay Him with evil and selfish actions?"

He's right. Why did I do this?

I know why. Because I'm not ready, because…

"I-I'm scared."

"Your fear is misplaced, child. You should fear the condition of your soul. I will not allow impurity within the walls of the Anointed Land. You should fear all the evil in the world outside the protection of this compound."

He wouldn't send me out there, would he? He and other members of the holy bloodline are the only ones permitted to brave the dark, new world since before my father was a boy. If anyone knows how bad it is out there, it's the Prophet. He's threatening to cast me away without my family, without my friends, without Zaaron, and without Zeb. I can't let that happen.

Excommunication is not an option.

I nod my head as fast as I can. "Yes, Prophet. I want to do whatever it takes to be pure again. I yearn for forgiveness. From you and from Zaaron."

Suddenly, he closes his eyes, turning his head to the ceiling. He stands that way for a long time. I've seen him do this before. He's speaking to Zaaron. Everyone in the holy bloodline is kin to our God, but only the Prophet can audibly hear His voice.

After what feels like an eternity, he lets out a long slow breath and murmurs, "Thank you." Opening his eyes, he looks into me. "I know what must be done to rid your soul of this evil." He turns to my father. "There is no need for her to live in the placing dorms."

Pa tilts his head to the side. "I apologize, Prophet, I don't understand. Why?"

He looks back at me, and when he smiles, I don't feel the comfort I should feel from my Prophet.

"Because she has already been placed."

For a second it feels as if I'm falling backward. It's like I'm not breathing, regardless of my chest beginning to heave. There's nothing I can do. This is Zaaron's will. If I want to remain in His grace and protection, I must honor it.

Clasping his hands together, my father cries, "Praise Zaaron!" Sister Mary is equally thrilled. My mother though, she doesn't look happy or sad. She is a statue of herself.

My father rarely smiles, and if he does, it's subtle. Right now, he's grinning like little Phillip did when he got into the bowl of icing Sister Mary left on the counter last summer. "This is fantastic news! May I ask who is to be her husband?"

A soft, small smile creaks from the Prophet's lips. "I am."

WHAT?!

Zeb's face falls in horror as he jumps toward him. "Father!" The Prophet glares, stopping him cold. He drops his voice to a whisper, slowly shaking his head. "No, please…"

"You have served your purpose here. Go home to wait for me. You and I also have much we must discuss."

They stare at each other until finally Zeb mumbles, "Yes, Father."

He walks to the door, turning to me one last time before

walking out. This can't be happening! Why would Zaaron want this? Zebadiah is my closest friend. I can't be his mother! I look over at Mia, and I hate her for this. I rationally know it isn't her fault, but I may have been able to lie my way out of it otherwise.

Tears begin to form in her eyes, the ribbons used to curl her hair bouncing as she rushes to me. "Laurel Ann—"

"Thank you for your honesty, Mia. It's time for you to be in bed." Pa pats her head and slightly raises his voice. "The same goes for the rest of you hiding in the hallway, listening!"

Sure enough, a bunch of little giggles and foot patters sound.

The Prophet chuckles, "The joys of children." He gives me a quick glance and adds, "It breaks my heart when they disappoint us." I hate having to listen to them talk about me when I am sitting right here. "Before Laurel Ann can come into my home and bear my holy children, her soul must be cleansed."

My father listens to the Prophet as if he's terrified to miss a single word, nodding his head in full agreement.

"Of course."

In a quick motion, the Prophet pulls on his right ear and wipes his mouth before he says, "Her cleansing ritual will take place at six p.m., Wednesday evening. As you know, during the time of questioning, she is not permitted to leave this house." He stands next to me, placing his hand on my shoulder. "Our union will protect her eternal existence. She has clearly been tempted by the Devil, yet my holy influence will help her to remain pure. We will hold the binding celebration Saturday afternoon, following services."

I don't care about the soul cleansing ritual. All I can think about is Saturday. Saturday is when everything will change. It doesn't matter what I, Mia, or anyone else did or didn't do.

Because Zaaron's will is impenetrable.

"While I am ashamed by the actions of my daughter, this is still such glorious news. I am grateful to you and to Zaaron for your overwhelming forgiveness and kindness. Thank you, Prophet."

The Prophet flicks his wrist to toss away my father's words. "It is my blessing and purpose."

His hand slides off my shoulder, his fingers sending a cold shudder through my skin as he slowly moves them down my back. He steps away, leaving me with my stomach turned to sludge as it rolls around, climbing its way to my chest. I slowly breathe in through my nose, so I don't vomit in front of the Prophet.

He turns to my mothers. "Have a blessed evening, Sisters."

They all nod as they mutually respond, "Have a blessed evening, Prophet."

He shakes my father's hand. "His plan burns through all evil, Brother Benjamin. Have a blessed evening." He walks to the door, carrying the box with the last of my childhood as he faces us. "May the holy fire of Zaaron cleanse you."

"May the holy fire of Zaaron cleanse you, Prophet." I say it with them because I know my father is watching.

As soon as he walks out of my house, the air instantly weighs a thousand pounds, requiring all my strength to remain upright. My father's face, which moments ago was soft and understanding, is now pressed into hard lines. His rage pours from his eyes as he marches toward me, ripping his belt from his trousers.

My mother rushes to stand in front of him. "Benjamin, please, this isn't necessary. She will pay her penance at her cleansing. And now we have a daughter who will give birth to children in the holy bloodline."

I love my mother so much for trying to save me. Having a

person of your family be bound to someone in the holy bloodline is a high honor, but having a daughter that will birth the Prophet's children? It's the most any family could hope for. She's reminding him of that.

He ignores her as he folds the belt in half. His eyes are on me, and while every single part of me wants to run, my feet are melted into the floor.

"I did not raise you to lie and hide from your calling as a woman of Zaaron. You have outright disobeyed Him, your Prophet, and me. You will pay for your sins against our God and the Prophet with your cleansing, and now you will suffer for your sins against me."

He grabs me by my dress collar to turn me around, and shove me to my knees. I know what's coming. This isn't the first transgression I've committed against Zaaron and my family. Still, the eruption of pain from the impact makes me cry out. He is very angry, so there isn't any relief of time between blows.

Shoulder.

Neck.

Waist.

Back.

The intense sharpness shoots through me, the volume of my screams is the only way I can tell the individual hits apart.

My mother is crying, begging him to stop, yet it's like I'm hearing her through a window…far away and small. Finally, the intense bolts of agony disappear, and all that's left is a dull radiation of pain spreading across my back. His heavy footfalls are loud, and although I can't lift my head to look at his face, I am able to see his boots.

"You are no longer my concern."

My cheeks are hot and wet with tears as I allow myself to lie down, sobbing against the floorboards.

Tender hands hold my arms, pulling me up. "Come on, Laurel Ann, sweetie. You need to get up. Let's get you to bed." My mother helps me to my feet as I look up to see Sister Mary forcing a frown. She's probably thrilled I'm almost gone. Sister Esther and Sister Lydia look at me with pity, and Sister Julia doesn't look at me at all. My mother leads me down the hall to the washroom where she opens the cabinet to pull out a box and an odd belt. She removes a thick white cotton pad from the box and hands it to me.

"Place it inside the belt, and change it every few hours while you have your blood."

With my eyes still wet from tears, I nod as she leaves me to it. Once I finish, I follow her to my room where Mia is sleeping. The moonlight allows us to see enough for her to help me out of my dress, and I bite my lip to stop the tears when I lift my arms. She removes my bonnet, taking the pins out of my hair to let it fall in waves down my back. I hold on to her shoulder as she takes off my shoes, stockings, petticoat, and bloomers. I wince in pain, though I don't make any noise. She quietly opens the dresser to remove a nightgown, gently gliding it over my head and arms. Giving me a sad smile, she takes my hand, sitting me down at my vanity. She slowly brushes my hair, and it's so still and quiet that when she speaks, I jump.

"I do remember how scary this was for me. I didn't know your father other than in passing, and I didn't want to leave my family. But that's what Zaaron wants to teach us, to be selfless for the good of everyone. Our emotions and feelings are miniscule in comparison to the bigger picture. We need to remain pure so we can make it to the Paradise Star together and spend eternity in Zaaron's love. You will get through this, Laurel Ann. And one day, you will be grateful for it."

I feel her finger sectioning off my hair as she puts it into a braid. "Pa hates me now."

She sighs. "He doesn't hate you. He loves you, and it terrifies him that someone he loves won't spend eternity with us. That's why he is angry. He's furious that you would risk that. Risk your soul."

"Yes, Mother."

She smiles at me in the mirror and kisses the top of my head. "Good night, my darling. Go to bed."

My bare feet slide between the sheets as she leaves the room. I roll over to face the wall.

"Laurel Ann?" Mia whispers. I don't know what to say to her. Too tired to hear her apology, I say nothing. There is silence for a long while until she says, "I'm sorry. I just don't want you to go to Hell."

I'm angry, sad, and scared. I look at the old, ripped, floral wallpaper on my wall. This is it. This is the last night I will sleep in my bed. This is my last night in my home.

This is my last night free.

4

THE PROPHET'S SON

Zebadiah

THE TEARS ARE LIKE FIRE, SO I PRESS MY PALMS TO MY EYES until spots sprinkle my vision. He's doing this to hurt me. I don't think Zaaron told him shit about Laurel Ann. I think he's trying to punish me for assisting her in breaking spiritual law.

I knew it was wrong from the moment I suggested it. I just couldn't sit by and let it happen to her. The terror on her face when she saw the blood of innocence put a physical heaviness on my chest. It seeped into my skin to pull out my own fears.

With the thousands of prayers I've prayed, I truly thought she would be my wife someday. I thought I could feel it. Now every hope of that is crashing down.

It's true, I helped her to not only protect her, but to protect myself. I can't handle the thought of her laying with someone else. Her little belly becoming round with child. The mental image of her body being touched and infiltrated by my father claws my mind to shreds.

I kick the dirt, cursing that I was born to the Prophet. Though I know I should be grateful to be a member of my holy family, we don't feel holy. My father is cruel, my mothers are weak, and most of my siblings are liars. I'm not saying I don't love my family, I'm just saying we don't seem all that spiritual to me.

Feeling the cool air on my face, I take the long way through the woods. What time I go home is irrelevant. My father will make sure I'm punished either way. The night is silent other than the sticks crunching beneath my boots as the moon shines through the trees. I wanted so badly to go to her at the soul cleansing, to warn her of what was to come. The betrayal in her expression was enough to turn my stomach when she saw me at her door, holding the evidence of her womanhood.

Although I know it's a pointless thing to do, I still wonder what I could have done differently to have altered the outcome.

I went immediately to the waste site after I left the creek with her. Maybe that was my first mistake. Maybe I should have let the water take her underclothes away.

While we repurpose things as much as possible, there are still items that must be disposed of. Those items go to the community waste site. Since everyone in the compound uses it, I thought it was the safest place to get rid of her clothing.

My uncle Cyrus had come upon me before I was able to place her bloody garments on the pile that, ironically, is burning right now. He ripped them from my hands, and held them up. It somehow felt like he was violating Laurel Ann, the way he sneered at them. After many times of refusing to tell him whose they were, he dragged me to my father.

Never once did I name her. It was Zaaron who told him. Even if He hadn't, every follower in the compound has seen that we've been inseparable lately. My father is no different.

I still feel like I've been betrayed by my God.

How many times have I begged you for her to be mine? I have told you every night for years how much she means to me. How could you want her to be with him? I know I'm not the Prophet yet, but why won't you just talk to me?

Are all my prayers falling on deaf ears? Are my desires and dreams completely irrelevant? Why does He allow me these affections for her if He refuses to allow me to act on them? And why my father?! I don't understand how he could be better than me. We are both of holy blood. She wouldn't have been so scared if it were me she was to be bound to.

My thoughts take my feet to where I'm going before I know that's what I want. I walk up to the little box holding Benji Johnson.

"Benji? It's Zeb. Are you okay?" There is only silence. Knocking on the door, I whisper, "Benji?"

"Zebadiah? What are you doing here? I'm meant to be in solitude. You're gonna get us both in trouble."

I hear the fear in his voice. I know I'm asking him to soil his newly cleansed soul by talking to me. I also know I need advice from someone I trust.

"I know… I just need to talk to you. I don't know what to do."

"Why? What's wrong?"

I hear a thump from inside the box's walls. I feel guilty for some of the less than kind thoughts I've had about him and his family because he's never been anything besides there for me. After Laur, he's my best friend.

"Laurel Ann received her blood today. We tried to hide it, and my father found out."

With a heavy sigh he says, "Being cleansed is a lot worse than I imagined. I don't know how she'll handle it."

"The soul cleansing isn't the worst part. She's to be placed with my father." My words get stuck in my throat, causing me to cough on them. "How am I supposed to spend every day with her in the same house, acting as if I'm her child? I see the evidence of what he does to my mothers, and he is no kinder to us kids. I don't want that for Laurel Ann. How could Zaaron?"

A dragging sound slides down the wood, and I think he is leaning against the wall. "Would you want her with anyone? I understand it being your father makes it worse, but what if she was to be bound to my father? Or one of her other uncles? Would it be any better?"

"No, but I wouldn't spend every day witnessing it! And at least your father isn't cruel."

His laugh sounds pained. "You see what he wants to show you."

Sitting on the ground, I lean against the box. "Are any of them what they say they are?"

"I don't know. Before my mother left, she told me lies overflowed this compound. She said she felt safer with a wolf that bared his teeth than one hiding beneath sheep's clothing."

I scoff at his pointless remark. "Well, your mother was possessed. The Devil says many things to confuse us. She was as trustworthy as a Philistine. You can't take her words to heart." He says nothing so I lean my ear against the wood. "Benji?"

"I think you better go, Zeb. You don't want to end up here too."

I nod even though he can't see me. "This is only temporary. You'll be out of there soon." When he doesn't respond, I stand to brush the dirt off my trousers, making my way home.

The common ground is empty as I pass it to get to my family's ranch. In the distance, the candlelight is burning, and I wonder who will still be awake to witness my lashings.

I cross through the gate, and something hard lands against my back, causing my chest to bow out as the air is forced from my mouth. I fall to the dirt, and barely catch myself in time.

"You shamed me today, Zebadiah." I flip to my back, struggling to breathe. "Of all my children, I expect the most of you, and you have let me down repeatedly."

He hits me in the arm with what I now see is a cattle encapsulator. The long, brass tool, intended for feeding our cattle their meds, slams against my leg, and I let out a yell. "I know, Father."

He kicks me in the ribs before pulling me to my feet by the front of my shirt. "Your relationship with the Henderson girl is offensive and sinful. I will not have it." Bringing the encapsulator hard against my side, yet still keeping me upright, he speaks through closed teeth. "I don't want you to have anything to do with her outside of what is appropriate with any of your mothers, do you understand?"

He throws me to the ground while I double over and grab my side, spitting the excess saliva into the dirt. "Yes, Father."

"You know how I feel about the family receiving public cleansings, so this is not something I am pleased with. However, you will be made an example of." I nod because I fear it will hurt to speak. He throws the encapsulator to the ground as he walks past me. "You sleep outside tonight. A bed is a right for those who are obedient."

Lying on the ground, I allow myself to groan at the pain shooting through my body. I roll onto my back and look up at the stars, wondering which one is the paradise we suffer for.

Water lands in large droplets on my face, forcing my eyes open. The sky is still dark as the rain pummels me. It's coming down so hard, I don't make it to the porch before I'm soaked all the way through. My side hurts something awful. I hold my hand over it involuntarily and sit on the porch chair.

Laurel Ann is usually one of the first things I think of upon waking up, and today is no exception. I wonder how her father reacted to what happened last night. Surely knowing she will be bound to my father would soften the blow. He seems prideful, and nobody wants the entire compound looking down on their family for the actions of one.

I'm going to have to do better. It's no secret in the Fitch house that when Father is angry at one of us, we all pay the price. I would never want Laurel Ann to get the brunt of his fury for something I did. After last night, I'm sure none of my family is too happy with me.

The rooster will be waking up the entire ranch soon. I might as well get a head start on my chores and maybe get my father in a better mood.

I've been at it for what feels like hours when I hear the *cock-a-doodle-doo* of a new morning starting. I look out the barn window, wiping the sweat on my sleeve. Since I finished my own chores about an hour ago, I started on my brother Ezekiel's. I would have been finished sooner, but my side and back hurt terribly, making me move slower.

As I finish mucking out the final horse stall, the barn door opens.

"You didn't have to do that," Ezekiel says, holding out a glass of milk.

I gulp it down in one drink before wiping my mouth. "Yes, well, I wasn't getting any sleep anyway."

He nods toward the house. "Your ma had a rough night last night with Father. You might want to go check on her before we head to school."

Anger bubbles in my veins like water on a stove. His

problem was with me, not my mother. The worst part is, she'll take it and apologize just like the rest of them.

"Fuck."

"Don't let Father hear you curse like that."

I scoff as I head toward the house. What else could he take from me that he didn't take last night?

I walk up the porch steps and pass a few of my mothers and sisters in the dining room. Sister Karen, Ezekiel's birth mother, gives me a sad nod.

"Blessed morning, Zebadiah."

"Blessed morning, Sister Karen. Where's Ma?"

Nodding down the hall, she turns back to her cleaning. "She's in her room, dear."

"Thank you, ma'am."

I leave her to go to my mother's chambers. Walking into her room, I find her at her vanity. As soon as I see the bluish bruises around her neck, in the mirror, I hold down a sob.

"I'm so sorry, Mama."

She gives me a small smile that does nothing to comfort me. "Come here, baby."

I roll my eyes. "I'm not your baby, Ma. I'm nearly a grown man."

"You'll always be my baby. Now come here."

I go to her and do my best to mask my own discomfort as I kneel on the floor at her feet. "He hurt you because of me."

She reaches out to hold my face. "Why did you do it, sweetheart? Why would you risk your soul for that girl?"

I love my mother more than almost anything, but I hate her talking about Laurel Ann like this is all her fault. "'That girl' is my best friend, and she was terrified when she got her blood. Rightfully so, look what happened!"

"This is her purpose, Zebadiah. I know you care for her, just know that this, too, shall pass."

"Yeah…"

"Zaaron always has a plan. You know that."

Sometimes I get the sense that she can't have a single original thought. All of her words are my father's. I often wonder who the twelve-year-old girl who was bound to him was.

"I need to get to school."

She nods as she turns back to her vanity. "Of course, sweetheart. Have a blessed day."

I stand and kiss her temple. "You have a blessed day, too, Ma."

Leaving out the back to minimize my chance of seeing my father, I walk to the schoolhouse. On the way, I realize I've never been to school without Laur. I don't want to go without her there, and in this moment, I decide I'm not going to.

I slip behind the general store, watching across the common ground until Sister Madeline closes the schoolhouse doors. The area will become run with people if I wait much longer, so I sprint across the dirt and run between the tabernacle and the school. Once I'm behind the tabernacle, I clutch the slicing pain in my side and press my back against the wooden shingles. I take a big breath and crouch down to crawl beneath my father's office window at the back of the tabernacle. Slowly lifting up to peek inside, I look just long enough to see my father sitting at his desk.

My feet take off as fast as they will go, and I attempt to ignore the sharpness intensifying in my side until I get back home. When I reach the road in front of my house, I finally slow down.

I climb the porch steps, walk through the front door, and nearly run into Sister Karen.

"My goodness, child, why aren't you at your lessons?"

Clutching my stomach and groaning, I say, "I'm feeling ill. I don't think I can make it through a whole day at school." It's not exactly a lie.

She presses her hand to my forehead. "You are flushed and a little warm." She nods her head toward the hallway. "Go lie down. Get some rest."

Walking to my room, I look over my shoulder to make sure she isn't watching me, and cross the hall to my father's study. Once I'm behind the closed door, my eyes scan the room for Laurel Ann's clothes. I hate that he has them.

I search through his desk when my eyes land on the closet door. Swinging it open, I see the box Mia gave him, on the top shelf. I step on a stool to reach up and grab it. Once it's safely in my clutches, I lift the lid and find Laurel Ann's bloomers laying on top. I take them from the box, ripping off a small piece of the fabric, and shoving it in my pocket. My heart pounds at what could happen if I were caught, and the fear adds to my urgency. Quickly tucking the rest of her bloomers and petticoat under my arm, I close the empty box, and return it to the closet. The door creaks when I open it, causing me to freeze and listen for my mothers. I stick my head out, seeing the coast is clear, and sneak back across the hall.

My stomach spasms at nearly completing my task. Quietly closing my bedroom door, I creep over to my bed and reach into my pocket to pull out the piece of bloody fabric. The material is soft between my fingers as I shove it beneath my mattress. Once I roll the remaining undergarments into a ball, I wrap one of my older shirts around it. With a tender touch, I slowly open my window and push myself through. I land with a *thud* on the dirt and bite my cheek to stifle my groan.

With a stroke of luck, I escape my ranch unseen. Throwing the bundle of clothes over my shoulder, I run to the waste site.

5

TIME OF QUESTIONING

Laurel Ann

DURING A TIME OF QUESTIONING, THE ACCUSED IS NOT TO have contact with anyone in the compound other than immediate family and persons from the holy bloodline. This time is primarily to ponder on what I desire most in life. Is it the wants of my own flesh, or is it to serve and obey Zaaron, our God? There is no better way to soul search than hard work.

I am made to deep clean every part of inside the house. I scrub the floors that the children keep tracking on, clean every single window, polish all of the furniture, and do about four hundred other tedious tasks that make my body ache. Since I can't leave the house, I help Sister Esther with the children. I make them food as she breastfeeds baby Paul, wash out the dirty diapers while she tries to get two-year-old William to stop eating baby Bridget's hair, and run little Phillip to the washroom so he doesn't soil his trousers.

I wish I could speak with Zebadiah. I want to know what happened after he left and how he got caught in the first place. I have been secretly praying I wouldn't get the blood for at least three more years, because then Zeb would be a man in the eyes of Zaaron and could be bound. A man being bound that young is extremely rare, but not completely unheard of for a future Prophet. I asked Zaaron to please let Zebadiah be who He chose for me.

That won't ever happen now.

My sigh fills the room…it doesn't matter anymore.

What will it be like to be Zeb's mother? The thought makes me want to be sick all over the clean clothes I just folded on the bed. I wonder if we will stay friends. It will be impossible to spend the time together that we used to. I will miss being alone with him, and he will eventually start spending his time with someone else. My chest hurts. I want to cry when I think of him with another girl.

Things with Zeb were starting to change. It was different, and though I don't really want to admit it, I liked it…a lot. It made my body tingle with warm waves of soft vibrations dancing up my skin. Now, when I think about what our relationship will be, my throat tightens and my head hurts.

I pull the golden knobs on the oak dresser, the drawer squealing in protest. The pale pink flowers painted on the cracked wood are chipped and worn. This has been my dresser my entire life. This is the last time I will ever use it. I rest my head against the edge, letting the tears fall into the drawer of clean clothes. I'm scared. I'm scared to be bound to the Prophet, I'm scared to have children, and I'm scared to leave my family.

I ask Zaaron to help me want this, help me desire it. Help me realize His plan is so much greater than the small speck that is my time on Earth.

Please Zaaron, help me be what I'm supposed to be. What you want me to be.

Closing the dresser isn't any quieter, and when I turn to

leave my room, Mia is standing in the doorway. Tears are bulging from her eyes, about to fall at any moment.

"I don't want you to hate me." Her lip quivers, and she lets herself cry. "I don't want you to leave."

I want to yell at her and tell her she should have thought of that before she brought the proof of my lies to the Prophet, but I don't have much time left with her. I will only see her during services, gatherings, bindings, cleansings, and maybe the occasional passing by, and that will be it. I don't want hurtful words to be the last ones I speak to her. Besides, that lip quiver she does is the saddest thing I've ever seen. I know her biggest fear is that everyone she loves won't make it to the Paradise Star. She just doesn't want to spend eternity without me. I don't want to spend it without her either.

I go to her, taking her hand and sitting both of us on her bed. "I will never hate you, Mia. Ever, ever." I pull her onto my lap and make sure I experience every sensation of it. Her head against my chest, her bonnet ruffle tickling my chin, her warm breath against my arm, the way her legs dangle over the edge of mine. I will never hug her like this again. "I know you were just being obedient. You are a good girl. I know Zaaron is proud of you." She wipes her nose as she looks up at me with a hopeful expression. "I will miss you too. I'll still see you every Saturday and Wednesday, okay?"

She nods, though she is far from being herself. "Okay."

"Come on. Let's go help mothers make dinner."

I haven't seen my father since last night, and when he walks into the kitchen I wish I could go hide. He doesn't speak as he kisses my mothers and sits at the table. Nobody else seems to be paying attention to him when he's all I'm paying attention to. I want him to look at me while at the same time, I'm terrified that he will.

The food is put on the table, and everyone sits before Father speaks. "I know you are all aware this is Laurel Ann's last night with us. I had prayed this would be under more celebratory circumstances, although I am still pleased she is to be bound to our Prophet. Sometimes, Zaaron's plan is not always clear. We will all attend her cleansing tomorrow evening with the exception of your mother, Julia, who will stay back with the children." He finally looks right at me, making me want to slide under the table. "I want Laurel Ann to be an example as to what happens when you sin against Zaaron and break spiritual law."

The room remains silent as Father continues in prayer, thanking Zaaron for our food, His blessings, for our Prophet, and asking that He will grant me forgiveness.

Nobody speaks of my cleansing again. It's almost time, and even though I haven't eaten since lunch, I can't bring myself to swallow much of my food. I expect my wasting to be pointed out, especially by Sister Mary, yet I hear nothing of it. I'm not able to focus on the conversation around me, which makes me sad because this is the last night I will get to be a part of it.

The knock on the front door causes time to halt. Everyone freezes in their positions until my father stands to answer. I know who is at the door even before I look up to see him.

Apostle Keaton removes his hat as he nods to my mothers, and we all stand to greet him.

"It's time for Laurel Ann to be taken to the holding room. Is she ready?"

No! I'm not ready!

I want to scream how sorry I am. How I wish I could take

it back. Before this moment I was worried, but now I'm so petrified that my feet are sunk into the floor, and my lips are sewn together with invisible thread.

"Yes, she is." My father gestures for me to stand. "It's time for us to say our goodbyes."

I want to fall to the floor. I want to cry and plead, beg them not to do this, but all my younger siblings are watching, and I must be an example to them. I get up to go stand by the Apostle.

The little children are too young to understand what is happening, and still, one by one all my siblings hug me, telling me they love me. When it's Mia's turn, she clutches at my apron as she cries against my stomach. "I will miss you, Laurel Ann. I love you. Thank you for forgiving me."

I kiss her head. "I will miss you too, and I love you. Be a good girl and keep studying hard, okay?"

She nods at me before falling into Robert's embrace. My mothers hug me, even Sister Mary seems sincere. My mother kisses my head while she cups my face. "Be obedient, Laurel Ann, and everything will fall into place." The tears are choking me, so I let some of them fall. "I love you, sweetie."

The only one left is my father. As he looks at me, I think he's going to let me leave without saying goodbye. Finally, he says, "Be an honorable wife to our Prophet, and you will honor our God."

He doesn't hug me, he doesn't tell me he loves me, or he'll miss me. He just nods in dismissal. I'm not allowed to bring anything. Taking one last look at my family and home, I follow Apostle Keaton out my front door, still hearing Mia's sobs all the way down the steps.

The Apostle barely speaks to me the entire way to the common ground, and even then, all he says is, "Try to keep up."

Looking at the schoolhouse brings tears to my eyes, and

my heart aches at the idea of never being able to go again. The Prophet doesn't let his wives remain in school. Things won't be the same with my friends; it never is when a girl gets placed. I always thought it felt like they had grown up and left us kids behind, but now it feels the opposite.

I look at the box of repentance as we pass by the cleansing station. Benji is still in there, and soon I will be.

We climb the steps of the tabernacle to walk into the foyer. The meeting hall has windows all along the sides, and now that the sun is beginning to go down, it casts an orange glow on the room. There are around fifteen long rows of pews all facing the pulpit at the front. Apostle Keaton leads me down the center aisle and onto the stage, taking me to the door in the back, left corner. I have never been in this part of the tabernacle before.

The short hallway has five doors: one to our left, three to our right, and one directly in front of us. He turns to the last one on the right, guiding me into what looks like a small bedroom. There is a blanket and a pillow on the bed with *The True Testament* sitting on a small side table. There are no windows in the room, but there are two oil lamps allowing for more than enough light. An open door showing me the toilet, tells me it's a washroom.

Click.

I fling around to see the closed door as the lock turns into place. I let out a sigh and take a lamp into the washroom where I pump a handful of water to wet my face. Without anyone to talk to and nothing to do, I lie down. Suddenly, I feel exhausted. I pull the wool blanket up to my chin, already wanting my own bed.

I awake to one of Zeb's younger brothers bringing me break-fast. He doesn't speak a word to me as he sets the food on the table, leaving the way he came, and locking the door once it's closed.

I take my time eating to have something to do for as long as possible. My thoughts float to my family. I wonder if they miss me and if they've already divided up my things. If they haven't, they will by this evening.

I sleep for most of the morning, and when lunchtime arrives it's in the hands of one of the Prophet's daughters. I try to speak to her, though she comes and goes just like her brother.

The third time I hear the door unlock, I assume it's for my dinner. My assumption is wrong. My gaze travels to the door where Apostle Keaton is standing.

"It's time to prepare you for the cleansing."

I follow him into the room directly across from the entrance of the meeting hall. This room has a window, allowing me to see it's about the same time as it was when I came here yesterday. It appears to be an office with a desk, two chairs, a worn bookshelf, an oil lamp, a large chest, and a water basin.

"Sit and lift your arms." I obey as he reaches behind my chair for the ox yoke. He lowers it over my arms, leading them through the bows, until the beam sits across my shoulders, holding me captive. He then ties two ropes through the chain rings on either side, letting the ends fall to the floor.

"Remain in this seat until the Prophet comes for you."

He closes the door, and I gasp when I attempt to lower my arms, causing the beam of the ox yoke to dig into the back of my neck. The more I try to get comfortable, the worse it becomes, so I move as little as possible.

Through the window, I watch the sky transfer from golden

to purple. It doesn't take long for the light in the room to fade.

The time oozes away at a leisurely pace, giving my mind space to roam. It's silly that part of me is mortified my friends are going to be watching. It's embarrassing enough to get in trouble in school. This is going to be much worse. People will be talking about me afterward, just as I am sure they are talking about me right now.

My neck and arms are aching as I think of what I am about to endure. I hope it makes me feel better afterwards–more grateful and not so self-centered.

The more time that disappears, the more nervous I get, until I'm tapping my boot against the desk. The window is open, making me grateful for the cool air the evening brings. I haven't stopped sweating through my bloomers since I came in here. This room is small and driving me insane. How long has it been?

Finally, I hear the *creak* of the knob. I try to turn my head to the door as the Prophet slides into the room, and even that hurts.

He looks down on me for a few long, torturous moments before he speaks. His voice is loud in my ears, seeming to echo in my head.

"I am going to remove your boots and stockings."

I'm in no position to be pushing boundaries, but if he removes my stockings, my ankles might show beneath my dress.

"Prophet…"

He steps closer, narrowing his eyes and removing all traces of their softness. My stomach flips as goose bumps dance across my flesh. He kneels down to undo my laces, rolling my stockings down my legs. I feel like this should be an intimate moment, yet he's doing it with such coldness, it causes a sense of shame.

"You will not be the recipient of another cleansing ritual

after this, do you understand?"

I don't really. Does he know for a fact I won't ever mess up again? Did Zaaron tell him that?

There is none of the kindness that is usually apparent on his face as he rests his hands on his knees. He looks into me, my heart bouncing against my chest. Is He telling him what I'm thinking?

"I will not have sin in my home, nor will I have any of my wives be made into a public spectacle."

I feel myself swallow. I'm still not entirely following, and I'm also thinking I don't want to. I nod in compliance. He snatches the ropes, pulling me up with him and pressing the beam against the back of my neck. Following him into the meeting hall, I am sure to stay close. He orders me to sit in the same pew Benji sat in. I become invisible to him when he walks away, leaving me unsure. He didn't tell me, but I doubt I'm supposed to move. I stay still, watching Joanna Fitch, soon to be my sister-wife, lighting candles up and down the hall.

The big wooden doors boom open as people pour inside, in their orders, moving through the pews like ribbons. When I see my family, I want to cry again. I do regret lying about the blood. If I could go back, I would do it differently, even though that's probably because I got caught.

The first person I make eye contact with is Samuel. He signs, *It'll be over before you know it.*

I'm not really able to sign in this thing, and I wouldn't want the Prophet to catch me anyway, so I nod to him. I look to Mia next. Poor thing. I can see from here that she has been crying—probably since I left.

The Prophet stands in front of me, behind the pulpit. I glance over to the front row to find Zeb taking his seat with his family. He sits awkwardly, holding his stomach, looking pained. Is he ill?

The Prophet holds up his hand, the small amount of chatter and whispers immediately dying down.

"The Devil is trying to take over the adolescents of this compound. He is attacking us through our youth. Children of Zaaron, we must fight this evil. Twice in three days' time, one of our flock has been led astray." Distasteful head shaking across the hall almost makes the room look as if it's pulsing. "Laurel Ann Henderson, arise, child." I obey, and he gestures for me to stand by him. "In the darkness, Zaaron's light burns bright. He blesses us while the Devil attempts to doom us. His holy voice has made it clear that Laurel Ann's soul is in peril. To protect her place in the Paradise Star, He has commanded I make her my wife."

Everyone instantly begins clapping. There are whispers of *Praise Zaaron*! as hands raise to the heavens all across the meeting hall. The Prophet allows them a moment to rejoice then he continues, "However, before we can receive the blessing of a binding, we must wash away the filth of sin." He turns to me. "You were given the gift of blood, yet you rebuked that gift by lying to me, your family, and everyone in the Anointed Land." My face and neck are hot. I never considered I was betraying everyone I've ever known. How many of them hate me? "Do you deny this?"

"No, Prophet."

"Do you understand this is a serious transgression that requires the holy fire of Zaaron to rid you of the stain on your purity?"

"I do."

"Will you accept this penance?"

"Yes, Prophet."

The room erupts into praise and cheer as he leads me between them. Every pull he gives on the ropes nearly causes me to fall and my ears to burn in humiliation.

Once the pillars of the cleansing station come into sight, bile raises into my throat. Sweat bursts through my pores, and my vision blurs, on account of my heart pounding behind my eyes and the unavoidable tears. He leads me down the rough steps of the tabernacle as I nearly trip off the last one, my feet slipping in the soft dirt. Squeezing my eyes shut, I allow the tears to fall on my cheeks.

I will get through this. Zaaron wouldn't ask His children to do something they couldn't. I chose to act outside of His grace, and this is how I am to remain inside of it. The air is cool in my nostrils as I inhale. I want to be pure. I want to obey Zaaron's laws, and I definitely want to remain in the Anointed Land. I can do this.

I have to do this.

The Prophet leads me to the cleansing station as the Apostle and the Counselor stand on either side, throwing the ropes over the pillars. Slowly they pull, until my head threatens to be pushed off my shoulders. Though my toes are touching the earth, I have to stand on the tips of them to relieve the pain in my neck. The murmurs sound loud in my pounding ears, causing the agony in my shoulders to shoot to my stomach. Attempting to lift my head, I make eye contact with my father. He looks just as he did at Benji's cleansing: passive and neutral. I could be a complete stranger. My mother has tears streaming down her cheeks, glittering from the light of the fire. Her face softens when she realizes I'm watching her, and she signs, *I love you.*

Almost my entire family is here, and I'm grateful they are standing in front of me when the *rip, rip, rip* of my dress from the Prophet's knife allows the air to whip across my bare back.

Zeb isn't in my line of sight, so his eyes must be among those I feel on my exposed skin. I know this isn't meant to be pleasant, still, I want nothing more than to disappear. I'm confident this humiliation is a worse punishment than the pain.

"Laurel Ann Henderson. You will receive eight lashings with the holy fire and thirty-eight hours in the box of repentance. Will you pay this price to be purified once again?"

My breathing burns through my chest and shoulders.

The burning hasn't even begun.

"Yes, Prophet."

In my periphery, the Prophet removes the whip from the pillar. Although I can't see him soaking it in kerosene, I can hear the *slosh, slosh, slosh* of something wet and the *whoosh* of the flame igniting the whip.

The anticipation is daunting, yet the pain that shoots through my body comes fast as my voice screams in my own ears.

"BE CLEANSED OF THIS EVIL!"

The world tilts around me, people becoming a distortion of faces and colors. The tears are hot in my eyes, stinging my irises. My back is overtaken with heat as the fire kisses my exposed skin, small pieces of flames landing on my arms and face like scorching pinpricks. I'm unable to regain my breath before more torture, in the form of the Prophet's new locust tree whip, consumes my body. There is screaming in my head...no wait, not my head... The screaming is in my throat. The base of my spine splits open as I try to reach for anything, anything to grab onto, but there is only the night air.

"BE CLEANSED OF THIS SIN!"

The warmth of the fire pulls sweat from my skin and it drips into my eyes. Pressing them closed is my only option as I freely weep. I don't try to be strong. Another lash rips at my flesh while my body arches in protest. I need this to be over. How many was that? I can't open my eyes. White light bursts behind them and my back explodes once more. Slowly pushing up my eyelids does nothing for my vision when the white turns black…

Reality becomes broken pieces of glass. The light breaks through the darkness only to be swallowed once again by night. I am overtaken by agony until the freedom of the blackness throws me into reprieve. It isn't long before I'm sucked back into my body where every inch is wailing to be relieved of the torment.

"THE SPIRIT OF ZAARON WILL BURN FROM WITHIN!"

Air slices its way down my throat with every breath. Time doesn't make sense.

The Prophet's voice seems to clear my mind, and the world comes back together like a puzzle. "Any sinful thoughts or temptations you have will be washed away by Zaaron's grace and the holy fire."

My head refuses to support itself anymore and my sight is reduced. My eyelids are heavy, and even with them closed, the smoke burns my eyes when it blows against my face. I think I cry as I try to push them open, watching my dirt and red speckled feet dragging across the ground, no longer strong enough to serve their purpose.

The rope attached to the right pillar loosens, making the ground jump closer. The other rope is undone, and I am unable to catch myself, getting dirt in my mouth and hitting my hip as I fall.

My body fights, wanting nothing more than to stay on the ground. The Prophet yanks on the ropes, taking me with them. He's pulling too hard and walking too fast, causing me to trip over the hem of my dress. Whispers are in the background as he tugs me to the box of repentance. When he removes me from the confinement of the ox yoke, my arms fall limp, screaming in relief.

"You have rebuked the prophecy of our God, Zaaron, and you have paid what was asked. Now it is time to be in solitude with Him, explaining why you would betray Him and us. Plead for His forgiveness, child. You have thirty-eight hours to convince Zaaron that you are truly remorseful and fully understand the error of your ways. Is there anything else you would like to say?"

I have a lot to say. I know I do…at least I think I do. I can't think straight while my throat fights me, so I inhale through my nose. My eyes struggle to open and my voice comes out scratchy.

"I'm sorry. I won't…I won't disappoint you again."

I am speaking to the Prophet, to my God, to my father, to my family, to Zeb, and to all the fellow children of Zaaron.

I am also speaking to myself.

The Prophet walks me up the plank, opening the door to show nothing inside. It's endless darkness. His hand pushes against my back, his fingers digging into my wounds, making me cry out. My shoulder slams against a hard floor as I fall inside, the last stream of light evaporating when he closes the door.

The wood pokes against my wet cheek. My arms and legs are twisted into an uncomfortable position, but my body and mind are too weak to care. The land of dreams is pulling me away, and I am all too willing.

The Prophet's voice slips through the cracks around the door. It's the last thing I hear before I drift away from here.

"There is much to celebrate this night. Another child has been saved from the clutches of evil. Let us rejoice in Zaaron as we commence the gathering!"

6

BOX OF REPENTANCE

Laurel Ann

LAUGHING, A ROGUE HOLLER, SOME TALKING TO BREAK IT UP, and then, more laughing. Opening my eyes makes no difference. There's only black. While I may not see anything, I feel everything. My body shrieks in protest with every movement, and my limbs don't feel right…unattached.

Wiggling my toes helps me get into a sitting position without too much agony. The wounds are tender and sensitive, sending bolts of sharpness down my spine with every move. I slowly take in air, breathing and allowing my eyes to adjust. Then I see it: light.

A flickering, thin, long, horizontal light. My grunts and groans give me a boost as I pull my legs beneath me to crawl to my only escape from the darkness. The floor beneath my hands splits every few inches, scraping hard against my knees. Suddenly, my head slams against the door, causing a ringing in my ears. I lie back down so my face is directly in front of the sliver of dancing illumination. Making out any shapes is impossible, so I listen to the rustling footsteps, the talking, and more laughing. I don't know how late it is, but the gathering is clearly still going on. All the young children should have been sent to bed by now.

It feels like I listen for hours before the noise dies down.

I fall in and out of sleep until an orange glow brightens behind my eyelids. My awareness of the heat and the dampness of my dress from sweat brings about my bearings. A sharp stab pulls tears from my eyes when I try to open them. My eyelashes are dried together. I lick my lips, coaxing a small amount of moisture into my mouth, and use it to rewet my lashes. They flutter open, and I'm instantly blinded by a stream of yellow.

"Ugghh!"

I roll away from it, forgetting about my back until it presses against the wooden floor. Tears spring out to run down my cheeks. Pushing myself up, I hear the softest noise.

Splat, splat, splat.

As I listen closely, I'm able to see a little better than I could last night. The room is short and small. I could stand, though my head would touch the ceiling. I focus on following the sound when my eyes fixate on something in the corner. I crawl to it and reach out to touch it. It's smooth and cylindrical, like a large barrel. It feels somewhat cool so I press my cheek against it, and while the relief is miniscule, it's still existent. My fingers find their way down to discover a long, skinny metal piece. At its end, I trace the pads of my fingers over the tip, and my heart leaps into my throat when I feel the wetness. I know what this is. I laugh regardless of my less than comical situation.

It's a water tank!

I attempt to move quickly and carefully, situating myself beneath the tank, and getting my mouth as close to the nozzle as possible. I feel around for the lever only to cry out in frustration when I realize the handle has been broken off. The water only comes out drops at a time, and still, I'm grateful for it. I lap at it like a cat drinking milk until the scratchiness is out of my throat and my thirst is no longer at the forefront.

Now my hunger is.

I squint to look around the room as if I will find a pantry. I know it's bare— I was lucky to get the water, yet here I am, crawling around, feeling my way across the room, hoping to find something.

All I find is an empty bucket, and I allow myself to wallow in my unfortunate predicament. The sweat is stinging my fresh wounds, and the rip in my dress is making it difficult to keep it on my shoulders. I wish I had been wearing my bonnet when the Apostle came to get me. It would have helped keep some of the perspiration out of my eyes. I settle for tying my apron around my head, but after a while, it makes me too hot to bear. My feet are nicked, cut from walking barefoot. My stomach pangs from hunger, and I feel hopeless in the fact that after all of this, I still have to be bound to the Prophet.

Last year, I followed Benji to the edge of the compound without meaning to. We were walking, lost in our conversation, and before I knew it, he clamped his hand over my mouth as he held a finger up to his own. He took the finger from his lips to point only a few yards away through the fence to where I saw them.

Philistines.

The anger I had for them rolled in my stomach. Treacherous heathens. They were the first and only ones I've ever seen. There was one male and one female who appeared to be a little older than us. I was shocked into silence because they were playing, laughing, and kissing. They chased each other around until finally, the boy tackled the girl in the field. I thought he had hurt her until her giggle rose up to slow my heart. Every once in a while, when they would sit up, I could see their arms wrapped around each other as they kissed. I remember thinking they didn't look evil or wicked.

They looked in love.

Since receiving the blood of innocence, there are things that I wish weren't the way they are. I don't understand all of Zaaron's laws, and although I believe in them, there are things I have begun to question in my head.

Bindings for example. Why must we be bound before we are ready to be? Why does Zaaron wait so long to place men, yet He places women within a year of receiving their blood? I know it's partly because women are unable to have children as late in life as men. We don't live as long either, and I understand it's our duty to populate the Paradise Star, but why can't it be with whom I choose? And with someone who chooses me back?

Voices distract me from my self-pity, and I ease back over to the line of light. This is the first I've heard anything since waking up. I still can't see other than a bit of the earth, and I can't make out what's being said either. It's too far away.

That's the point I suppose. Seclusion. Just me and Zaaron.

I know lying about the blood was wrong. Please, please forgive me. I was frightened, I didn't know what to do. Why won't you take away this fear if this is what you want from me? I desire to be a holy woman for you, I just need more strength. There were still many things I wanted to do before being bound. I...I just really like Zeb. I had hoped he was who you had in mind for me. Now that I know it's the Prophet, I am scared of losing him. He's my best friend. It's the fear I beg you to take away. I can't feel this way forever...

I don't know if I finish my prayer. I zone in and out, the heat and the hunger pangs making everything feel like a half existent reality...half of a dream.

My tongue is dry, and my lips are so tight I fear they will tear if I open my mouth too wide. The fullness of my bladder has become painful, and I don't know what to do until I remember the bucket.

I push my bloomers to my knees as the sweat rolls down my temple, dripping to my neck. Although it's too dark to see, I can feel the dried blood on my thighs, and I wonder if I bled through my mother's cotton pad. I was supposed to change it yesterday.

After I finish with the bucket, I feel around for the mouthpiece on the water tank. I can barely breathe, the muggy air sticks in my throat, and I could cry when a single drop falls onto my tongue. It does little to sate my thirst, yet the moisture is a small relief nonetheless.

I don't know if I will make it to this evening. Sweat flows from every pore in my body. Since my dress is barely staying up anyway, I pull it down off my arms. There is an instantaneous, momentary ecstasy of relief when the stale air hits my flesh. Pushing my dress down, I toss it against the wall. I tug my bloomers as high up my thighs as I can, and it's still not much better.

I spend my entire day drinking from the water tank. My tongue is completely raw, and my jaw hurts with the water being my only sense of relief.

Thunk... Thunk.

What was that?

Thunk.

It's coming from right next to me.

Thunk. Thunk.

I get up, my fingers leading my way to the sound, and I press my ear against the wood. "Hello?" *THUNK.* The panels shake, and the sound is so loud against my head I jump away. There's someone out there—I can hear footsteps and talking. "H-hello?"

Their voices sing, *"Your soul stinks! We can't stand the smell.*

We think you belong in Hell. The stench of your sin makes our stomachs turn. We want you to burn, burn, burn."

It's children from the sound of it, but that doesn't make the sharpness in my chest any duller. I don't know what to say. It doesn't matter anyway when I hear their laughs receding.

People tend to keep their thoughts to themselves in public, though I know in my own home, the opinions of my mothers and father are made clear. There are those who are surely disgusted with my actions. As they should be.

I never thought the Devil could get me…worm his way into my mind to trick me. Maybe I was wrong. Maybe that's why I'm feeling scared like this. The Devil is making me feel this.

A wretched smell floats its way into the box. Manure. That's what the children were throwing.

The emptiness in my stomach turns at the unwanted aroma. I let my mind wander to the creek with Zeb in an attempt to distract myself, but with the heat and being in such a small space, the smell is quickly becoming unbearable.

I am frantic in my search for my dress. When my fingers grasp at the fabric, I thank Zaaron. I cover my nose with it as I crawl back to the water tank. The dress does little to help, and soon my empty stomach can't take it anymore, forcing me to gag and dry heave.

I haven't eaten since lunch yesterday, and very little comes up, making me more nauseous.

Lying beneath the mouthpiece, I almost cry with relief every time a drop of water drips from the nozzle onto my face. I'm so thirsty, and only receiving droplets at a time begins to drive me mad. I would do the cleansing ritual all over again just to have a cup right now.

My mind shifts over in my half consciousness. I think maybe I've been too focused on my fear to look at this the right way. Maybe my mother was right. Maybe Zaaron's plan will take time to see. I might fall madly in love with the Prophet, wanting nothing more than to give him as many babies as I can. Maybe I will look back at this time and be grateful this is happening the way it is. Maybe this will make me happy.

But I was happy before.

The stream of light has dimmed with what must be the evening. The manure has lost its effect as I can no longer smell it.

Crickets begin to chirp in the distance, and though at first, it's somewhat relaxing, now nothing would please me more than to stomp on each one of their high pitched, squeaky little heads.

My line of vision has all but disappeared. Touch is my only form of navigation around the room. With the temperature dropping in the evening, it's become much more comfortable, so I curl up in my spot beneath the water tank.

"Laur!" My eyes shoot open at the whispered yell. "Laur! Can you hear me?"

I almost vomit up my heart. I scramble to the door as fast as I can, no longer concerned with the agonizing ache.

It's Zeb.

My fingers claw at the seams in the door, trying to get it to give a little. "Yes! Yes! I'm so happy to hear your voice!"

"Are you okay? I've wanted to speak with you since Monday after I got caught."

I can't lie to him. I've never done it before, and I tell him everything. "I don't want to be bound to the Prophet."

There is a dull thud on the wood, and his sigh creeps in

through the cracks. "I…I don't want you to either. I don't want you bound to anyone, least of all him." He sounds so defeated, it makes my chest hurt. "I wish I was already the Prophet. Things would be different."

"How do you know? If Zaaron wills it, it will be."

Grunting in frustration, he says, "I don't know. I just want to stop this more than anything."

I'm grateful for the wall between us because I'm sure the grin stretching out my cheeks looks ridiculous. My thoughts travel back to the night my life changed, sobering me quickly as if being doused with ice water.

"You tried to stop it, Zeb. There's nothing more you could do. Just…promise me we can try to stay friends once I'm your mother?"

His chuckle is heavy with sadness. "I still can't believe this is happening."

That's not an answer to my question, though the urgency of my next statement feels dire. "I like you, Zeb. I like you a lot. And not the way a mother should like her son," I blurt.

"Can you stop calling yourself my mother? We're not there yet. And I like you too…a lot. I just don't see what we can do about it now."

"There is nothing to do about it. I simply wanted you to know. I've wanted you to know for a while."

He's silent for a long moment before he says, "Put your fingers down here, along the bottom of the door." I do what he says, running the pads along the seam. When my fingertips touch his, my stomach dances with my heart. "You will always be my friend, Laurel Ann. You think getting away with things is difficult in your family? It's twice as hard in mine. It won't happen often, but I promise I'll make sure we get time together without anyone knowing, okay?"

"Okay." My voice only allows a whisper. I don't know

how to express the relief coursing through me at his words. "That's… Thank you. And thank you for coming to see me. I've missed talking to you."

"I've missed talking to you, too. I hate to go, but I'm already in a heap of trouble. I just… I had to speak with you."

"Are you going to be all right?"

"Nothing that won't heal. I'll be in there in a few days too. My time of questioning begins Saturday after…the festivities. My cleansing is on Monday."

I had hoped being the Prophet's son would get him out of a cleansing. The Prophet seems less than thrilled to have his family members' sins made public, something I'm still confused about.

"I'm so sorry. I shouldn't have put you in this position," I say, holding back tears.

"You didn't put me in any position. I did what I thought was right. I'll gladly pay my penance for that." He breathes out a thick sigh. "I need to go. You're almost done, Laur. You can do it."

The wood of the door is rough as I press my head against it. "Thank you, Zeb."

Each of his footsteps is quieter than the last until I can't hear them at all. It's odd that I'm smiling, considering where I am, yet Zebadiah sneaking out to see me makes me want to laugh, or yell, or jump, or something to release the swarm of bees in my stomach.

"Thank you, Zaaron. Thank you for letting him come tonight."

The prayer is a hymn in my soul. It releases a pressure on my chest to know Zeb will do what it takes to remain friends and spend time together. While I may not ever be able to be with him as man and wife, at least he will still be a big part of my life. Zaaron has a plan for all of us. I wish so badly that

I could see in the future, then I'd know what it is for me and Zeb.

I don't understand how I can be this tired when I've been sleeping almost all day. Not that there is anything else to do. I make my way back to the water tank, adjusting myself on my stomach. Closing my eyes, I replay our conversation in my mind.

I don't want you bound to anyone.

I like you too…a lot.

You will always be my friend, Laurel Ann.

My fingers are soft against my chapped lips, and I smile in spite of it. Zebadiah Fitch snuck out just to talk to me…and he said he likes me.

A lot.

7

DAY OF REST

Laurel Ann

CLICKETY-CLANK. CLICKETY-CLANK.

I lurch at the disruption of silence, causing pain to shoot through my body. My eyes barely adjust to the darkness when the door swings open. Sunlight explodes through the room, making me whimper and smack my hands over my eyes.

"Cover yourself, now."

I force my eyes into slits to see the dark figure in the doorway. The brightness of the light cascading around him makes him a shadow of a man. Not that I need to see him to know it's the Prophet. His voice is unmistakable.

I scramble to find my dress, releasing a breath when my fingers clutch around the soft cotton. He clears his throat as I shove my arms into the sleeves, my slick skin sticking to the fabric. After tying my apron, I stand as straight as I can to smooth out my dress. The quick movement causes my head to feel dizzy and my stomach to roll with nausea.

When his face comes into view, he doesn't seem much happier with me than he was before my cleansing.

"Did you make yourself right with Zaaron?"

I think of the most honest answer I can give. Since Zaaron doesn't speak to me as He does the Prophet, all I can do is look for signs. Zebadiah coming to see me last night was a sign of His forgiveness, I just know it.

"I did, Prophet."

His nod is harsh and curt. "I am pleased to hear it." He doesn't sound pleased. Looking over his shoulder, he says. "You may take her now."

He turns away, walking down the wooden plank as the Apostle takes his place.

"Follow me."

I nod at him in greeting. Giving me no acknowledgement, he leaves the same way the Prophet did. I try to keep up, but my body moves in slow motion, every muscle stretching to its capacity just to allow me to walk.

The grass stabs my feet, the soft dirt a welcome reprieve between my toes. The bright sun makes me lightheaded when I turn to see a few people loading up their buggies outside the general store. I see my father and Sister Mary leaving the medical hall, and I freeze. Our eyes meet, staying connected for only a moment before they both look away, and Father nods to the Apostle. They act as if they don't know me at all.

Apostle Keaton turns in the direction of the schoolhouse and placing dorms. I get choked up thinking of Zebadiah, my friends, and siblings all sitting in class.

We walk up the dirt path, taking the single wooden step that leads to the placing dorms. This and the adjoining nursery are the only buildings in the entire compound that I have never been, so I admit some curiosity. The wind catches the screen door from the Apostle's grasp and it slams against the side of the building. He turns the knob to the wooden door, opening it to a room almost as large as the meeting hall in the tabernacle. Rows and rows of beds are lined across the room, all neatly made. There are linens and clothing folded beneath many of them. The room only has a few people in it since the girls under eighteen are still allowed to attend school until they are placed, if they choose. Many women are here for the second time because their first husbands have passed, though if they still have young children, they stay in the nursery.

The back of the room has dividers with the smell of food snaking around them, causing my eyes to water and my stomach to jump in excitement. Immediately after we pass the thin partitions, I can see into a large kitchen where a few women are bustling around. There are rows of tables and seats with a few ladies sitting at them, eating. My hope for food is demolished as he leads me past the delicious scent through another door. There is an open hallway to my right and two doors to my left. The second door on the left is the one he chooses. He taps on the wood with light pressure, opening it without waiting for a response.

"Hello, Apostle Keaton. It's a pleasure to see you as always." The woman's voice is difficult to place until I am ushered further into the room to see Sister Evelyn Taub. Everyone in her family is either a seamstress, weaver, or a tailor, and they clothe everyone in the Anointed Land. Since it doesn't take an entire family to run the placing dorms and nursery, she, along with a few other women around the compound, control them. I go—well, used to go—to school with her sons and daughters. "And hello, dear!" She reaches her arms out to me. "A clean soul looks good on you, but it takes its toll on the mind and body. Why don't we get you cleaned up and fed, then I'll show you to your bed?"

"Yes, ma'am."

Apostle Keaton turns to leave after adding, "I will be here to fetch her in the morning, before services."

She curtsies. "She will be ready."

The door shuts behind him and she smiles. "Let's prepare you a bath."

While the warm water of the bath hurts as it stings my wounds, it still feels incredible. Being clean makes me feel more like myself, allowing my body flexibility. Upon finishing in the tub, I am pleased to see the blood has stopped. I can't believe that's going to happen every month now. Since the belt is no longer necessary, Sister Evelyn hands me only a night gown before she sits to watch me braid my hair.

"Are you hungry or would you prefer to rest first?"

"Yes!" I lower my voice an octave when she jumps. "Yes, I would like some food first, please."

The floor is cool against my feet as I follow her back into the large room. She guides me to a table with three women, all older than my own mothers.

"Hello, ladies. Laurel Ann will be staying here until services tomorrow morning. Let's make her feel welcome, shall we?" The moisture from her hand seeps through the fabric of my gown when she places her hand on my arm. "I'll fix you a plate. Take a seat."

I lift the nightgown to swing my leg over the bench. It doesn't matter if my ankles show, there are only women here. They look familiar, but my mind won't let me place them.

"Hello," I greet them.

They all smile at me when a red-haired woman with sun spots on her face speaks. "Hello, dear. Are you feeling well?"

"I am now, thank you."

The one in the blue bonnet swallows her milk before

turning to me. "You are the one to be bound to the Prophet tomorrow, are you not? That's quite a blessing. You must be thrilled."

Seeing as I just cleansed my soul, I don't want to tarnish it by lying, so I let my smile be my only response.

A plate of eggs, potatoes, bacon, and bread appears in front of me, my hunger making me forget to pray. I grab the fork to stab into the eggs when I feel four sets of eyes on me. I move my utensil to the plate in slow motion and fold my hands together.

I say my blessing and shovel in four bites before I remember to thank Sister Evelyn.

"Thank you for breakfast."

Her smile isn't quite as bright as it was a moment ago. She nods and wipes off her hands on her apron. "When you are finished, you may lie down in bed number twenty-four."

I nod with my fork halfway to my mouth.

Speaking no more than a few words, I am more interested in my food than conversation. Not that my company minds. Once they mention it, I remember their husband passing a few weeks ago.

A full belly and my clean skin make my exhaustion apparent as I take my leave from the chatty widows. I walk between the aisles, looking at the paper signs attached to each bed. I search for the number twenty-four, like Sister Evelyn told me. When I see it, a number has never been so beautiful.

I don't even know if my head touches the pillow when sleep hugs me tight.

I don't awake until after noon, and I only do so because I need the washroom. I eat my lunch alone and ask Sister Evelyn if there's anything she needs help with. She just tells me to rest. It's odd for me to not have any chores or tasks to do. The evening seeps by as I read *The True Testament*, but the words are scribbles to my eyes.

Even though the women I have spoken to are nice on the surface, I can sense a level of hostility in their voices. When the younger girls arrive after school, I'm relieved at seeing some of my friends.

Dawn Garret received the blood of innocence only two weeks before me, and when she sees me, she waves and makes her way to my bed. She quirks her lips into a sad smile and sits next to me. "Hey. How bad was it?"

I shrug, attempting to appear brave. "I'm glad it's over."

"Yeah, I'm sure. Are you excited for tomorrow?"

I chew on my lip as I contemplate my answer. Her eyebrows raise in question, and I spit out a response. "I am excited to fulfill the plan of Zaaron."

"Well, congratulations." She stands, holding her books to her chest. "Have you eaten dinner already?"

I shake my head, and she grabs my hand. "Come on, I'm starving."

While my mind won't entirely focus on our conversation, I am still thankful for the distraction talking with Dawn brings.

I feel a hot hand on my back as Sister Evelyn's voice cuts through our discussion. "It's time for you to rest, Laurel Ann. You have an early and eventful day tomorrow."

Smiling at Dawn, I nod to Sister Evelyn. "Yes, ma'am."

Dawn's fingers wave to me before I walk past the dividers and back to my bed.

It may be because I've had so much sleep the past few days or it may be because of what tomorrow brings that I toss and turn through most of the night.

"Laurel Ann, it's time to wake up."

Sister Evelyn's tired whisper is in my ears. Dread consumes me, and I want nothing more than to roll over. I don't want this day to be here.

It's dark, other than the moonlight shining through the room in a beam. I follow her through the sleeping bodies, envious of their dreams.

She leads me into the washroom where three of Benji Johnson's mothers are waiting. They fill my bath with a fruity, sweet oil, washing my skin and hair with soap that smells of wildflowers. They put salve on my wounds and rub my rejuvenated skin with an oil that tingles every bit of flesh it touches.

Their family makes all the hygiene and basic remedies for the compound. They don't speak other than to tell me to move this way or that. My hair is braided, and my body is rubbed down with more creams until they pat me from head to toe with powder. The room smells divine, and I know I do too.

They wrap me in a blanket, ushering me to the room next to Sister Evelyn's office. The back wall has two windows where the rising sun shines onto three small tables covered in flowers, ribbons, jars, and brushes. Stacks of chairs are shoved against the wall with a few strays sitting throughout the room. There is a large mirror in the corner, and hanging next to it... is the most elegant and terrifying dress I've ever laid eyes on.

They push me into a chair, applying bits of color to my lips and cheeks. My eyes keep going to the dress that seems to mock me until one of them removes it to carry it over.

They don't let me do a thing. Not even put on my own undergarments.

Slipping a leg into each hole, I stand still as one of the women pulls the white fabric up my body. The bloomers are thin and trimmed in white lace that dangles mid-thigh. The drawstring is a satin ribbon, and while they may be soft and pretty, it takes me a moment to process why anyone would put so much craftsmanship into an item nobody will see... It's because someone *will* see them.

My husband.

The Prophet.

I'm going to be sick.

One woman is quick to the draw and has a bucket beneath my mouth before any bile leaves my lips.

"There, there. Shhh. Let it all out, child. It's just nerves."

Nerves? Is that what the doubt and fear have been?

Half of my breakfast is gone, allowing my stomach to relax for the moment. "Is it normal to feel this way?"

"Absolutely." She dabs my mouth with a handkerchief. "You should have seen what a mess I was on my binding day."

Her statement is a comforting one, and it unties one of the knots in my chest. They continue as if nothing happened, having me step into a full body petticoat. It's sleeveless, besides the thin strip of lace tickling my shoulders. The blonde-haired one, Sister Kelly Johnson, fastens the small, white buttons down to my waist. More lace separates the horizontal panels at the bottom of the petticoat. If I wasn't shaking and trying to keep the rest of my breakfast down, this would be a fantasy.

The dark-haired woman holds up my binding gown, and I gasp. From far away it's beautiful, but close up...it's stunning.

They lift my aching arms, sliding the dress over my head. The bottoms of the sleeves are fitted from my wrists to my forearm with more buttons in a line down the sides. From my forearm to my shoulder the laced fabric is loose, creating a slight billowed effect. The dress tightens around my torso as the back is fastened. The entire bottom is layers of scaffolding lace with a pink ribbon woven through at the hem.

Fingers remove the braids from my hair, and the light red waves cascade over the ruffled trim along the bodice of the dress. They tie it up in white ribbons and pink flowers after sliding white, crochet stockings up my calves.

The blonde woman holds out a pair of white ankle-height boots with a short heel. I have never worn a pair of new shoes before, much less ones like these. As they are slipped on, yet more buttons are fastened up the sides.

All three women stand in front of me to admire their work.

"You are a lovely bride." The dark-haired one smiles, gesturing to the mirror.

With a deep breath, I follow her invitation. I don't recognize myself, though I must admit I look beautiful. The lace neckline is tight around my throat, making me appear very sophisticated. I wish there was a way to remember what I look like right now.

"Thank you," I whisper before turning to them. "I've never looked this pretty."

"Do you have any questions about your vows?" The blonde wife asks.

I've heard vows exchanged enough times I could say them backward in my sleep. "No, ma'am."

A *tap* at the door pulls all of our attention toward it as Sister Evelyn sticks her head into the room.

"The Apostle is here for Laurel Ann. Is she prepared?"

Hands nudge me forward when one of the Johnson wives reply with a lie.

"Yes, she is ready."

8

THE BINDING CEREMONY

Laurel Ann

THE APOSTLE IS WAITING FOR ME AT ONE OF THE TABLES NEXT to the kitchen. Sister Evelyn greets him, barely receiving a nod in return.

"We must leave for the tabernacle," he informs me.

He mutters in annoyance at the girls who continue stopping us to compliment me on my ensemble. I follow him outside and hold up the delicate dress as not to dirty the hemline. Upon stepping out the door, I see the common ground has been transformed for the binding celebration after the ceremony. Tables and chairs adorned with ribbons and flowers are arranged in a circle around a large open area. Paper decorations are streamed from wooden poles, the binding pyre right in the center of it all.

The doors of the tabernacle are a heavy oak, carved in an intricate illustration of Zaaron consuming the vessel and preparing the Anointed Land. I've always found it comforting, until now. Today it makes my stomach turn.

The tabernacle is hollow with empty pews and an eerie silence. The tapestries and paintings on the walls seem haunting in the light of events transpiring. The pulpit stands as a beacon for my fate through the doors of the foyer. I walk behind Apostle Keaton, and he leads me to the bride room at the left of the entrance.

"You will await the service in here, with the family."

Once the words leave his lips, he opens the door, putting me face to face with the Fitch family. The wives all swoon, telling me how wonderful I look, but when my eyes lock with Zebadiah's, my heart falters at the heartbreak in them. He doesn't appear to be breathing as his gaze roams over my ensemble. The last time we spoke he made me feel secure in our friendship, but seeing his expression brings doubt into my mind.

While I carry on conversations with my soon-to-be sister-sister-wives, my thoughts remain in the corner of the room with Zeb.

There's a tap on the door, and the Apostle pokes his head inside. "Service is about to start."

Sister Ava Fitch, Zeb's mother and the Prophet's first wife, ushers everyone in their order. The air evaporates from my lungs when Zebadiah stops next to me. His scowl heats up my skin, and he seems to be struggling to force out the words.

"You look beautiful, Laur."

He doesn't wait for my 'thank you'. He just walks away to take his place in the order. I try to swallow back my urge to cry, making my throat feel raw. I don't understand. He knows I don't want this.

Taking my place last in line, I stand behind Sister Cora Fitch holding her baby boy. Hundreds of eyes are burning into me as I follow the family to the front row of the meeting hall. I know the Prophet has taken the pulpit from the sound of steps crossing the stage, yet I can't force myself to look up at him.

"Welcome, children of Zaaron. We have been blessed

with such a lovely day for this most joyous occasion. Today I will take a new wife. Laurel Ann, please stand." My face heats up at the mention of my name, and I am shaky as I obey. I keep my gaze upon the wooden floor when the room flares up in applause. "I hope you will all stay for our binding ceremony and celebration immediately following today's service. The rest of you may stand."

The room is loud with the shuffling of feet while one of the Prophet's younger daughters takes her place at the piano.

I sing along with the hymns and say the prayers, though I'm not feeling anything I say. I'm simply going through the motions, numb to the presence of Zaaron. I watch the Prophet perform the ritual of blessings at the sanctorum altar, holding up the Anointed sigil to the heavens in prayer.

I don't know what the Prophet teaches in his sermon. I think it may have had to do with the blessing of servitude. I just hope nobody asks me about it.

We stand for the closing hymn, but I can't find the words with the pounding vibrations in my veins. The Prophet releases the followers, reminding them to take a candle on their way out. Family by family they file out until it's just me and the Fitches. I look at the Prophet for the first time. I'm not above admitting he looks nice. His black hat is new and matches the crisp jacket he's wearing over his white, button down shirt. His boots are freshly polished, and his face is clean shaven. The family lines back up in their order, and everyone over the age of understanding takes a candle, with the exception of myself and the Prophet.

We walk out of the tabernacle to find the entire compound waiting in four circles, one inside of the other, the outside one being the largest. They break hands to allow us through each ring. The Prophet and I walk to the now lit binding pyre as the Fitch family creates the smallest circle around us, holding hands to close it.

The Prophet performs all of the binding ceremonies, including his own. His cold hands wrap around my clammy ones.

"Zaaron has chosen Laurel Ann for me and me for her. Our souls are to be bound in His presence for all of you to bear witness. It has been prophesied that as children of Zaaron, we are to multiply under His holy guidance, preparing a population for when He burns this world to ash and brings us home to the Paradise Star." He looks right at me, his eyes wide and kind. I see the Prophet that I have come to love and respect. His finger traces my chin in a moment that should be touching and intimate, but instead it makes my gut turn inside itself. "Our union will bring forth many children born with holy blood, and our immaculate descendants will one day help lead us all back to Zaaron."

I get it, all right? I'm going to have a million babies. I just wish everyone would stop reminding me.

I force my lips into a smile, hoping it doesn't look like a snarl. He squeezes my hand before he walks me around in a circle to present me as unbound for the final time. Turning us to the fire, he places his free hand above the flames. He drops his head back to face the sky, and his lips move with murmured prayers. Once the fire is blessed, he picks up the two candles from the ledge.

He gives me one, never releasing his grasp on my hand. We hold our candles over the blessed fire until the flame licks them to life. Two by two we light the candles of my almost sister-wives and children.

When I stop in front of Zeb to light his candle, I can't keep myself from looking at his face. It proves to be an unwise decision for the sake of my heart. He glares at me in a way that makes me queasy. I don't understand what's going on with him. He knows this isn't my fault, so why does it feel like he's mad at me? I plead with him as much as I silently can within the split moment it takes to light his candle. The time comes to move on to the next until the circle encompassing us is a ring of holy flames.

Dispersing to the rest of the compound, the Fitch family uses their candles to begin lighting the next ring. Once this sacred ceremony is protected by the five rings of fire, the Prophet wraps a satin white ribbon around my wrist and up my hand.

"Laurel Ann Henderson, I vow that the purity of your soul will be my utmost concern. I will lead you and our family down the holy path prophesied by Zaaron. I vow to be a righteous husband and Prophet to you and our family. Your best interests will always be my intent in whatever I do. I will obey our God and do whatever is within my power to assure that you and the rest of the children of Zaaron arrive at the Paradise Star."

I wish I had more faith in myself than I do. It is my turn to say my vows, and while I was somewhat confident about them this morning, now I wish the earth would quiver and split, allowing me to fall in.

My grip on the ribbon is shaky as I wrap the other half around the Prophet's wrist just like he did with mine. I take a deep breath, and the air vibrates down my throat. I am about to make a promise in front of Zaaron, my Prophet, and fellow followers that I don't want to make. I had hoped the nerves the Johnson wives had spoken of would have dissipated by now, but in this moment, they are worse than ever.

Please don't let me cry in front of everyone.

I make the mistake of looking up, meeting the angry gaze of Zebadiah. I don't know what he expects me to do. I push with everything I have to keep the tears down.

Will you tell him I'm sorry? That I am just being obedient to you? Please, Zaaron, will you help him understand and forgive me?

"Hiram Fitch, my Prophet, I vow to serve Zaaron, our gracious Messiah, by honoring you in all things that I do. I will obey you without question and join you in our task in populating the Paradise Star. I will bear your holy children and lead our family down its righteous path. I vow to accept your words as Zaaron's words and absolute truth."

The few that have tambourines shake them in a unified beat while we tie the ends of the ribbon together.

He walks us around the final circle and says, "On this day and every day, our souls are bound, never to be separated or broken."

I lick my lips, allowing the needed moisture into my mouth. The words I am about to promise become razor blades in my throat.

"Though our bodies may parish into the ground, our souls will remain together with Zaaron, for all of eternity," I finish.

Reaching into his pocket, he pulls out a silver cuff bracelet with intricate vines carved into the metal surrounding a small pale stone. He slips it over my free wrist. "We are now one." Allowing his fingers to slide between mine, he holds our bound hands in the air. "Let us celebrate in the glory of Zaaron's many blessings!"

The booming of cheer makes my chest squeeze so tight that, for a moment, breathing is impossible.

That's it. It's over.

I'm bound…to the Prophet.

The guests place the candles in the holders on the tables, switching them for fistfuls of flower petals to throw at us. The food is brought out, and while it looks delicious, eating isn't going to happen right now.

Though the term being 'bound' is in reference to the

spiritual sense, in this moment, it's one hundred percent literal. Our wrists remain tied together through the entire celebration, abolishing any chance of getting a moment alone with Zeb.

All night it's been one congratulation after another. My family greets me with open arms, my father smiling at me for the first time since before I received the blood of innocence. Mia goes on about how pretty I look, and my heart aches at how much I will miss her. My muscles relax after seeing them. I allow myself to try and enjoy the festivities, and it works…if I don't look at Zebadiah.

All the girls are acting like I landed the prize husband. I suppose by logical standards I have. It's just to me, my prize husband is now my son. Still, I giggle as they swoon over my dress and bracelet. Being the center of attention has its perks, and I am enjoying them until the Prophet's voice whispers in my ear.

"It's time to show you your new home."

It's as if the ribbons snake from my hair and wrap around my neck when he pulls us to standing.

"Children of Zaaron, I am humbled by your love and kindness this night. Please stay. Enjoy the evening while my new bride and I continue our binding night."

Forming a pathway, every person in attendance stands to send us off, throwing flower petals until we pass.

Cheers and applause fades into the background, pushing me into silence with my new husband. I've never been alone with him for more than a few moments.

"You did well tonight. I am pleased. As is Zaaron."

I can't decide between 'you're welcome' or 'thank you', I just know I'm grateful he isn't angry with me. "I am relieved to hear you say that, Prophet."

"That was the very lesson I was teaching in my sermon

this morning. There is freedom in servitude. You will quickly see that relinquishing your trust and decision making to me is a powerful type of deliverance. And please, you are now my wife. To you, I am Hiram."

I don't know what to say, but compliance is always honorable. "Of course, Hiram."

We walk in silence. I am about to speak to relieve the awkwardness of it all when he sighs.

"I do know things started out rough between us. Understand, I can be a fair and just husband as long as you live within spiritual law."

"I desire to be a holy woman. I want you to know that."

"I do know, Zaaron has told me as much."

His fingers squeeze my hand, and we take the dirt road that leads to the Fitch ranch. This is the biggest house on the compound, by far. To even call it a 'house' doesn't do it justice because it's closer to three houses that are attached together.

We walk into what appears to be the main entrance of the home. He ushers me across a dining room that leads to a kitchen, and then through a seating area. I wonder how long we are going to stay tied together as we keep going through this never-ending house.

Stopping at a door, he pushes it open. The evening has begun to ascend, painting the sky in dark violets through the floral curtains. The room is smaller than the one Mia and I shared back home.

He lights a match to ignite a lamp, placing it next to a copy of *The True Testament* on the nightstand. There is an open closet, but I don't have any clothes to fill it besides my binding dress. The white vanity table begs me to sit down on the matching stool. I yearn to run my fingers over its golden accents and the designs carved into the wood. The quilt and pillows adorning the bed look fluffy and soft.

The bed.

The bed brings back the fear with a force so harsh, I am grateful for the ribbon's part in keeping me standing.

"These are your sleeping quarters. On the nights you sleep alone, you are to be in this room at ten o'clock and must remain here until you are told you may leave the next morning. Use of the washroom is permitted during these hours. However, I suggest you keep the frequency to a minimum."

It's not uncommon for a husband to give his new wife strict rules when first bound, but this narrows my chances of getting time alone with Zeb.

I nod. "I understand."

He holds up our bound hands and unties the ribbon, freeing me from him for the first time in hours.

"Though tonight there is no need to worry about that."

The room begins to shrink around me. The walls are going to squish me flat. He closes the door, removing his hat and jacket before hanging them on the pegs on the wall. When his thumbs hook under his suspenders to pull them down, I can't stop the tears from blurring my vision.

He stands in front of me, lifting my chin. Not looking up at him is impossible, and when I do, the kindness present in them moments ago has vanished.

"Do not cry. This is your duty."

Please, help me be strong. I don't think I can do this.

The more I try to quell the tears, the quicker they fall. His fingers unbutton his shirt as he barks, "Turn around."

I do what he says with my tears refusing to subside. The dress loosens while he works his way down the back of the gown. I push the sleeves off my arms and step out of it before turning to face him. My ears burn when his gaze moves across my exposed flesh, and I instinctively lift my hand in an attempt to cover myself.

He rips the beautiful dress from my grasp, tossing it on the vanity chair as he closes in on me. Reaching into his pocket, he removes a hunting knife and presses the sharp edge of the blade against my shoulder.

"It is told to us by our God, Zaaron, in *The True Testament*: 'Blood is the most sacred form of love. As a husband takes the blood of his wife, he takes her into him, forevermore.'" He swipes the blade across my skin, and I gasp. Lurching forward, his tongue traces along the wound before he suckles at the split flesh. When he becomes satisfied, he stands straight and hands me the blade. My blood is bright on his lips when I push the sharp side of the knife against his chest. He continues, "'Furthermore, as the life force of the groom is ingested by the bride, the Anointed bond becomes unbreakable—an impenetrable circle.'"

Squeezing my eyes shut, I pull it across his flesh. Slowly, I open my eyes and watch the crimson blossom from his skin. His impatience wears thinner with every passing second, so I lean forward, pressing my mouth to the cut. Once the metallic taste hits my tongue, I suck out the warm liquid until he seems appeased.

Pulling back, a large sob jumps from my lips. "Stop crying!" He raises his hand and brings it across my face. "Ungracious bitch."

I cry again at his curse, hating that I'm not stronger and more obedient.

"I apologize, Pr- Hiram."

He grabs my arm, pushing me on the bed before he undoes his trousers. I crawl up the quilt when he grabs my ankles and yanks me back to the edge. Ripping off my boots, he pushes up my petticoat and tears down my bloomers.

"I had wanted this to be more pleasant, but regardless, you will serve your purpose."

He pushes my legs so far apart I fear they will dislocate from my hips. I sob as he lies on top of me. The heaviness of his weight is suffocating me...crushing me. I claw at his back, begging for the air to reach my lungs, when my body is ripped down the middle. I open my mouth to release my scream, though it's cut short by his hands around my throat.

"This is a divine gift!" He hits me once more, and the pain is so excruciating, I wonder if I'm dying. "I won't tell you again. Stop crying or I will fucking make you."

His sigil pendant rubs against my chest, and I accept that my rebellion is making this worse for me. While the tears continue to fall, I stop fighting, lying still.

I let him take my body and soul as I stare at the beautiful white vanity with the golden accents.

9

MARKED WITH BLOOD

Laurel Ann

THERE AREN'T ANY DRY SPOTS ON MY PILLOW. NOT THAT IT matters. Sleep isn't on my side and wants nothing to do with me. His back expands with his steady breathing. I shouldn't feel this way toward my husband and Prophet, but in this moment, I hate him.

My first time with a man was the worst experience of my life. It hurt more than I could have fathomed, and when he finished, he didn't speak a word. He climbed off of me to roll over and go to sleep, leaving me to silently weep.

Your unwillingness to obey is revolting.

His words slide around in my mind causing tears to sting my eyes. My ribs ache and my thighs burn. I just want to stop crying. A rooster crows, and Hiram stirs. I need out of this room before I choke. I need away from him. I lift the heavy quilt off my legs and slip from the bed. Picking up my binding gown and bloomers, I adjust them as much as possible and sneak into the hall. Every step hurts, and I have no idea where the washroom is.

"Laurel Ann."

Zebadiah's voice, even as a whisper, is unmistakable. I don't know what to expect from him, I just know I can't handle his anger right now. I turn to him, and his head falls before he shakes it back and forth.

"Fuck."

His curse shocks me, and I cover my mouth to quiet my gasp. "Zeb—"

"He hit you. He couldn't even wait to let your binding night pass." I don't understand how he could know that. As if reading my mind, he answers my unasked question. "Your face, it's bruised."

I touch the tender spot beneath my eye.

Stop crying! You are being touched by holiness!

I know I don't have much time to speak with him. I don't know what I'm going to say, even as the thoughts are forming in my head. Last night isn't something I can keep reliving. The realization of that makes the words almost too thick to speak.

"I can't stay here…with him. I'm going home."

My statement hangs in the air between us, and now that I've said it aloud I know it's what I have to do. I don't want to ever feel the Prophet's touch again.

His eyes stretch out so wide I think they might pop out. "What are you talking about?!"

I use my hands to shush him. "It was horrible, Zeb. I'm going to ask my father to take me back."

He shakes his head like he's organizing my words in his brain. "It doesn't work like that. You said your vows. You're his forever."

I'm surprised I can still produce tears, yet they pour out in a stream. "I can't live this way. I'm sorry…maybe I'll become un-boundable."

He rubs his forehead in frustration. "Un-boundable? That's not a thing! You have to accept this."

"I…I can't." I ignore the aching in my body and wrap my arms around him, laying my head against his chest. "I'm sorry." I don't know how this is going to turn out, I just know that anything is better than repeating last night over and over again. I lean back to cup his face. This is a sin and I know it. So is leaving my new husband. I pull him down to me as I push up on my feet, pressing my lips to his. My heart patters violently in my chest, and I pull back to look in his bewildered blue eyes. "Goodbye, Zeb."

I turn back the way Hiram led me last night with Zebadiah following after me, pleading with me to stay until I reach the front door. He can't leave his house; this is his time of questioning. I lift my skirt and run. Standing in his doorway, he no longer attempts a whisper, yelling my name.

"Laurel Ann! Don't do this! Laurel Ann!"

The Fitch ranch is on the opposite side of the compound from my farm. I wish I would have picked up my shoes, but this decision wasn't a thought out one. The rocks make running difficult, so I cut through the grass patches as they come. A sharp pain stabs my side, and I slow to catch my breath once I reach the common ground. I pass Henry Taub and Doc Kilmer who both give me questioning looks.

The sun is tired in the horizon, and I know my father must be awake by now. The sight of my farmhouse is a comfort to my tattered soul. I pick up my dress, revealing torn stockings, and sprint up the dirt path. Hurrying across the yard, I climb onto the porch with desperate steps. I shove open the door, and crossing the threshold is a relief on my cut-up feet.

My father is sitting at the table eating eggs and toast when he jumps from my entrance. His face flashes through shock before it settles on fury. He shoots to standing and barrels toward me, raising his hand but changing his mind mid-strike.

"What are you doing here?!"

I fall to his feet and grasp at his boots. "Please let me come home, Pa. I can't be bound to the Prophet...please don't make me go back."

My eye hurts worse when I cry, though it's not my concern at present. I need him to understand.

His fist clenches around the fabric at my shoulder, yanking me to my feet. "You are no daughter of mine!" He pushes me out the door, and I fall backward down the steps, sending more agony through my already aching body. "Get up."

I push myself to my knees, and he doesn't wait any longer. He grabs me by the arm, dragging me to the side of the house where the horses are already hooked up to the buggy. I don't wait for him to tell me to get inside. This was a mistake. I don't have any idea what gave me the inclination that he would bring me back into the family.

Imagining what the Prophet is going to do mixed with the bouncing of the buggy turns my insides, pushing them into my throat. I jump up to lean over the side, watching the sick hit the dirt behind us. Father turns and glares at me, saying nothing.

He doesn't even get the buggy stopped in front of the tabernacle when Hiram walks out.

"Prophet, I cannot apologize enough—"

The Prophet holds up his hand to stop him. "It is not your fault, Brother Benjamin." He looks at me with repulsion. "She has made her choice."

Apostle Keaton walks out of the tabernacle. "What do you need from me, Prophet?"

Hiram barks at me, "Get out of the buggy." I scramble to obey. I don't think anyone has ever had two cleansing rituals within a week before. "Take her to the holding room and meet me in my office."

Apostle Keaton nods. I step to follow him when the

Prophet grabs my wrist, yanking off my binding bracelet. My father scoffs at me. I am nothing to him anymore. The Apostle marches me into the tabernacle and shuts me in the first holding room. This isn't how it was done last time, which causes an uneasiness to creep into my pores.

Excommunication has always been a fear for me, especially as a child, but I have never seen it happen to anyone. I think part of me didn't believe they would ever really do it. Sitting here, I don't doubt it anymore. I'm not receiving another cleansing. Zaaron forgave me, and I threw it back in His face.

Oh, Zaaron, please don't rebuke me. I'm sorry. Sorrier than I've ever been about anything.

Plenty of time has passed, yet to me, it could have been moments. In this room I am safe, and I am in no hurry to change that. My ripped stockings stick to my bloody feet, so I peel them off, whimpering at the pain. The lock on the door *clinks* and the knob turns. My eyes slam shut, refusing to let the next few moments pass.

"Remove your binding gown."

The Prophet speaks to me as if each word is beneath him. If I take off my dress I'll be in nothing besides my bodice petticoat and bloomers. Of course, he knows that.

I reach behind me, unfastening as many latches as I can before I push aside my humiliation and obey. Regardless of the warmth of the room, when the air hits the exposed skin of my arms, chills spread through my body.

He rips the dress from my fingers, taking the rope tucked under his arm and tying it around my wrists, tight enough to jab into my skin. Yanking the door back open, he pulls me through the empty meeting hall. I'm tempted to fight him and not let him do this. I just know any attempt would be futile.

The tabernacle doors open, and the exact same faces that were congratulating and complimenting me last night, are now snarling and glaring. They all hate me. It is written clear as glass all over their expressions. He leads me through the crowd spewing their repulsion at my actions.

Something hits my stomach, and the smell twists in my nose. I look down to see a red, rotten tomato smeared across my white petticoat. The first becomes an invitation for more. My already weak body is pelted with old food. They are all yelling at me about the tortures awaiting me in Hell and in the outside world. The humiliation brings more tears than the pain. I hate that they can see my flesh and know my sins.

They all follow us as he leads me to the main gate of the compound. He turns my body to face the crowd, and the first person my eyes find is my father. He's steps in front of the angry followers to spit at my feet.

Removing the blade from last night, the Prophet holds my bound hands and slices the knife across my right palm, making me gasp from the sting. He pushes his finger down into the cut, covering it in crimson as I cry out. He draws the X of excommunication on my forehead, marking me with blood. I hear Mia's screams from the crowd. I look across the furious faces to see my mother holding her back as she reaches for me.

Benji Johnson works his way to the front of the mob. His chest is heaving, and terror consumes his features. He's obviously wishing he could speak to me. I haven't gotten to see him since before his cleansing.

My heart shatters to the dirt around my feet, and the consequences of my actions weigh heavy on my shoulders. Zebadiah's not even here, he's confined to the ranch. The knowledge that I will never see him again threatens the strength of my legs and hollows out my chest. Why did I do this?

I'm so sorry...

"Laurel Ann Henderson. You are hereby excommunicated

from the Anointed Land." Those words echo in my brain, consuming everything that comes after them. "Your soul has been overtaken by the Devil, and your sinful decisions have given him access into this compound. You will no longer be under the grace and protection of Zaaron. You are destined to walk this earth for the remainder of your days in the absence of His holy presence. You will not meet us at the Paradise Star, and you will never again feel peace. Your soul will forever be tormented."

The gates are opened, and as I step over the edge of the compound, my body is consumed in shivers. The desire to drop to my knees and plead is overbearing, but it's already done. It would do nothing more than add to my mortification.

The field in front of me stretches on for miles. I turn back to the only place I have ever known, watching the people who used to be my world walk away from me. I stare at them until they disappear, and I'm truly alone.

Blackbirds fly across a bright, blue sky unaware of my world shattering. I don't know where to go, and there is no way to avoid the Philistines. This is their world. My feet move me forward, and I let them. It doesn't matter where they take me.

It won't be home.

The edge of the field is cut off by a tree line, so I follow it until I reach a road. Open land and fields spread around me in every direction. My heart stabs in my chest, and I don't know if it's from panic or heartbreak. I'm nothing now. I turned from my God, losing everything as a result. Even if the heathens accept me, I won't accept them. I won't allow them to darken my soul any more than it already is. I would rather be by myself for the rest of my life.

Other than the occasional house in the distance, there's nothing around. I no sooner think how lucky I am that I haven't seen a Philistine when I hear a noisy rumble. It gets louder with every second that passes. I whip my head around for someplace to hide, but there is nothing besides emptiness. It's right behind me, and though my mind begs me not to, I turn around. It starts as a black dot that gets larger at a terrifying speed. A cloud of dirt trails behind it, and no matter how fast I run, it will be on me before I even get a few yards. I still have to try.

My tied wrists inhibit me more than I anticipated. Rocks jab into my feet, and my leg gives way, causing me to fall. The sound begins to slow until a metal machine that resembles a horse on two rubber wheels, pops and spurts to a stop right next to where I lie. A black boot attached to what is certainly a Philistine, lands in the dirt next to my bound hands. My heartbeat is so quick and loud I can't make out what he says. Lifting up my hands, I block the sun blinding my vision. The man is in all black, apart from the silver metal he's wearing. His dark hair is pulled back, and his beard is the longest I've ever seen.

Crouching down in front of me, he smiles. "You okay, little lady? Where ya headin'?"

He reaches out to me, and I snap my hand back. There is no way he's getting his filthy hands on me. "Don't touch me. You're a bad man."

His laugh shakes his whole body, and I slowly try to scoot away. "That I am. Lucky for you though, not to little girls who look like they've had it rough enough already. Why don't you get on the bike, and I'll untie your hands and take you to a police station, okay?"

"I'm not going anywhere with you!"

He reaches for me again, so I use all my strength to kick his knee with my heel.

"Ah! Shit, girl, I'm trying to help you!"

I crawl backward as his fingers grasp at my petticoat. I

don't look to see if he's chasing me when I flip onto my knees and push to my feet. My speed picks up once I step upon the field, but I know I can't outrun him.

If you are still listening, please don't let him hurt me.

The roar of the man's machine brings me to a stop. I look over my shoulder to watch him zoom away.

I'm okay. I'm safe.

Thank you, Zaaron.

As my heart rate slows, the fear dissipates, and momentary relief takes over. Is this how it's going to be now? Every minute of every day running and hiding from the evil covering this place? Will terror replace the love and happiness I once felt? The shame, regret, and fear tie together in a knot to climb up my throat. The tears pour out like rain as I fall to the ground and weep.

I allow myself a few moments to mourn the loss of everything I have ever known because I need every bit of strength that remains to survive here.

Body and soul.

I tug and pull on my bindings. For once I'm grateful that I'm sweating when my hand slips free of the rope. Breathing out a relieved sigh, I release my other wrist. Finally, I stand, brush off the debris, and continue my journey to nowhere. I make it back to the road where I'm left to the peace of being alone.

My feet hurt, my legs ache, I'm hungry, I'm drenched in sweat, and I think I might dehydrate soon if I don't get some water. The knowledge that I have no bed to lay my head on tonight brings the nausea back.

Beep-boop. Beep-boop.

My skin jumps from my bones at the intrusive sound. There are voices that sound small, like they're trapped. I turn to see blue and red lights flashing around in a circle on top of a white metal box on wheels. A man in black pants, shirt, and hat is walking toward me with one hand on his hip and the other outstretched. There are more *beeps* and voices, but I don't see anyone else around.

I move my feet, running before I even turn around.

"Stop!"

His footsteps are close, urging me to run faster. It's pointless though because his hands wrap around my shoulders.

"Don't touch me!" I try to break from his grasp, my strength nonexistent in comparison. I kick and scream, and although his palms are slippery with sweat, he's still able to hang on.

"Ma'am! You're bleeding! Stop! I am here to assist you. I'm just going to take you to the station."

"Assist me by leaving me alone!" I stomp on his feet and elbow him in the stomach. He grunts and struggles, yet I still remain in his clutches.

"This is your last warning. Stop moving. I don't want to cuff you, but I will." His arm wraps around me, passing by my face, so I clamp my teeth down onto his wrist, biting with all my strength.

"Fugh! Damn it!"

He rips his arm from my mouth as he bends my own behind my back. Something hard digs into my wrists, and I can't separate them.

"What did you do to me?!"

I haven't been out of the compound a day, and I've already been captured. I try not to think of the terrifying things that await me once I arrive at 'the station'.

"What did I do to *you*?! You broke skin, you little delinquent. You'll be lucky if I don't press charges."

He pushes me in the back of the metal box which has *Kiowa County Sheriff* written on the side, and slams the door next to me. This must be some type of buggy because when he sits in the seat in front of me and it shakes to life, we begin to move forward. I don't know how because there aren't any horses to pull us. Within moments, the fields are passing by me in a blur. I don't like the way this is making my body feel. I bet this is some kind of Philistine trick.

"Where are you from?" I'm sure he would love to know that. I don't answer him. He may be able to force me to go to 'the station', but he can't make me talk to him. While there's a gate separating us, I can still see his shoulders lift with his sigh. "Do you come from that weird cult place a ways back?" I keep my lips closed and glare at him in the tiny mirror above his head. "It's just your clothes. They're...different. 'Vintage' as my stepdaughter would say." I don't know half of the things he speaks of. He huffs, "If you don't tell me where you're from, how am I supposed to get you home?" For some reason, in his twisted heathen brain, he thinks my silence is an invitation to keep asking questions. "What's your name?"

The fields have dispersed, replaced with homes and buildings. The metal buggies are everywhere now.

We stop at a red flashing light, and he turns in his seat so I can see his face. "Will you at least tell me where you were going?"

His questions scrape over the already raw reminder of my predicament. I hate this man. I hate him for abducting me. I hate him simply for what he is: an evil, dirty sinner.

"Your soul is a heap of bile. It makes me sick. I'm not telling you anything."

His head snaps back before turning around to resume driving. "Fine. Then I have no choice other than to call social services."

We aren't allowed to know hardly anything about the outside world. It is forbidden, and that was just fine with me until now. I don't know what he's talking about, and it could mean anything.

"Are they going to hurt me?"

"What? No." He shakes his head, and the strange buggy slows down until it completely stops. The rumbling quiets, leaving us sitting in silence. "They'll take you to the children's home in Tipton until a foster family becomes available. Unless you want to start talking?"

Children's home? That doesn't sound so bad. Maybe Philistine children are not yet as corrupt as their adult counterparts. Why am I acting like I have a choice? This is where I will live and die. Alone. I am no longer protected by Zaaron. However, I still know the truth. I will keep my soul pure. I will not allow these heathens to tarnish it. I will live as holy of a life as possible outside the gates of the compound, and maybe when I die, I will still make it to the Paradise Star. I know the prophecy states that those cast out of the Anointed Land are destined to forever starve for the presence of Zaaron, but I have to try. I have to.

Please, let me show you how I yearn to be Anointed once again.

10

WHITE AND YELLOW FLOWERS

Zebadiah

I'M STUNNED IMMOBILE. THE WAY SHE'S SPEAKING TERRIFIES ME, yet her taste is all I can think of. Her lips are touching mine for the first time. I have thought of kissing her so many times, I just knew it wasn't fair to push that sin on her. I didn't want her angry with me. Now, I wish I would have risked it.

Her lips pull away, and she whispers, "Goodbye, Zeb."

My heart freefalls to my stomach as she spins around to leave. She can't do this. He'll make her pay, and it will be ruthless. I rush to follow her. She just needs to calm down.

"Look, I know you're scared, and I'm sure he put you through a lot of pain, but if you obey him, he can be bearable. Please listen. If you leave, things will be worse." I rush out my words while she ignores my attempts to make her see reason. She can't understand the extent of the damage she's about to cause. Pushing open the door, she runs from the house, the fear of how he'll react turning my stomach sour. "Laurel Ann! Don't do this! Laurel Ann!" She's already reached the edge of the yard. For a split second, I consider breaking my time of questioning to chase after her, but she's clearly made up her mind. Angering him more would only make this harder for the both of us. I can't believe she's doing this. I slam my hand against the door frame.

"Fuck!"

The collar of my shirt constricts around my neck as I'm flung around and shoved against the wall. My father stands in front of me, seething. Shirtless and barefoot, he wears only his trousers. The back of his hand lands hard against my cheek.

"Do not speak that way in this holy house!" He glances over my shoulder, out the open door. "Where is she?"

I swallow any words I may have had. I want to knock him to the ground, hit him over and over, turning his face into nothing but bloody features. I hate him for taking Laurel Ann as his wife, I hate him for laying with her, and I hate him for hurting her. I reach out to shove him.

"She went anywhere she could to get away from you!" I scream at him, clenching my fists so I don't hit him again.

Wrapping his hand around my neck, he squeezes tight and slams my head against the doorframe. "WHERE IS SHE?!" he roars in my face.

I choke, my throat threatening to collapse. I claw at his hand, unable to answer him even if I intended to. My vision becomes spotty, and my mind loses focus.

My mother screams for me in the distance until, finally, I am released from his clutches. I collapse to the floor, wheezing in my attempt to refill my lungs.

Before I can regulate my breathing, he's grabbing me by my arm and yanking me down the hall. I look over my shoulder at Zeke, in only his union suit, frowning at me with concern. Jacob is next to him concealing his smirk. Internally rolling my eyes, I'm dragged further down the hall to my room.

He tosses me inside, and I fall to the floor. "You will not leave this spot until Keaton brings you to the holding room."

The door slams behind him, and he stomps back down the hall where I hear my mothers asking what's happening.

Crawling on my bed, I rub my throat, groaning as I lie down and look at the wooden beams across the ceiling. Part of me is proud of her for standing up to him. She's never been afraid to speak her mind, at least not to me, and it's one of the million things about her that make her my favorite person in the Anointed Land. I've always wanted my mothers to be stronger and defend themselves, although I logically see why they don't. Now, I'm wishing she would have been more like them.

If only I was already the Prophet. Then Zaaron would tell me what is to become of her. His wrath can be gruesome and vengeful. I often wonder what it will be like to share a mind with Him.

Just last month, Rose Taub was caught stealing fruits from the general store for the third time. Henry Taub has the habit of using food as a tool to keep his wives in line, and Rose was being starved for disrespecting him. For the sin of thievery, Zaaron ordered my father to remove the three middle fingers on her right hand.

If He would do that to a woman who was only hungry for food, what will He do to Laurel Ann for spitting His blessing back in His face?

I unknowingly doze off, awakening to my bedroom door slamming against the wall.

"Get up," my father barks.

Scrambling to my feet, I look into his angry face. "What are you going to do to her?"

His nostrils flare as he stares at me for a long, tedious moment. "I only do what is ordered of me by Zaaron. Now, move. Your uncle is here to take you to the holding room."

"Just tell me she'll be okay...please."

He flinches like he's going to hit me, but instead takes a step closer. "You listen to me. You are Zebadiah Immanuel Fitch. You have a destiny. A plan set forth for you by our God!" Grabbing my arms, he shakes me. "Do you not see, by fighting me, you are fighting Him? Things are going to change, my son. Now, if I have to repeat myself, you will not enjoy the outcome."

Losing my footing, I stumble back. I don't care about my fucking destiny. I just want to know she's going to be all right.

I scoff and pass by him to leave my room. "Yes, sir."

When I arrive in the dining room, my uncle Keaton is with my mothers. He grunts at me in his way of greeting. My mother rushes to me, hugging my neck and kissing me.

"Be obedient, baby. It can't happen to you, I couldn't bear it," she whispers urgently.

My throat tightens, my eyes widening at what her comment could be referring to. "What can't happen to me, Ma?"

Just as my father appears in the doorway, my uncle says, "We must go, Zebadiah."

It's hard to find my breath. My father's been bugging me for the past few months to study *The True Testament* and other religious texts. It's important that the Prophet has extensive knowledge of everything involving our belief system. I've been putting it off, but now I am angry at my procrastination. If I knew spiritual law inside and out, maybe I would have a better idea of what horrors are awaiting her.

Turning from my father's glare, I do as I'm told and follow

my uncle Keaton out the front door. We walk down the pathway, and I wait until we are a good distance from the house before speaking.

"Will you tell me what is to become of her? Please, Uncle Keaton?"

He sighs and steps ahead of me. "I was specifically ordered to not give you that information."

Hurrying to keep up, I walk briskly beside him. "Just tell me, is she to remain bound to my father?"

With a frown, he grunts. I don't think he's going to respond when he finally says, "No."

My pulse thumps at my temples, and I wipe my hand over my mouth. She's being stripped of her position as the Prophet's wife, which to most would be a devastating loss. Not to her though. My father knows that, and Zaaron does too. There has to be more in store for her.

"Will she receive another cleansing?"

He shakes his head, walking faster. "Enough about the girl. No more talking."

I bite my tongue at the desire to call him my father's dog. Insulting him would get me nowhere.

As we walk through the common ground, I search for any sign of her. My uncle doesn't speak to me again until he's leading me into my holding room. He uses a match to light the lamp before walking to the door.

"Your choices go far beyond you. Everything has a consequence." He doesn't speak that often, so his words surprise me. He tips his hat as he backs out of the room. "Get some rest, kid."

She wasn't there.

My breath comes out wheezy as I rub the back of my neck. I think the ox yoke may have cut me when it dug in. I'm hunched over in the corner of the box of repentance, next to the water tank. Even with my body in agony, my thoughts refuse to leave her.

I scanned the crowd for her face through my entire cleansing. I screamed as my father burnt and cut my back, all the while, I just wanted to see her eyes.

My siblings followed their apparent orders by refusing to speak a word to me when they brought me my meals in the holding room. The few moments I had with my father before the ritual were filled with nothing more than threats and insults.

The worst possible scenario keeps haunting me. I've never seen an excommunication besides Benji's mother, and that was her choice. I have to believe Zaaron wouldn't cast her out for this. She wants nothing more than to go to the Paradise Star.

She's probably just in the other holding room. She has to be.

Shifting my body to lie beneath the water tank has me gritting my teeth in pain. I would like to believe every decision made by my father, when it comes to spiritual law, is sanctioned, but today felt personal. Twelve lashings and forty-five hours in the box is excessive, even for the worst offenses. He was making an example of me.

Using my torn shirt as a pillow, I lie beneath the spigot and open my mouth, waiting for a drop of moisture.

I try imagining all the best outcomes of this. Maybe I'm getting scared for no reason. Still though, there's a disquiet that refuses to dissipate.

I close my eyes as a drop of water falls into my mouth,

and I savor it. I realize, with the water tank being the only source of relief in this box, she likely spent her time lying in this exact spot. It makes my chest feel raw to think that she went through this. I'm used to my father's abuse, yet it did nothing to prepare me. There were moments when the whip was ripping apart my flesh that I feared my ability to survive.

Guilt hits me in the chest, and I can barely breathe. She never would have lied about the blood if I hadn't suggested it. This chain reaction of events falls on my shoulders. Whatever is happening to her is my fault.

Please don't let her suffer for my actions. While she responded out of fear, my choices were born from selfishness. If anyone deserves your wrath, it's me. She means so much to me that I was thinking of my own desires and not the good of the Anointed Land. I know I must do better if I am to be an honorable Prophet, and I vow to make holier choices. I simply ask you to spare her. I know I am destined to rule this compound, but I have not taken the responsibility of it. Please, show her your grace, and I will be the man you want me to be. The man you prophesied I would be.

Light I haven't seen for what feels like days burns my eyes as my father arrives to release me from my confinement.

"Go immediately home and wait for me in your room." His voice bounces off the walls of the wooden box.

I nod my head and bite my tongue until it hurts to keep myself from asking about her. He wouldn't answer me anyway. My shirt hangs open, baring the sensitive flesh of my back. The glaring sun turns my vision black, and my legs haven't been walked on in hours. They are wobbly beneath me, and I fall off the plank as I try to leave.

My father doesn't attempt to help me up or speak to me at all. I force myself to my feet before turning my back to him and walking to the ranch.

In the distance, the school bell rings. The sound used to ignite joy over the end of another school day, and now it only brings anxiety.

It's never taken me this long to get home before, and it's getting more difficult to not stop and lie down on the ground. The only thing driving me is the possibility of getting answers from someone in my family.

Grass rustles behind me, and I groan as I turn to see my brother, Jacob, running up to me. "So, you're finally out, huh?"

"You're clearly the one with the brains in the family."

He doesn't laugh at my sarcasm, he just grinds his teeth and taunts me. "Too bad it was all for nothing."

My blood turns to stone in my veins. "What do you mean?"

Shrugging, he continues walking. "I just mean you're the future Prophet. You risked your soul for that tainted bitch, and Zaaron excommunicated her anyway."

My body is consumed with a burning as hot as the fire from my cleansing. My exhaustion is swallowed by vehemence, fueled with heartbreak.

Excommunicated?! You fucking excommunicated her?!

A roar rips from my throat before I tackle him to the ground. I don't notice the pain from moments ago. I don't feel anything past betrayal, grief, and rage. Somewhere in my mind, I know that my brother is not who I really want on the receiving end of my fury, but I allow my fists to rain down onto his body anyway.

I know I'm screaming at him, yet I can't recall the words that last left my mouth. He attempts to cover his face, tucking his knees to his chest. Something wraps around my arm, pulling me off him.

"Zeb! Zeb! Stop!" The tremors behind my eyes cease, allowing me to focus on Zeke. "Are you crazy?"

Jacob spits on the ground and wipes his lip. "Wait till Father hears about this."

Ezekiel's jaw clenches as he points a finger at our brother. "You will keep your deceitful mouth shut or I'll shut it for you." His anger is rare, however, if he's pushed far enough, his temper can be vicious. Turning back to me, his expression softens. "What are you doing?"

Of all my siblings, I am by far the closest to Zeke. He's teased me about all the time I spent with Laurel Ann, but he was always there to listen, and he's the only one who knows how I truly feel about her.

I don't have to be strong in front of him, so I'm not. I let the tears freely fall. "Is she really gone?"

He closes his eyes, giving me the slightest of nods. My chest heaves, and I shake my head as if my denial can undo what's been done. Ire is the life source of my newfound vigor as I run from my brothers toward the fence. Zeke calls my name, and I block it out, using every scrap of my energy to get to the edge of the compound.

My fingers grasp the fence. I scan the field beyond for any sign of her, and find only emptiness. Looking down shatters me even more when I see yellow and white flowers growing against the wood of the fence. A smile appears through my sobs at the memory of the day I finally worked up the courage to talk to her.

My palms are sticky and sweaty around the bouquet I hold in my hand. She reminds me of a shooting star, the way she glows when she smiles. Her laugh tickles my stomach as I walk up to her among the wildflowers. I hope she's pleased with the ones I picked for her. The white and yellow against her red hair would make them look like they were on fire. Why do I feel so funny? I can't decide if I'm scared or excited.

She raises her head, and our eyes meet. Her freckled cheeks turn rosy, and her full, pink lips lift into a smile. Tucking her hair behind her ear, she flutters her long eyelashes.

"Hello, Zebadiah,"

I think I'm going to throw up.

"Uh, hi, Laurel Ann...I picked these for your crown." I hold them out to her, and my heart flips at her sweet expression. "I thought they would look pretty in your hair."

She accepts them with a gentle smile. "You got these just for me?" I nod to her and stuff my hands in my pockets. "They're perfect. Thank you."

She wraps me in a hug while my grin stretches my cheeks. She smells like the flowers we stand in.

Falling to my knees, I weep as I curse my God.
How could you take her from me?

I know I'm going to regret my disobedience tonight. The pain from my lashings and the intense need for food have once again consumed by body. I don't know how I'm going to handle the steps to the porch much less more of my father's beatings. I just can't stop staring out of this fence, as if there's a chance of her appearing.

"Hey...are you okay?"

I jump at the unexpected voice and turn to see Benji Johnson. He moves to sit against the fence next to me.

"I can't believe he really sent her out there." Shaking my head, I can hear the tears in my own voice. "What if they hurt her?"

His expression softens with a small smile. "She's strong. I

have no doubt she can take care of herself."

My anger may be misplaced, it just feels like I'm the only one who understands we will never see her again. Do they not realize that she's gone not only in this life, but the one after?

"She's your fucking kin, Benji! How can you not be more upset about this?!"

He ignores my outburst, resting his head against the fence. "She's only my second cousin, no more kin than most people. And I am upset; she was my friend too. If I could have done anything to stop it, I would have."

The inevitable guilt for snapping at him seeps over me, and I wipe my hands across my face. "I'm sorry. I know you care about her. I'm angry at Zaaron and my father, not you."

His head tilts as he wraps his arms around his knees. "How is this the Prophet's fault? He's only obeying Zaaron."

I'd been unknowingly clenching my jaw so I force myself to relax. "He didn't have to! Zaaron makes it clear that the penance for sin is a cleansing, yet the members of my family don't get a quarter of the cleansings they should. He could have chosen to make his own decision. He could have kept her here."

Looking lost in thought, he stares toward the common ground. "Would you have? When you become Prophet, will you obey everything Zaaron tells you?"

It's hard for me to admit to even myself that I don't possess the desire to be Prophet. I don't want to spend my life being Zaaron's henchman.

Standing, I brush the dirt from my trousers. "I don't know. I just know I'll be a better Prophet than he is. I'll rule with kindness, not cruelty."

He raises his eyebrows and quirks his mouth to the side as if struggling to believe me. "I hope you do. You'll probably be the one leading us all to the Paradise Star."

My father reminds me of this fact quite frequently. I'll be

sixty-four years-old when the Abolition comes to pass and very likely, the final Prophet.

"I better go, my father's expecting me."

I struggle to make my way back to the ranch. I'm so hungry and tired that my bed and the possibility of food are the only things that keep my feet stepping in front of each other. I reach my porch steps, and I dread climbing them. I feel on the brink of collapsing.

As I reach for the door, it swings open, and Sister Karen helps me inside. "Zebadiah, where have you been? I've been expecting you for over an hour." My brothers and sisters sit at the table, but I don't look up to see which ones. She leads me to the washroom as quickly as I am able. "Your water will now be cold, and you must eat in the tub if you want food. Hiram will be back soon."

Every time my mothers speak of him there's an underlying tone of fear. Like they're walking on a frozen lake, and one wrong step will make them fall in.

"I just...I just found out about Laurel Ann."

She holds my face in her hands and kisses my forehead before pulling my shredded shirt from my arms. Undoing my trousers, I unbutton and remove my torn union suit as she takes off my shoes. Once I'm nude, she helps me into the barely lukewarm bath.

"I'll be right back with some stew."

She hurries back into the hall, and I do my best to clean myself. Even with the water cool, it heals and washes away the dirt. When Sister Karen returns, she shoves a bowl in my hands and orders me to eat.

With the first bite I feel relief in my stomach. Physically, I begin to revive as she washes my hair.

After I'm clean, she retrieves the salve from the cabinet, and I wrap the towel around my waist, moving much quicker now. Her gentle fingers rub the medicine on my wounds. I groan from the sting, but I know that it will feel much better tomorrow. The jar clangs as she closes the lid.

"Go to your room, and wait for your father."

"Yes, ma'am."

She rushes by me to bring my empty stew bowl into the kitchen, patting my arm before I walk down the hall to my bedroom. I enter to be immediately greeted by Ezekiel, as if he's been waiting for me.

"Hey."

His voice is filled with pity, and it flames the already simmering fire. I don't want him to feel sorry for me. I want him to be angry for me. For her. I go to the closet for a new pair of trousers and a shirt. Opening my dresser, I pull out a fresh union suit.

"Did anyone even try to stop him?! Did anyone fight for her?"

I drop the towel to step into my underclothes and pants. He scoffs, looking out the window before meeting my gaze. "What were we supposed to do, Zeb? None of us could have stopped it."

Marching over to him with my shirt still in my hand, I point a finger at him while my fury bubbles up again.

"You should have tried!"

"Zebadiah!"

My father's voice sounds behind me, igniting my vehemence. I spin around on him, and seeing his face propels me forward. I shove him as hard as I can, once, twice.

"How could you?! How could you send her out there?!" I scream at him, spit flying and tears falling down my face. "You've taken everything from me!"

His response is his fist against my jaw. I fall back only to be yanked up by my hair, hard jabs landing against my ribs.

"Father, stop! He's mourning. He just found out about her."

Zeke's hands are on my arm to try and pull me away. His interference switches my father's focus to him. He's backhanded so hard his head slams against the wood floor. I try to regain my breath as Father drags him by the shirt and kicks his boot against his back. He looks up at me, his face twisted in a mix of agony and fury.

"This is not your concern and not your place to intervene. I will deal with you momentarily." He rips his belt from the loops of his trousers. "Do not *ever* lay a hand on me again."

Landing the first blow across my chest, he pulls back for another, and I spit at him. "Beat me all you want, you hypocrite. You chose to excommunicate her, and I will never forgive you for it."

The belt lands against my stomach, forcing me to yell out as I double over. His fist is in my hair, yanking my head back to look at him.

"I have no desire for your forgiveness."

11

FRIENDS WITH A PHILISTINE

Laurel Ann

THEY LOOK ALMOST HAPPY IN THEIR LIFE OF GODLESSNESS. Picking at the bluegrass, I watch the children in the courtyard. You would never know by looking at them how horrible they really are. In the six weeks I've been away from the compound, I've learned this place is just as evil as I was taught. The children are crueler and more selfish than the adults. Either that or the adults hide it better.

I'm used to them all making fun of me. Since I had no clothes or belongings with me, I had to use what was on hand at the children's home. There wasn't much I could wear because modesty is not a virtue these heathens possess. One of the women who runs the children's home took me to a place called a 'thrift store'. I was thrilled at some of the dresses and skirts I was able to find. I even got a bonnet. The children haven't stopped teasing me about my clothes since. They call me 'weird' and 'freak'. They mock the way I talk and how picky I am with my food. At first, I didn't care what they said. Their opinions have no bearing on my soul. Now, my stomach twists, and tears spring up in my eyes. I refuse to let them know they have that power over me, so I mostly try to distance myself as much as possible.

The *buzz* that sounds in the courtyard is the signal for lunchtime. I don't get up though. I'm always the last one to enter the cafeteria and the last one to leave. When the final child abandons the playground, I stand to brush the grass from my skirt and make my way inside. I'm sure to keep my head down, and I still get kicked in line while I await my food. Lifting my gaze to search for an empty table, I am relieved to find a small round one in the corner unoccupied.

I sit close to the wall, poking at my greasy, square, cheesy piece of 'pizza'. It's terrible and can barely be considered food, but it's either that or starve. Even the green beans are hard to choke down.

"Hey, you gonna eat that?"

I look up to see a short girl with black, curly hair pointing at my tray. Plopping down in front of me, she tilts her head, waiting for my answer.

"What? My food?"

"Just the brownie. I ain't stingy."

I keep waiting for the cruel comment as I push my tray toward her. "Please."

"Wicked. Thanks." She shoves the brownie in her mouth, bouncing in her seat like she can't sit still. "What's the deal with the getup? You Amish or somethin'?"

I've been asked that question multiple times since coming here, yet I'm still not any closer to knowing what it means.

"What does that mean? Amish?"

"So, that's a no... Amish people don't live like we do. They don't drive cars or have TVs or anything. They dress funny, kind of like you do." My heart leaps into my chest, and I feel excitement for the first time since leaving the gates of the Anointed Land. I want more than anything to find these Amish people to ask if they will let me live with them. The thought makes me want to cry with my first sliver of hope. She gestures around the cafeteria. "Why are you in here?"

Lies have poured from my lips more in the last few weeks than the rest of my life combined. Philistines are not to know of the compound. They would most certainly try to take it, defiling it with their modern devices and evil ways. This girl though, she doesn't seem like much of a threat. What is she really going to do? She's the first person my age to talk kindly to me. I want her to continue doing it.

"I come from a place called the Anointed Land. I rebuked my God and was excommunicated because of it. That's why I'm here, living outside of grace."

Her eyebrows jump to the middle of her forehead. "Whoa…ease up. You're a serious one, aren't you? If they kicked you out, then why do you still dress like the cast of Little House on the Prairie?"

"Because I believe in spiritual law. It's forbidden for me to allow a man that is not my husband to see the skin above my wrists and ankles. Though I may be cast into a world of sin, I will still follow the commandments of Zaaron."

Her eyes widen, and she leans back, crossing her arms. "Um…okay. That's cool. Whatever paints your pallet. What's your name anyway?"

"I'm Laurel Ann Henderson. What's yours?"

Her lip quirks, making her appear mischievous. "Kaila Paisley." Sparkling nails covered in chipped, glittery polish are in my face as she holds out her hand. I'm hesitant, but I shake it anyway. "Want a cigarette? We won't get caught if we go by the trash bins."

I've only stayed at one other place besides the children's home since coming here, and it was with a family. It was only for a week and that was more than enough time for me. The father of the home smoked something called cigarettes. I hated the way he would blow the smoke in my face as he spoke. While I definitely don't want one, I do want someone to talk to, and she is interesting…for a Philistine.

I miss my family, I miss Zeb, I miss my friends, and I miss my life before the blood of innocence ruined everything. I don't have the choice to not associate with these people. If I must spend time with a filthy Philistine, I think I'd like it to be her. Besides, from what I've seen, she's the best option by far.

"Okay."

I follow her out of the mess hall and through the lobby. It's meant to be cheery, when instead, it's utterly depressing. She stops by the front desk, greeting Jaida, one of the women in charge. My heart trades places with my stomach. She's setting me up. She's going to get me in trouble somehow. I should have known. None of them are trustworthy.

"Hey, Jaida," Kaila sings.

Jaida's skin is the same stunning dark color as Kaila's. I'd never seen skin that color before leaving the Anointed Land. Philistines may all be evil, but that doesn't mean they can't be beautiful.

Jaida looks to Kaila, and her expression is a paradox. Her eyebrows are scrunched together, yet her lips are upturned in a smirk. "Uh-oh. Here's trouble."

Kaila presses her hand to her hip, blowing her a kiss. "You know you love me, Jaida."

"What I would love is for you to call me Ms. McElroy."

Kaila claps her hands together. "Ooh! I like this game. My turn. What I would love is…another TV in the rec room. I need my 'American Idol' fix. Okay, now you go."

Jaida shakes her head and laughs. "Get out of here, Paisley."

Grinning, Kaila hooks her arm in mine. "Let's go. I know when I'm not wanted."

We walk through the doors that always know when we're coming because they open for us every time. All by themselves, as if being controlled by the Devil.

Walking outside, we pass the playground where there are young children swinging in the middle of the yard. A few boys, including the ones who have picked on me, are playing a game where they bounce an orange ball, and then try to throw it through a net. Bucketball, I think.

Kaila sings some ridiculous song about getting her 'sexy back' as she takes us further from the yard, around to the side of the building. There are three large, blue, metal bins where the trash is disposed of. She leans against the wall next to them, removes two white cigarette sticks from a white box, and hands me one. I'm curious what brought her to this place of unwanted children. Why isn't she with her parents?

I copy her actions and put the stick in my mouth. She holds up the little, pink cylinder containing the flame. A lighter. She lights mine, though instead of catching on fire, it suppresses the flame like charcoal. Smoke that tastes like burnt toast floats into my mouth. It fills up my throat, blocking my airway, making me cough and choke. Tears burn my eyes, and I crouch over to ease the attack on my body.

Kaila laughs. "Haven't you ever smoked before?" Every time I open my mouth to speak, I cough again, so I shake my head. She puts her cigarette to her mouth, blowing the smoke out without even clearing her throat. "Don't feel like you have to smoke it if you don't like it."

Oh, thank goodness. I hand it back to her. "I'm sorry."

She snubs it out on the side of the building and puts it back into the white box. "No worries." She smiles, and her cocoa eyes sparkle in the sunlight. "I still like you."

"Why are you here? Where are your parents?"

She has a relaxing energy about her, so I ask before

thinking. Just as the words fumble out, I regret them. I'm being intrusive. She did ask me, yes, but she's a heathen. You can't blame her for not having social manners.

The smile falls from her face, and she kicks the rocks off the sidewalk with her 'flip-flop'. I think they call them that because of the sound they make when walked in. I'm told it's a shoe. Hardly. It doesn't even qualify as a sock.

"My mom's in rehab. She's been in and out for years. And my dad...well, my dad loved me a lot." She raises her eyebrow. "Too much, ya know?"

I'm completely lost. I have no clue what a rehab is or how a father could ever have 'too much' love for his daughter. I wish my father had loved me more.

"That's bad?"

She sighs and squints into the sunny sky. "It wasn't real love. He did things. Made me do things. Ya know, sex stuff."

My fingers still smell like smoke when I cover my mouth. My stomach twists at the thought. Her own father? I know people in the outside world are evil and wretched, but this is repulsive.

I suddenly want her to know that while it may not have been with my father, I know what it's like to be made to do those things with someone you revere and love.

"I, uh...I had to have sex once. It was horrible."

I'm grateful for her consciousness to blow the smoke in the air above her and away from my face. Her eyes go wide as she cocks her head to the side.

"With who?"

Why am I telling her this? She is a Philistine for goodness sake! Yet, I continue to speak. "My husband. He was my Prophet."

"No shit? Now that's messed up. What are you? Like thirteen?"

I nod. "Yes."

"Damn. Are you still married to him?"

"Not in the eyes of Zaaron."

"Who the hell is Zaaron? Is that his name?"

"No, that is my God."

She blinks a few times. "Right... Anyway, I eventually told my gran about it. She took me away and called the police. I haven't seen him since."

"Why aren't you still with your gran?"

She drops her cigarette on the ground before stepping on it. "She died last year."

"Oh...that's sad."

She sighs as she wraps her arm around my shoulder. "Come on, prairie princess. You said it's only men that can't see your arms and shit, right?" I nod, and she does a shake with her hips. "Good, because I am going to give you a secret makeover."

Her room is shared with five other girls, two of which are in the room with us. One has on a pair of the electric earmuffs that play music, the other is flipping through pages in a book, and both are ignoring us.

Kaila wraps a band around my hair to make a 'pony tail'. Why everyone around here wants to make their head look like a foal's backside is beyond me. Philistines. I don't try to understand them. She pulls a basket out from beneath her bed, digging through it as she tosses articles of clothing in disarray around her. She hands me her choices before rummaging through a small, blue bag with yellow stars on it.

I hold up what she gives me, and I'm disturbed that anyone would wear this. There is hardly any fabric here at all. What exactly are these going to conceal? I lift up the heavy, blue bottoms that appear to be some kind of bloomer with pastel rainbows on the back pockets.

"These are covered in holes."

She chuckles, arranging an array of colorful powders and brushes on her bed. "Just put 'em on."

My undergarments cover more than these do! The frayed edges are the only reason they're as long as they are. I pick up the next item. Is this a brassiere?! I yank the flimsy, black fabric over my head and hold out the bright pink shirt. There are no sleeves, and it says 'Another Day of Not Being Rich and Famous' in curly black letters. The material is thin and doesn't cover my stomach. The arm holes almost dip to my waist, and I don't know if there is even a point to wearing it. These clothes are so bright. My dresses at home were never flashy colors like this. Wearing such things is a clear sign of vanity. She puts goop and powder all over my face before tying a pink bow in my hair. She throws me a pair of pink and black sparkly sneakers with white toes and laces. A clunky, multicolored necklace finishes her 'makeover'.

She brushes something off her shoulder before pushing me in front of the mirror. "Ta da!"

I hardly recognize myself. I can't help but think how horrified my family would be if they saw me right now. I look much younger than I normally do, and though I hate to admit it's kind of cute, I still want to cover up the exposed skin.

"Whatcha think?"

"Uh…I don't know. What do you think?"

She taps her chin. "I think you look adorably uncomfortable."

I laugh. "Yes, a little… Thank you. This was fun."

"That's what friends are for."

The smile refuses to leave my face.

Friends. With a Philistine.

I never thought I'd see the day.

I have spent every day this week with Kaila, and while she seems to break a lot of rules, they are Philistine rules that I have no use or respect for. Even now, we're sneaking to the basement with a bunch of other kids, and it's well past lights out.

Their loud whispers and snickers are going to get us in trouble. An uneasiness rolls in my stomach, and I hold my knapsack tighter to my chest.

"Relax," Kaila whispers. "If we get caught, all they will do is send us back to bed."

I nod to her as we descend the stairs. The room is large, mostly filled with boxes and storage. Following Kaila, I copy what the other kids do by laying my knapsack on the floor.

Everyone seems to like her. The boys are always smiling at her and the girls seem to mimic her. She either doesn't notice or doesn't care because she mostly ignores them.

One of the boys with a shaved head comes over to us, holding out a bottle to Kaila.

"You want a drink, K?"

She takes it, bringing it to her lips and taking a large gulp. Her face twists up, and she wipes her mouth. "Ugh." Holding the bottle to me, she says, "Here."

I take it from her, but it didn't look like it tasted too good. "What is this?"

"Tequila."

"Alcohol? No, thank you."

I hand it back to her, and the boy snorts. "Your loss, Bible thumper."

Biting my tongue, I settle for glaring at him. In the short time I've been here, I've heard plenty about their false God and blasphemous text. I don't appreciate being compared to that.

Kaila scoffs, "Thanks for the liquor, Patch. Now go away. I'm not into guys who talk shit to my friends."

"Oh, come on. Don't be like that, girl. I was jus' playin'."

She smirks at him, and lifts the bottle back to her mouth. "See ya later, Patch."

He grabs his chest like he's wounded before grinning and turning back to his friends.

"Thanks for standing up for me."

She plops down on her blanket. "I wouldn't be much of a friend if I didn't."

"You're not like them, are you?" I ask her. I don't know how she's different, she just is.

"Like who?" She gestures to the other kids. "Them?"

I nod. "You're not as evil as the rest of the Philistines in this place."

She takes another drink without looking at me. "They're my friends, too, ya know. You calling them evil is no different than them calling you a freak."

Guilt presses against my chest. Is she right? Zaaron teaches us to be kind, but he didn't mean to them. Did he?

"I apologize. It was not my intention to offend you."

She shrugs. "I mean, they *can* be assholes."

I narrow my eyes in confusion, and she starts giggling.

It's getting really late, and I can't believe we haven't gotten caught with how loud they've gotten. I think I'm the only one who can still speak and walk correctly. It amazes me that there's a couple openly kissing and touching in the corner. Any one of us could look over there and see them. I can't believe their lack of shame.

They keep smoking weeds for some reason, making the room stink with the odd stench of it. My eyes are getting heavy, and I've felt like an outsider this whole night. I'm ready to go to sleep, so I can laugh with my brothers and make flower crowns with my sisters. I spend my slumbers at the creek with Zeb and walking the fields with Benji.

When I dream, it's of home in the presence of Zaaron.

I tell Kaila I'm going to sleep, and even though she tries to get me to stay, she finally lets me go.

I'm so tired, and it still takes me forever to fall asleep. The noise and hard floor making it difficult to get comfortable.

Pain. It's the first thing I register. Someone is stabbing me. Cries pour from my throat, and my hands fly to my stomach, finding no knives. My eyes flutter open to see Kaila kneeling next to me, crying. Her hands are shaking and wet. As my eyes adjust, the shade of red comes into focus. She has blood all over her.

I try to sit up when the excruciating feeling in my stomach intensifies, causing me to cry out before she shushes me.

"Don't move. You're going to be okay."

I suddenly realize I'm wet. Ignoring her instructions, I yank off my blanket. When I see the blood pooled between my legs, bile rises up my chest. I throw myself to the side, releasing the contents of my stomach.

"Eww. Gross!" One of the children yells.

Sweat is all over me, sticking my clothes to my chest. I've seen enough miscarriages to know that's what's happening to me. Zaaron had blessed me with a child before I turned my back on Him. Now He's taking back what's His.

Kaila's arms are around me, keeping me up as she whispers, "Jaida's on her way. She'll help you."

True to her word, Jaida comes running down the stairs. When she reaches me, her fingers brush her lips in an attempt to contain her shock.

"Oh, Laurel Ann, sweetheart." She kneels down next to me. "Are you okay?" I nod even with the tears drenching my cheeks. "Come on, hon. Let's get you cleaned up, all right?"

She helps me stand, and Kaila rushes to my other side. "How can I help?"

"By getting everyone back to their rooms. I'll deal with you tomorrow, Paisley."

I can't move very fast, though Jaida is gentle as she assists me up the stairs. If I weren't in so much pain, I would question why we aren't going to the girls' wing. Instead, she guides me through the door behind the front desk that leads to a long, white hallway.

"This is the employee's wing," she informs me, opening a door that says: WOMEN.

The room is similar to a public bathroom besides the fact that there are rows of showers. Jaida walks to a line of lockers, and opens one without a lock on it, removing two towels and a rag.

"Do you need help, or will you be all right to shower alone?"

Going to the locker below it, she takes out two bottles. I try to smile at her in thoughtfulness as she sets the towels and bottles on the bench.

"I'll be okay."

She lightly rubs my shoulder and says, "I'll be right outside if you need me."

Slowly I make my way to the shower. I do have to say, of all the evil their technology brings, they got something right with instant hot water.

I wash the remnants of my unborn baby from my thighs,

wondering who it would have been if I wouldn't have sinned. I put my face in the water and cry a silent apology to him or her.

I'm sorry I took away your chance at life.

I know its soul is in the Paradise Star because it was conceived within the Anointed Land inside of a sanctioned binding. Its flesh had never entered the world, and therefore was never tainted—protected by the womb.

If I don't make it there, just know I would have loved you.

I take my time washing my hair and skin because once I step out of the water, I'm scared I'll feel different.

Turning the shower knobs, I step out and wrap a towel around me. I look at my reflection in the long mirror, wondering if I appear the same.

"We have to do something! That poor child." Jaida's voice rises behind the door, and I know she's talking about me. I walk closer to hear what she's saying.

"We don't know the circumstances of the pregnancy. There's nothing to do." I'm not able to place the other voice, though it sounds familiar. I think it might be Peggy.

"Oh, come on, Peg! Does she look like she's the type to sleep around?"

I press my ear against the door, hearing Peggy say, "Look, I respect that you're in this to help the kids, but you're too young to understand how difficult it is to get shit like this through the system. Especially without evidence. Unless Laurel Ann has said something and is willing to go on record with it, then you're wasting your energy, Jaida."

"Then what's the freaking point? If we can't help them, then why are we here?"

"We do help them, just maybe not as much as we'd like to be able to. I'm sorry. I feel bad for her too."

"Fine. I'm going back in there to see if she needs anything."

I rush back from the door and sit on the bench, grabbing

the towel to start drying my hair.

Jaida smiles as she walks in and takes a seat next to me. "How are you feeling?"

"It doesn't hurt that bad anymore. I'm just cramping."

Leaning forward, she rests her forearms on her knees and sighs. "Can I ask you…" she pops her knuckles, "when you got pregnant…what were the conditions like? Was it something you wanted to do? Was it with a boy your age?"

My mouth freezes shut. My head begs to shake no, so I hold still. I mustn't speak of anything to do with the Anointed Land to a Philistine, and I'm regretting ever telling Kaila.

Jaida's hand holds onto mine, making me realize my silence is saying more than I intended.

"Did someone force you? You can trust me."

I close my eyes because I wish that were true.

"No, Ms. McElroy. I was willing."

12

THE JOHNSON BARN

Zebadiah

3 years later...

"LISTEN, ZEKE, THIS ISN'T ABOUT YOU. THIS IS BETWEEN ME and him. There's no point in getting your hide tanned too."

I tug on Mable's teat, squirting milk into the Mason jar. Ezekiel clicks his tongue. "I hate the old man just as much as you do. You're bringing him to the edge of his sanity, and I'm gonna help you push him over, so name it." I can't stop my grin. I've been pretty proud of some of my 'stunts' as Father calls them. Screwing the lid on tight, I shake up my concoction as he points to it. "What's in there anyway?"

I hold up the Mason jar, swirling the contents. "Eggs, milk, and vinegar. I'm gonna leave it in here for a couple weeks, then I'm gonna pour it in the chalice before services." He laughs as I hide the Mason jar inside Dandelion's stall.

"That's disgusting."

I cross my arms. "You really want to help?" His grin is huge. "Fine. I already have an idea, but it involves Philistine trinkets."

He adjusts his straw hat with a whistle. "Whoa. That's going a little far, don't you think? I mean, Zeb, come on. That's literally playing with the Devil."

"We won't actually use them. We just need to make sure someone finds us with them in a public place. Then Father can't punish us in private."

"Where would we even get something like that?"

"I know someone. Just let me go alone because he might not give us anything if he gets nervous."

Though he nods, the idea clearly has him uncomfortable. I leave the barn, climb up on the hay bale, and jump over the fence to go to Benji's.

As I pass through the common ground, I wave back at those who raise their hands in greeting, grinning at the debacle I'm going to make.

With or without Zeke.

I vowed to my father I would never forgive him for Laurel Ann, and I have kept my word. From that day on, any chance I get to humiliate him, I take. Most of the things have been small, just enough to require public penance—things he couldn't brush under the rug. I'm taking away his ability to choose, just as he's taken mine.

Benji doesn't live far from the Henderson farm. It still makes my chest ache as I look at it, kind of like when I go to the creek. It's the only place I feel close to her, but it hurts something awful. I wonder who she is now. Fear tickles my spine with the thought that she may not even be alive anymore. Not a day passes that I don't think of her and regret not attempting to search for her. I could have protected her. While I know I probably wouldn't have found her, possibly damning myself for no reason, the idea of living in the dark, new world doesn't seem so terrible if I could be with her.

I pass by Benji's barn when my steps are halted at the

sound of muffled screams and cries. Careful to watch the twigs beneath my feet, I sneak to the partially open barn door. The smothered screaming hasn't stopped for even a second. As I peek inside the barn, my eyes widen in horror, releasing tears I haven't cried in years.

Benji is bent over the workbench with his trousers around his ankles and a handkerchief stuffed in his mouth. Tears wet his red face as his fingers claw at the wood of the bench. My feet sink further into the ground, making me immobile. All I can do is watch as his father, Jameson Johnson, shoves the wooden handle of a pitchfork deep into his ass.

"Is this what you want? Do you like this, you fucking sodomite?!"

Benji wails around the cloth in agony as the pitchfork is jammed back into him, jolting his body forward. I plead with my feet to move as he pulls the farm tool out of Benji, throwing it on the hay-covered ground. The blood dripping down the handle makes my insides twist to the point of nausea.

"If I ever catch you doing something like that again, I'll kill you myself before the Prophet gets the chance to cleanse you. No son of mine will be a Nancy-boy." Shaking his head, he spits on Benji's back. "Your mother's perverse, dirty blood runs through your veins. I should have made her take you with her."

As if released by an unseen force, I'm finally able to uproot myself as Brother Jameson walks toward the door. I hurry around to the side of the barn, wiping my tears as I wait a few moments before peeking around the corner to watch him go inside the house.

Taking a big breath, I rush back into the barn. Seeing Benji sobbing and bleeding on the floor has me falling on my knees next to him. He's removed the handkerchief from his mouth, his cries now much quieter. I reach out for him, but I don't know what to do. I don't want to make this worse.

"Benji," I whisper. "It's Zeb." He sobs harder as my mind battles with my heart between confronting Brother Jameson and my need to tend to my friend. "Please, tell me what to do."

He tries to lift himself with shaky elbows. "Help me up."

I put my arms beneath his to assist him. "I'm so sorry, Benji. I should have stopped it. Why would he do that to you?"

"Help me with my pants," he coughs.

"You're bleeding."

"I know, Zeb!" He cries, "Please, just help me get dressed."

His blood is everywhere, and it gets on my hand as I adjust his trousers. "You're really hurt. We need to take you to Doc Kilmer."

"NO!" He lurches at me, immediately wincing in pain. "No, he'll tell the Prophet."

"Maybe my father should know! There's nothing you could have done that would be worse than this."

He shakes his head. "I'm fine, I just need to rest."

I pace the floor, physically unable to stay still right now. I want so badly to grab that bloody pitchfork and return the favor to Brother Jameson. If I could only go back five minutes to stop this sooner. I just want to take away his pain.

I need to make this right.

"Benji—"

"You really want to help?"

"Yes, yes, anything."

He leans against the workbench for support. "I have a place...my safe place. If you swear to never tell a soul, I'll show you where it is."

"How far is it?"

"Past the common ground, at the edge of the compound."

My shoulders fall. He'll never be able to walk that far.

"Don't move. I'll be right back. I'm going to get the buggy."

I look out the barn door, making sure I don't see Brother Jameson. As soon as I'm confident it's clear, I run as fast as I can.

I don't think I've never gotten to my ranch this quickly. My side burns as I hurry around to the back of our barn and see the buggy isn't harnessed.

Shit!

The barn door bangs open as I burst through to get a horse. I don't have time for this.

"What are you doing?"

My heart bangs against my chest before I see Ezekiel leaning against a post, eating an apple. I rush out a breath in relief.

"You scared me. I thought you were Father. I need the buggy."

"Why? What happened with the Philistine trinkets?" Taking the collar off the hook, he hands it to me.

I place it over the horse's head and grab the lead. "Come on, Dandelion." I click my tongue while I take her from the stall. "I just need it to help a friend. And I don't know about the trinkets right now."

"What friend?"

I sigh as we reach the buggy. "I'm not able to tell you that."

He frowns at me. "Tell me, or I tell Father you took the buggy without permission."

The response is so un-Zeke-like it would have made me laugh under better circumstances.

"Are you a child?" I buckle the traces as he crosses his arms.

"You're clearly shaken up about something, and I want to know what it is."

My nostrils flare. If I can trust anyone, it's Ezekiel. "Help me finish this then you can see for yourself."

Once Dandelion is harnessed, we jump inside. I gather the left rein and tug on the right.

Ezekiel tips back his hat with a raised brow. "Are you going to give me some idea of where we're going?"

I realize I'm grinding my teeth as I try to figure out how to repeat what I saw. "Benji was who I was going to ask about the trinkets." His open mouth matches his wide eyes as I snap the reins. I know she can go faster than this. "When I arrived at the Johnson place to ask him, I found his father...hurting him."

He frowns. "Like lashing him?"

I shake my head, my chest hurting as I remember the horrible look of terror and torture on Benji's face. "So much worse. He's real messed up. He asked me to take him somewhere to heal in peace. Believe me, he's in no shape to be walking."

"I don't understand. Why would Brother Jameson do that?"

Someone yells behind us to slow down as we ride through the common ground. "I don't know."

I yell at Dandelion to hurry up until I'm tugging on the reins to stop the buggy on the road behind the Johnson barn. "Come on, he's back here."

Running to the side of the barn, I hold up my hand to stop Zeke so I can check for Brother Jameson. When I see that the yard is clear, I wave at him to follow me. Once we're inside, I find Benji lying on the ground. Fear wraps around me at the sight of his still body.

"Benji?" I whisper.

He groans, allowing me to breathe. Hurrying over to him, I feel sick when I see the blood seeping through his trousers.

"Holy fire of Zaaron! What did he do?" Ezekiel gasps. I nod to the bloodied handle of the pitchfork laying in the hay. All the color slips from his face as he shakes his head. "No…"

"Zeke, come on!" I yell, and he snaps out of his daze enough to help me hoist Benji to his feet. "Can you walk at all?" I ask him.

"Yes," he coughs as more tears fall, soaking his cheeks. "I think so."

We let him use us to lean on as we carry him back to our buggy. We try to be gentle, but every few steps he wheezes in pain. Finally, we get him inside, and I tug the reins.

None of us speak until we pull up to the common ground. "Where is this place?"

Benji points behind the medical hall. "Stop here. We'll need to walk the rest of the way." I do as he says, and Ezekiel is quick to help him down. "I don't usually come here when there's still daylight…so both of you need to…keep an eye out. Walk straight until I tell you."

Every word seems to be more painful for him than the last. I wish I knew where he could be taking us because I don't want him to have to talk.

We no sooner take five steps into the open field when Sister Madeline's voice sounds behind us. "What on earth are you boys doing?"

We all glance at each other as I stumble over my words. "We—er…we're um…"

I turn to look at her just as her eyes travel to Benji's trousers. She covers her mouth before rushing over to us. "My goodness, child what happened?!" Her eyes bounce between all three of us as her face falls. "Come along, hurry, get inside."

She guides us through the back entrance and into the clinic. After assisting us in laying him on the bed, she instructs that we go into the waiting room while she works.

"What about Doc Kilmer?" I ask.

"He's at the Garett's house tending to one of the children's broken leg."

I know Benji doesn't want this to get out, so I have to know. "Are you going to tell my father?"

She shushes me as she runs her hand over my hair. "I need to tend to Benji. The Prophet will not hear of this from me. You have my word."

I sit in silence with Zeke for what has to be over an hour. The sun has begun its descent, casting a dark shadow across the room.

"What do you think he did?" Zeke asks in a low voice.

I scratch the itch on my brow and my stomach rolls.

If I ever catch you doing something like that again, I'll kill you myself…

"From what I heard, Benji did something to give Brother Jameson the impression that he's a sodomite."

His initial expression holds horror, though his face quickly hardens as I stand to light a lantern. Sister Madeline emerges from the back, and we both meet her as she approaches us.

"There are many cuts and tears as well as a number of splinters that needed removed, though the bleeding has slowed." She looks between us with sorrow in her eyes as her shoulders slump. "This was Brother Jameson, wasn't it?"

I nod before I consider I'm betraying Benji, but to my relief she just sighs. "That was my assumption."

"Is he okay?" I can't tell if Zeke sounds sad or angry. If he's feeling anything like I am, it's both.

Reaching into her apron pocket, she removes a stack of thin cloths. "I gave him some laudanum, and it would appear he's getting around easier. Since this is to remain between us, I am trusting you two to keep an eye on him for any sign of infection–vomiting, fever, fatigue, or if the pain doesn't recede." She places the cloths in my hand. "These should last him until the bleeding stops."

The door behind her opens as Benji walks out in clean clothes and wet hair. Shoving the cloths in my back pocket, I rush to assist him.

He holds up a hand to stop me. "I'm fine. Let's just go." He turns to Sister Madeline. "Thank you…for everything."

She gives him a small smile, placing her hand on his back. "Now, come along. My husband will be returning soon."

Leading us out the back exit, she gives us one last smile before shutting the door behind us. Benji is standing straighter, and though he's still going slowly, he's moving much faster than he was.

"It's dark enough now that we shouldn't be seen. Follow me."

Ezekiel looks at me, and I shrug as I trudge behind Benji. Just as we're about to reach the large fence surrounding the compound, he drops to the ground. Brushing away dirt and sticks, he reveals a large, wooden cellar door. He takes a key from his shoe to unlock the lock.

"Give me a hand with this."

I kneel next to him. "Nobody else knows about this?"

"No."

I pull back until the door hits the ground with a *thud*. Benji turns around, slowly climbing down into what looks like a black hole.

Within moments, I hear the *snick* of a match as light shines up from the ground. I look down to see him holding an oil lamp. A ladder leads into the cellar, so I do as he did and climb down. I can't believe this place. I stare around in awe. The craftsmanship is not only impressive, it's amazing that he was able to do it alone while keeping it a secret. Thick pieces of wood line the walls in panels to keep the hole from falling in on itself. There's even a mattress at the opposite end of the space.

"Close the door behind you," Benji tells Ezekiel as he climbs down.

Jumping off the last step, Zeke asks, "How long have you had this place?"

Benji takes tentative steps to the back of the room, careful to sit on his hip as he lies on the far side of the mattress, leaving enough room for me and Ezekiel. "A couple of years."

As I sit next to Benji, Zeke scoots next to me and says, "It's remarkable."

The silence between us is making the already small room suffocating; I can no longer keep the questions inside.

"What happened, Benji?" The visions of earlier in the day assault me. "Why the hell would he do that to you?" He blows the air through his nose and shakes his head. I add, "You can trust us. I swear, whatever you tell us won't leave this place." I look to my brother. "Right, Zeke?"

He nods at Benji. "I swear."

Leaning against the wooden wall, he drops his head, releasing a long sigh. "There's a…guy." His voice strains over the last word. "I won't tell you who, so let's just call him my 'friend'. At first that's exactly what it was, a friendship." Shifting around, he winces, clearly still in a lot of pain. "Then about a year and a half ago, I realized I desired him…in a way a man shouldn't desire another man."

He refuses to look at us, keeping his stare on his feet. My mind spins, and my stomach twists. Brother Jameson was right.

"I learned the feeling was mutual, and eventually, I laid with him." A small smile peeks through his pained expression.

I want to look at Zeke's reaction, but I don't want Benji

to stop talking to us, though I now have a good idea of what happened.

"We've kept it a secret ever since." He clenches his jaw as his hands clutch the mattress between his fingers. "We were careful. We're rarely seen together in public, and we never meet at the same time or place. Today my father was supposed to be at the common ground, making his delivery, so we planned to meet in my barn." The tears roll down his cheeks as his words become strained. "He returned much sooner than he should have and found us in the barn while I was…on my knees…sucking him." He sounds repulsed at himself. I force my mouth closed and attempt to keep my eyes from widening at the mental image I'm trying not to picture. "I've never seen him that angry. He told us to get dressed and to wait for him …" More tears fall as he wipes them feverishly and whispers, "I wish I would have made my friend leave. He was terrified, and it was all my fault." Ripping a string off the mattress, he sighs. "When my father returned, it was with my little sister, Serah. He told me he was going to 'purge the perversion'. I didn't understand until he took off her clothes and told me to do the same. He said I needed to be with a woman, and since Serah is the eldest having yet to receive the blood, there was no chance of impregnation." Now, I do look at Zeke, and he's paled even in the yellow light of the lamp. Benji's sobs force my attention back to him. "I couldn't do it…physically. I wasn't able to get myself to…" he gestures to his lap, "you know. He tried making her do a few things to me, and nothing helped." He rips at his hair, and I place my hand on his back as he rocks. "She did everything he told her to because she's a good girl and just wanted to be obedient. But I saw her eyes… she's fucking terrified of me now." His shoulders heave, and I wait for him to scream at any moment as I watch his anger rise to the surface. "My *friend* sat there, watching all of it until finally my father made them both leave, taking matters into his own hands." He tilts his head, though not enough to look at me. "You arrived shortly after that." Finally, he lifts his gaze to us, his eyes glistening with moisture. "And here we are."

Zeke and I are both shocked into silence. I don't think either of us knows what to say at this point. My brain feels like it's going through a meat grinder. Brother Jameson can't just get away with this, and now, I'm worried about Serah. She's probably scared and confused. I fear for her safety with a man that could do this to his children. And what about when she gets bound? She won't be pure for her husband. If that fact comes out, she will be punished as an adulteress while the true evil remains to fester.

What I do know is Benji has to stop what he's doing. He can't get caught again.

"You're not going to see *him* again, are you? Your 'friend'? Please promise me you're done doing that, Benji."

He scoffs, and I think I've angered him when his face suddenly falls passive. "Yeah, well, you don't have to worry about that. I saw the way he looked at me. We're done." He's completely heartbroken over...whoever he is. I hate that he's in pain, but what he desires is a sin.

Nodding to the ladder, he says, "You guys don't have to stay here with me. I'm sure the Prophet will be wondering where you are."

"I'm not going anywhere. Sister Madeline said we need to watch out for infection." I move further back on the bed and look to Zeke. "Go home. We need to get the buggy back anyway. I'll talk to you tomorrow."

He hesitates before dropping his shoulders to relent. Scooting to the edge of the mattress, he looks at Benji.

"I'm really sorry. You need to know you didn't deserve it."

Benji simply nods. Giving me one last glance, Zeke climbs

the ladder, closing the cellar door behind him.

I blow out a large breath from my lips. "I really think you should get some sleep."

He shifts himself into a lying position, leaving enough room for me at the end of the bed. "Do you think I'm a disgusting sodomite now?"

"No, of course I don't. I think you sinned and paid well beyond your penance for it."

His father, however, has many sins yet to answer for.

13

SINS OF THE FATHER

Zebadiah

I TAP MY FINGER ON MY THIGH, CONTINUOUSLY STEALING GLANCES at Serah Johnson while my father gives his sermon. She rarely looks up from the ground since what happened a couple weeks ago.

I've made sure to make my presence known at least once a day at the Johnson house until I figure out how to handle Brother Jameson. I'm sure he's less likely to do anything when he knows I might be around.

Benji seems to be handling what happened really well besides the fact that he refuses to talk about it. He just wants to forget it ever happened. I can't forget it though. I won't ever get the image of that pitchfork out of my mind. I've tried to talk to Serah a few times to see how she's doing. She has no idea that I know, and she's still less responsive to my questions every time I approach her.

Finally, my father makes his closing statements, and once he says, "May the holy fire of Zaaron cleanse you," I'm out of my seat, bee-lining for Serah.

I catch up with her in the common ground standing by

herself while everyone else in her family is enjoying their individual conversations.

Shoving my hands in my pockets, I walk up next to her. "Hi, Serah. Your dress is pretty. Is it new?"

She nods and whispers, "Hi." Her eyes still locked on the dirt.

"How are your lessons coming?" It's a stupid question, but I just want her to talk to me. I need to know she's going to be okay. I think if Laurel Ann were here, she'd know what to say.

"Fine."

I sigh, looking up to see Benji making his way toward us. He looks down at Serah as if she's crushing him from the inside out.

"Hey, cricket." He wraps her in a side hug, and she stiffens, causing him to drop his arm and look away before addressing me. "Hi, Zeb."

"Hey, Benji."

There hasn't been a gathering since it happened, and I'm counting down the days until the next one, so I can ask Zaaron why he would allow this to happen to Serah and Benji. Why he would let such an evil man like Jameson Johnson remain inside the gates of the Anointed Land, yet he would cast out Laurel Ann?

I've only had the chance to talk to Zaaron once, and I wasn't at all prepared. The last gathering was my first as an adult, and it was the most incredible experience I have ever encountered. While I wasn't able to hear His voice, I did feel His touch. I had no idea we had that ability.

I glance to my father who is gesturing for me to come to him. I look down at Serah and bend over to be at eye level with her.

"Sometimes it's hard to talk to our families about things.

If you're sad and want to talk to someone, I happen to know Sister Madeline Adams is a great listener. She's the best at keeping secrets."

She doesn't respond or look up from her feet. I sigh, patting Benji on the back before I walk to my father. He's speaking with Brother Benjamin Henderson, and I wonder if he thinks about Laurel Ann with the frequency I do. I partially blame him for her being sent away, even though I know that's completely unfair. It would have happened regardless.

My father holds his hand out to me as if he hadn't beaten me with it this morning. "Ah, the future Prophet. Come here, my son."

I do my best to conceal my grimace and hold my hand out to Laurel Ann's father. "Blessed day, Brother Benjamin."

He shakes my hand. "Yes, blessed day, my boy."

"Brother Benjamin's youngest has been very sick this past week, and Doc Kilmer is at a loss. I will be laying hands on her after we leave here, and I would like you to accompany me."

It almost makes me laugh how he says it like I have a choice. "Yes, Father."

He yanks on his ear before wiping his lip and clapping his hands together. "Wonderful. We will make our way over whenever you're ready."

Brother Benjamin bows his head. "I praise Zaaron for your holy graciousness."

I hate going to the Henderson farm. Waking up every morning knowing I have to go another day without seeing her is bad enough. Being inside her family home will rip the scab off of the never healing wound.

The sun is climbing its way up the sky as I kick a rock across the Johnson's yard. I don't even make it to the porch when Benji busts through the front door.

"Serah!" he calls. Pounding down the wooden steps, he searches frantically in every direction. "Serah! Where are you?!"

The shrill panic in his voice sends a coldness through me, and I run to meet him. "Benji! Wait! What's going on?"

"My mothers can't find Serah anywhere." I have to jog to keep up with him. "Her bed hasn't been slept in, and she's going to be late for school."

"Serah!"

He runs to the greenhouse when I tell him, "I'll check the barn."

Yelling her name again is his only response. I sprint across the yard and yank open the heavy, wooden door.

Little boots suspended in the air are the first things my eyes land on before traveling up to the young girl hanging from the rafters. A rope is around her neck, her vacant eyes staring into the abyss.

My vision obscures, and my head spins as I brace myself against a hay bale. I heave and gag until I hear Benji calling for her behind me. I meet him right in front of the barn, and when he sees my face, he shakes his head and lunges to go inside.

Grabbing his arms, I pull him back, doing anything I can to keep him from seeing her. "No, no, no! Don't go in there, Benji!"

His strength and determination outweigh mine, and he breaks free to bust through the doors.

"SERAH!" He runs up to the loft before he grasps for the rope. "Fuck, Serah, what did you do?!" He pulls her up and removes the rope from her neck, falling to the floor with her in his lap. He attempts to revive her, but from the color of her skin, she hasn't been alive for hours. "I'm sorry, cricket. I'm so sorry." He squeezes her to his chest, rocking and wailing into her hair.

"NO!" A feminine voice screams behind me.

My own tears are running down my cheeks when I turn to see Serah's birth mother behind me. Rushing past me, she holds up her skirts to climb up to the loft. She howls in pain, falling to her knees as she arrives next to her dead child.

Desperate to get out of here, I back out of the barn and run.

I just keep going until I'm in the common ground in front of the death dealer's shop. Banging on the door, I can't keep my heart from beating out of my chest.

Dealer Gunter Adams swings open the door with a frown. "What is it, Brother Zebadiah?"

"There's been…someone died…at the Johnson place."

He grunts, turning to a work table and grabbing a bag before he brushes past me to the coffin shed. "Adult or child?"

I choke on my own words. "A child. It's Serah Johnson."

Serah didn't get a soul releasing ceremony. Suicide is a one-way ticket to the pit, regardless if it's man, woman, or child. They buried her outside of the gates, and nobody speaks of her. Everyone acts as if she never existed at all.

Benji has barely spoken a word to me since her death, and he refuses to talk to Zeke either. I know he blames himself, but why he isn't making his father pay for this is what I don't understand. I can barely look at the man without wanting to hit him until my wrists break—scream until my lungs burst.

I've been sitting on this hay bale for hours. My stomach

rumbles in hunger, and my mouth is dry from thirst. I do my best to ignore my discomfort because I'm not moving until I do what I came here to do. I don't know when Brother Jameson is coming back, and it doesn't matter. I'll be here waiting when he does.

I stare at the barn doors as I spin the pitchfork in my hand and look at the rafters. I can still see her little body hanging there.

The door creaks open, and I tense, wondering what I will say if Benji catches me in here. Brother Jameson walks in, and when he sees me, his eyes narrow.

"Zebadiah Fitch? May I ask why you're in my barn?"

Clenching the pitchfork in my hand, I stand to hold it out to him. "I'm here to make you pay for your sins."

He laughs. The evil prick laughs and walks closer to me. "*My* sins? You're exhibiting violence toward your elder. So, ask yourself, young man. Who between us is the one sinning?"

"Serah killed herself because of you. Benji was in pain for days because of what you did to him. These are your children. Zaaron gifted them to you to love, care for, and protect. Not to rape and abuse!"

"Zaaron also gave me the right to run my home as I see fit. My son is a sodomite. It was my duty to put an end to his perverse actions. And Serah made her own choices."

Gripping the pitchfork, my palms are slick against the handle. I seethe, "She was barely over the age of understanding! Why involve her? She had nothing to do with it!"

"Serah was a tool given to me by Zaaron."

How can he be so callous about the death of his own child? I barely knew her, and the very thought of her makes it difficult to breathe. "Your lack of remorse sickens me."

"I will not weigh down my soul with the sins of my children."

I didn't come here with a plan. I thought he would show some sorrow, some pain. All I'm seeing is a man serving his own purpose, not Zaaron's. He takes his next step, my fury over the fallout he caused, burning in a whirlwind up my body. Once it reaches my eyes, all I see are flames, and I lunge forward. I yell as if it will release the rage, but my movement is halted the moment the pitchfork pierces his stomach. Blood pools in his mouth, dripping over his lips and down his chin. His wide eyes move to his stomach before becoming vacant.

Instantly, what I have just done snaps me into reality like I was hit by my father's locust tree whip.

I drop the pitchfork, and his body falls forward, the prongs stabbing deeper when he hits the ground.

Oh, Zaaron, please forgive me.

14

THE NEW PROPHET

Zebadiah

9 years later…

MY FATHER HAS HAD ME ASSISTING HIM A LOT MORE LATELY, doing things the Apostle would normally do. He's grooming me for the day I become Prophet, and the thought is one I think I have finally accepted. The Anointed Land has proven to not be what I thought, and I yearn for the day I can speak with Zaaron myself—to ask Him if this is how He desired His plan to unfold.

Things came to a head with my father about five years ago. I had just had my forty-sixth cleansing in less than seven years… I'd gone a little crazy after Serah's death. At that point, it became less about what my father did to Laurel Ann and more about my anger at Zaaron and the unfairness of it all. I thought I had nothing left to lose, but I was wrong. My father will always find ways to threaten me.

I realized that all my childish pranks weren't ever going to bring her back or change anything. I decided the best way to make a difference was to prepare to be the best Prophet I could be. I put all my energy into studying Zaaron's laws, and I can finally say that I think I'm following the path He desires for me.

I climb the steps to the tabernacle with *The True Testament* tucked under my arm. Ezekiel's birth mother, Sister Karen, has taken ill these past few weeks. It's been emotional for all of us, watching our mother's health dwindle. Father told me yesterday that he fears the worst. Then, this morning, I was awoken by him knocking on the front door of my home, announcing Zaaron had spoken with him and told him to gather the compound.

We're to have a revival.

He ordered me to make the rounds through the Anointed Land, and inform the followers of the events taking place. It's been many years since we've had a revival. The week-long service is constant worship of Zaaron, stopping only to eat and to get a few hours of sleep. The women of the compound take shifts cooking the meals, and anyone can ask for healing whether the ailment is physical or spiritual. On the final day, we present our animal sacrifice to Zaaron for all that he does for us.

While the tabernacle is currently empty, within the hour that will change. Every man, woman, and child will be filling these seats.

My father stands at the pulpit as my mother lights the candles around the room. He doesn't look up from his notes to address me. "Has everyone been informed of the revival?"

"Yes, sir. They are all making the necessary arrangements for the week."

"Wonderful. I need you to make sure there's plenty of oil available for this evening. Bring out three jars from my office. Once you finish, check that there are plenty of candles, and then see if your mothers need assistance. I'm going back to the ranch to prepare Karen for the services."

Picking up his papers, he steps from behind the pulpit and walks past me between the pews.

"Father?" He turns to me, so I continue. "Will Sister Karen be okay? Has Zaaron told you?"

"I do not know, my son. Zaaron reveals what He believes to be necessary."

"Of course."

He turns his back to me before I finish speaking, and I make my way into the back hall that leads to the offices. I look everywhere for the damn oil, and all I can find is one jar. I don't want to piss him off, he's got a lot on his plate right now with Sister Karen. I'll just run back to the ranch and sneak into his study. He always has extra jars of oil in there.

I'm out of breath by the time I run from the tabernacle to the ranch, so I allow myself to catch it before I creep in through the back door. The last thing I want is to see my father and give him a reason to think I'm too incompetent to perform such a menial task. I'm in such a hurry to get the oil and get out that I almost storm into the kitchen without realizing he's standing inside.

I stop and wait behind the wall as he makes Sister Karen some porridge. I peek around the edge, tilting my head in confusion when he kneels on the floor and pops up a floorboard. What the hell is he doing? Removing a blue bottle, he holds it up over the porridge bowl. Blue liquid comes out, pouring into the food. He mixes it with a spoon before returning the bottle back beneath the floor. I duck behind the china cabinet as he passes to take the food to Sister Karen.

Once he's gone, I slip into the kitchen and grab a butter knife to loosen the board. I reach in, feeling an odd texture. I'm not sure what I'm looking at exactly. *Antifreeze and Summer Coolant* is written across the front. This didn't come from the

Anointed Land.

Shoving it into my pocket, I hurry to replace the boards and rush to my father's study for the oil.

I get out unseen, but it feels like everyone I come across knows about the bottle of 'antifreeze' in my pocket. Why did he bring it here? I want to think it's a type of Philistine medicine, yet there's a feeling in my gut that says it isn't medicine at all.

I need to find Benji. If anyone can tell me what it is, it's him.

He sits on his mattress, looking at the bottle as if it's a priceless gemstone, and I roll my eyes. "Well, do you know what it's for?"

Quirking his mouth to the side, he rubs his nose. "I'm not sure, I can easily find out though. Where did you get this?"

"I found it."

His expression tells me he's unamused by my less than truthfulness. "I think I've earned a little more trust than that, don't you think?"

"Are you ever going to forgive me?"

He scoffs. "Are you ever going to admit to it?"

"Benji—"

"He was stabbed to death by a pitchfork. *The* pitchfork."

We've gone around and around with this. He's never going to let it go, and he's never going to stop asking. I shove my hands in my pockets.

"He must've fallen."

"Yeah, so you've said. Don't you think that's a pretty big coincidence?"

"Zaaron's plan will always prevail."

His nostrils flare with his harsh breath. "I have the right to know this shit, and I want to hear it from you. Did you kill my father, Zeb? Yes or no? That's all I'm asking."

I turn to climb the ladder out of his secret cellar. "I'll be looking for your attendance at the revival."

When I close the door, a loud clatter sounds as if he threw something. I sigh and make my way back to the common ground.

On more than one occasion, I have thought of just admitting it to him. At this point, I think he's angrier that I continue to lie to him more so than what I'm lying about. The truth is, telling him would give him something on me. Deep down I know that isn't who he is, but I've used blackmail as currency multiple times, and I feel safer not giving him the chance. Besides, him thinking he knows is one thing, him actually knowing is something else altogether.

The worst part is, the remorse I was expecting never arrived. Instead, I gained a sense of duty. Honor. The Anointed Land is a holier place without Jameson Johnson.

My father has noticed my minimum participation in the revival. I just can't seem to look at him without my mind thinking up worst-case scenarios regarding his reasons for using the Philistine concoction. While he hasn't mentioned that it's missing, he's not a stupid man. If I don't pull myself together, he'll figure it out before I know what I'm dealing with.

I'm regretting my choice of declining his offers to go with him outside the gates. Maybe if I would have, I would already know what antifreeze is.

I served myself an abundance of food since I hadn't eaten since breakfast, and now I'm regretting my greediness. Forcing another spoonful of potatoes into my mouth, I look up to see Benji grinning at me.

I swallow to properly glare at him "What's that smile about?"

"I found out what your little blue bottle was."

The milk I'm drinking goes down the wrong way, and I cough. "Not here, you idiot."

Carrying my plate and my glass to the dirty dish station, I wave for Benji to follow me behind the tabernacle.

After one last check that nobody is around, I let out a sigh. "All right, what is it?"

He clicks his tongue and crosses his arms. "Not so fast. If you want me to tell you what I know, you're going to have to tell me where you found it."

My jaw drops in shock. Maybe blackmail isn't beneath him.

"Are you serious, Benji? It's important that I know what that is."

He tilts his head. "I'm not unreasonable. I'll let you choose. You can either tell me where you found it or you can admit to me that you killed my father."

I rub my hand across my stubbly chin, reminding myself I need to shave before my father says something about it. "Fine. I found it beneath the floorboards in my father's kitchen."

His smugness is exchanged for confusion. "I don't understand…it's for a Philistine contraption. A *vrehickle*. It's like a buggy without horses."

"What does it do to people?"

"Nothing good. The bottle says not to drink it and to reach something called 'poison control' if you do."

"Shit. I gotta go. Did you bring it?"

He pulls it out of his pocket, and I snatch it from his hand before he grabs my arm. "What's going on, Zeb?"

I pull away without answering. How would I begin to say the words anyway? My father has been poisoning one of my mothers so he could 'heal' her? Why would he do this? Why would he need to? The entire compound kisses the ground he walks on. What does he have to prove by nearly killing Ezekiel's mother?

I walk as fast as I can without running while I search the common ground for Zeke. I finally find him talking with our younger brother, Jacob.

"Hey, Zeke, I need to talk to you…now."

Jacob frowns at us, and Ezekiel steps to follow me. I lead us in the direction of the ranch. "Where are we going? The revival is about to start back up."

"We're not going to the revival."

"What?" He runs in front of me to get me to stop. "What's going on?"

I sigh and look over my shoulder to make sure we're far away from nosy eyes and ears. "I saw Father doing something today." The words are thick like sludge, and I'm struggling to push them out.

"And…?"

I take the antifreeze from my pocket, handing it to him. "I watched him put this in Sister Karen's porridge. According to Benji, it's something Philistines use on their machines. It's dangerous to people."

He's looking at the bottle, yet his eyes aren't focusing, they're just getting darker. "Why would he do that?"

"I think he's making her sick so he can make her better. Perform a miracle."

When his eyes shift to mine, I feel a chill, and it's not from the breeze. Even at his most furious, he's never shown rage like this. He drops the bottle, storming behind me, back toward the common ground.

"Wait, wait, wait. Let's get him alone. Who's to say what lies he'll spin to turn the followers against us? We must be patient until he returns home tonight."

His Adam's apple bobs with his swallow as he brushes past me toward the ranch.

The hours stretch on with every *tick-tock, tick-tock* of the clock. The moonbeams shining through the window are our only source of light. We don't speak. We simply sit with our thoughts and let the betrayal fester. Has he ever loved any of us? He always comes to his study before he retires to bed, so it's here we will confront him.

I must fall asleep because I am awakened by voices. I hear the 'blessed evenings' from my mothers, and see Zeke's shadowed form in the darkness. When the knob turns, my heart stops, and neither of us move as my father makes his way across the study. He lights an oil lamp on the wall that illuminates his face before stepping to his desk.

"She could have died," Ezekiel murmurs, emerging from the shadows. "What if she would have died?!"

My father jumps at the unexpected intrusion of privacy. "Son," he grabs his chest, "you frightened me."

"You should be frightened. You tried to kill my mother!" He whispers with rage as he slams his fist on the desk.

"Sit, boy. You're on dangerous ground. You know nothing of what you speak."

"Then explain it to us, *Prophet*," I say from my place in the corner of the room. "Was my mother next?"

My father's head jerks in my direction just as Sister Wanda calls through the door. "Hiram? Are you all right? I heard something."

His eyes flip to Zeke before snapping back to me. "All is well. Go on to bed."

We all three stare at each other, listening to the retreating footfalls. Zeke is the first to break the silence when he pulls the belt from his trousers. My lip tugs itself into a smile. He's gonna beat him with it like he's done to us endless times.

"You have abused every single person in this family under the guise of being our Prophet and have allowed others in the Anointed Land to do the same. I don't believe you're blind to what goes on within these gates, you just allow what doesn't directly affect whatever agenda you have."

Father's eyes don't leave the belt. He holds out his hand, and it's clear he's nervous even without the evidence of it in his voice.

"I am not only your father, I am also your leader. Your Prophet! You will sit down, and I will tell you how you are confused. I don—"

"Confused?" Ezekiel stalks toward the back of his desk. "No, Father. There are many things I'm feeling at present, though confusion is not among them."

Whipping his belt around our father's neck, he squeezes it tight. My eyes widen, watching him eliminate his ability to breathe. This was not the direction I thought this was going.

Father grasps at the belt, and I feel no pity for him. All I feel are recycled emotions from the past. The terror and pain of the beatings, the humiliation of his constant demeaning, and the white-hot fury for what he did to Laurel Ann.

Killing my father was never an option I truly entertained. Yes, fleeting thoughts of it have crossed my mind, but until this moment I never considered it a real choice. Watching him fight in Ezekiel's grasp gives me a pleasure I wasn't prepared for.

The moments seem to skip as I walk toward them. The next thing I know, I'm beside my father, looking into his horrified, bulging eyes.

Whether he is attempting to speak or yell I'm not sure, and it doesn't matter. The time for listening to his lies has come to an end. I reach for the knife in his pocket, and squeeze the hilt. My skin burns hotter with every beat of my pounding heart.

Bending over, I look in his red, watery, evil eyes while he spits and flails in the chair. "What does *The True Testament* say about those who speak with a false tongue?" His head shakes, and he tries to scream. Zeke's expression holds wonderment, and he nods his head, ever so slightly, in approval. I force my father's mouth open to pull out his tongue. He tries to wiggle it from my grasp, so I dig my nails into the slippery flesh to get a better hold. "'The deceiver continuing to bear false witness loses all credibility, becoming unable to recognize truth.'" I press the blade against the side of his tongue, sawing through the muscle and watching it split and bleed. He attempts to shout, and Zeke straightens his arms, pulling the belt tighter. Once I'm halfway through, I tug harder to add tension, slicing through the slimy organ much easier. With the meaty tissue removed from his mouth, I throw it on the desk before walking over to the water basin. "'Truth is imperative,'" His attempted wailing has faltered with the belt constricting his oxygen. I fill the large bowl with water and turn back to my father. "'We must rid the Anointed Land of his falsehoods by removing that from which he speaks.'" I place the bowl on the table before turning back to face him. His eyes are droopy, and he's fading. "23:4D and E." I grab a fistful of his hair as blood drips from the sides of his mouth. "This is for our brothers and sisters." Twenty-seven years of hatred for him forces fire through my veins, and I shove his head into the bowl. Blood ruptures in the water, blooming like a flower. Ezekiel keeps a firm hold on the belt. "For our mothers and everyone you've let down in this compound." He thrashes beneath me, and I use all my weight to drown every bit of the man that has caused me only suffering. "This is for Laurel Ann."

I close my eyes and imagine Zaaron's energy leaving his body and entering mine. He scratches my hand and pulls at my jacket. The more he resists the harder I hold him down and the tighter Zeke squeezes. It seems like forever until his limbs hang lifeless beneath me.

It's suddenly hard to breathe, and my heart ricochets hard in my torso. I look up to Zeke expecting to see remorse and sorrow. His smile is crazy and wild, his chest rising with heavy breathing.

Fuck! Now what? I didn't think past this point. Releasing my hold on his hair, I press my hands against my eyes.

I expect Zaaron's voice to be instant, to feel Him consume me, but there is only silence.

You can talk to me now. Tell me what to do...

I pace the floor, waiting. Zeke looks to me for the guidance that is now on my shoulders, and I spew out the first solution I can come up with.

"We can't let anyone find him." I glare at my lifeless father, and there's not an ounce of love lost. Even dead, he's a scourge. "We'll come back early, before the rooster crows, and tell mothers we have business with him. After we 'find' him, you go to Dealer Gunter and pay him whatever you need to for him to keep the details to himself. Tell him we don't want to incite fear within the followers. As far as anyone else will know, he died of natural causes."

He scoffs with an impressed smile and pulls my father up, bloody water landing on his shirt. Ripping the sigil pendant from his neck, he holds it out to me with a bow of his head.

"Of course, Prophet."

15

STURGIS COUNTRYSIDE MEATS

Laurel Ann

"**W**HOO! GO BEARCATS! THAT'S WHAT I'M TALKING ABOUT, Bronson!" Kaila screams from our seats in the stands. I shake my head at her theatrics as I sip my sweet tea through a blue striped straw. "Take that shit, Mangum," she adds, pumping her fist in the air.

I'm not sure what the appeal of watching teenage boys throw around a leather ball is, but football is a favorite pastime among Philistines, Kaila included, so I indulge her.

"Hey, Kaila." I look up at the voice of Ricky Willis who is grinning at me. "Hey, Laurel Ann." I hold up my hand in a wave which he takes as an invitation to sit next to us. "You guys going to Bedlams after the game?"

Inwardly groaning, I look to see Kaila wearing the expression I was worried about. "Count us in," she says.

I have work in the morning, and I was really hoping to get a full night's rest. It's obvious Kaila has made up her mind though, and there's no way she would let me skip it.

"Great." He gives us a big smile that used to make the girls in high school lose their oversexed minds. "I'll see you guys there."

He climbs down the bleachers to his friends, and I narrow my eyes at her. "What about Brently?"

She goes through boyfriends quicker than I go through shampoo. Brently is her most recent conquest, and they're still hanging on after four months together.

Monogamy is the standard practice among Philistine couples, and the concept intrigues me. Running a family with only one mother seems impossible, yet the idea of another woman in the relationship is seen as negative.

She scoffs and tosses a nacho in her mouth. "What about him? I asked him to come, but he would rather play video games with his loser friends. And it's just Ricky Willis. We've known him since high school. Besides, I think he's more into you than me."

I smooth out my skirt and laugh. I'd sooner shave my head than date a Philistine. "Well, too bad for him. You know I don't date...people."

She sighs. "Yes, I do. I just keep hoping you'll grow out of it."

Her issues with my beliefs have been the main struggle in our relationship. It frustrates her, and as hard as she tries to understand, the truth of it is, she won't ever be able to.

And that frustrates me.

"You were hoping I would 'grow out of' my faith?"

Dropping her head back, she groans as the people around us jump up and cheer. "I'm not having this discussion tonight. All I'm saying is I don't want you to look back and wish you had done some of these things you've missed out on."

I nod my head and bite my tongue because what I really want to say is: *What about all the things you've done that you can't undo?*

Trumpets from the band sound, and everyone around us

erupts into the school song. I lean around the woman blocking the scoreboard. Hobart wins forty-three to twelve, and I feel guilty because I stole the moment from Kaila with our conversation.

Lucky for me, she's always quick to forgive. She loops her arm through mine, leading me down the bleachers.

"Come on, there's no way I'm walking all the way there. I'm using the car card tonight. We'll get a ride with Ricky."

She knows how I feel about vehicles, so she walks with me most of the time, but every once in a while, I let her pull the 'car card'. It's not an actual card, and neither of us keeps count. She uses it very sparingly for when she's feeling especially lazy or we need to get somewhere in a hurry.

Dragging me behind her, we catch up to Ricky as he's climbing into his truck. Waiving her arm at him, she yells, "Hey, Ricky! Can we catch a ride with you?"

He pops his head over the hood with a grin and jogs around to open the passenger's side. As I climb into the cab, he tips his cowboy hat to me. "Ma'am."

I grin at his country cheesiness and look at Kaila smirking while I get in the truck. She curtsies to him before climbing in behind me. "Mister."

Chuckling at her sarcastic response, he closes the door. It takes five minutes to drive what would have taken twenty minutes or so to walk. The bar is pretty packed tonight on account of it being game night and the only bar in town.

I follow Kaila to a barstool, and Ricky asks us what we're having. "Wild turkey shot for me and a vodka tonic for her."

He gives us a finger gun and turns to the bar. Kaila combs her hair back. "What are the chances you're actually going to drink that?"

I shrug and watch an older woman grinding against three different men on the dance floor. "About the same as you not drinking at all tonight."

She laughs as Ricky returns with our drinks, setting them on the table. "Here ya go, ladies."

Kaila throws hers back and points to the jukebox. "Whatcha say you go put on some tunes from this decade?" He backs up with a wink, and Kaila grabs my drink to down it. "Go get your tonic water before he gets back."

We do this every time she takes me out to drink. Since I refuse, I order a tonic water and say it's vodka. Nobody has ever questioned it.

I look at the Budweiser clock on the wall and groan at the fact it's already nearly one o'clock. Kaila is having the time of her life on the dance floor when Ricky scoots next to me at the bar. "Want to dance?"

"No, thank you."

I take a sip of my drink, and he leans closer, slurring, "I'd be willing to bet you aren't as innocent as you put off." His hand goes to my thigh, and all I can do is stare at him in shock. "Why don't you show me what you keep hidden under here?" Sliding his hands between my legs, he cups my sex over my dress.

My mouth drops open, and I bring up my hand, slapping his face for his audacity. I stand up to storm off, pointing my finger in his face. "I wouldn't go to bed with you if it was my last chance at the Paradise Star, you Philistine pig."

I go to spit at him before deciding that might be too much. I spin to see Kaila stumbling over herself. It's time to go. I run to the washroom because I've had a ton of tonic waters, trying to keep up with Kaila. This is going to be a long walk home.

Returning to the bar, I search for her. I look through the entire establishment, even the bathrooms, both of them, yet she's nowhere in sight. I bust through the doors to run outside, searching for any sign of movement. As I walk to the back of the bar, I hear the sounds of heavy breathing near the Bearcats high school football shrine. Bands play there sometimes in the summer, and it's hidden in the alcove behind the neighboring businesses. It's too dark to see right now, but I've been here enough times to know HOBART BEARCATS #1 is painted on the corrugated tin sheets lining the wall, and pans painted in the school colors of blue and gold are hung behind where I see shadowy, moving figures.

Tiptoeing around them to get closer to the wall, I hear a whimper that has to be Kaila. I realize I never saw Ricky when I was looking for her inside. I reach to lift one of the pans off its hook, accidently banging the tin sheet.

"What the hell?" A man's voice says. I bring the pan over my head, hitting him somewhere on his body. "Arrrgh!" He screams in pain.

Good.

Kaila jumps up next to me and cries, "Brently! Are you okay?"

Brently? Oh no.

Oops.

I hang the pan back on the wall, embarrassed. "I'm really sorry, Brently. I thought you were Ricky."

In the darkness, his shadow stands straighter. "Why the fuck would you think Ricky Willis was out here with *my* girlfriend?"

"That's what I want to know," Kaila adds.

"Because he was very rude to me earlier, and when I couldn't find Kaila or him, I assumed he was trying something with her. I'm truly sorry."

"Wow, Laurel Ann. Sometimes you surprise me. It's good to know I can count on you to protect my girl." He begins walking back to the bar, and he rubs his shoulder, apparently where I hit him. "Want me to kick Ricky's ass? It would be my pleasure. I've never liked that cocky prick."

Kaila is next to me as I follow him. "No, violence accomplishes nothing."

He scoffs, "Says the girl that just hit me with a pan."

"Shit, Laurel Ann, do you know what time it is?" Kaila pulls her curly, black hair over her face to block the light.

"I know exactly what time it is. Do you?"

She rolls over on the couch to get her phone off the coffee table. "It's before noon. Too early for you to be waking me up on my day off."

I've never understood how she can sleep all day, regardless of whether she works or not. Rolling my eyes, I pick her bra up off the floor and throw it at her. "You have a bedroom. I would appreciate it if you and Brently used it when you do your sinful sex acts."

She throws her head back against the couch, laughing. "God, girl, I love you."

I squint my eyes at her even though I can't help grinning. "There are some eggs and bacon on the stove and some fresh bread in the bread bin, but you better eat it soon or it'll go cold."

"Thanks, Mom."

I reach past her shoulders, tugging my gray, crocheted hoodie out from between her back and the couch. Tossing it over my head, I untuck my hair. "If I were your mother I would be sure you wouldn't curse as much as you do."

She winks at me, lighting a cigarette and walking to the TV to turn on one of her 'exotic yoga', 'striparerobics', or 'dance like a whore and call it exericiseilates' videos. I pick up the cash jar and stuff a few bucks in the pocket of my patch-work maxi skirt before backing up toward the front door. Grabbing my keys off the hook, I watch her bend over and shake her rear while still puffing on her cigarette.

"Isn't that counterproductive?"

Her head peeks at me from between her legs. "Nope."

I grin at my friend and begin the fifteen-minute trek to work. Walking along the uneven sidewalk, I spot one of my fa-vorite people to watch. I often see her near the Saint Peter and Paul church on my way to and from the butcher shop. She's a religious woman called a 'nun'. I love watching her clutch at her cross as she prays to her God.

I never considered that there were other belief systems when I left home. I assumed they didn't believe in anything, never thinking past the fact that they were all heathens. The truth is, they think they're on the right path, and I can respect them for trying, even if they are misguided.

She wears the same dress every time I see her. It's modest, covering all the appropriate areas, so the repetition seems irrel-evant. I admire her ladylike body language and the polite way she walks. There is a white statue of a man in a crown directly above the wooden paneled double doors of her church, and she stops to look up at it before going inside the brick building.

I pass Molly's Doughnuts and Café, waving to Crackhead Mike who is smoking a cigarette and spinning in circles on his rollerblades. I feel like that's a mean nickname considering that as far as I know, he doesn't even smoke the crack, but it's how he introduced himself. He tips his cowboy hat as he dances to whatever he's listening to on his headphones, wearing shorts that are way too small.

I get to Jefferson Street, finding the butcher shop door propped open. Rushing inside the Sturgis Countryside Meat's entrance, I mumble, "Pardon me," while weaving through the customers.

"You're late again," Cameron spouts off when I rush behind the counter for an apron.

"Yeah, I know, I know. I—"

"Be grateful that we're slammed, and I'm short staffed."

I roll my eyes. His definition of 'slammed' is eight people, and 'short staffed' means he only has one employee. Me.

"I am."

The customers keep piling in since everyone in town is getting ready for their Labor Day parties. It's one of their more normal traditions, not as odd as Easter. During their Easter celebrations, the adults hide plastic eggs filled with candy for the children to find, and sometimes people dress up like human-size bunnies. That part is quite terrifying, actually. There seems to always be some type of holiday tradition going on. They even celebrate the day they were born, as if it's some sort of crowning achievement. That's how vain they are.

Of all the Philistines I have met, my boss, Cameron, is one of the harder ones to figure out. Some days he's outright mean to me, yet on others I almost get the notion he cares about me. I have worked here for over a year, and I'm no closer to understanding him.

Finally, the last customer leaves, and Cameron turns to go to his office. "I have some things I need to look over before my new distributer gets here."

I nod to him, logging into the computer to pull up customer orders. There are things I have to do on a daily basis that tarnish my soul. Electricity, computers, cash register, telephone... While of course I don't like it, I have my own ways of trying to cleanse myself.

Inside the meat locker, I pull out five pounds of beef flank steak. I love the feel of raw meat against my fingers, it always soothes me. It reminds me of home when I would help my elder brother, Benjamin Jr., prepare the meat from the pigs and chickens, and I wonder if my heart will ever stop aching at the thought of my family and my home. Sighing, I wrap the steak in the butcher paper as the door chimes, announcing a customer.

I put on my kindest smile to greet them, but looking up paralyzes every muscle in my body. I don't understand… How is this possible?! My words run for the hills, and my hand is still on the half-wrapped meat when he sneers at me.

"I am Zebadiah Fitch. I have an appointment with Cameron Sturgis."

16

TWO WORLDS COLLIDE

Laurel Ann

MY EYES ARE THE ONLY BODY PART CURRENTLY WORKING AS they stare. If he recognizes me, he's hiding it well. He's gotten very tall, and he's no longer the boy I would sneak to the creek with. His hair is hidden under his hat, a few little, tawny wisps around the brim. He resembles the Prophet much more now. His crossed arms are considerably larger, and those suspenders are wrapping around his chest a lot nicer than they used to. His once boyish face is now defined with a square jaw and strong features.

On either side of him are two other men—Oh my gosh, are those his brothers? Ezekiel is still as handsome as I remember, just much bigger. Jacob though, he was a squeaky little mouse last time I saw him. Not anymore.

Why are they outside the gates? My heart seems to catch up with the situation, picking up pace and pumping the sweat from my pores. I should say something, anything, but all I want to do is run to him and take his face in my hands. I want to look in his eyes to confirm they are the same bright blue. I want to tell him how much I've missed him, and I still dream of him every night. I want to ask about my family, I want—

"Did I not speak clearly, girl? I have an appointment with the owner of this establishment."

My stomach drops so hard, I buckle my knees to keep them from giving way. He's looking at me as if I'm the manure on his boot. He's never spoken to me with that tone.

"I...I...u-um..."

"Laurel Ann, can you come here for a second?"

Cameron's voice halts my blubbering, and if Zeb didn't know who I was earlier, he does now. His expression fades from neutral to shocked before it contorts into disgruntled, hard lines. He looks at me, really looks at me, for the first time, and I don't know why it makes me want to duck behind the counter. I lower my gaze from Zebadiah to Ezekiel and Jacob glancing at each other with raised eyebrows and slacked jaws.

The walk back to Cameron's office is agonizing. My throat will only take in little bits of oxygen at a time, causing me to breathe faster and with difficulty.

I push his door the rest of the way open to find him tapping away on his cell phone. They seem to be the worst, the cell phones. You should see the way everyone walks around as if they are drugged, staring into their Devil's boxes, clueless to the earth around them. He looks up at me about to say something when he leans his head to the side.

"Are you okay? You look pale."

I stand up straight, composing myself. "Yes, I'm fine. Zebadiah Fitch is here to see you."

I don't want Cameron to know that Zeb and I have history, at least not before I get a chance to talk to him by myself. Philistines have no need to know anything about us or our world, but now...

I am a Philistine.

The thought jumps around my head hard enough to cause a headache. My insides turn, threatening to resurrect this morning's eggs. It has always been me against them. I have never fit in with them, besides Kaila. Yes, there are a few good people out there and some that I would go as far as to call 'friends', though there's no real loyalty there. I have never felt like I belonged in this world. Even knowing it's been undone, I still feel like a child of Zaaron. I still pray to Him every day, striving to be the person He originally intended. Even when it feels impossible, being surrounded in a world of so much sin, where nobody understands my beliefs.

Seeing Zeb and his brothers again makes it all too clear that I am not like them anymore. To them, I'm just another heathen living in filth.

In my mind, I always assumed Zeb would miss me as much as I have missed him. I never imagined he would blame me or think poorly of me. In that look he gave me, I saw it, his anger at what I have become. His disappointment. I want to relieve the burning in my eyes by letting the tears fall, yet I pull them back in.

"Oh, good." He stands, stretching his arms. "He has the best deal on beef I've seen in years, but he's a weird ass motherfucker." Looking at me, he smirks. "I bet you two would get along." He laughs and then must realize he is being offensive because his grin falls off his rosy face. He clears his throat and says, "Go ahead and send him in. After you check the dates for all the pork products in the display case, you can head out."

"Okay, thanks, Cameron. I'll see you tomorrow."

"On time though, yeah?"

I already apologized. I'm not doing it again. "Yeah."

My feet know how I am feeling because they drag on the tile as I make my way back to the lobby. I don't want to face him again if he's going to continue to look at me that way.

The three men stand in the exact same position they were in before I left: Zeb in front with Ezekiel and Jacob behind him on either side, in a triangle. I open my mouth to speak when the words get tangled in my vocal chords. The more steps I take, the thicker the air becomes. I don't want him to see me falter. He may see me as evil and repulsive, but he won't see me as weak. I push back my shoulders, and my throat opens up, allowing the air to freely flow.

"Cameron is ready to see you, Mr. Fitch. You can go on back."

It is the weirdest thing in the world to call him that, but it's what I would call a normal customer, and Cameron can hear us if he's listening.

He glares at me, nodding his head for his brothers to follow. I don't move a single inch when they pass by me, and I couldn't even if I wanted to. I half expect them to spit on me. Though Jacob and Ezekiel ignore me, Zebadiah stops next to me. I can't force my eyes to meet his, and I prepare for whatever verbal abuse I have coming. He stands there long enough for it to become awkward, making me jump when he speaks.

"Be outside when I leave." His tone is harsh and low. What happened to the boy I left at the compound?

I give him a quick nod because it's all I can muster. He steps behind his brothers, and they disappear into Cameron's office. I double over, grabbing my knees to regulate my breathing. Slipping my hand over my mouth, I feel my pulse thumping in my fingertips.

I can't believe this. He's here. Zeb is here. Never seeing his face or hearing his laugh again was a truth I had accepted. He said to wait for him. That has to mean he wants to talk to me. Of what he plans to speak of I have no idea. I just know how I am perceived now. I have to hope that if he hated me or was disgusted by me he wouldn't waste his time. That if he thought of me as a Philistine, I would be all but invisible to him.

I hurry through the pork with my organs twisting inside me all the while. I log the two pounds of meat that's gone bad into the computer, cringing the entire time. Using this thing so close to Zeb makes me feel all slimy.

I toss my apron into the hamper and wash my hands before I rush out the front door. The fall wind spins around my hair, blowing it in front of my face.

His buggy sits right out front, next to Cameron's Toyota, looking lost in a world it doesn't belong. The horses whinny, and I miss being able to be around them every day. I cross the sidewalk with confident, steady steps so as not to startle them. I'm sure they're already nervous around all the cars. The black one with a white mane shakes his head and paws at the ground. I hold my hand out, touching his nose with tender, secure fingers.

"You're sick of being tied up out here, huh?"

I glide my hand down his shiny coat that looks like ink when the chestnut horse does his own show of neighing and pawing.

"Awe, are you feeling left out?"

Petting them both with equal attention, because they will let me know about it if I don't, I watch the people coming and going. I've lived in and around Hobart for the last twelve years, yet it still feels unfamiliar. The only place that has any sense of home is my house, though I'm sure that has more to do with Kaila than the living space. I've never really belonged here. Seeing Zebadiah makes that fact rise to the forefront, bright with clarity.

I just don't understand why he's here at all. Why is he outside the gates? Maybe the Prophet has given him more responsibility, grooming him for when he takes the title.

"Hey! What are you doing?! Get away from the horses!"

My feet back up at the warning while my mind is still registering who's yelling at me. Jacob bounds toward me, and Zeb grabs his arm, shaking his head.

Jacob throws his hand out at me. "She's a Philistine!"

Zebadiah looks at him as if he is a confused child. "She's Laurel Ann. She can pet the horses if she desires." His response takes away my oxygen. My heart pumps blood full force through my veins. Ezekiel stands behind them, watching their exchange with crossed arms, and Jacob looks like he's about to stomp his feet. "Both of you, wait for me in the buggy."

Jacob's mouth drops open, and he narrows his eyebrows before obeying. Zebadiah removes his hat and hands it to Ezekiel who follows his brother to the carriage.

"Walk with me."

He's slipped his hands into the pockets of his trousers, making him appear more relaxed and more like the Zeb I remember. My palms are sweating. I have no idea what I am going to say to him or what he's going to say to me. I try to keep in step with his long legs, and I smile. Some things never change.

We walk for a few moments in silence, to the point it's making me anxious. Twelve years is a long time. He turns in the small space between the American Legion Bingo Hall and BancFirst. There's nothing back here besides a trash bin, though I'm sure that's the point. He turns to face me; his blue eyes are dark in the shadows as he stares down at me.

"Your clothes…they are appropriate."

My clothes? Twelve years, and he wants to talk about my clothes?! I ache with the need to wrap my arms around him and press my head to his chest, not talk about my wardrobe choices. Still, seeing the pleased expression on his face makes me proud of myself.

"Thank you. I do still try to follow spiritual law, but it has not been easy."

His eyes sparkle, and he gives me the smallest of smiles. "I would imagine not."

I can't hold it in anymore. I've fantasized about this since I was sent away. What if the Prophet comes to deal with the meat next time, making this my only chance to ever speak to him again? Even if he rejects my words, at least I will know I've said them. I don't try to stop the tears. The relief of his presence overwhelms me.

"I have missed you every single day. I should have listened to you and stayed with the Prophet. I am so sorry."

His eyes flash and his nostrils flare when he says, "What's done is done."

The crassness and shortness in his voice takes me aback. "Zebadi—"

His lips press together, making his jaw pulse. "I don't have time to discuss it right now. I brought you back here to ask you one thing." He swallows as if he's scared to continue while I devour his every word like a starved child. "Do you desire to regain your place in the Anointed Land?"

The alleyway closes in, and I can almost feel the wall of the Bingo Hall push against my shoulders. This was always a clear answer before. Of course I want to come home, but Kaila has become like a sister to me. I can't imagine not having her in my life. If I come home, I won't ever speak to her again. His irritancy at my hesitation causes me to blurt the first answer that climbs onto my lips.

"Yes."

His shoulders and eyebrows relax with his nod. "Good. We will speak more of this in one week. Is there a place we can meet privately? Do you have a home?"

It's difficult to process what's happening, and I'm shocked

by his suggestion. For a man to be alone with a woman in her home, to whom he is not bound, is most definitely a sin.

"That would be inappropriate." In part I'm teasing him, attempting to lighten the tension, though his narrowed brows say he's not in the teasing mood. "We could meet at Bedlams bar. Believe me, it will be a lot more private than at my house with my roommate around."

His lip lifts in disgust. "You share a home with one?"

The reaction is expected, yet it heats up my belly all the same. I would never have wanted them to meet in the first place, and now that feeling just multiplied. They'll surely not get along. I can't stand the thought of being torn between them.

"Yes, I do. And she is the only person who has stuck by me in this terrible place."

I think he's about to ask me a question until he straightens his jacket and turns to go. Panic creeps up my back that he's rescinding his question, but when I reach for his arm he adds, "Be at your home a week from today at six o'clock. No later. One Philistine is better than a room full, and I will not step foot into an establishment that serves liquor."

He faces me, his harsh expression causing me to jerk my hand back. "It's a restaurant."

"It's a brothel," he snaps.

It's hardly a 'brothel'. Their primary clientele are middle aged farmers and their wives.

"All right then, my house is the green one at the corner of Third and Randlett Street."

"Very well. One week."

This is all almost too much to bear. I woke up this morning thinking it was going to be another regular day. I have my fears about leaving Kaila, though right now my elation is at the forefront. Everything I've ever wanted could be happening.

As quickly as it came, my excitement is pushed away by trep-idation. Will I be expected to return to my binding with the Prophet?

"What about your father?"

With none of the grief I would have expected, he states, "Zaaron has taken him home."

Wait…Hiram is dead? Then that means…

Oh my goodness.

"*You're* the Prophet?"

His nod is curt as he turns from me, his footsteps taking him away. My body sags against the brick wall when his voice floats through the alley. I look up to see his back to me.

"I prayed every single morning and night that Zaaron would bring you home. I've missed you more than you could ever know."

17

CHANGED BY TIME

Zebadiah

I KEEP MY HEAD HIGH AND SHOULDERS STRAIGHT UNTIL I TURN behind the first building I reach. I can't believe this. She's here. My heart pounds so hard I feel the need to undo the top button of my shirt. This was not a reunion I was prepared for. I all but promised her she could return to the Anointed Land. What the hell was I thinking? While I've fantasized about her coming back for many years, it was never really something I actually believed would happen. The words were out before I could stop my mouth from saying them.

Was that you speaking to me?

I chuckle despite the fact that my mind won't stop racing. Time has done wonders for her. I would have never recognized her as the cute little red haired, freckled-face girl I fell in love with. Her words were just as perfect as she is. She has tried to obey Zaaron's teachings, and she still wants to come home.

This morning I was dreading this meeting because I despise leaving the compound. It makes my hair stand on end and my skin feel covered in dirt. Who would have thought a few extra pregnant cows would bring me to her? Zaaron bless-ed us with multiple successful inseminations of our livestock earlier this year, and the calves will be ready for slaughter next month. Cameron Sturgis is the nearest butcher to the com-pound, and I came in last week to discuss his interest in be-coming a buyer. I was under the impression he ran the place himself, so the last thing I was expecting was to come face to face with a very grown up Laurel Ann Henderson.

Seeing her stirred up emotions I would have never dreamed of. She's absolutely breathtaking. Seeing her again, missing all of those years, awoke the sleeping fury I had for not only my father, but myself for setting it all in motion. Still, I'll never forget the blast of energy that surged through my body once I realized the girl behind the counter was the one who took my heart with her when she left.

I'm struggling to force my lips out of a smile as I make my way back to the buggy and climb inside.

"What was all that about?" Jacob asks, his nosiness never failing.

"If it's necessary for you to know, then you'll know it."

Zeke snorts and tugs the reins to take us back to the Anointed Land. Leaning back in the buggy, I place my hat over my face. They take the hint, talking amongst themselves and leaving me out of it.

Philistines have machines that give them the ability to trap time into something called a photograph. Her face looking up at me from behind the counter is now etched into my mind a lot like that. If I was being completely truthful with myself, I wouldn't be waiting to talk to her if Zeke and Jacob weren't with me. Even though I do really need to think this through.

There is always a period of slight mistrust with a new Prophet, especially one as young as I am. It's not ever blatant or public disrespect, but there are whispers. I can't do anything to disrupt the tender balance right now. There's also no way I'm giving up until I have her back in the compound where I know she's safe and pure.

We arrive at the gates, and I lift my hat, tapping Ezekiel on his shoulder. "Drop me off at the tabernacle."

He does what I say, and when I enter the dark place of worship, I light the lamp next to the entrance. I make my way to my office, and even knowing I'm alone, I still lock the door behind me. Kneeling behind my desk, I open the bottom drawer, move the service notes from the previous Prophets, and pull out the bloody piece of torn fabric. I hold it to my nose. It's long since lost her smell, so I invoke her scent from earlier today, imagining it still on the old cloth.

My cock grows against my leg in my trousers, and I grip it as I inhale again.

Is this what you desire? Did you lead me to her today?

I undo my pants to free myself, stroking at her memory.

Show me. Talk to me! Please, Zaaron, tell me she's meant for me.

I wrap the scrap of her childhood fabric around my erection, and it instantly makes me throb. My balls rise up at the memory of her womanly curves that were apparent, even beneath her modest skirt.

Tell me, Zaaron. Tell me how to keep her here.

Her little hand would feel so soft wrapped around me. The image has me pushing my trousers down for better access. My thoughts flash to her licking her lips in the alley. How would her tongue feel, moving against my tip? Pumping faster, I close my eyes, conjuring up what she would look like bare, beneath me. In my mind, I enter her body, and the pressure is blinding as I pulse beneath my fingers.

"Oh, fuck, Laur."

My come flows over my hand and splashes across the long-dried blood of innocence on the cloth.

I use it to clean myself off before rinsing it in the water basin. I sit at my desk and pull out *The True Testament* along with sermon notes from the bottom drawer to try to come up with a way to make this feel legitimate.

My head falls as I nod off. I don't know if I'm any closer to an answer. Every ritual I can find that would be hefty enough to make the followers trust her again is brutal. The idea of putting her through any of those things makes me nauseous. I still have five days to figure it out. Maybe Zaaron will finally decide to weigh in between now and then.

Closing the tabernacle door, I walk through the empty common ground and back to the ranch. Everyone is asleep, and I am more than ready for that myself.

Keeping my footsteps quiet, I walk inside my home, and carefully close the door. My eyes are heavy with exhaustion. After removing my shoes and hat, I quietly make my way down the hall. Slipping into my room, I pull down my suspenders and get undressed before sliding into the fresh smelling sheets. I roll over, kissing my wife as I slide my hand beneath her nightgown. She shifts onto her back with a sleepy sigh.

"Hello, husband."

I get up to hover over her, lifting her night gown and lowering my flannel drawers. When I push inside her body, I pray I will finally get my chance to do this with Laurel Ann.

18

PERSONAL CLEANSING RITUAL

Laurel Ann

T HE FIFTEEN-MINUTE WALK HOME FEELS MORE LIKE TWENTY seconds. I need more time to think about what happened, but it still feels like I dreamed it. Kaila knows all about Zeb. I talk about him all the time though the boy I told her about is quite different from the man he is today. He has hardened and is the Prophet now. That one I'm having a hard time wrapping my head around. It's difficult to imagine him performing cleansings, bindings, and services. I can't fathom the pressure that is now on his shoulders. All the people looking to him for guidance.

I may have a real chance at going home. I just won't know for sure until I speak with him next week, and next week is going to take months to get here. Knowing for sure that I will see him again feels like a feather is tickling my insides.

If I get to go back, I will at last see my family again. I ache to see my mother and siblings. Most of my brothers and sisters will be grown now. I have often wondered if they think of me as I do them, and what has become of them.

With Hiram gone, I no longer have to worry about the

consequences of dishonoring our binding. The idea of not having to be forced to use computers and electricity, to listen to the sinful music and see violent television shows, would be like a rope loosening around my chest. Being the only one who cherishes modesty and purity is maddening. Once again surrounding myself with those of my same beliefs would be such a relief to my soul.

If I'm honest with myself, there are reasons I don't want to leave, or at least not be secluded from it all. There are things about this place and their modern life that I quite enjoy. I fight hard to not like a lot of these things, but Kaila has a way of making me give in. Like when she forced me to watch a movie with her. It didn't even have people in it. Well, not real people, more like moving drawings of them. Halfway through, I found myself giggling at the snowman that wanted to live in the summertime. Kaila's smirk was smug, and I would never admit I had fun watching.

It is clear in *The True Testament* that alcohol consumption is forbidden, and it has never touched my lips. Tobacco is also a sin against Zaaron. Had I known at the time that cigarettes are the same thing, I never would have smoked that day with Kaila, and I haven't had one since. I do not curse, date, or dress inappropriately, and I'm still surrounded by so much sin on a daily basis. Now, after seeing Zeb today, my desire to cleanse seems urgent.

My front door is a few steps away, the need to purge myself of my weekly transgressions becoming dire. I lift my skirt to run up the steps, my hand digging through my pockets. I grab hold of the two keys on the ring and shove the required one into the lock. The house is empty, yet every single light in the living room and kitchen are on.

I walk through the bottom floor, switching off all the lights before I turn on the faucet for a glass of water. There are little packages of apple chips in the bowl next to the fridge, and I grab one on my way up the death stairs. We call them that because they have never been updated, at least not in our lifetime, and sound as if every step you take is killing them.

Kaila's bedroom light is on, her door is open, and her room has to be infested by now. I don't remember ever seeing her clean it. Turning off her light, I close the door.

My friendship with Kaila has taught me a lot of things, one of them being that caring deeply about someone means it's possible to waver between wanting to hug them and strangle them with your bare hands.

My room is the polar opposite of Kaila's. Where hers is covered in completely pointless junk, like a hunk of wood that spells out 'Love', mine is only the necessities. Her bed is covered in a mountain of pillows, which she doesn't even sleep on, while mine has a single pillow, linens, and a quilt. My walls are as bare as hers are cluttered, and my closet is modest and organized where hers is in a state of disarray with half of her grossly extensive wardrobe crumpled at the bottom. I don't think she has seen a quarter of her clothes in over a year.

I kick my bedroom door closed behind me with my boot, toss the chips on my bed, place the glass of water on the nightstand, and yank open the drawer.

The first time I attempted a personal cleansing was a few months after I came to this dark, new world. Zaaron wasn't done punishing me. To show Him how much I still desired His grace, I placed my hand on my foster mother's stove. I had to go to the hospital though, so after that I began to use hot needles, metal hangers, and even tried one of Kaila's cigarettes once—anything to melt away the sin. Over time, I learned how to care for the burns and make sure they don't get infected.

Now I use a small, metal bookmark. It's roughly an inch and a half long, a quarter inch thick, and curves at the top to save your place when reading. I lay it next to the water to pull out my small, hand-held torch. Picking up a handkerchief, I place it inside the glass of water until it is entirely submerged, ready to cool my skin once I'm finished.

When Kaila learned I was doing this, she got extremely angry. It took a while for her to comprehend why I needed it. Eventually, she began to soften and understand, suggesting I do them in some sort of design so I'm not covered in random scars. She was right. Putting them in an orderly fashion not only is more aesthetically pleasing, but allows for more markings in a smaller area.

I pull off my left boot and stocking to inspect the space on my ankle. The long, straight scars lay at a forty-five-degree angle, one right after the other, creating a ring of lines all the way around. I have a completed ring on my right ankle and right wrist, two on my left wrist, and I'm finishing the second circle on my left ankle. The second ring is tilted the opposite way from the one beneath it, creating an arrowed, zigzag effect. I don't want to do it next to my most recent mark with it still being tender, so I position myself to reach the space on the opposite end.

I press the button on the torch and hold the long end of the bookmark beneath the flame.

Cleanse me of this evil.

Cleanse me of this sin.

Let your fire burn from within.

I repeat the words in my mind. Over and over, faster and faster, as if the more I say it, the more likely He will answer my plea. The metal burns bright when I press it to my flesh. The smell of burning transgressions fills my room while the popping sound of the melting epidermis comforts me, regardless of the tears streaming down my face. The familiar pain sears through my leg, and I whisper my prayer through my groan.

Tap, tap, tap.

I look up at the sound. My door creaks open and Kaila pops her head in. "Hey, do you need anything?"

Removing the metal from my ankle, I shake my head. "No. I'm finished. How was your day?"

I don't know how to tell her about Zeb. She's never been keen on the compound. I want to get her talking about herself, which isn't exactly difficult, until I can figure out what in the world I'm going to do.

I press the wet handkerchief against the fresh burn, and relief washes over me. As I place the bookmark on the nightstand to cool, she sits on the bed.

"It was good. Brently took me out shooting cans, and we saw a movie. How about you? Was Cameron pissed you were late?"

I avoid her russet eyes, pulling my stocking and boot back on. "It was fine, and yes, he said it's my last warning. Did you happen to get any food today?"

"I ordered a pizza." I stop myself from complaining about the junk food and place the torch and bookmark back in the drawer. She plops backward on the bed, ripping open the bag of apple chips. "That's it? You usually love to bitch about Cameron."

I knew I wouldn't be able to be around her long without spilling. She does that to me. It's as if she can suck my feelings right out. I lie down next to her, and we both look at my asbestos ridden ceiling while she munches on the chips. "Someone came into the butcher shop today..."

"You know I don't do guessing games."

The flutter in my stomach at the mere thought of his name ignites a smile across my lips.

"Zebadiah."

She flies up to an elbow, and at any moment her eyes are

going to pop out and roll onto the bed. "Like *the* Zebadiah?! As in your religious Romeo?"

I snort. "Stop."

"So, what happened?! What did the sanctified stud say?"

I groan before I get up to head downstairs, but she's right beside me with a mouth full of chips, her hair bouncing all the way down the steps.

"I'm not telling you anything until you can be serious."

She follows me into the kitchen and jumps up on the counter while I search for something appetizing to eat. I glare at her when she tosses the empty chip bag in the sink and open the refrigerator.

"I am being serious. You've never liked a single guy besides this holy hunk." She claps her hands together, fluttering her eyelashes. "He's your spiritual sweetheart."

My eyes can't roll any harder. "Okay, you're done."

There's nothing to eat in this house, leaving me with the pizza. I pull it out from under the leftover Chinese food and ignore her amusing herself.

"For real, what happened?"

I take a big bite of the cold pizza as if speaking with a full mouth will make the words easier. "He wants me to come back."

All traces of humor are gone. She knows how much I've desired this, though neither of us ever thought it was an actual possibility. Kind of like her winning one of the talent shows she watches on TV.

"I thought you could never go back. Isn't that what excommunication means?"

"It does." I swallow my bite and wipe my mouth on a napkin. "I don't know what he's thinking. He's changed a lot... He asked me if it's still what I wanted. He'll be here next week to talk about it."

She points to the floor. "Here? He's coming to our house?"

I shrug. "That's what he said."

She jumps off the counter, takes the cigarette pack out of her purse, and sits at the table, before lighting a cigarette. "What did you say? When he asked you?"

I don't want to hurt her, and I know my answer will. It's not as if I've made up my mind, I just know that I'm being offered something I've wanted for half of my life.

"Kaila…"

She has only been angry at me once. We have our bicker fights that we end up forgetting what we're fighting about halfway through, though she's only been honest to goodness angry at me once. It was over a dirty jerk who treated her terribly, and she, for whatever reason, was head over heels for him. I didn't go about it the right way, but she wouldn't listen to me when I told her he was a disloyal liar. I took it upon myself to prove it to her. I set it up so she would catch him kissing me. That's the only Philistine boy I ever kissed, and the only time she has ever looked at me like she is now.

"Yeah."

She walks into the living room, and I follow her. What do I say to make her understand? "You know this is what I've always wanted. If you got the opportunity to go to California and be famous, I would want you to go."

She scoffs and falls onto the couch. "If I went to Cali, I'd take your ass with me." Her head whips back to me as she glares. "Not to mention I wouldn't be forbidden to leave or to see you. I get that you miss your family, but you're just ready to leave me behind forever, without a second thought, to go back to a cult that controls you."

I suck in a breath from the heated pang in my chest. When I started school in Hobart, I was completely shocked to learn the people in the town were aware of the Anointed Land.

None of them had ever seen it, of course. Kaila and I kept my being from there a secret, but I heard the derogatory way they spoke of my home—like we're all crazy and stupid.

"You know how I feel about that word."

"It's what it is, Laur! I've tried to keep my opinions to myself because I know you care about that place, but it's all bullshit! I mean come on, nobody has even heard of this Zaaron douchebag. Don't you think if he was 'God' people would know about it?"

"That's blasphemy! Do not speak that way in front of me! And you don't know about Him because you are a Philistine!"

She has never blatantly spoken against my beliefs or my God. While she may have been angry with me before, this is the first time I've had the desire for her to leave. I don't like the mix of hurt and fury I feel for her right now. She can joke about my clothes and the things she doesn't understand, however, outright degrading His name I cannot tolerate. What hurts the most is she knows that. That's why she said it.

"That's all I've ever been to you, isn't it? A 'Philistine'. You've always thought you were better than me, but you're not. You're just brainwashed." She gets back off the couch, storming toward the stairs. "So, you know what? Go back to the family that forced you into a marriage at thirteen to a man three times your age. That when you tried to tell them you didn't want to be fucking raped, sent you into a world they taught you to fear. Just go, because for the life of me, I don't understand why you would ever want that over freedom and someone who loves you more than a sister."

She pounds harder with each wooden step until the force of her door slamming knocks the tears from my eyes. She's wrong. I don't think of her that way, not really. I love her too, and leaving her would be heartbreaking for me. Yes, I want to see my family. I miss Zeb and want to be surrounded by those with like values. Mostly though, I want to make it to the Paradise Star and protect my soul from Hell. She can't understand because she doesn't have beliefs. At least not ones she takes seriously. I grab her pillow that's shaped like a tube of pink lipstick and weep into it. I don't know what to do. I always thought if I was ever given this opportunity, it wouldn't be a choice.

Are you testing me? You know how much she means to me.

I don't think I'll be able to make a clear decision until after I talk to Zebadiah, and I can't think with this going on between me and Kaila. I need her to know what she means to me. That she's the only reason I haven't gone crazy in this world.

She really loves chocolate chip cookies, and miraculously, we have all the ingredients I need. Well, besides the extra egg and the chocolate chips. I luckily find quite a few snickers in our old Halloween and Christmas candy. Out of all the Philistine holiday traditions, those two are my favorite. I mash up the candy into a bowl before mixing them into the batter.

While they are baking, I pull out the bottles of vodka, Baileys, and Kahlua. We may barely have any food in the house, yet somehow there's always a full supply of alcohol. I pour it all into the blender with some milk and ice. I'll confess that the blender is a fantastic device. It can shred, chop, or liquefy just about anything in a matter of moments.

I pour the drink into a pink, plastic cup we got from the Wal-Mart once I remove the cookies from the oven. They are gooey, almost falling apart when I place them on a plastic plate to carry both items up the stairs.

Her music is loud through the door as I tap it with my foot. "Kaila? Can we talk?" I wait until she doesn't respond to add, "I have cookies and a mudslide."

One breath later, the door swings open and she yanks the treats from my hand. I follow her without invitation and wait until she has a mouth full of cookies.

I still have no words chosen, though I pray Zaaron will show them to me.

As she slurps on the mudslide, her inability to speak gives me courage. "You are the only reason I haven't made up my mind. You are much more than a friend to me, Kaila. You have been my storm shelter in this place. I have never fit in here, and while it is surely not what I imagined, there is still so much sin. It's become easier to deal with over the years, and that terrifies me. I don't want to burn in Hell. I want to spend eternity with my family in the Paradise Star. I can't do that outside of the Anointed Land."

Her shoulders slack, and her eyebrows relax. "I don't want to be disrespectful to your beliefs. You know I've always tried to support you, but listen to what you're saying. Everyone in the entire world, besides the few hundred people who live within those three-square miles of Oklahoma are going to burn in Hell forever?" She shrugs. "I'm just sayin'. It's going to get crowded."

It hurts terribly to know that her soul will suffer such agony when the world ends, and I wish more than anything I could save it.

"Zaaron gave your ancestors a chance to follow Him. He asked them to give up their wickedness and live under His grace in the Anointed Land. They were warned that they were dooming the souls of their children and their children's children, yet they mocked Him. They sealed their fate and yours by doing so."

"So even if I wanted to join this…family of yours, I can't, and my eternal existence is still fucked?"

My skin goes rigid as my heart skips a beat. I never entertained the idea of bringing her with me. Zeb is the Prophet now. If she is willing to follow spiritual law…

"You would do that? You would leave all of this to live a life of purity with me?"

She shoves another cookie in her mouth. "Fuck no."

I huff. There goes that. "I don't know what to do. I feel lost without my God, without my family, without Zebadiah. But I would feel lost without you, too. I've lived each half of my life in opposing worlds. I'm scared for my soul, and honestly, I'm a little scared to go back. I need you through this." I let out a big breath. "I am asking you to support whatever choice I make."

She pushes off the bed. "I really do want you to be happy. That's all I want for both of us. I had just hoped it would be together." She walks over to me, embracing me against her short frame. "I will back you up, no matter what." Pushing off me, she spins around and flops back on the bed. "But only because you make a killer mudslide."

19

BAKED WITH EVIL

Laurel Ann

TODAY IS THE DAY.

Zebadiah will be at my house within the next three hours. The entire week, Kaila has been not so subtly reminding me of all the wonderful things that make up the Philistine world, while unintentionally just enforcing all of the darkness. I barely slept an hour last night. I've been feverishly cleaning all week, and last night I went over everything for a touch up. I'm not sure if I'm nervous or excited or a hybrid of both, but the man at the counter has had to repeat his order twice already.

"I apologize, sir. I have three pounds of flank steak, two pounds ground lamb, five pounds boneless pork butt, and eight pounds prime rib roast?"

He sighs. "Four pounds of ground lamb."

"Right. Give me about ten minutes."

"I'm obviously in no hurry," he grumbles at my back.

Make it twenty minutes.

I slip the last wrapped pieces of the man's order into a

Sturgis Country Meats bag as Cameron walks out from the meat locker.

"I don't know where your head has been today. If you can keep it on long enough to clean the slicer before you go, I would appreciate it."

I nod and internally mimic him. Maybe if he wouldn't be so passive aggressive, he would have a girlfriend by now.

Once the slicer is clean, I mop the floor behind the counter and clock out. The weather is lovely, not too hot or cold. I run as fast as my lungs will allow, rushing home to make sure everything is in order by the time he arrives. Kaila got off work two hours ago, and I pray she hasn't destroyed the house.

The living room is still clean, and whatever dishes Kaila used in the kitchen have thankfully been put away.

Zeb's favorite pie is apple, and I'm going to make him one. The thought of baking something just for him gives me a thrill. I melt the butter before I preheat the oven, adding in the flour and sugar mixture. I use the Granny Smith apples, hoping he likes the tanginess they provide, and I admire my perfect lattice work once I drizzle the filling into the holes.

My skin sings at the removal of my jacket, and I run up the stairs to shower. I don't want to smell like raw meat when he arrives.

"Fuck, yes! Oh my God, fuck me, Brently! Yes!"

Kaila's moans float through her closed door, and while they are nothing new, this can't be happening when Zeb gets here. In fact, Brently needs to be gone altogether.

I hurry through my shower, taking a little extra time on my hair. Wrapping myself in a towel, I rush to my room and pick out my clothes. I've narrowed it down to three dresses I think he'll like, but I can't decide. I need to make sure the nastiness going on down the hall is wrapping up anyway, so after throwing on my sweater and night dress, I march to her room, and pound on the wood to ensure I am heard above her moans.

Swinging open her door, she greets me in the nude. "Ugh, Kaila!" I look away, making the mistake of choosing the bed to land my eyes. Brently is sprawled out on her blanket, his erection pointed straight to the ceiling. His stare meets mine before he smirks and wraps his hand around his cock, sliding it up and down. I spin around, putting my back to the both of them. "Zeb is going to be here soon, and I need your help with my clothes. Also, you're going to make him uncomfortable enough, I don't think Brently would help the situation."

"Oh, I wouldn't want to make his royal righteousness uncomfortable in my own damn house."

I roll my eyes so hard I feel it in my temples. "Will you please put some clothes on? I'd like to talk to you."

"God, fine." I hear the door slam behind me, and I have the unfortunate luck of not getting away fast enough to miss her saying, "Looks like you get to put it in my ass. I need you to bust it A.S.A.P. all right?"

Gross.

I put the pie in the oven, setting the timer before I make sure we have milk. Zeb used to drink an insane amount of milk. Maybe that's how he got so huge.

I hear her bedroom door open and their goodbye, which consists more of making out than actual words, as I fluff the pillows on the couch and straighten the coffee table for the fiftieth time. Since I don't have my sweater on, I head back into the kitchen until I hear Brently leave through the front door.

Kaila is pulling her shirt over her head when I return to her room, and she has yet to get into her pants. Probably because Brently just did.

"There are three dresses I can't choose between. I need you to tell me which one you think looks the best."

"The pinkish-burgundy one." How did she know that was one of my choices? "It's my favorite thing you own. It looks incredible with your hair and eyes." I feel my lips lift. Her compliments are so genuine, they always make me feel good. "Come on, let's go pick out some jewelry."

I follow her out of her room, keeping my thoughts to myself about her leaving the light on. Once in my bedroom, I take off my nightgown, and she holds up the cameo necklace I got from Now and Then Antiques.

"This one. I wish you would have let me pierce your ears. I have some ivory earrings that would look killer with this."

I slide the dress over my head. "Altering the body for vain purposes is a sin."

"Of course it is." She attaches the necklace before smoothing my hair. "There. You look perfectly virginal."

If only.

"Thank you for your help. I didn't cause any problems with Brently, did I?"

She shrugs. "He got his rocks off." Ugh. She covers her mouth and giggles. "Oh my God, I love your face when I talk about sex shit."

I scoff, yet I still can't help myself from smiling at her. The knock at the door is loud and hammers me to the carpet. I stand frozen, unable to move a muscle. It's what I imagine paralysis to be like. I can feel my limbs, they are just useless.

"Are you gonna get that or am I?"

He's expecting to predominately deal with me. The less interaction he has with Kaila, the better.

"I-I will."

Her eyes look around the room, and she rocks back on her heels. "Today?"

"Shut up."

The heaviness of my feet gives way, allowing me to run

down the hall and stairs.

Either the door feels bigger than normal, or I feel much smaller as I wrap my fingers around the cold knob. I swing it open and am met with a very handsome-looking Zebadiah.

Black suspenders bow out from his chest, covered in a cream, thermal shirt that does nothing to hide his abs and pecs. His jacket is draped over his arm, and the eyes I know are blue are hidden beneath the shadow of his hat. My mouth suddenly feels dry, so I swallow.

"Hey, hi… erm, hello."

His lips tweak into a subtle smirk. "Hey, hi, hello to you too."

I don't doubt my cheeks are pink as I hold out my arm to invite him in. He hesitates for the slightest of moments, which gives me a twist in my gut, reminding me that what we're doing is wrong.

He removes his hat, allowing the light brown strands to fall into his eyes before he smooths them back. His skin is darker than it once was and has taken on a lovely golden glow. It's odd to see him with a five o' clock shadow, but I like it. The last time I saw him, he was barely shaving. Not to mention, cleanliness is extremely important in the Anointed Land. He'll be required to shave soon, regardless of being the Prophet.

I hate how nervous I am. He should be the only other person in the world, besides Kaila, who I'm completely comfortable with.

I hold out my hand. "May I take your hat and jacket? Would you like a glass of milk? Oh, and I made you an apple pie. It should be done soon."

My words tumble out on top of each other, and I feel the heat crawl up my neck. I'm relieved at his smile and flustered by the way it pulls out the shine in his eyes.

He hands me his things, and as I hang them in the closet,

he says, "Milk would be wonderful. Thank you."

I gesture to the living room, wishing I had something other than our thirty-year-old couch for him to sit on. "Take a seat, I'll be right back."

Turning toward the kitchen, I'm grateful for the escape from his gaze. I check on the pie and pour his milk before I return to find him frowning at the blank television.

"You have one of these in your home?"

I place the milk in front of him on the coffee table and sit next to him, though at a polite distance.

"It's my friend Kaila's. There are a lot of sinful things I'm forced to associate with, so I do my best to pay my penance for it."

He arches a curious eyebrow. "And how exactly do you do that without the presence of holiness?" He picks up the milk, and as soon as it hits his lips, his face twists in repulsion. "Oh Laur... Please tell me I didn't just drink milk that has been run through a machine."

Oh, no. I forgot about the milk. It took some getting used to for me too, but since Kaila hates unpasteurized, I didn't think to get some.

"I am so sorry! I-I wasn't thinking." The timer for the apple pie goes off, and I could almost cry with gratitude. While his face softens to neutral, he pushes the milk away. I stand to fetch the pie. "Excuse me."

Stupid! If we were in the Anointed Land, this would be a serious offense. Though it may have not been intentional, I still caused him to ingest a sin-tainted substance. He won't want this pie either. It's been put in an electric oven. A pie baked with evil.

So far, this night is going terribly.

I toss the pie on the stovetop. No more food or drinks. I want to hear what he has to say and how he thinks my returning home is possible. Smoothing out my dress, I stand up straight, assuring myself the rest of the evening will go smoothly.

"Oh, hey! So, you're the pious prince! I'm Kaila."

Oh no, no, no.

"Excuse me?"

I run into the living room to see Zeb leaning away from her outstretched hand as she wiggles her fingers for him to take it. I hadn't outright asked her to stay out of sight, though she knows it's what I would have preferred.

I throw her a glare to which she responds by widening her smile. She drives me nuts sometimes. I am going to hide all of her tweezers. She will freak out if she can't 'maintain her brows'.

"She's joking." I frown at her. "She's just not very funny."

Dropping her hand, she shrugs before she rubs her palms together. "Do I smell pie? You want some, farmer Zeb?"

"If you must address me, I insist you do so as Zebadiah. And no, I do not break bread with Philistines."

Her eyebrows jump up her forehead, and her open hands fly up by her shoulders. "Oh well, damn. It's like that, huh? Okay then." This isn't good. She can be a bit of a scrapper, especially with men. She's always been like that, but if she hits him, this visit will come to an unfortunate end. She leans forward enough that I know he can see down her shirt. He's looking at her like she smells bad, and her posture is screaming fight mode. "Here's how it is: I don't give a fuck what you think of me, but I swear to any God besides yours that if this isn't legit and you do anything that hurts Laurel Ann, I will destroy your precious 'Anointed Land'. And this Philistine keeps her fucking promises, you dissembling dick."

She spins toward the kitchen and looks at me to see if she crossed a line. While of course I wish she would have stayed in her room, she has a right to be offended. Zeb could have kept his thoughts to himself, even if she did come on strong. She did nothing besides enforce his opinion of her.

I close my mouth and nod her on. Right now, I just need her out of here. Zeb scowls at me in silence, and Kaila stomps around in the kitchen. When did he get so grumpy? I know he's outside of the compound, but he is with me. That should count for something. At least it used to.

The backdoor out of the kitchen slams. I'm not looking forward to how long I'm going to hear about this from her tonight.

He looks around my home as if we are standing in a cesspool. "How do you live like this?" If I were in his position I would feel the same way, yet his words physically sting my chest. I would rather him spit on my face than judge me the way he is. "With *her*?"

The fact that he's speaking of Kaila more than the sins runs through my spine. I march over to him, and he stands to greet me. "She's just trying to protect me, and you were very rude to her. She doesn't like being looked down upon."

He shakes his head like I'm speaking French. "She's a loud, obnoxious Philistine. There is no reason to be kind to her."

Oh, wow. She's right. He *is* a dick. I fight the urge to poke him in his incredibly hard chest.

"How about because she is my friend? And I thought you were too? I have done my best here, but I never could have done it without her. She's always supported me, and she has been my only source of love and affection in this evil place. You don't have to like her, though I would appreciate you being cordial."

Why is he smiling like that?

"You're right. I apologize for my unfriendliness. I have no

idea what you have gone through these past years. Though in part, that's why I'm here." He gestures to the couch. "Please sit with me."

Were his moods always this extreme? I take his invitation to sit while he does the same. He's just looking at me. Am I supposed to talk first? He lifts his hand, and my dress has become a furnace. He's going to touch me.

His palm is much bigger than it used to be as he cups my face. "You were always beautiful, but now...you're simply breathtaking," he whispers. I can't stop the smile from lifting my lips at his unexpected words. My stomach flies around inside me, and I hope my face isn't red. He leans forward, and for a wonderful moment I think he is going to kiss me. "I want you to come home."

I nod quickly to avoid appearing hesitant. "As do I, but how? Excommunication is permanent."

"It is Zaaron's will."

I nearly jump up with a rush of excitement that explodes into every cell in my body. "He told you that?"

"I am the Prophet."

I want to simultaneously laugh, scream, cry, and pray. Finally, I give in to what has been the constant desire to hug him. His body heat radiates into mine when I wrap my arms around his large frame and lay my head on his shoulder.

"This is everything I've dreamed of since I was cast out."

He vacillates at first, then his body relaxes to embrace me. I hear him quietly inhale as he places a small kiss to my head.

"Tell me how you have kept yourself pure."

I pull back from him, insecurity worming its way into my thoughts. What if he sees my methods as ridiculous or worse, ineffective?

"I need you to understand, there are evil things I have to

do on a daily basis, almost constantly. All I knew to do was to try to atone for them all, periodically."

"There are many sins, Laurel Ann, and most can be forgiven. However, there are a few which are impossible to come back from." I nod because as far as I know, I have not committed any unforgivable sins. "Have you, in any way ingested the blood of a Philistine?"

"No."

"Have you ever rebuked Zaaron as your God and Messiah?"

"No."

"Have you ever had a Philistine man inside your body?"

My face flames although I'm glad I can say, "No."

The thought of him touching another woman batters my mind, and I clench my dress in my fists. He's very possibly bound to at least one wife by now. That is his purpose. I've always known that, so why is this feeling in my stomach making me want to scream into the lipstick pillow he keeps staring at?

He smiles and his eyes roam down my dress. "Please, continue. What is your source of cleansing?"

I unfasten the buttons on the cuff of my sleeve, pulling it up enough to show him the bracelet of scars.

"I pray to Zaaron to cleanse me while burning my wicked flesh." I quickly cover myself. "I have many more."

His eyes slightly widen as he appears to be fighting a smile. "This has saved your soul."

The words sound so final, like the decision has been made. "I can come home?"

"It will be a bit of a process, but yes, I suggest you tie up your loose ends."

Questions begin to overflow my mind, climbing over one another. "Where will I stay?"

"This is an unorthodox situation. While you paid penance with your flesh, you have been in a constant place of sin for years. It will take something much more extreme than a cleansing to purify you of its tainting. You will also need to apologize to all of the children of Zaaron. You will first stay in the holding room. Once you are again pure, you will live in the placing dorms until Zaaron's will becomes clear."

"Do you think they will accept me? I'm scared I'll be shunned."

He lifts his hand, hesitating for a moment before he tucks a strand of hair behind my ear. "I can't promise this will be taken with approval, at least not right away. However, the children will not defy their Prophet or the word of Zaaron." He takes my hand. "I will undo what was done by my father."

Feeling his touch closes a door in my throat, requiring considerable effort to speak. "What happened to him?"

"Zaaron desired him at the Paradise Star. How his physical body died though, we don't know."

"When?"

"Next week will be four months since we put him into the ground."

"I'm so sorry."

He shrugs with indifference. "It was meant to be." I want to ask if I will be eventually placed again, but considering my history, I don't want to come across as ungrateful. "I must take my leave. Either I or Ezekiel will call on you, informing you of when to be ready and where you will be picked up."

I am going to guess, for now that Ezekiel is the Apostle, if Zeb is sending him on tasks. He stands, and I follow him to the door.

"This means everything to me, Zeb. Thank you."

He spins back to me, pushing my chin up to meet his stare. "Prophet. I am your Prophet." His harsh tone and hardened face forces me to gulp a big ball down my throat with my nod. His fingers trace up my cheek, pulling the air from my lungs. He leans down, and I can feel his lips barely touch my ear. "I want you to say it."

My heart *swooshes* in my chest, and I lick my lips.

"Thank you, Prophet."

20

A FINAL FAREWELL

Laurel Ann

I CLOSE THE DOOR BEHIND ZEB AND LEAN MY HEAD AGAINST IT. What just happened? I agreed to come back without so much as a single thought. Now that he's gone, and I know Kaila will be back any minute, guilt grows in my chest, overtaking my joy.

I don't know how I'm going to tell her. It's really happening, and the thought of never seeing her again is crushing. Doubt consumes me. The desire to go to my room to sleep overtakes me.

I don't bother with a nightgown or covering up with my quilt. The sobs are muffled by my pillow, and I never would have imagined feeling this way after receiving the only thing I've wished for years. I can honestly say I love her. It's similar to how I feel for Mia and my family, but since we chose each other, there is something more between us.

She's never going to forgive me, and I won't blame her. I have to go back. While I know that, this is going to tear my heart in two.

Tap. Tap.

Kaila's head peeks into my room. "Hey. How'd it go with the divine dickhead?" I sniffle and roll over to face her. Once our eyes meet, her shoulders slump, and she climbs on the bed, lying next to me. "Are you okay?"

My vision is obscured with tears when I squeeze my arms around her. I hold her as tight as I can. After she finds out, I may never get to again.

"I don't want to leave you." I bawl into her hair. The agony in my heart makes me question if I can do this. She's been my entire world for almost half my life.

"You're going back." She doesn't pull away. She doesn't scream or get angry, she just holds me tighter. Her tears wet my neck as we cry with each other. She pulls her head up and clears the wet hair from my face. "What am I going to do without you?" Another floodgate bursts through my eyes at her words. "I'll be right back."

My body curls into a ball. I clutch at my pillow and thank Zaaron that she doesn't hate me. Leaving her that way would have been unbearable. After returning with an envelope, she sits back down.

"Here's what we're doin'," she says. When she opens the paper package, a stack of photographs falls out. "We are going to stay up all night reminiscing and saying a proper goodbye, okay?"

I force a smile as I take her hand. "Thank you for not being angry."

"I'm not sure what I feel, but it's not angry." She straightens the photos, handing me the stack with a sigh. "I know how you feel about getting your picture taken, but I've still snuck in a few clicks here and there."

The only photographs I've ever seen of myself are the ones I've been forced to take for identification purposes and class photos. I refused to smile in them, hating that they were proof of my sins. As I flip through these photos though, I'm laughing or smiling in all of them, unaware of the moment being stolen. Seeing these joyful memories in my hands makes me choke on a laugh. A lot of them are 'selfie-style' with Kaila in the corner of the photo wearing her beautiful smile. The last one is of both of us laughing about something, on our couch.

She points to it. "Brently took that one last month. I hope it's okay I have these. I know you can't take them with you. I just wanted to show you that you were happy here. With me."

I wipe my face. I don't want to get the photos wet, and I don't want to let go of the one with us. It would be a horrible idea to bring it back with me. Not a good way to start off my return by bringing something as modern and soul damaging as a photograph into the Anointed Land. And yet, the idea of having this piece of her to hold and to look at when I miss her is one of the strongest desires I have ever felt.

"Please, can I keep this one?"

Her face brightens a shade. "Of course, I just didn't think they'd let you."

I rub my fingers over the glossy copy of her face. "They won't."

She giggles. "Try to not get excommunicated again in your first week, okay?" That shouldn't be a funny thought, and it really isn't, but a laugh pops out anyway. "And let me get a copy of it before you...how long do you have?"

"He didn't say. He just told me to get my affairs in order."

Her eyes go glassy when she squeezes my hand. "Well then, we'd better make the most of what we have."

It turns out I have two 'loose ends': Kaila and work. Cameron is more upset that I can't give him a date for my last day than the fact that I'm quitting. Never mind it's been almost two weeks since I told him. He grumbles about having to hire someone on short notice and how he hopes they are more dependable. I think he's being a little unfair. I haven't been that bad of an employee. Sure, I've been late a few times, but I have never missed a day in the year I've worked for him and have agreed to come in on my days off plenty of times. Plus, he's said himself I'm a hard worker. He is just like so many others in this dark, new world—unhappy with everything.

I think of all the Philistines I have met during my time here. They all do unholy things, but they aren't all cruel. They aren't all killers, rapists, or thieves. They are mothers and fathers, teachers and healers. They get sad and happy, just like we do. I wonder if I should tell anyone how I feel about them now, when I go home. Home. It's surreal that I am going to get to see Samuel and Mia, the twins, Robert, and Benjamin Jr, my mother and Benji. It's what I've dreamed of for years, so I don't understand why my stomach gets nauseous and jumpy every time I think about going back.

I don't know if they will welcome me with open arms or if they will rebuke me for living outside of grace for all these years. I still question if I'm able to be bound. I wonder what my purpose will be, and if I'm destined to be husbandless and childless for the rest of my days. The idea of that makes me terribly sad. I have always wanted children. I shake the thought away because that is more than I can consider right now.

Cameron tells me he has work to do in his office, and that I can leave once I wipe down the counters and mop the lobby.

The mop water has taken on a brown-gray hue when the bell *dings* from the door being opened.

"Hel-" I look up to see Ezekiel standing at the front of the shop "-lo."

He looks around as he marches up next to me and speaks quietly. "Are you alone?"

I nod my head toward Cameron's office. "My boss is in there."

"Be at the east edge of town, by the city sign, tonight at sundown."

"Tonight?" Flutters behind my belly button have me holding my stomach.

He crosses his large arms, and his eyebrow arches beneath the brim of his hat. "Is that a problem?"

"Of course not. Thank you, Ezekiel."

In almost a concerned tone, he softly says, "Please, address me as Apostle."

I nod to him. Well that answers my question about Zeb naming him for the position. "I will be there. Thank you, Apostle Ezekiel."

I finish mopping and try my best to explain to Cameron that I won't be returning. To my complete surprise, he pats me on the back, telling me he enjoyed my working for him. He sure had an interesting way of relaying that emotion. I smile and thank him before I leave Sturgis Country Meats for the last time. I have an odd sense of sorrow as I look back at the place that has paid for my home for an entire year. Though Cameron and I may not have been best friends, I am saddened at the fact that I won't ever see his dorky face again.

I get to the end of Randlett Street, passing by the church that I always see the nun coming and going from. The statue above the doorway has always intrigued me, and this will be the last chance I'll have to admire it.

The first time I was ever taken to a Philistine church was when I was living with one of my first foster families. No matter how much I fought them, they forced me to attend.

"I'm not going! I won't set foot in that evil place!"

"You will go, and you will pray to Jesus to forgive you. You have been nothing but a disobedient pain in the ass since you came to us."

My foster mother, Claudine, sneers at me. She has another thing coming if she thinks I'm praying to anyone besides Zaaron.

"Your Jesus was a blasphemous, false Prophet, and I will never utter a word of praise to his name."

She brings the back of her hand across my face. "You watch your mouth! You just lost your right to a bed tonight."

I don't care if she makes me sleep with the dog. I refuse to do what she demands.

"When your flesh melts from your body and your screams of agony never end, I'll be with my family and my God in the Paradise Star. So, make me sleep wherever you want, filthy Philistine!"

Her face puffs up with rage as she pushes me up the sidewalk. Her son, Marvin, is around my age and has gotten quite the thrill from watching me and his mother butt heads. He is a gluttonous, pimply boy who is self-centered and full of demons. He snickers behind me, and she shoves me in front of their 'church'. A white, stone woman in a veil and gown looks down on us at the entrance. Her hands are frozen open in a welcoming gesture, and I wonder if the living version of her will be inside.

"Please be quiet, and do what we do." My foster father whispers in my ear. He hasn't been unkind to me, but he doesn't stop his wife from treating me like dirt either. It seems that she treats him just as badly sometimes. Marvin though, he gets away with everything. The way she coddles him is nauseating. He speaks to her with horrible disrespect, and she still acts like he's perfection personified.

"Who is that?" I point to the statue before my foster father ushers me inside.

"That's Mary. If you don't want to pray for your own sins,

maybe you could ask her to do it for you."

That's not going to happen. I don't care about a nonexistent, pretend God that has no bearing on my soul.

The flesh of her is not inside, but a woman in a black veil and dress trimmed in white stands at the pulpit reciting their lies. Her dress and demeanor are to be revered, and I find myself unable to take my eyes from her until a man in black with the white square on his neck takes her place. He drones on and on about their evil prayers and demonic Bible. I try to block out the words, yet I can't deny the familiarity of the ritual and the bond apparent in those with like beliefs. He speaks of love and forgiveness, though if my foster parents are any indication, it's not being heard.

I make it through their 'mass', wasting no time getting out of there. I don't even wait for my foster family. As soon as we're dismissed, I rush back outside, turning to look at their 'Mary'.

"Don't you dare murmur a single word of your poisonous prayers for me. It is I who will pray for you."

I gladly sleep on the floor. I won't let them break me.

I will not let them tarnish my soul.

"Are you all right?"

I jump at the voice regardless of its softness. My eyes are connected with hazel ones not much older than mine. It's her. The 'nun'.

"Oh, yes. I was just thinking."

She lightly places a hand on my back, leading me to the building next to the church. 'Parish Hall' is written in black letters on the brick building. She sits on the steps and smiles at me. "It looks to be something confusing from your expression."

These people really like their statues. There's a small, gray one on the top stone step of a bald man holding a cross. I don't want to sit next to the statue, but I feel odd towering over her, so I sit on the step beneath her.

"It shouldn't be."

"Is it something you want to talk about? I'm a fantastic listener."

I laugh. Seeking advice on my soul from a Philistine. That's quite comical.

"Do you like being a nun?"

She smiles. "Yes, however, I'm not a nun yet. I'm a Sister." I'm shocked at the title. It's the same as adult Anointed women. "I have dedicated my life to The Church, and there is no doubt in my mind that it's what God desires for me. So yes, it makes me very happy."

I know my mouth is hanging open. I can't believe that I can relate to this woman.

"Do you really believe you're right? That your God exists, and you're not damning yourself?"

Now it's her turn to gape. Slowly, she pulls her lips back into a smile. "Well, yes, I do know that my faith is placed in the one and only God. I absolutely believe that he exists, but…"

"Do you believe that I am going to Hell because I don't believe in your false God?"

Her nerves are apparent in her chuckle. I don't know why I'm grilling her. I'm angry over my feelings about going home, not this woman's belief system.

"Goodness… Okay, well, first of all, my name is Sister Emma. I feel like you should know my name before I confess this to you. Second, I don't believe that people do or don't go to Hell based on their religion. I think trying our best to follow our conscience and being kind to others is all that God really asks of us, though many will not agree with me. While my principles and the answers to my prayers tell me I am to devote my life to God, I know not everyone will have that calling. There are evil men in The Church, and there are good and pure men who have never stepped foot inside a chapel."

I don't know what to say because I know she's wrong, but she says it with such conviction, I don't want to tell her so. Nothing she can do at this point can save her soul. What's the harm in letting her live blissfully in her ignorance?

She gestures behind us. "It's pretty warm out here. Would you like to come inside and cool down?"

The truth is, a part of me does want to stay and talk with her. I just don't have much time left, and I want to spend it with Kaila. Plus, there is no way I am going inside that building.

"I'm sorry, I can't. Thank you for your kindness." I stand, brushing off my dress before I hold out my hand. "It was nice to meet you, Sister Emma."

She looks a bit disappointed, yet curious. "The pleasure was mine…"

"Laurel Ann."

"Laurel Ann. That's a beautiful name. Please, come back anytime."

I'm delighted to have met her and enjoyed speaking with her. I don't want to soil that by telling her I won't be returning. Flashing her a smile, I turn around to finish my walk home.

Kaila is sitting on the couch filing her nails, watching the television set, when I walk in. My heart aches as she smiles up at me. This is the very last time I will ever come home to this. How am I supposed to tell her that I'm leaving? That after tonight, we will never be able to laugh, talk, or eat burnt popcorn together ever again.

"Hey, Laur, what's up?" She holds her hand out, admiring her work. She must be satisfied because she sets down the file in exchange for a cigarette.

"Hey."

My voice sounds mopey and whiny, even to myself. She scrunches her eyebrows, patting the couch. "What's wrong? Is everything okay?"

I flop down, hearing the springs groan. "Zeke, Zeb's Apostle, came in today. I'm leaving tonight."

Ripping the cigarette from her lips, she looks at me with heartache. "Tonight?!"

Breathing in through my nose so I don't cry, I quickly nod. "Yes. At sundown."

"I can't believe this." She shakes her head, taking a drag. "What in the hell am I supposed to do without you?"

She's attempting to be strong, yet her voice cracks, and tears leak down her face. I wrap my arms around her as I break down, giving us both permission to cry.

"I will never forget you. You will forever be my best friend."

"I can't believe you'll be gone."

There isn't a single thing I can think of to make this easier. "I would say, 'I'll write you', but...you know."

"Can I at least wait with you until you go?" She sobs against my shoulder, and I wish I could tell her yes.

"I'm sorry. I must meet them alone."

She looks toward the window, then to her phone. "We only have a few hours."

"You do understand why I'm doing this, right?"

She wipes her nose as she snuffs out her cigarette. "Understand it? Yes. Like it? Fuck the fuck no."

"Must you curse so often?"

"See? Who the fuck is going to say shit like, 'Must you curse so often?' to me now?" I laugh in spite of her filthy mouth and hug her again. "Do you need to pack?"

"No. There's nothing I can take with me. Your photograph is all I'm bringing, and it will be hidden beneath my dress."

She pulls back from our embrace. "This is what you truly want, right?"

"This is what I *need*. For my soul."

She rests her head back on my shoulder, squeezing me tight. She doesn't let go until the sun begins its descent. It breaks my heart to peel her fingers from their grasp.

"I'm sorry, Kaila, I have to go. I love you."

I try to be strong for her as I shut the door behind me. I keep my composure until I'm across the street, where sobs overtake my body. I have to mourn her now because being seen crying could be mistaken for uncertainty in my choice.

The sense of melancholy I get walking through Hobart is unexpected. For the first time, I wonder if I have grown to love it here more than I want to realize or admit. This was the first place I saw outside of the Anointed Land. I spent three years living here with my foster parents, Curtis and Jordan, and went to Hobart schools for the majority of my Philistine education. I've lived here with Kaila for years. Never seeing the familiar buildings and people again makes me mournful for reasons I'm not sure I understand.

I brush my fingers over the stone of the Hobart City sign and allow another tear to fall. Softly wiping it from my face, I press my finger against the sign, imagining it seeping into the rocks, keeping a part of me forever.

The outline of the horse and buggy shows in the distance. Although the horizon behind him is darkening his face, I know it's Zeb. Air pushes out of my lungs with relief while my heart picks up pace. I was worried he would send Ezekiel, or worse, Jacob to bring me back.

How long am I going to feel this way around him? Before, our relationship was fluid like a river—natural and peaceful. Now I don't know what to expect from him. So much time has passed, and he's much colder than he used to be. What is he expecting to happen once I'm back inside the gates? Has he prepared the followers?

The horse brays as he tugs on the reins and jumps down from the buggy. He isn't wearing his hat, and in the street lights, I see his smile.

"Hello, Laurel Ann. Are you eager for your return?"

He's happier than I've seen him since we were kids. I look up to his face, and he startles me when he pulls me to him, wrapping me in an embrace.

"I have dreamed of this," I whisper.

He releases me, and his smirk brings back the Zeb I remember. "As have I." He takes my hand, guiding me into the buggy. Being back inside of one makes the bubbles in my stomach pop. He climbs in behind me. "Are you hungry? I know it's late, but I thought we could have an evening picnic. I don't know when the next chance for privacy will arise." As if trying to convince me, he adds, "I brought you some of my mother's strawberry-rhubarb pie."

This is a completely different Zebadiah than the one who was at my home and the butcher shop. This is how I pictured him in my dreams. I feel the smile stretch my cheeks as the lit lantern hanging in the back casts a shadow across his hopeful face.

While I think I'm too sad, excited, and nervous to eat, the fact that he planned a picnic fills me with glee. It's almost like a date a Philistine would go on. 'Dating' doesn't exist in the Anointed Land. Once placed, the binding will occur within the week. Unless a woman is a first wife, her personal time with her husband is reserved for their bedroom.

If I would have stayed, would we have found ways to sneak off and have secret picnics? Now that I'm coming back will we?

"That sounds perfect. Thank you."

We are still about a mile from the compound when he tugs on the reins, causing the horse to whinny as the buggy slows to a stop.

"Here we are."

He turns to unhook the lantern, handing me a couple of blankets and picking up a large wicker basket. He holds up the lantern, and it gleams off his eyes, making them sparkle when he grins. Gesturing his head for me to follow, he leads me into the field. It's almost completely dark, and with no one else around we stay close to the buggy. He puts the lantern on the ground, smoothing out one of the blankets next to it.

He points to the other one, made of thick lamb's wool. "In case you get cold."

"Thank you, Zeb."

His grin melts from his face, revealing a glare in its place. "I have told you, you are to address me as Prophet. Once you're back within the gates, I won't tolerate it. I can't give you special treatment. You need to understand that."

I resist my desire to cower in embarrassment by holding my head up high. I truly do understand. That still doesn't change the fact that it hurts. I don't even know what else I expected from him. Of course, he has to uphold spiritual law, regardless of our friendship. I'm struggling to see him as my Prophet, but he's right. It is borderline blasphemous to call him by a name other than his title, unless it is done so by his children or his wives.

I sigh. I don't want to make this harder on him than I'm sure it already is. "I do. And I apologize. I must confess to feeling a little conflicted with your position. It won't happen again."

His demeanor relaxes once more with his nonverbal invitation to sit on the blanket. "Please."

I adjust my dress as he takes cups and plates from the basket. He removes sandwiches and potato slices from a cloth, placing them on the plates. Using a glass jar of milk, he fills our tin cups.

I look up at him and bite my lip. "Can I ask you something?"

His smirk is a little sad. "When it is just you and I, you can always ask me anything."

I have a book of questions, though there is one that sits in the front of my mind. "Does my family know I'm coming back? Does the rest of the compound?"

He brushes the hair out of his face. "I wasn't completely secure in the fact that you would come tonight. I didn't want to disrupt order if you were going to change your mind. So, no, beyond you and me, Ezekiel and Jacob are the only two who know."

I can't decide if that makes me feel better or worse. "What's it like? To talk to *Him*?"

He laughs. "Enough questions for now. Eat your sandwich."

Surprisingly, I'm able to eat. The deliciousness of the ingredients nearly has me moaning. Crickets chirp in the distance as we silently chew. Tomato, chicken, and lettuce on rye. He inhales deeply in the silence before he takes my hand.

"Will you make me an oath?" My curiosity is piqued, but I'm not about to agree to something before I know what it is. I tilt my head in question, and gust of wind blows my hair around my face. The heat beneath my skin ignites when he tucks the stray strands behind my ear. "I want you to make me the promise that no matter what happens after we enter the gates, you will know I still care for you deeply. Though you may not understand my methods, I need you to know that whatever I do is in your best interest."

I don't particularly like how this is sounding. I also knew it probably wasn't going to be easy. He's preparing for the worst, as should I. Not a single soul has ever been brought back into the protection of the Anointed Land once cast out, so opposition from the fellow children is an understandable reaction.

The fact is, I made the choice to come back. I must shift my thinking to that which is expected of me. Whether I am comfortable with it or not, Zebadiah is my Prophet, and trusting the Prophet is synonymous with trusting Zaaron. If he says he will only do what is best for me, I can accept that.

"You have my word. I trust you...Prophet."

His fingers are long and have a slight roughness to them as he rubs his thumb over my knuckles. The light of the lantern makes him appear to be glowing. His lip lifts into a half-hearted smile before he turns and digs into the basket. Presenting a full pie and two forks, he sets them on the blanket.

"We can't bring anything back, so have at it."

I laugh, stabbing my fork right into the middle to scoop out a large bite. The filling and rhubarb pieces are sweet and tangy while deliciously topped with a flakey, buttery crust.

"Mmmm." My mouth voices its pleasure as I revel in a taste that will always make me think of my childhood. "This is delicious."

He chews his bite and smirks before he reaches out, brushing his thumb across my lip. Stray filling sits on his finger, and he looks at me, bringing it into his mouth. My heart stutters, and another feeling in my stomach, but...lower. I untuck my legs, and cross my ankles, keeping my mouth full of pie so I don't have to occupy it with awkward words.

"I don't remember looking forward to anything with the excitement that I have for today. Thank you for coming home."

"Thank Zaaron. He's the one who made it possible."

Leaning closer, he reaches out to touch my face like he did before, but this time, he presses his lips against mine. My chest explodes, sending aftershocks through my body as his kiss turns from tender and cautious to deep and desperate. His hand moves from my face to the nape of my neck.

My mind is dizzy. I have barely been kissed, much less kissed like this! The ache below my stomach is now throbbing between my legs. This is wrong. We are not bound, and we are not trying to have a child. This is an act reserved for husband and wife. I know I should push him away, but Zaaron forgive me, all I want is for him to keep going.

He groans against my lips and puts me on my back before lying on top of me. His erection is hard against my thigh, and I have the urge to scoot lower. What are we doing?! My mind hands over control to my body, and I gasp, rocking against his belly.

Suddenly, he stills. He pulls his mouth away, nearly causing me to cry. I have never experienced anything like this.

In the lamplight, his jaw ticks as he shakes his head. "We can't do this. I'm sorry." I nod because I have no oxygen to speak or brain function to produce a response. He pushes himself away from me. "It's time for us to go."

We silently gather the non-food items before I follow him back to the buggy. Once we're both seated, he clicks his tongue and pulls the right rein.

He seems uncomfortable, and while in my mind I know we just sinned, in my heart, I don't feel the guilt that usually comes with it.

"You know I won't tell anyone about our picnic, right?" He nods at me, but I don't think it relaxes him at all.

The fence that wraps around the compound is difficult to make out in the dark, yet it's still one of the most comforting sights I've seen in years. The buggy pulls up to the gates as the night guard yanks it open. Since I can't see his face, I'm sure he can't see mine. I would still guess he's curious.

Being back inside the compound gives me a tugging feeling throughout my body, and I can't quite place if it's unpleasant or not.

We stop in front of the tabernacle, and he grabs the lantern, pointing toward the doors. He steps out of the buggy, and I follow him up the wooden steps. There are no candles lit inside the building, leaving the moonbeams and Zeb's lantern our only sources for light.

He leads me to the same holding room I stayed in before my soul cleansing twelve years ago. Ezekiel is sitting in the chair next to the bed reading *The True Testament* by lamp light.

Zebadiah places his hand on the small of my back, nudging me in ahead of him as Ezekiel stands and nods. "Blessed evening, Prophet."

"Blessed evening, Apostle."

Zeb turns to me. "You are to give every article of your clothing to Apostle Ezekiel. I want you stripped of everything tying you to the outside."

I feel a twist in my gut at the memory of the photograph in my undergarments. "Yes, I understand."

He backs toward the door, looking to Ezekiel. "Bring her clothing to the waste site on your way home."

"Yes, Prophet."

Ezekiel exits the room to wait in the hall, leaving Zebadiah to stare at me. After a moment, he gives me such a genuine smile, returning it is automatic.

"Welcome home, Laurel Ann."

21

THE PRODIGAL DAUGHTER

Laurel Ann

THIS ISN'T MY QUILT…THIS ISN'T MY BED.

Opening my eyes, I push myself up, allowing yesterday's memories to flood over me.

I'm here.

I'm home.

Last night Ezekiel gave me a long, button-down petticoat and bloomers to wear in exchange for my Philistine clothes. Reaching beneath my bloomers, I pull out the photo of me and Kaila. I hope she's all right this morning. I have to believe that she will move on, and eventually, I will become a distant memory in her mind. Although that very thought causes the tears to prickle my eyes, her sadness would make me even more sorrowful. She has Brently, and if they don't work out, she will find someone else who makes her happy. Getting a guy has never been a difficult task for her. I run my fingers over her glossy, frozen smile.

"I miss you already."

Returning the paper piece of time to my bloomers, I push the blankets off my feet. I run my fingers over my personal cleansing scars and smile at that time in my life being over. There is a knock at the door before Ezekiel lets himself inside. I attempt to cover my arms as he places a plate of toast and a glass of water on the table.

"Hurry and eat. We must go."

Go? Go where? The placing dorms?

I eat my bread along with my questions. I wash it down when I notice the rope in his hands. My stomach falls even though I expected it. Zeb had said I wouldn't be able to walk back in here without paying some type of penance.

He beckons me with his hand, and all hope for receiving a dress is demolished. I stand in front of him, and he wraps my wrists together with the rope, tugging me out the door. I expect the meeting hall to be full of people, but it's bare. I don't even get past the pulpit before I hear them from outside—angry voices urging one another on. The doors are pushed open, forcing me to close my eyes to protect them from the bright rays of sun.

"This is not right!"

"She doesn't belong here!"

"I don't want her evil near my children!"

Ezekiel leads me down the steps and through the angry crowd. As I strain to open my eyes, I see Zebadiah in the center of them. He is dressed in his hat and black jacket, looking every bit the Prophet that he is. They spit on me and hiss in my ear.

"Children, I know this is a territory we have yet to discover. I am asking you to trust in me, and furthermore, to trust in Zaaron. This is His will and desire. If anyone wants to question His plan, you will see yourself at the receiving end of a cleansing ritual." Their cacophony dies down into undistinguishable murmurs. "Zaaron has told me of His plan for Laurel Ann. Her soul has survived the dark, new world. When surrounded in sin and the absence of grace, she did everything possible to keep the tainting at bay. She obeyed spiritual law, and for twelve years never committed an unforgivable sin. Could any of you guarantee the same had it been you?" My heart swells at his defense. It's working; they have all but fallen silent. He takes the rope from Ezekiel and holds up my wrists, showing the crowd my personal cleansing scars. "Though the fire may not have been Anointed, she paid with pain and scars to prove her devotion. I do understand your hesitance. She broke one of the most sacred of spiritual laws by denying the path Zaaron had laid out for her. He works in mysterious ways, does He not? He has a new path for her now. He wants you all to accept her back into the folds of the Anointed Land as if she had never left." He pushes me to the ground, uncaring of the abuse to my knees. My eyes travel to the shallow hole in the ground forcing my heart to pound in my chest. I've never seen a demon exorcised, although I know what it entails. "I understand your fear of the evil she has brought with her and the possibility that she is possessed, looking for a way to taint our holy land." Why would Zaaron choose this as my punishment? He must know I'm not being controlled by the Devil.

Looking up reveals Ezekiel and Jacob carrying the tomb of abolishment. It's no bigger than a coffin, and I feel nauseous as they remove the wooden lid.

"I would never risk the safety of you or our land. If any darkness or evil resides in her, Zaaron will see that it is removed. Once this night has passed, any ill will you have toward her must be dissipated or a cleansing will be in order."

I inhale a breath so sharp I can feel it slice down my throat. I'm not secure in the fact that I can survive this. Shortly after my excommunication, I developed an aversion to small spaces. I don't like things covering my face or being enclosed. I had something called a 'panic attack' in one of my foster homes when one of the other kids trapped me in a blanket. They wouldn't let me out, and I thought I would die inside that place.

This is where my faith must come in to play. Surely Zaaron's wrath is vicious, though I do not believe He would dole out a penance I could not pay.

My heart tries to escape my body as I watch Zeb's boots disappear to walk behind me.

I understand Zebadiah has to do this, but even knowing he has to remain a holy example, I still can't push away the sting in my chest.

"She will remain in the tomb for no longer than two hours. That is more than enough time for any evil she has obtained to be removed by the envoy."

I have to believe the time limit is a safeguard to try to protect me. Whether it's Zaaron or Zebadiah, I'm not sure, though I suppose in some ways, they are one in the same. While the sun is too bright for me to look at their faces, I hear their whispers. Zebadiah instructs them to make a circle around us and the tomb of abolishment. Are my mother and father among them? Mia? She is a grown woman by now. This will be her eighteenth year. Will I even recognize her?

Suddenly, my face is covered by what feels like a gunny sack and secured around my neck. There are holes that I can see through, obscuring my vision. The small opening for my mouth seems to do nothing to assist in my breathing. The sack puffs out from my lips every time I exhale, making me feel suffocated. My chest rises and falls rapidly as Ezekiel approaches me, lifts the ropes, and brings me to my feet. Everything inside me wants to fight him, to pull away and run, but this is what's required for my soul. I will not deny it this time. He leads me to the tomb, and I lift my foot to step inside. I make the mistake of looking at Zeb in time to watch him take the envoy's cage from Jacob.

I feel like I'm going to be sick when I hear a familiar voice. "You have disgraced this land, me, and our God. I can still smell them on you. May Zaaron cleanse your disgusting soul."

It's rougher and hoarser than I remember, but there's no mistaking it's my Pa. I know seeing the disappointment on his face will crack me, yet I look anyway.

After all these years, he still hates me. My tears trickle down my face at the confirmation that I will not be welcomed back into my family without an abundant effort, and perhaps not at all. His words begin a downpour of hate, the children of Zaaron crying out their disgust.

"Disgraceful!"

"Filthy!"

"Corrupt!"

"Wicked!"

"Shameful!"

"Evil!"

"Sinner!"

They spew their judgments, confirming my mistakes and failures. I knew there would be some discord, I just never imagined this level of abhorrence. Their words may be different, yet what they say is the same:

You are not welcome here.

Ezekiel helps me lie down in the tomb, and I shut my eyes as if it will make the dread more bearable. It only makes the anticipation worse, so I look up at the clear Oklahoma sky.

I can't see him from my position, but Zeb's voice fills the tomb. "The envoy is a miraculous creature. In Zaaron's wisdom, He has given us the ability to remove the demons that may inhabit our fallen Sister. If she is possessed, His envoy will bite her, consuming any evil within her, allowing us to destroy it once and for all."

As he stands over the tomb, my breath becomes too thick to leave my body. He lowers the tarantula inside with me, and I freeze, trying to stay perfectly still.

He looks down at me and whispers, "Keep your eyes shut."

I do as he instructs and hear him close the lid. My heart moves to my throat when the light weight of little legs crawls up my shin. The tears fall, and a whimper escapes to the sound of the followers praying for me. The tomb is lifted, and suddenly, I'm floating. My stomach flips as I feel myself being lowered into the hole. I try to slow my breathing as my heart hammers in my chest loud enough that I can hear it.

Wait…that's not my heart.

Thud. Thud. Thud. Thud.

The dirt drops against the lid as they bury me in the earth. Little hairs brush against my ankle, startling me and causing me to cry out. I involuntarily kick my foot at the sensation of light legs moving frantically around my feet, trying with all my might to stay motionless.

Thud. Thud. Thud.

The more dirt that falls, the faster my pulse quickens. I'm sweating like I'm being baked in an oven, and my throat is twisting closed. The harder I try to breathe, the more difficult it becomes. I gasp and attempt to lurch out from the closed space, enraging the creature more. A piercing pain stabs my leg, and I scream. Faster up my body it moves. I shriek, squeezing my eyes tighter closed. The hair of his legs touches my chest, and I can't stop myself from choking. Cries bursts through my diaphragm making the intake of oxygen impossible. Snot and tears roll down my cheek beneath the mask, and I claw at my throat, not only to breathe, but to knock off the spider.

In my mind, I know the thrashing and screaming only

makes him angrier. I also know I need out of this tomb, or I'll die. I bang against the lid, praying for the darkness to take me, yet my mind forces me to hang on as if Zaaron Himself desires for me to feel every moment of this incursion. Bile rolls in my stomach, making my throat burn. I need out of here! My screams become razor blades in my vocal chords, and I imagine the tissue bleeding from tearing. Agony is from head to toe, and my lungs have stopped expanding. I don't know if I can make it through this. The name 'tomb' is only to signify the death of the demon, though in this moment, I know I will spend eternity in this hole in the ground.

Then suddenly, time temporarily stops. Well, it doesn't stop, I just stop experiencing it before being flung into chaos. My body has taken over, and I am just the observer watching through cracked glass as my limbs flail me around the tomb.

Back and forth.

In and out.

Here and gone.

"Try to open your eyes, Laurel Ann. If you can hear me, open your eyes."

As much as I want to obey the command, the weight on my eyelids refuses to dissipate. It's a masculine voice that I think I recognize, but cannot place. I try to communicate with my voice, though my throat feels swollen closed.

"Will she be all right?" Zeb asks.

I wish I could speak because I want to yell at him that I'm not all right. I'm just too tired. I know a penance was necessary, but he's the Prophet. Couldn't he have negotiated for a milder punishment? Zaaron has to know I was never possessed. Was I?

Every part of my body aches, including my heart. How could Zeb put me through that? Seeing as there is no way what happened at our picnic last night was sanctioned, I know he is not unwilling to make his own choices.

"The tomb has taken a lot out of her. I suggest you give her a night of rest before continuing with her castigation."

I want to hear what they say, it's just taking all my remaining energy to fight sleep.

"If that is what you suggest, then that is what shall be done. Thank you, Doc Kilmer. May I request she spends the night in the clinic?"

"Of course, Prophet. I will have Madeline stay with her tonight. I know she always liked Laurel Ann."

Doc Kilmer Adams. That's why I recognize his voice. He and his family supply the medicinal and educational needs to the compound. He is speaking of my old school teacher, Sister Madeline. Knowing I'll be seeing her again makes me smile in my mind, though I'm sure it doesn't translate to my body.

"Call on me if her condition worsens. I will send the Apostle tomorrow to collect her."

"Yes, Prophet. Have a blessed evening."

"You as well."

Commotion and voices dance in and out of earshot, but I do not know what they say. There are moments when I feel scared and angry at Zeb, and others when I am desolate. I shut myself out of my body, putting the pain in a box where it can't touch me. Sleep holds out its hand to me once again, and I take it, gladly.

"Laurel Ann? Do you remember me?" It's Sister Madeline. If I had control over my skin, I would lift my lips into a smile. I think I am able to move my head and nod because she softly caresses my cheek. "Shhh. Rest now."

Having a familiar person who doesn't hate me is a soft bed for my soul. My muscles relax, and I obey her request to rest. Her voice is a warmth that finally makes this place feel like home. She sings me back to sleep with one of my favorite nursery rhymes.

One day, child, there'll be no more pain,
No more suffering and no more shame.
One day, child, when your body's in the ground,
And your lips can no longer whisper a sound.
One day, child, you'll be free of sin,
In the Paradise Star when we're together again...

My face is being wiped with a wonderful, wet, cold cloth. Chills run beneath my skin, breaking the smothering heat pressing on my chest. My lungs expand, and I greedily suck in the air.

"Slow breaths. Relax."

I am able to open my eyes with significant effort. Once the blur of the room comes into focus, I see a slightly older Sister Madeline.

"Thank you." The words have spikes on them, scraping their way out and taking my voice with them.

She cups my neck, slowly lifting my head. My body aches in protest, and a whimper forces its way out as she continues to adjust and shush me. A tin cup is pressed to my lips, and cool water trickles down my throat, cooling the raw burn. I grasp at the cup, drinking ravenously.

She helps me move my legs off the edge of the bed before stopping me from getting off. "Take it easy, not too fast." Moving around and quenching my thirst does wonders for my mobility, and my words flow out much easier.

"Thank you for being kind to me."

She sighs. "As a woman, I've always understood your fear

and why you did what you did. I know you're a good girl, and you have always done your best to follow spiritual law." She lowers her voice to a whisper. "And between you and me, I believe your excommunication was based on the wounded pride of our former Prophet, not your sins." She smiles and returns her voice to normal. "I am so glad you're home."

She leads me to the tub filled with deliciously warm water fresh off the stove. I dip a leg in and see a swollen red mark on my shin. I rub my finger over the tender skin of the bite.

Sister Madeline dips a cloth into the water and helps me sit. "There's one more here." She runs the cloth over my neck, and I wince from the sensitivity of it. "How's that?" The heat from the bath is a respite I can't express, my moan being my only response. "You gave the Prophet quite a fright." She lifts my arm to clean beneath it. "Me as well."

My ears tingle at the mention of him, and I turn my head to face her. "What happened exactly?"

Using a jar, she fills it with water before dumping it over my head and soaping up the dirt covered strands. "You stopped screaming and banging on the tomb. You made no sound at all. The Prophet paced around the hole, constantly, until the time came to dig you out. When he took off the lid, you were unconscious. He lifted you out immediately to rush you here."

She dips me back to rinse my hair, helping me up once she finishes. I try to recall what she's saying. "I don't remember anything, really. I was just so scared. I couldn't breathe, and I didn't feel right. I thought I was going to be sick. Everything after that is hard to remember, like when you wake up from a dream." She nods and gives me the cloth. I was bitten. My heart feels like a stone in my chest, and I break into tears. When could it have happened? How did I not know? "Do *you* think I was possessed?" I cry.

She shushes me and wipes the hair from my face. "I don't

know. I don't have any other explanation for you being bit, but you're pure now, child. It's over." I want to curl up in a ball and sink to the bottom of the tub. Instead, she pulls me to my feet and wraps me in a towel. "You'll feel better soon. I promise."

Once I'm finally given a dress, we sit at the table and eat the stew she made. The food fills my stomach, and I feel a heaviness weighing on my eyes once again. My mind drifts off, and Sister Madeline helps me from the table.

"Why don't we lie you back down?" Just as I am about to get the billowy reprieve of the bed, a knock on the door gives me a jolt. Her eyes are sad when she says, "Stay here."

Leaning against the bed, I hear her voice laced with synthetic cheer. "Blessed Evening, Apostle Ezekiel. Please, come in."

"Is she prepared?" Ezekiel's low voice trails into the room.

"She is still exhausted, though I assume the Prophet is aware of that."

There is a moment of silence before Ezekiel says, "I trust he knows what's best."

"Of course. I will fetch her."

She appears in the room, holding out her hand with a smile. "You are where you are meant to be, Laurel Ann. Welcome home. This will all be over soon."

She leads me out of the safety of the clinic to the waiting area where Ezekiel gives me something close to a smile. Opening the door, he nods his head for me to follow him. The common ground is mostly empty as he leads me to the cleansing station.

He hasn't spoken to me once, and when he does, it startles me. "The Prophet is very pleased to have you back."

"That comforts me to hear, Apostle Ezekiel."

Ahead of us, Jacob is waiting, holding a rope in each hand

and scowling at me. I nod my head in respect when we reach him. He grips a tight hand around my arm and jerks me to his side. I never knew Jacob that well, but from the rough way he's tying the rope around my wrist, I would assume he hasn't forgiven me for leaving his father.

Ezekiel is kinder in his task of tying my other wrist, allowing more room. Jacob pulls me between the pillars, and each of the men slide their end through the grooves at the top, fastening me to the cleansing station. My body droops, and while the discomfort is immediate, it's not painful. The holy fire burns in the side of my vision, and just as I wonder if it has been blessed yet, Zeb's voice sounds behind me, sinking from my ears to my stomach.

"Leave me with her."

Their murmurs recede until the only sound is the wind in my ears. Why isn't he speaking? I hate feeling so much smaller than him. So much less. I am tainted, yet he is the Prophet. My body hangs in front of him, a drawn-up sinner in the presence of holiness. I know he has the blood of Zaaron within him, and I know he is the holiest person on this earth right now, but I cannot seem to make my mind focus on that truth. The exhaustion is going to take me at any moment, and though the anger I have for him is unwarranted, it boils within me just the same.

Why won't he speak to me?!

"Do you feel power in my humiliation, *Prophet*?"

I say the words through my teeth. I'm furious that he isn't making this easier for me, while at the same time, I know he has to follow what is desired by Zaaron.

Still, he doesn't let a sound pass his lips. His steps are only heard because of the eerie silence of the common ground. They are slow, and I can sense his eyes trailing down my neck and back. The touch of his hands on my sleeves causes my body to jump in surprise, and there's no stopping the pounding of my heart.

His lips are at my ear as he brushes them against the lobe. "Hush." Gentle fingers press against the fabric of my dress, trailing slowly to my ribs. "You gave me your word." Despite the sweat dripping from my forehead, chills snake through my veins when he drapes my hair over my shoulder and places a kiss to the back of my neck. "I know this is demeaning. That's the point. You said you trusted me, so do it now. This is what's necessary for you to be fully accepted back here. I am doing this because I care for you, Laurel Ann."

He steps away from me, and I don't understand why the absence of him makes moisture pool in my eyes. I am left to be a beacon and a warning of what happens to those who disobey.

At least an hour has passed, and the aching in my arms is past bearable when Zeb returns with Ezekiel and Jacob. I desire sleep more than my next breath, yet I know there's no hope of that until I'm released from my bondage. I can't turn my head to fully see, but in the edge of my sight, Zeb is facing the fire with his hands stretched to the sky.

His voice is deep beside me. "Zaaron, our God. Our Messiah. We are the blood of your blood and the flesh of your flesh. We thank you for your protection from evil and the forgiveness of our sins. You have provided us with the tools to remain Anointed and pure, and we ask for this fire to burn with your cleansing grace." There is a pause, then he adds, "Thank you for your infinite mercy."

I see his hands lower to reach for something. Once the Anointing iron comes into view, he lays it in the fire, and I realize what's happening.

When a baby is born as a child of Zaaron, they must be

marked accordingly. I don't remember my first Anointing, and it won't be any worse than my personal cleansings, yet the symbolism is paramount. There will be no question if I belong here once I re-receive the mark. Nobody can doubt it.

The voices get louder with the arrival of the crowd. They stand around the cleansing station looking down on me. I can't hear what they say, though their murmurs are all around me. I lift my eyes regardless of my mind screaming at me not to. They connect with green ones that are twelve years older than the last time I saw them. Mia is a full-grown woman now, and the sight of her sucks the little amount of oxygen I have from my body.

She has the same sad look she had the day I was excommunicated, though now it's tainted with pity. I don't remove my gaze from hers until Zebadiah's voice seems to boom from behind me.

"Welcome, children. I know this has been difficult on all of us. This is a situation to which we are not accustomed. The outside world has temptations that we do not want to be confronted with. I know many of you have your reservations about your own souls and the souls of your family. I ask you to think of this: When a child is born, their souls are as tarnished as that of a Philistine, yet we do not fear an infant. Think of Laurel Ann as that infant. She has no ill will toward us and desires only to be welcomed into the Paradise Star upon her flesh resting beneath the dirt."

Water rushes over my head, the coolness of the liquid dripping down my body. While it feels incredible, it runs into my mouth, filling my lungs and making me cough with the need to breathe.

"Wash away the filth of this world. Purify this child so she is worthy of your grace and protection." Zeb's practiced prayers get louder as he circles me, continuing to splash me with water. "You were rebuked by this sinner, yet you desire her in the Paradise Star. We are in awe of your infinite compassion and will honor your will of an Anointing." He lifts my right foot and pours the remaining water across the pad. His slick fingers massage my foot with what I know is blessed oil. He softly touches my toes before grasping my ankle. "We ask you to bless this child as we mark her as one of yours, from now until forevermore."

The water and oil cause the burn to sizzle much louder than when I did it on my own. The heat of the iron consumes my foot, and I try to pull it away, but Zeb's grip is tight on my ankle. The sharp sound that climbs up my belly and shrieks from my throat, slices through the air around me before I know it's happening. Zebadiah presses the Anointing iron harder into the arch, and my screams become blurred with sobs. The scent of burning skin and oil is offensive, turning my stomach. The bottoms of my feet have always been sensitive, and when the heated metal melts into my foot, thoughts of doubt enter my mind.

We do this to infants?

Once he is satisfied, he removes the iron, and I wish more than anything I could grab hold of my foot and wrap it in a wet cloth.

As he stands in front of me, I don't have the energy to lift my eyes higher than his chest. The muscles cause lines in his shirt, and I focus on them in hopes it will distract me from the pain. His hand holds my face so tight, his fingers squeeze my cheeks.

"You have been forgiven because we worship a merciful God." Releasing me, he steps to the side to present me to the crowd. "Her excommunication is to never be spoken of. I ask each of you to place your hands on her and pray that she will never again be tempted by evil thoughts."

The hope that he will release my aching arms is obliterated when he puts his palm on my head and looks to the sky.

"I ask for you to guide this child. You clearly have plans for her soul, and I trust in your decision. Thank you for her safe return, my God. Your kindness is infinite."

One by one, the very people who were rebuking me just yesterday, lay their hands on me and offer words of love and acceptance. How could their feelings have changed so rapidly? I don't hear their individual sentiments, just lies on repeat.

The pain in my arms has gone numb. I don't feel them until Ezekiel and Jacob untie me from my bondage, and I fall to my knees. I moan out my relief at the ache of freedom overtaking me. I fight with the decision to massage my shoulder or hold my burning foot, but I'm pulled back to standing before I'm able to make my choice.

Zeb's hand is on my back as he gestures to the crowd. "Do you have anything you would like to say, Laurel Ann?"

I swallow, and the lack of saliva does nothing to soothe my scratchy throat. "I am truly remorseful for the suffering I have caused you all. I will forever be grateful for your willingness to forgive me and welcome me home."

My response is expected. I just wish I could have said it with more conviction. How much could they have really suffered? None of them were cast out alone and confused. Zebadiah removes the ropes from my wrists, while all I want is to fall into the dirt and sleep.

Apparently, that won't come for some time.

"Let us rejoice the freshly Anointed soul of our prodigal daughter and commence the gathering!"

The voices all begin at once, the crowd blooming like a flower as they disperse. Chatter and excitement for the monthly celebration surrounds me. I am beyond grateful when Zeb drapes my arm around his neck, and Zeke does the same.

They are gentle in their assistance in helping me to a chair amongst the festivities.

"You may sit here until you feel confident you can move around."

I nod to him and sink into the chair. The aroma from the food floats beneath my nostrils, and I'm surprised at my stomach's desire for it. I smile at a group of small children chasing each other in a game of tag and the women talking and giggling in a circle.

Finally. I am home.

I look up to see Mia walking toward me with a young girl skipping next to her. The girl is too old to be her daughter, and that comforts me. The girl runs up to Zeb, hugging him as he smiles down at her.

Mia greets them. "Zebadiah, your holiness never ceases to amaze me."

My skin beads with sweat at the use of his first name, the moisture from my tongue all but evaporated.

His smile never leaves his face, though it's the trained smile, not the genuine one in my dreams. "I am but an instrument to see out Zaaron's desires."

He turns to me, his smile faltering. His brows knit together, and his jaw strains before he gestures to Mia. "You are clearly acquainted with my first wife." I'm either going to hyperventilate or puke when he runs his hand over the hair of the young girl hugging him...the child hugging him. "And this is Marybeth Adams. My second wife."

22

SPEAKING WITH ZAARON

Laurel Ann

I FIGHT TEARS AND THERE IS A TWISTING IN MY CHEST MAKING IT hard to breathe. The one thing I am feeling above all else is anger.

How could he have forgotten to mention the fact that he's bound? To my sister?! And then there is the onset nausea when I think of him being with that child. In the Philistine world, women don't consider marriage until they are well into adulthood, and even then, they choose their own mate. The sight of them together is jarring and unsettling.

I'm sure he didn't tell me because he was worried I wouldn't come back. I don't know how I would have reacted. What happened at the picnic definitely never would have transpired. The tears climb their way back into my eyes at the thought. Until now, there was a part of me that had hoped Zeb and I would someday be together under spiritual law, but now, thinking of his hands on them...I want no part of it.

I may not be able to express my feelings in this moment, however, the next time we have our privacy, Prophet or not, he's going to hear what I have to say.

The girl, Marybeth, startles me when she wraps me in a hug. "Mia has told me so much about you! It's such a pleasure to meet you!"

I place my hands on her back, stabbing my eyes into Zeb's. I want to scream at the top of my lungs, yet I must sit here and be joyous in my newly pure soul. His face softens as if begging me to understand.

I don't understand, and I won't. As far as I'm concerned, he lied to me.

The girl releases me, and Mia holds out her arms for an embrace. "I have missed you, sister. Welcome home."

This is not how I imagined our reunion. I thought I would be overcome with happiness, not envy and resentment. Why am I having these feelings toward her? She can't help who she's bound to. Still, my hug is half-hearted, and I'm barely able to force myself to speak.

"And I have missed you, sister."

Zeb's voice interrupts our embrace. "I'm sure you two are eager to get reacquainted. I would just like to bandage Laurel Ann's foot first, so she will have an easier time participating this evening. I will have her back out shortly."

Why doesn't he have Sister Madeline do it? Mia looks at me with uncertainty before the little girl pulls her toward the celebration.

He once again drapes my arm over his shoulders, wrapping his hand around my waist to help me to standing. I put as much pressure on my foot as I can and limp next to him on the way to the medical hall. Neither of us speaks, even when we are out of earshot of the attendees of the gathering. If it wasn't for his holding me being a necessity, I would have already pushed away from him. I don't want to be anywhere near him right now. The steps of the medical hall are a trick, but he's gentle in his assistance.

Once the doors are closed behind us, I can no longer stand him touching me. I shove his hands away and stumble backward, thankful that I am able to remain standing.

"How could you not tell me?! Mia?!" I'm yelling, and I know I need to quiet down a little or else I will be heard outside. "You are bound, and you kissed me. You touched me and deliberately kept this from me."

"I didn't see it as relevant."

I know I am gaping at his idiocy. "You didn't see it as relevant?! Are you freaking serious?!"

I'm confused as to why I'm so angry. I've always known he would be bound to other women eventually. Regardless of all that, imagining him in their beds makes my insides swelter and boil.

He closes in on me, and my foot doesn't allow me to move away quickly enough. His hands squeeze my waist to lift me up and shove me into a chair.

"Do NOT speak to me that way." He grips the armrest and leans in, inches from my face. "Just as you had no choice in fucking my father, I had no choice in being bound to your sister. Or Marybeth for that matter."

His curse startles me although the low blow he just landed demands more of my attention. He's bringing his father into this? Okay, if that's how he wants it.

"You are no different from your father! Marybeth is younger than I was! You have been going to bed with a child, Zebadiah."

"I do not go to bed with her!" he barks, his knuckles whitening from his grip on the chair. Once the words leave his lips, his regret is apparent. He cups my face, and his tone becomes gentle. "I would never force her to lay with me, just as I never forced Mia."

His words shock me into forgetting my anger. "You

haven't been with her? How are you to have children?"

His nostrils flare when he presses his lips together. "Do not ever speak of what I just told you." He drops his voice to a whisper as if trying to keep a secret from Zaaron Himself. "I did what was ordered of me by my father. They've never meant the same to me that you do. You understand that, don't you?"

I can't stop the tears from prickling my eyes. "I don't know."

Staring at me for a long moment, he stands to retrieve a bowl and a pitcher of water from the washbasin. He silently places my feet inside, pouring cool water down my shin to my toes. The water surrounds my Anointing mark, and I can't decide if it's blissful or torturous. He dunks a bar of soap into the water to wash my foot. His fingers caress over my personal cleansing scars with a gentle touch as he tenderly cleans the wound.

This very act goes against spiritual law. What kind of Prophet sins this much? The words are written in *The True Testament*, clear as a summer day: *It is not our Prophet who washes the feet of the children, but the children who wash the feet of the Prophet. –3:4A.*

Upon finishing, he softly places my foot on the clean towel to dry it off.

I blurt, "Have you gone to bed with her? Mia?" I don't know why I ask, of course he has. She's beautiful.

He doesn't look at me when he answers, "Yes. She gave herself to me last year."

As he wraps my foot in a cloth, fury salted with self-pity bubbles inside me. She's the reason I was excommunicated. It's because of her I had to have that horrible night with Hiram, and now she's rewarded by being able to openly be with the only boy I have ever wanted. She also got to choose when to have her body entered. She may have been bound as a child, but for years Zeb waited for her to be ready. I can't even think about the sins among that because I am angry it isn't me in her place. How many times did I pray and beg Zaaron to be bound to Zeb?

Endless times.

"Do you love her?" I despise the spite in my voice. I thought I had forgiven her for all this.

"I love her as I love Marybeth and all of the children of Zaaron."

He stands and walks behind me to a cupboard. My smile is fighting to show at his words. They are nothing more to him than what is required of him by his station. Yes, he cares for them, just not in the way I care for him.

Stockings are draped over my shoulder. I reach for them, freezing when he moves my hair away from my skin and his lips softly brush against the back of my neck. "I couldn't protect you before. I was helpless. The day I found out you were gone was the worst day of my life." I try to focus on his words, yet his mouth against my skin is the only thing I'm able to register. His whispered voice is rough and almost strained. "That's changed now. I never thought you would come back to me, yet here you sit."

He's barely touching me. His hand trails softly down my neck to my chest, and my breathing completely stops when his fingertips begin to disappear beneath the hem of my neckline.

The click of the door and the voice of Sister Madeline are simultaneous. "Prophet? Is ev—"

My heart is in my throat, and I get as far from him as the chair will allow. He jumps from me as if ejected from a cannon, and Sister Madeline is stunned frozen.

While I'm still panting and my heart is threatening to explode, Zeb brushes himself off, and acts like we were just seen praying, not committing a lustful sin.

"Yes, Sister Madeline?" he says in almost a flirtatious tone.

We all know what she walked in on, yet she straightens herself and seems to wipe it from her memory.

"I wanted to make sure you were finding everything properly." He may be the Prophet, but Sister Madeline has known us since we were children. There was a time when she took a switch to him for disrupting class. She narrows her eyes while her words remain respectful. "I can finish here. Your presence is being requested by Sister Mia, your *wife*."

Her tone is drenched with disapproval. Not that Zeb is in the position to point it out.

"That is appreciated. Thank you, Sister Madeline."

He slips out the door, leaving me alone with her. I pull on my stocking to avoid looking at her face, hearing her sigh on the way to the closet, where the spare clothes are kept.

"Size seven?"

"Yes, ma'am."

She hands the boots to me, and I take them, meeting her eyes. I'm expecting to see judgment and disappointment in them, when instead there is sorrow.

"You cannot do this, Laurel Ann. I know you two were always close, but if this were to get out...for goodness sake, child, you just got back! Imagine what this would do to Sister Mia."

My face is most certainly burning from shame and embarrassment because I know she's right. Since I can't find any words that will improve the situation, I choose honest ones.

"I don't know what to do here anymore."

I hadn't realized that truth until speaking it. Hurrying to lace up the boots, I'm thankful for something besides her to focus on.

She chuckles, and I look up into her sensitive, blue eyes.

"Of course you don't. Twelve years is a long time to be out from under the grace of Zaaron. You must give it time...and make holy choices. Your penance has been paid, so let's go rejoice in it, shall we?"

Holding out her hand, she helps me up. I'm surprised at how the support of the boots alleviates enough of the pain, making it much easier to walk.

She helps me out of the medical hall to find the celebration in full swing. There are very few things that we are allowed to have for the purpose of pleasure and musical instruments are one of them. The eyes of the followers are sticking to my back while Sister Madeline assists me into a chair. She stands next to me, fidgeting with her sleeves and shifting on her feet.

I take her hand. "Sister Madeline, please don't feel like you need to spend your evening looking after me. Go, celebrate with your family."

Her touch is gentle against my back as she leans down next to my ear, her hair tickling my cheek. "I am trustworthy," she whispers quickly. "If you need someone, I will be that for you." She stands and steps toward the party. "Welcome home, Sister Laurel Ann."

I nod to her and scan the crowd for my family. Zebadiah, Mia, and his child bride are impossible to miss since everyone seems to gather around them. My heart aches from simply looking at them, so I make sure to avoid doing it. The air smells divine, and the breeze blows cool against my face as I revel in my momentary solitude.

"Well, I'll be. Laurel Ann Henderson, look at you."

Turning in my seat, I stare at the owner of the masculine voice. He sits next to me and crosses his arms. When he grins, I finally recognize him.

"Benji?!"

"In the flesh."

He's huge now. Actually, all of the men on the compound seem much larger than most men on the outside on account of Philistine men generally being much more sedentary. His auburn hair has darkened, and his once boyish face is now sculpted. That smile though. That's not changed a bit.

I wrap my arms around him. This is the excitement and happiness I've been waiting for, and I'm grateful to him for giving it to me. "You have no idea how good it is to see you."

He smirks, sticking his thumbs under his suspenders. "I have a pretty good idea. I look in the mirror a lot." I roll my eyes as he chuckles.

"I'm glad to see you have your vanity in check."

He jerks his head to the dancing crowd. "Not in the rejoicing mood?"

I've always been able to tell Benji anything, or at least I used to. "This just isn't going exactly as I imagined."

Standing, he holds out his hand for me to take it. "Come on, let's get out of here for a little bit. Besides, a walk might loosen you up."

Being alone with a man that is not my husband isn't necessarily a sin if we're not in either of our homes, but it's not a favorable action and may not be the wisest choice on my first night back. I glance at the crowd of people that are now mostly strangers. A break from it all does sound nice.

I smile at him and accept his hand. "Lead the way."

He wraps his arm around my waist for support as he takes me behind the death dealer's shop and away from the common ground. We keep walking across the open prairie, and it isn't until the sounds from the gathering become quiet murmurs that he speaks.

"I can't believe you're back. I never thought I'd see your freckled face again."

I scoff. I hate my freckles. "Shut up, I don't have that many anymore."

"Aww, I always thought they were cute."

He nudges my shoulder, and I realize my steps are much more secure. "I think I can walk by myself now." I try to see ahead of us, but it's dark. We're going to come to the edge of the compound if we go much farther. "Where are we going anyway?"

His arm hooks around mine. Cupping his hand next to his mouth, he says in a loud whisper, "My secret space of solitude."

I laugh at him. He's still the same old Benji. "And that would be?"

"It's a storm shelter," he responds flatly. "Way to suck the fun out of it."

I laugh and squeeze his arm. "And what makes it so secret?"

My eyes have begun to adjust to the night, allowing me to see him grin at me. "Because only a couple of people know about it." I'm about to ask how the heck he was able to do that when I hear a *thud.* "Here it is." He bends over and moves around some two by fours as if they are twigs. "Built this about a year or so after you were...uh...left."

He pulls out what I assume is a key, from his pocket, before a lock *clicks.* Hinges creak as he pulls open the large wooden door, dirt clouds kicking up in the moonlight when he allows it to fall to the ground.

"You did this without anyone finding out? How?"

"I went a lot of nights without sleep. Wait here." He drops his feet into a large, open space where all I see is blackness. There's a *thud* when he steps on something. Slowly, he disappears deeper into the ground.

Tink. Thunk.

"Damn it."

I'm not as bothered by cursing anymore, since Kaila made me somewhat immune, but hearing it here, from him, oddly makes my lip quirk into a smile.

"Are you okay?" I call down.

"Yeah, I just can't find the—oh, here it is." A quiet *tick, tick, tick,* sounds before suddenly, a light flickers and blooms from the hole, allowing me to make out Benji's form holding a lantern. "Do you think you can get down here with your foot?"

"I don't know, but this is too good to pass up." I lift my skirt and kneel down to place my good foot on the first step.

He sets the lantern on a small table next to him, holding out his arms. "Just fall forward. I'll catch you."

"Are you out of your mind?"

"I promise I won't drop you. Come on, we can't be gone too long."

He waves his hand to hurry me up. I release a breath and let go of my grip on the ground, allowing myself to fall forward. His body is hard and warm when I land against him. That wasn't so bad.

"Umph! Philistine food makes you weigh a ton."

My mouth drops open, and I hit his arm as he sets me down with a grin. The space is probably eight feet deep, and the room is long and narrow. We can stand comfortably next to each other while I can easily reach the table with the lantern behind me. The walls are lined with thick, wood panels.

"How did you do this all by yourself?" Even if he was able to get this much wood without anyone becoming suspect, carrying all of it alone would be nearly impossible.

"I never said I did it by myself."

He walks to the back of the underground room, passing a mattress on the floor, to go to the shelves lining the back wall.

Boxes are stacked up all across them.

"So, who is it? Who helped you?"

He runs his fingers along the boxes' edges, and I make my way to join him. Shaking his head, he smirks. "Sorry, freckles, I can't tell you that."

"Okay then, what's in all the boxes?"

Releasing a deep breath, he takes down a dark green one. "What was it like?" He turns to look at me, all of his light-heartedness from earlier completely dissipated. "Out there, with them?"

I step back and sit on his mattress. "There's a lot of sin. And in the beginning, it was really scary…" I scoot myself to lean against the wall, and he joins me. "But there are some amazing things too." He's gripping the box tight, just as he is every one of my words. "You know the loud metal birds that fly above us sometimes?" He nods with urgency. "I've been in-side one."

"No way!"

His eyes are wide, and his excitement flows into me, mak-ing me smile. "They're called planes. Oh! And they have these things called microwaves. It can cook almost anything in less than five minutes."

"Wow," he whispers.

He's definitely not a kid anymore, but right now, his fasci-nation makes him look just like the boy I knew all those years ago.

I point to the box in his hands. "What's in there?"

My curiosity is at its peak when he lifts off the lid, tilting the container to show me. His green eyes sparkle, and his smile is full of pride. I look down and gasp. Is he crazy? It's full of Philistine things. A phone, batteries, a driver's license, a key fob…the list goes on and on. My eyes lift up to match his hesitant ones. "Where did you get all this stuff?"

He shrugs, and his shoulders slump. "I met a Philistine. He brings me things." He raises his brow. "You aren't going to tell anyone are you?"

"Oh, Benji, of course not."

"Not even our *Prophet*?" He snickers the word as if it's a joke.

I roll my eyes and sigh. "Definitely not him. I still can't believe it. Zeb is the Prophet."

"Yeah, he's changed a lot since you've been gone. Just be careful. Don't trust him until you know you can, okay?"

I'm shocked at his words. He and Zeb were always close friends, and I wonder what has happened between them in these past years.

"What happened to him after I left?"

"He kind of lost it after he found out you were gone. He had more cleansings over the next few years than I've ever seen anyone have. He did everything in his power to humiliate and defy his father. Then suddenly, he became the perfect child of Zaaron."

I always wanted Zeb to miss me, but I never wanted him to suffer. His father had a cruelness in him that I have no doubt he showed Zebadiah. It breaks my heart to know he was hurting because of me. Even if Benji isn't outright saying it, I've seen with my own eyes some of the traits he's inherited from his father. "I've changed, too, you know."

He grins. "I can see that." Pushing into the mattress, he scoots himself off. "We should probably start heading back." He holds out a hand to help me up. "I just wanted to show you this place in case you ever want to come here and take a break from it all. I'll be sure to leave it unlocked until we figure something else out." He's always been a kind soul, and it makes me feel warm that he's trusting me with this. His head tilts a little as he crosses his arms. "Do you think you'll miss it?

Living with Philistines?"

I don't have to think about my answer, and I love that I can be honest with him. "I know I will."

He nods toward the ceiling of the room. "Come on, let's go."

Basically carrying me up the ladder, he helps me out of the cellar and keeps a hold of my arm while we walk. I've been dying to ask, and we are almost back to the gathering. "Have you been bound yet?"

He chuckles and shakes his head. "No, Zaaron has been gracious to me in that regard."

"What do you mean? Don't you want children and wives?"

His sigh is heavy as the noise from the gathering becomes louder. "I'm not quite ready to have a family."

I can understand that. I wasn't ready twelve years ago, and the thought is still somewhat scary to me. "Does Zebadiah know you feel this way?"

He shrugs. "I haven't exactly hidden it from him."

I squeeze his arm to let him know we don't need to speak any more of it.

"I just wish I knew Zaaron's purpose for me. Why He brought me back."

We walk around the front of the medical hall, and Benji's feet slow as he leans down to whisper in my ear. "This is your first gathering since being an adult, isn't it?"

He pulls back with an impish grin spreading across his cheeks. I smirk, raising an eyebrow. What's that ornery look for?

"Yeah, so?"

"Because now, you can ask Him yourself."

23

GATHERING OF THE ANOINTED

Laurel Ann

IMMEDIATELY STOP WALKING TO STAND IN FRONT OF HIM. "What do you mean?"

"Just wait and see." Benji smiles, but once he looks behind me, his grin falls into a hard line. "Fun's over, freckles."

Frowning at him for the nickname, I turn around to see Zebadiah marching over to us. And he doesn't look happy.

When he's close enough to speak, he glares at us both. "Where have you two been?"

What in the world is he so upset about?

"We just went on a walk, Prophet. Wanted to catch up after all this time." I have to bite my tongue at the patronizing tone in which Benji responds.

Zebadiah's false smile is doing nothing to cover up his anger. "You are free to go back to the gathering, Benji."

I scoff before I can stop myself. His dismissal of Benji makes me want to punch him. As soon as I think it, shame clouds my soul. I should never think violent thoughts toward anyone, especially not my Prophet. The dark, new world really has tarnished me.

Benji places his hand on my shoulder. "I'm glad you're back, Laur. We'll talk more later."

Walking behind Zebadiah, Benji turns and flips him off behind his back as he smirks at me. I quickly look away from them both, forcing out a cough so I don't laugh.

"It doesn't look good for you to disappear alone with a man who isn't your husband." Zebadiah's harsh tone sobers me and turns my attention back on him.

"I've been alone with you quite a few times," I snap.

He closes the gap between us, lowering his voice. "I am not just a man, I am your Prophet. Do not do that again. It's not a request."

My eyes are begging to roll around in my head, even if there is truth to his words. "It was only Benji. It doesn't get much more platonic than that. How can you tell me to not spend time with a friend I haven't seen in over a decade?"

His fists clench as his body stiffens. "Then do not make a damn spectacle of it."

There is stress in his voice, and he just cursed so I'm obviously upsetting him. I don't want that. He's not just Zebadiah anymore. He's the holiest man on the earth. I need to accept that and stop these thoughts of doubt and rebellion.

"I apologize, Prophet. I was not thinking."

"No. You weren't. Now hurry, there are those who wish to speak with you." His shoulders relax. "Do you need help walking?"

"No, I'm feeling much better. Thank you."

Turning around, he walks back toward the celebration. I follow behind him, and just as we reach the edge of the common ground, a woman rushes toward us. When the lights from the gathering glow on her face, my heart attempts to jump through my chest, tears instantly filling my eyes.

"Laurel Ann!" she calls to me, picking up her dress to run.

I fight through the pain to move my feet as fast as they will go. Our bodies crash together, and our arms wrap around each other in a tight embrace.

"Mama." It comes out blubbery through my tears, and she squeezes me tighter. "I missed you terribly."

She pulls back to hold my face. She looks much older than I remember. There are lines and creases that weren't there before, and the gray in her hair glints in the lights. "You're finally home." She kisses my head. "And more beautiful than I ever dreamed."

While we break from our embrace, she keeps her arm around me as we make our way toward the crowd. Zebadiah has already rejoined his brides, and I don't see Benji. My eyes look ahead of me, finding Sister Mary and Sister Esther. There are many children around them, and none I recognize. Most of them didn't exist when I left. I know my father is standing next to Sister Esther, but I refuse to meet his gaze.

"Laur!" My steps falter when I connect the voice to Dawn Garrett. She hands a baby to Sister Esther before running to me. Her arms tighten around me in such a fierce hug that I can't prevent my laugh. Knowing she's bound to my father unsettles me, so I shake my head, pushing the negative thoughts away. "I can't believe it!"

She drags me over to the people who were once my family. I am genuinely grateful for her acceptance, and I feel guilty for zoning out when she rattles off the names of all of her children.

"They're gorgeous, Sister Dawn."

My father steps next to me, and I still won't look at him, but I can see him in the corner of my eye.

"I am pleased Zaaron has had grace for your soul, Sister Laurel Ann."

I honestly don't know how he would prefer I address him.

Brother Benjamin or Father? Definitely not Pa. Right now, I just want to keep the peace.

Turning to look him in the eye, I say, "Yes, sir."

That seems to appease him as he nods and bends down to pick up one of his children who have yet to disappoint him.

Dawn hugs my arm. "Come on, let's go get some food."

I smile at my mother and family before I follow her, yet I am relieved to be away from them. Why? Haven't I wanted this more than anything?

Dawn has barely left my side. She drags me around to see our old classmates, making it easy for me to succeed in avoiding Zeb and his wives. Most of the girls I used to sing and pick flowers with are now either with child or have already given birth, and all of them are bound. It makes me feel like an outcast—an old woman who will never know the joys of motherhood. Some of the boys I went to school with are also bound, but there are many who are not. I speak with my brothers and sisters, and I am surprised that both Faith and Hope are bound to Benji's older brother, Jethro Johnson. They seem happy and have clearly remained close.

"Brothers and Sisters!" Zebadiah's voice slices through the noise. Silence falls immediately, other than the occasional noise of a child. "The night has been full of fellowship and celebration. Zaaron is pleased. Let us take a brief intermission to put our children to bed before continuing with the evening's events. May the holy fire of Zaaron cleanse you."

"MAY THE HOLY FIRE OF ZAARON CLEANSE YOU, PROPHET."

The crowd disperses, and Dawn gives me a quick hug.

"Welcome home."

After everything that's happened the last few days, exhaustion returns with a vengeance. I use the time to myself to walk around the outside of the common ground behind the tabernacle and the schoolhouse.

Benji's words jump around in my brain. What did he mean about talking to Zaaron? To my knowledge that was an ability reserved for the Prophet alone. As if thinking of him is a summons, Zebadiah steps out in front of me, appearing from the side of the schoolhouse.

My heart leaps, and I tell myself it's because he surprised me. Opening my mouth to speak forces out my anger, his lack of truth about his bindings boiling in my gut.

I scoff. "Shouldn't you be with your brides?"

"They're helping my sisters with their children."

"What do you want, Zeb?"

"I want you to address me as Prophet! If someone hears you use my name then—"

"Then what? You clearly choose which laws you want to follow and enforce."

He walks forward, compelling me to take a few steps back. "What are you talking about?"

I stick out a finger to count. "Being bound means you reproduce. The fact that you waited for my sister and wait on your little girl bride is a sin. They know their duty, and you not making them fulfill it is a plight against Zaaron." My second finger rises, and he glares at it. "We are not bound, yet you put your hands and lips on my skin, you washed my feet. And finally, I believe Benji hasn't been bound because you know he's not ready, but Zaaron clearly doesn't care about that because *I* wasn't ready. If He wants you to bind him and you don't that's also a sin, but I just got here, so give me time, I'm sure I'll find more."

I march past him toward the tree line when he grabs my arm. "I'm doing the best I can, and I have to do what I think is right." His voice is low and deep as his words come out jagged. "The line I walk every day is nearly translucent. The spiritual crown lays heavy upon my head, and you can't comprehend what this is like for me…constantly being torn between righteousness and my own feelings."

I jerk my arm from his hand. "It's not about your feelings or what *you* think is right. It's about Zaaron's will."

Once I speak the words, I know I should take my own advice. The last few days and this evening's events have me wanting nothing more than to be alone. I brush past him, and he allows me to walk into the trees, even though I hear the twigs beneath his feet telling me he's behind me. I pick up my pace, putting plenty of forest between us.

I don't have a destination in mind. I look to the sky between the branches when an unnatural noise stops me in my tracks. What is that? I follow the sound, peering around a tree, and I am stunned to the point my feet freeze in their tracks.

My brother Samuel is leaning against the trunk of a tree with his eyes closed, his face flushed with pleasure. The man on his knees in front of him bobs his head quickly over Sam's penis. Sam grips his hair, shoving himself deeper into the mouth he's violating. I know I shouldn't watch this, I don't even think I want to, but I can't stop.

When the man slides his lips off of Sam, I finally see his face, and my jaw drops.

"I will make you moan someday, Sammy." Benji's voice is seductive as he stands and presses their cocks together, stroking them. He kisses up Sam's neck, leaning back to sign something.

Samuel grins. *Yes, fuck me.*

Benji grabs him by the shoulder, turning him around and

wetting the head of his erection with saliva. His fingers massage Samuel's anus before he presses his tip against the hole. His body jerks as he pushes himself into my brother. Sam of course doesn't make a sound. His hands grope at the tree while he rocks against Benji.

"Fuck, Sammy, I've been thinking about this little hole all day." He thrusts harder, a moan slipping out. Sam's face twists, and his white semen spurts against the bark. Benji groans, "Oh, yeah, your ass is so damn tight...fuck, you're gonna make me come again." Benji pulls Sam's head back by his hair, and I can't believe I'm still standing here watching this. "Does my cock feel good?" Sam nods, and Benji pumps harder. "I'm going to be walking around hard for the rest of the night, thinking about my come in your ass." He lets out a guttural sound with his quickened pace.

I hear the *crunch* of a stick, and I can sense Zeb standing behind me. "Laurel Ann—"

The moment he speaks, Benji's eyes meet mine, widening. Samuel scrambles away from the tree, nearly tripping, while Benji fumbles with his trousers and bites out, "Shit!"

Zebadiah's chest heaves as he storms past me, his shoulders tense. "What am I seeing here?!"

Samuel begins signing frantically, but it's been a long time since I've signed. I'm having trouble following most of it.

Benji pulls up his suspenders and pleads on the verge of tears, "Please, Prophet, this cannot become known among the other followers. I beg of you to punish us in private."

Zeb rips his hat from his head and stabs it toward him. "You promised, Benji." My eyes stretch out as I stare at Zeb. Did he know about this? Benji's mouth moves without speaking, and Zeb scoffs. "We will discuss this matter tomorrow." His words slide out between clenched teeth. "Tonight is for rejoicing. I will not have it sullied with...this. Now go. I would prefer not speaking to either of you for the remainder of the evening."

They both look at me when they pass, their faces covered in shame. I want more than anything to reach out and hug both of them. It's true, before I left the Anointed Land, this kind of thing would have disgusted me. Sexual intercourse with no chance of reproduction is a sin, and I was always taught that a man with another man is blasphemous.

Maybe I should still feel that way, but I don't. The longest I ever lived in a foster home was with two men. They were kind and loving to not only each other, but also to me. They forever altered my opinion on the matter.

"Laurel Ann, would you like to say grace?" The man named Curtis is smiling at me. I've only been here for a couple of hours, and he is already trying to get me to pray to their false God.

"I will not. Not today or ever. Your God sickens me."

The other man that lives here, Jordan, snorts before covering his mouth. "You got some spunk in you, don't you?"

Does he think this is funny? I clench my fists and glare at him. Holding his hand, Curtis looks at me. "My husband's just teasing, and I didn't mean to offend you. We apologize."

"How is he your husband? You're both men. You can't create children together. What you are doing is an abomination."

Jordan's stupid grin is wiped away. "Okay. She's not quite so cute anymore," he says flatly.

Curtis' kindness has slipped from his face, but instead of being replaced with anger, it's covered in sorrow. "In this house, everyone's beliefs and opinions are accepted as long as they stay deferential. You may pray to whatever God you like. Maybe you can teach us about Him. Regardless, you will treat us with respect in our home. You don't have to agree with it or like it, but you will be civil. Do you understand?"

I nod my head at him. "Yes, sir."

He is being kind even though I upset him, and this is by far the nicest home they've put me in. I'm the only kid here, and their house is clean. I can try to be cordial if they are going to be so to me.

"Okay, then. Why don't you say the prayers for the evening?"

I am grateful for the freedom as I close my eyes and press my palms together. "Zaaron, my God. I ask you to help me stay away from all the sin and evil in this world. I'm scared I won't be able to keep my soul untarnished. I want to stay Anointed and to go to the Paradise Star. It's all I want. Please let me prove to you that I can be pure, and I can follow your laws. I humbly ask you to watch over my brothers and sisters, Mama, and Zeb, and Benji. Please don't let them be too sad. May your holy fire cleanse me. Truth and purity, amen."

I open my eyes and both Curtis and Jordan are staring at me, wide-eyed, before glancing at each other.

"Th-that was, uh, very nice, Laurel Ann. Thank you." Curtis' smile is once again present as he stands to serve us our food. Chicken, green beans, and little potatoes cover the cream colored, square plate. My mouth waters at the sight of real food. The things Philistines eat are disgusting. Everything comes in a box or a bag, and it doesn't even look edible. This though, this is going to be delicious.

"I have to say," Jordan speaks, and I lift my gaze from my plate. "I've been trying to get Curtis to go organic for years. When your case worker told us about your aversion to processed foods, it was just the push I needed. I suppose I should thank you." He pops a little potato in his mouth and smiles.

He's a filthy sinner and a perverse Philistine, yet it's proving very difficult for me to not return his grin. I cut off a piece of my chicken, and it's so tasty I don't care that I'm moaning against the fork.

Curtis mixes his food all up into one dish as he asks, "Can we make a deal?"

Is this a trick? I narrow my eyes at him. "What kind of deal?"

"We will try some things your way, if you try some things our way."

I place my fork down and cross my arms as my curiosity takes a front row seat. "What do you mean?"

He brushes his hand over his short, black hair and down the back of his neck. "Well, if you agree to let us take you to an amusement park this weekend, next weekend we won't use any electricity. No TVs, no cell phones, no computers."

"What?!" Jordan asks with a mouth full of chicken.

Curtis ignores him, and raises an eyebrow at me. "So?" He holds his hand out across the table. "What do you say?"

I think that's fair, and something called an amusement park may not be too bad. I take his hand and shake it.

"Deal."

They were more in love than I've ever seen two people, and I struggle with believing that could be wrong.

Zebadiah spins to face me as if he's about to say something, but I get to it first. "You knew? What did Benji promise you?"

Shaking his head, he ruffles his hair and groans. "I didn't know what he was doing with Samuel, I just knew he had been with a man in the past, but he assured me he was finished with it." He sighs, and while he's made me less than pleased with him the last few days, the pain this is causing him is clear. I want nothing more than to comfort him. "How do I keep evil out of this place? Benji is my friend. Samuel is your and Mia's brother, so of course I don't want to cleanse them, but how am I supposed to ignore this?"

"Are you sure it is evil?" The question comes out before I think.

The frown on his face is marred with confusion. "What kind of question is that?" He brushes past me to walk back to the common ground. "Of course sodomy is a sin."

I sigh, following him past the tree line, in silence. A small group has begun to form in front of the tabernacle, and Zeb makes his way to join them. He laughs and smiles as he greets some of the followers. How quickly he can slip on his mask for them.

I leave him to go look for Benji and Samuel. I'm nearly positive Samuel is the other person who helped with the cellar. Making sure that no one is watching me, I walk across the open land to the compound's edge.

My body aches, and all I want is to sleep. In fact, I kind of hope they aren't there so I can lie on the mattress Benji has. I keep my eyes peeled for the two by fours, but because of the darkness the night brings, I'm really just looking for anything out of the ordinary.

I think I see it, and once I am close enough to make out the closed door on the cellar, light streams between the planks.

Softly tapping on the wood, I whisper through the cracks, "Benji? Sam? It's Laurel Ann. Can we talk?"

There's shuffling around before I hear footsteps on the ladder. "Get back, I'm coming up." I do as he says when Benji lifts the door to poke out his head. "Come on."

Samuel helps me down, and immediately after my feet hit the ground, I look at him. His gaze is on the floor when I reach out to touch his arm.

"Hey." Lifting his eyes to mine, he's barely holding back tears. I concentrate on my signing so I convey the right words. *You don't need to be ashamed with me. I love you.* While I'm aware he can hear me, speaking in his language shows my sincerity. Benji silently climbs off the last step and scoots by us to go to the shelves.

Samuel's eyes narrow in disbelief. *Really?*

I haven't had a chance to properly look at him yet. His hair is still dark, but much longer, with wisps over his honey eyes. He's considerably taller and broader than he once was, and his skin has taken on a tan. I cup his face and kiss him. My brother has grown to be very handsome.

Are you in love with him?

His smile stretches across his face. *Yes, yes, yes.*

I laugh. How can this keep them from the Paradise Star? This is love, not lust, and isn't love the purest thing on earth? I look over at Benji who has made his way to the mattress. He's digging through a box.

"What are you doing?" I ask, holding Sam's hand and walking to the back of the cellar. Benji pulls out a tiny bottle with *Jim Beam* written across the front, holding it up with a grin. "Benji Johnson, is that alcohol?"

"I've been saving it for an occasion such as this. If I'm going to Hell, I'm going out hard."

I sit on one side of him as Samuel sits on the other, leaning against the wooden wall, crossing his arms.

"Have you asked Zaaron if He's angry with you? You said you can speak to Him at gatherings."

Benji scoffs as he twists the cap. "I've asked Him every month for the past nine years, and He has never once given me a clear answer. I have no idea why I'm like this. I think women are beautiful, they just don't make me feel that juddering pulsation from the inside out like he does." He looks to Samuel and winks, causing him to blush. "We tried, Laur. We tried so hard to stay away from each other. We just can't."

I look to Samuel. "Have *you* asked Him?"

Squinting one eye like he's trying to remember, he signs, *He doesn't speak like you're thinking. It's more of a feeling.*

Benji takes a drink off the bottle and hands it to Sam as I frown at them. "How did you get a bottle of liquor?" Samuel takes a drink and tries to hand it to me. "No way."

He shrugs and gives it back to Benji. *He bought it.*

Benji throws his arms up. "Sammy!"

"What? You've left the compound?"

He sighs and finishes off the bottle. "No, my Philistine friend bought it for me."

"Benji..."

He pushes off the bed to return the box to its place. "It doesn't matter anymore. I doubt our Prophet will allow us to remain here now."

I cross my arms and shake my head. "He's not going to excommunicate you. He won't even cleanse you. He's going to keep his mouth shut."

Samuel pushes off the wall with wide eyes. *What? How do you know that? Did he say that?*

"He said he doesn't want to, but I will make sure of it. Our Prophet is not as holy as he seems, and I will remind him of it if he attempts to punish you."

Benji's laugh is loud in the small room. "You're extorting the Prophet for us? I'm touched. Any chance you'll tell us what he did?"

My cheeks heat up at the memory of his kiss, his touch, and his words. "He has been unfaithful to his wives."

They both drop their jaws. At the same time Benji says, "No way," Samuel signs, *With you?*

I nod, and my face burns. Sam is still standing there shocked as Benji laughs and puts his thumbs beneath his suspenders.

"I have a feeling that things are about to get interesting around here."

Though I'm not a particularly tall girl, I'm not short either, and standing between Sam and Benji makes me feel like a child. We are all assembled in front of the tabernacle as Zebadiah stands above us on the steps.

He's removed his hat, and the wind blows the hair from his face. He holds up the skull of the ox head that represents Zaaron's original form. He speaks of the first encounter, between Zaaron and the human vessel. How the arrival of electricity pushed humans into a spiral of sin, forcing Him to earth where He appeared as an ox to the man who would become His vessel. The vessel heard His voice in his mind and accepted Zaaron's request to inhabit his flesh. Zeb speaks of the body of the vessel erupting into Anointed flames as he was overtaken by the holy energy of Zaaron.

I try to concentrate on his words, but my eyes are watching the way Zeb's jaw looks when he speaks and the way his arms fill out his shirt as he holds up the skull.

"Tonight, we will go to the most sacred place on this earth: the burial grounds of Zaaron's human vessel." Suddenly, I'm focused on what he's saying. I've always known that when Zaaron returned to the Paradise Star, His human vessel perished and was placed beneath the earth. What I didn't know was that the body of the vessel lied within the compound. "Although you pray to Him, and He receives your prayers, you can't hear Him as I can. But tonight, my children of Zaaron, tonight you will hear Him!"

The followers clap and howl, yet I stand frozen. This won't be my only chance to speak to Him since this is apparently an occurrence at every gathering, but it is my first. This is honestly something I've never really thought about because I never knew it was possible.

Leaning over to Samuel, I whisper, "I'm scared. What am I supposed to say to Zaaron?"

He glances at Zeb to make sure he isn't paying us any attention before he signs, *He's not how you imagine Him. Don't be afraid.*

I smile and lace my fingers through his. "I love you, Sam." He kisses my temple as Zebadiah's voice breaks through the crowd.

"Think on your struggles, your heartaches, what causes your mind to drift from the glory of Zaaron. Reflect on these things, and bring them with you tonight as you taste a piece of Him. Now come, and let us rejoice on our way."

Once again, the followers let out their praises, laughter and chatter bubbling around me. Zeb gives the ox head to Ezekiel, and I watch him kiss my sister before taking his place beside her. While I've felt jealousy in the past, it was of another girl's hair, face, or clever wit. I've never felt it because of a person, and this is a whole new level of it. It's more than wanting my sister's husband. I don't feel like he's hers at all. He was mine before everything went so wrong.

I shake my head, feeling the urge to cleanse myself for my evil thoughts. That won't work anymore though because now I must confess my transgressions to Zeb.

I'd much rather do a personal cleansing.

Mia, Zeb, and his child-bride make their way to the front of the followers. As he passes, he softly brushes my arm, and I hate the tingles that run across my skin.

"Laurel Ann!" a man's voice calls. I turn around, and once again my stomach flips at seeing those I love for the first time in years.

"Robert!" I run to my brother who picks me up, twirling me around. I squeeze his neck tight, and he chokes with his laugh. He places me back on the ground. "You look completely different. You're not such an ugly duckling anymore."

I snort, looping my arm through his as we walk with the

followers. "Thanks?"

He's gotten tall and looks so much like Father it's a little unsettling, but then he smiles, and our mother shines through like a sunbeam. "I've attempted to talk to you all night. You keep slipping off."

"I've been trying to get my bearings back. It's all a bit overwhelming."

We walk toward the direction of the Fitch ranch as those around me break out in a hymn.

"We are the Anointed,
Those cleansed by fire.
We are the Anointed,
Those of holy desire.
We are the Anointed,
We will cast the final stone.
We are the Anointed,
We will follow Zaaron home".

I haven't sung this song in many years, and still, I remember every word.

"I want to have you over for dinner soon. I'd like you to meet my wives and children," Robert says between verses.

I can't believe how much I've missed. I won't ever get back the chance to be there for his first binding or the birth of his first child.

I squeeze his arm. "Oh, I would love that. How many children do you have?"

"Three children with our newest, and two wives, however, my second wife has yet to conceive."

"I'm sorry to hear that. Take comfort in the knowledge that Zaaron's plan is true."

"That it is." He kisses my cheek and smiles. "Have fun tonight. May the holy fire of Zaaron cleanse you, Laurel Ann."

"May the holy fire of Zaaron cleanse you, brother."

On his way back to his family, he passes Samuel and squeezes his shoulders.

The crowd's singing lowers to a quiet hum as we leave the Fitch ranch behind us and continue on to the river. Lit torches stick up from the ground, casting a haunting glow on the field and woods. As we come up to a large tree, I notice Zebadiah's mothers handing Mia and her sister-wife each a wicker basket. They both carry them away from the crowd and behind the tree.

Zebadiah stops, and in turn, so does everyone else. He holds up his hands, smiling his 'Prophet' smile before projecting his voice onto the crowd.

"Brothers and Sisters, welcome. Zaaron has gifted us such a beautiful night to bask in His presence. Tonight is a special night because we have a Sister who will be experiencing His voice for the first time. Laurel Ann, will you come up here please?"

There is a small amount of light from the lanterns, and I am thankful it isn't bright enough to show the color of red my face must be. I swallow and grip Samuel's hand before I obey. The stares of the followers adhere to me like sweat as I walk between them to get to Zeb.

He reaches out for me and takes my hand when I emerge from the crowd. "You have been through many trials and tribulations, yet here you stand, with a soul as pure as snow."

The crowd cries their praises with their hands raised to the evening sky. Zeb gestures behind me, summoning my sister to us. Reaching into her basket, he speaks loud enough to be heard over the crowd.

"When Zaaron finished writing *The True Testament*, He knew His mission on earth had come to its close." Since I have no desire to look at Mia, I don't understand why I do. She smiles at me before passing through the crowd with her sister-wife, handing out whatever they carry in their baskets. Zeb continues, "He had completed His task of laying out His desires for us and was to return to the Paradise Star. He told His wives that He would be leaving the mortal realm, and they were to place His empty human vessel in the ground beneath this beautiful Bur Oak. When His words came to pass, they honored His request, burying Him right beneath this very tree. Though His firstborn son, Lazarus Fitch, became our first Prophet and could hear Him, His wives felt lost without his presence. They visited His burial site every day, mourning and praying for Him to speak to them. On the fifth day after His passing, they discovered that He had left them a gift." He holds what he took from the basket between his thumb and his forefinger to show the crowd. "Out of pure faith, the wives consumed His gifts and found themselves once again in the presence of their husband and God." He turns to show me, and it still takes me a moment to figure out what it is... Is it a mushroom? "Open your mouth, Sister Laurel Ann." Wait. Are these what I think they are?! Kaila took mushrooms once, and that was the longest six hours of my life. I have never heard anything like this before, and I know every verse in *The True Testament*. I don't know what to do. How are these in the Philistine world if they are a gift from Zaaron? I don't under-stand. How is this not a sin?

Everyone is looking at me, and Zeb's jaw is ticking. I do what he tells me and open my mouth. He places it on my tongue and whispers, "Eat it." I bite down, and the taste is so vile I cover my mouth to keep from gagging. Oh, this is bad, so bad. He finally turns away from me and back to the crowd. "To this day, He still bestows us this gift. Now, go my children, and speak to our God."

Those who have already gotten their 'gift' disperse, and the last few are waiting to reach into a basket for theirs.

"Do you not partake?" I ask him.

"Why would I? I'm the Prophet." I wish I could hate the smugness in his voice and how handsome he looks. I also wish I could see him as the holy man he is.

"As you continue to remind me."

Once I say it, I know it's disrespectful, and when I look up into his eyes, I've clearly angered him. "I suggest you spend the evening asking Zaaron to help you remember your place here. I want you in the tabernacle tomorrow morning at seven, sharp. There are things we clearly need to discuss."

He stiffens and turns to walk away from me to go to his wives. My heart aches to watch them, so I look up to the sky and sigh. Maybe he's right. My soul may be pure, but my mind has lived outside of grace for half my life.

I want to be alone and somewhere that has happy memories. I walk through trees until I break through and reach the bank. My feet take me in the direction away from the Bur Oak, and it isn't until I cross over the hill that I realize where I am. The last place where everything was perfect. The last time I was blissfully without doubt, was in this very spot. Taking off my boots and stockings, I set them next to a rock. I lift my dress, careful of my Anointing mark as I walk into the creek.

The water is cold on my feet and makes me shiver, but I sigh at the memories I have of this place. There is a movement beside me, and I turn to see a fawn behind a tree. I hold my breath and don't move an inch. She makes her way to the creek only a few feet from me. As she bends down to drink the water, I very slowly move toward her. Holding out a tentative hand, I get mere inches from her when she looks up at me. We lock eyes, and when I close those last few inches, she allows me to touch her sweet little head.

A wave of emotion rolls over me, and in this moment, I know she was sent by Zaaron. I feel connected with her in a way I never knew was possible.

I can feel the wind as she runs through the fields, taste the berries she feeds on, and sense the desire she has to find her mother. A burst of incredible joy overtakes my body, and I weep because I can't contain the intensity of this feeling. This is Zaaron. He's talking to me.

My sniffle startles the deer, causing her to run back into the trees. I hope her mother finds her. The water laps around my feet, and I've never realized how magnificent it feels. I want the incredible pleasure all over my body.

I lie flat on my back in the shallow water, and I gasp at the sensations of tingling across my skin. The water lifts my dress as I look up at the stars coming out for the night. I can almost touch them.

24

WRITTEN ON SKIN

Zebadiah

MARYBETH GIGGLES HYSTERICALLY WHILE MIA COMBS HER hands through her hair.

"It tickles, just different," Marybeth says, rubbing the fabric of her dress between her fingers.

Mia smiles at me and shakes her head with a soft laugh. Before seeing Laurel Ann in town, spending time with my wives would be a fairly pleasant evening. They are both kind, holy women, and any man on the compound would be blessed to be bound to them. Now though, I can barely be in their presence. All I can think about is getting some time with Laur.

Things are not going as I had planned. Not that I really had a plan, I simply assumed she would be much more obedient. I've done what I needed to do to keep things peaceful on the compound, yet she shows up fighting me at every turn. I know I'm being hard on her, but that's only because if I appear to be giving her any special treatment, my credibility, along with her chances of acceptance, will be obliterated. I understand that she's upset about Mia and Marybeth, but I have done nothing that wasn't within my duty as Prophet. She acts as if I was bound out of desire. And I only kept it from her because I didn't want to alter her choice.

Then this shit with Benji. How does he expect me to react? Being a sodomite is one of the worst sins out there. And with Samuel Henderson of all people. When Benji first told me of his perverse desires, I tried to find whatever I could about it in *The True Testament*. It makes it clear that a man being with another man is an abomination. Zaaron's orders for atonement are clearly written: *And for three days, the sodomite must pay the same penance as that of an adulterer. Closing the orifice used with thread will prevent more sins from being committed before the cleansing of their soul. –12:16B.*

I wipe my hand over my face and watch the many children of Zaaron reveling in their divine bliss. They all look to me for the answers I don't have and words I don't hear. I do what I was born for, fulfill my calling, because otherwise, why didn't I try to find her? That question has been a permanent fixture in my brain for twelve years, and I have to believe it was for something greater.

Marybeth jumps up and shrieks with glee as Faith and Hope Johnson chase her with a frog. Mia gets up to follow, and I grab her hand.

"I have some things I wanted to speak to Ezekiel and Jacob about. I'll see you at home tonight, all right?"

She gives me a slight smile. "Of course, husband."

I kiss her and feel a pang of guilt when she leans in to me. My thoughts about Laurel Ann have been anything other than pure. Every moment I'm with her it gets harder not to break my vows. Even as the culpability chokes me, my hands trail down my wife's waist while I think of her sister.

If we hadn't been interrupted by Sister Madeline earlier tonight, how far might things have gone? My erection grows, tightening my trousers at the memory of Laurel Ann's flushed skin beneath my fingers.

Breaking our kiss, I back away toward the tree line. "Keep an eye on Marybeth."

She nods before spinning around to join her sister-wife in being chased with a frog by the twins.

I keep my eyes peeled for Laurel Ann, though I'm sure I know where she is. I get the occasional "Blessed evening, Prophet", but mostly people are lost in their state of grace. I slip over to the Bur Oak and put one of the mushroom caps in my mouth. I've eaten these on many occasions trying to get Zaaron to speak to me. The more I eat the more I feel Him, and the closer I get to the Paradise Star. It also pulls my mind from this world. Mia found me once, and she was terrified. She said I was speaking gibberish. She went to fetch Doc Kilmer, and I had to assure him it was a holy affliction. Zaaron never did speak to me, even then, so I've never consumed more than one at a time since.

I'm far enough away from Mia and Marybeth to comfortably grab a torch and slip into the trees. As I cross over the hill and arrive at the creek, my heart falls at her absence. I feel like a fool for thinking she'd be here.

I can't deny this place brings me a peace I need terribly, and being alone with my thoughts and Zaaron may be beneficial to my predicament. Walking closer to the river, my steps falter. My heart pounds like a gavel in my ribcage.

She's lying in the water, her hair floating around her like the ethereal creature she is, humming an old nursery rhyme. I swallow down my nerves and stick the torch in the ground to make my way to her. Taking off my boots, socks, and jacket before I reach the water, I stand over her until she opens her eyes.

She shoots up in surprise. "Prophet!" Scrambling to her feet, she flings water everywhere and backs away. "What are you doing here? I thought this was my time alone with Zaaron?"

I shove my hands into my pockets because I find it physically difficult to not touch her.

"I didn't want to wait until tomorrow to talk with you. I don't like things like this between us."

Her fingers trail up and down her wet sleeve as she lets out a sigh that is so close to a moan the hairs on the back of my neck stand on end. "I don't know what you mean."

I close the space between us and brush the wet hair off her shoulder. "Yes, you do. You're angry at me for Mia and Marybeth, and you're angry at me about the tomb of abolishment. So, tell me, what would you have had me do?"

Her mouth falls open before she snaps it shut and narrows her eyes. "I would have had you be honest with me about it. Not throw me in blind." She leans closer to me, and her body shivers as she snaps in an angry whisper, "The way you kissed me at our picnic actually had me believing that we might be bound once I came here."

I take in a breath because she has no idea how many times I wished for her to be my wife. My first wife. My only wife. Knowing it was impossible never took away from how much I've desired it.

"Is that what you want?"

Tears roll down her face as she shakes her head. "It's what I've always wanted, but now…seeing you with your other wives…with Mia, I don't know."

She's more sensitive because of the mushrooms. They force truth and take down the walls we put up. They may be magnifying her emotions, but they are still hers. She just can't hide them right now.

I try not to be offended at her words. This has surely been a difficult few days, and it will take her time to adjust. I take both of my hands and wipe the tears from her cheeks. "I have a proposition."

Tilting her head in confusion, she sniffs. "What kind of proposition?"

"The kind where we forget about everything that's happened since you returned...an armistice. Only for tonight. Tonight, we enjoy our time together, under the stars in the most beautiful place on the compound."

Her breath comes out shaky, and she moves her hand toward me before suddenly pulling it back. "I don't know. It's an awful lot to forget."

The fear of her turning away from me after all this time threatens to close my throat. I need these moments with her more than I realized. I need her to know that I don't want any of this; I just don't know what to do.

"One night. That's all I ask."

She chews on her lip as she looks across the creek. The silence is killing me. She grabs my hand, and I let out a quiet chuckle of relief.

"One night," she whispers.

Leading me to the water's edge, she sits down, and I follow. Her body is shaking more harshly now. The thought of her taking off her dress sends the blood rushing to my cock, though the real reason I want her to remove it is I don't want her getting sick.

"Maybe you should take the dress off. It's not making you any warmer."

A smirk blinks across her face before it slips away, and she lifts her hair off her shoulders. "Will you help me with the buttons?"

The Laurel Ann I know wouldn't have an inkling of how to seduce a man on purpose, making the lust rolling off her tongue so natural it's intoxicating. I allow my fingers to brush her neck, and she releases another one of those sighing moans, giving me the urge to reach down and stroke myself.

Zaaron's gifts are taking their effect, causing the hundreds of buttons trailing down the back of this dress to feel like they're pulsing beneath my fingers. With each one I undo, more of her pale flesh presents itself to me, the faint lines of her soul cleansing scars decorating her otherwise flawless skin. The lace trim of her white, bodice petticoat looks soft like the brushstrokes of a painting against her back. Lightly fondling the material, I push the wet sleeves of her dress down her delicate shoulders. Before I can stop myself, I press my lips to her back and inhale her scent. My senses become hyperaware of her skin tingling beneath my lips.

She whispers the softest, "Prophet," as I kiss up her spine.

Once her dress is down her arms, she pushes it the rest of the way off, leaving her in nothing other than her petticoat and bloomers which stick to her figure from being wet. She turns to face me, and the light from the torch shows her hard nipples through the white fabric. I have to clench my fists to prevent myself from brushing my fingers over them. My gaze travels up to her quivering lips before meeting her watery eyes. She reaches up, holding her hand against my cheek. Her touch feels so incredible, my cock twitches in my trousers.

I turn my head to kiss her palm when she says, "Does Zaaron tell you what will become of me?"

Honesty is on the cusp of my tongue. I want to tell her that I'm a fraud. That Zaaron doesn't speak to me at all. That the entire compound has put their faith and trust into a man who doesn't know what the hell he's doing. "He tells me what He feels is necessary." She looks up at me with those earnest, green eyes, and I wish I could tell her everything will be all right. "Your future has yet to be determined."

The challenge is subtle yet apparent when she asks, "Has

He told you what will become of Benji and my brother?"

I'm angry that they put me in this position, but I know I can't let the compound learn of this. Being branded a sodomite stays with someone. Even once they are cleansed, they are treated differently. I can't let that happen to them.

"He has been oddly silent on the matter. Until He tells me otherwise, I will take this as another example of His infinite grace."

From the expression I'm receiving, I'm sure she's questioning my response. I have to lie on demand so often that half the time I wonder how threadbare my falsehoods seem. If she doubts my honesty, she speaks nothing of it.

She nods and looks across the water in silence. When she finally speaks, she doesn't move her gaze.

"I was with child when I left the compound."

Vibrations on my skin make it come alive, as if it will separate from my body at any moment just to wrap around her. My tongue swells, and my head fills up with air, making me light headed. I've pushed away the thoughts of my father taking her body hundreds of times. Knowing that he put a child inside of her makes my hate for the dead man hotter than it has been since the day we killed him.

"What became of it?"

She doesn't answer, and I wonder if I asked the question at all or just imagined it when she says, "Zaaron ripped it from my body."

Women lose children all the time, on the compound. The situations can range from mild to fatal. The thought of her going through that all alone in the dark, new world has me wrapping her in my arms and pulling her into my lap. There aren't words that can be said for this. There is nothing to do besides hold her against me. She laces her arms around my neck, and as her chest presses against mine, each of her breaths flow into me, connecting us with an unseen chain. Our skin begins to mold together, and I smile against her shoulder. I have to believe that this is Zaaron's way of telling us that our souls are meant to be one. I don't know how, I don't know when, but the very core of our being recognize each other on a majestic level.

I hold her against me as my fingertips softly trail across her back. She lets out an erotic sigh and turns her body to wrap her legs around my waist. I can feel the heat between her legs through the fabric of my shirt.

"Oh Prophet...that feels really good," she whimpers. I have to swallow at the vision of her rocking against my stomach. "Every touch is like a tiny explosion." Her fingers fondle the chain of my sigil necklace, little puffs of air falling from her lips. My aching cock presses against her ass, and even without her touching it, the feeling is so overwhelming I'm worried she will bring me to completion just like this. "Is this Zaaron? Is He doing this?" she gasps.

I can't handle this anymore without coming in my trousers. Lightly nipping at her ear, I whisper, "I'm going to lay you down."

"I don't want to move," she groans in protest, making me chuckle and my dick throb. My restraint is waning as I press my lips to hers, tasting her desire.

I slowly lay her on her back, when like a flash of lightening in a stormy sky, guilt over my current acts of unfaithfulness flicker through my mind. My eyes trace over her lightly freckled skin, drowning my transgressions in my arousal. Her mouth is slightly open, and I give into my desire to trace my tongue along the inside of her bottom lip.

I grasp at the hem of her petticoat to push it over her bloomers. "What are you doing?" She lifts her head in a half daze of excitement and confusion.

I continue lifting the fabric, exposing her stomach, begrudgingly stopping before I reach her breasts. "We're going to play a game."

Her laugh is husky as she lays her head back on the bank and looks to the night sky. "Okay...what are we playing?"

My hand brushes across her stomach, and she quivers. "I'm going to use my finger to write something, and you have to guess what it is."

Her breathing becomes faster. "Okay."

I lie on my side, allowing me to see her body move as I touch my finger around her navel. "Ready?"

She nods her head, and a wisp of air leaves her lips. Tracing a vertical line across her flesh, I add two smaller horizontal ones, one at the top and one at the bottom. "I," she sighs. I draw a vertical line before dragging it down diagonally, up diagonally and down again vertically. "M." Once she guesses the next *I*, I make a snake-like motion across her torso, and she arches her back as she whimpers, "I missed you, too, Prophet."

I grin, pressing a soft kiss right below her belly button. "I think this is too easy for you," I murmur against her skin. Pressing continuous kisses up her stomach in a diagonal line I begin writing a *Y* on her skin with my lips. She doesn't guess the letters as easily, so I take my mouth lower on her body each time. Her pelvis thrusts on its own every few minutes until I can't take it anymore. Risking reaching down to rub the head of my dick over my pants, I groan from the sensation. By the time I get to the *U*, I take the chance and tug down her bloomers. Since she doesn't stop me, I pull them down a little further for the '*R* when something pokes out from her knickers. Grasping at the piece of paper, I slide it out of her undergarments before she jolts up and reaches to take it from my hands.

I yank it back and laugh, "What's this?"

When I look down and the light from the torch illuminates the paper, I realize what I'm holding and nearly drop it.

Real anger is not something I have ever felt toward her. Even when I had to watch her be bound to my father, even when she left him knowing there would be consequences, and even when I knew she was living with a Philistine. But this? She intentionally brought it into our sacred land, and she deliberately disobeyed our laws. "What are you thinking?!" I jump up to grab the torch, ready to see this unnatural blasphemy burn.

"No!" she screams, grabbing my arm. "Please, Zeb, please don't. It's all I have left of her. I won't ever see her again! Please!"

She looks about to fall to her knees to plead. The use of my name causes a pain in my chest, and the heartbreak on her face is almost too much to bear. I don't understand how she could have developed feelings for a Philistine. Regardless, the girl was clearly a lifeline for Laurel Ann. It's obvious how much she cares for her.

I sigh. This wasn't an act of rebellion. Photographs were created by men who tried to outsmart Zaaron and stop time, but even I can admit to having the desire to hold a moment in your pocket. Keeping the wet picture between my fingers, I hold it out to her, and she snatches it back, pressing it to her chest. The flame from the torch causes a glow around her partially dried hair, and I brush it back from her face.

"Since I told you that tonight wasn't about anything other than us, I'm choosing to ignore this. Just know, if I see it again I will destroy it. Keep it better hidden."

She nods, "Yes, Prophet."

Rushing over to her boots, she bends down to place the photo inside as I step behind her. She turns around quickly, nearly bumping into me. She gasps at my close proximity and covers her mouth.

"You scared me." Looking into my eyes with her wide ones, she steps closer and places her hands on my chest. "Thank you," she whispers, standing on her toes to kiss my cheek.

I grasp the back of her neck and press my mouth against hers before I grin. "We didn't finish our game."

She breathes out a soft laugh as I grab her to pull her back down to the bank. Once we touch the ground, I lean down, and her chest lifts when she wraps her arms around me, hugging me closer. My hand travels down the right side of her body until finding the hem of her petticoat. Her legs spread, allowing me to lie between them and kiss across her face and neck.

"Every night for as long as I can remember, I thought of this."

She stills, and her hands brush over my shoulders to my chest, slowly pushing me away. "What are we doing, Zebadiah? This is wrong, but it feels…everything just feels so much…more. I'm not strong enough to say no to you. I need you to stop this."

I lightly bite her ear before whispering, "Sorry, Laur. When it comes to this, I'm weaker than you are." Alternating between nipping and kissing, I move down her neck as she sharply inhales and grasps at the ground. "And this feeling is a gift from Zaaron." My fingers slide under her bodice strap to tug it over her shoulder, exposing her pretty, pink nipple. I look up at her, and she's watching me. I smile and lick the little nub. "So, fucking enjoy it." I suck the hardened flesh into my mouth, and she cries with actual tears.

"Don't curse."

Her hand goes to the back of my head, pressing me closer as I laugh against her breast. I slowly trace my fingers across her stomach until reaching the waist of her bloomers.

Flattening my palm against her skin, I slide beneath the fabric. When I reach the soft hair, my heart pounds, and she jolts, forcing my fingers to slide against her wetness.

"Prophet!" Allowing my hand to softly roam, I gently put a finger inside, her body clamping around it. I slide slowly in and out to let her adjust to the sensation. As she pushes herself against my hand, I move my finger faster. "This is...I've never felt this before...it's amazing..." she murmurs, her words fading under the fog of Zaaron's presence.

The very idea of her coming is almost too much to bear. This is the only chance I'll have, and I want so badly to know what she tastes like. Just the thought of such an act has me undoing my trousers and fisting my cock. Removing my hand from her bloomers, I run my wet fingertip up her stomach to her belly button.

"Why did you stop?" she pants.

Pulling the ribbon, I untie her knickers and tug them down her body. Her pale skin looks intoxicating in the light of the moon as I take in her natural form for the first time. Seeing her like this has been the subject of so many of my dreams.

My groan comes out soft when I ask, "Do you know what I was going to write earlier?" She gives me a slight shake of the head, and I lean down to kiss her. "You're beautiful." Smiling, she bites her lip, and I reach back down to run my thumb over her wet pussy. "Has anyone ever licked you here?"

Her eyes widen in horror and mild disgust. "Of course not! Why on earth would I let someone put their mouth there?"

Her reaction isn't surprising. I just want to experience her in every way possible. Mia has never let me do it, but I've always wanted to. I know that it's perverse, and for some reason, that's partially why I want to do it. I lean back to push her legs further apart as I move down her body.

When my mouth is inches from her clit, she shakes her head. "Prophet, this is—" My tongue darts out, softly licking the little bud. Her body tenses for a moment before relaxing completely. While I've never done this personally, I watched Ezekiel doing it to Gretchen Adams a few years ago in the loft. Since she seemed to like my fingers earlier, I slide one into her, and she moans, thrusting against my tongue. "Don't," she softly cries.

The little nub has gotten harder, so I suck it into my mouth. "Don't what? Don't stop?" I flatten my tongue and trace it from her hole to the sensitive spot. "Or don't keep going?"

She reaches for my head. "Don't stop."

It's not difficult to slide in another finger with how wet she is, so I do. I pick up the tempo and return my mouth to her pussy, using my free hand to stroke my cock. She threatens to scalp me as she shamelessly grinds against my tongue.

My dick throbs, the blood vibrating in my veins. I pump myself faster, and the wetness of my arousal seeps unto my thumb. I'm about to come all over the ground when she chokes out, "S-something's different." Her thrusting gets quicker, and with a whimper, she pulses around my fingers. Her taste gets sweeter as my mouth fills with the juices her orgasm gives me. "Prophet!"

As if her pleasure siphoned every drop of energy, her body slacks. Her chest rises and falls with a quickness. I wipe my mouth and move up her body, pressing my painfully hard erection against her slick entrance. I slide it between her lips, watching my length push them apart.

Looking up to her face, I brush her cheek, and her eyes flutter open. "Did you like that?"

With a shaky breath, she nods with a barely audible, "Yes."

She licks her lips, and a peaceful, dazed smile graces her face. "It was…I don't know how to explain it…" I look back down to watch myself gliding across her pussy, and she does the same. I think this is going to push me over when she says, "Are you going to…"

Her voice trails off, all but giving me permission. Excitement jolts through my body, and I lean back to wet the tip with her come. "I just want to feel."

I push myself into her, though she's too tight to get all the way in. The intensity of my pleasure is multiplied from Zaaron's gift, and I moan at her body constricting around mine. She cries at the intrusion, clawing at my back. I kiss her hard and thrust in deeper, her strangled cries escaping from her throat as I wipe her tears.

"Are you okay?" I ask her.

She pushes a smile through her apparent pain, nodding and caressing my cheek. While I may not be able to hear Zaaron, I can feel Him in this moment. She opens her legs wider to welcome me as I lift my ass, sliding back in, easier this time.

"You're the only boy I ever wanted," she says so quietly I wouldn't have heard her if her lips weren't next to my ear.

The sigil hangs from my neck as I hover above her to see her face, thrusting faster. "Funny, because you're the only girl I ever wanted."

Not for the first time, I wonder what could have been with us if we'd been born to Philistines. What it would be like to live freely together, without all the rules and responsibilities. What it would be like to sleep in her bed every night. I know this is just my flesh having these thoughts. What is the point in a life together here if we have to spend eternity apart?

Looking at her bright, green eyes and beautiful, taught body, mixed with her pussy squeezing my dick builds my orgasm, and I fuck her with years' worth of fantasies. The desire to want this to last forever isn't strong enough when my whispered name is falling from her lips. I wrap my arms around her shoulders to keep her in place as I pound into her. Moving inside the body I've dreamed of, thought of when I stroke my cock, is too much with her voice in my ear. I know I should stop now. I should pull out of her and come on the bank. I should...

The pressure builds a euphoric heat, and as it rolls through me, I groan. "Can you feel it? How full I'm making your body?" She moans, lifting her hips to take all that she can.

We're both panting when I look up to see her face covered in uncertainty, and I must say, I feel it, too.

What the hell did we just do?

25

LIES BEGET LIES

Zebadiah

WE LIE IN SILENCE FOR A LONG TIME, NEITHER OF US SURE where we stand or what this means. I know I must return home. Mia and Marybeth are surely wondering where I've been. I can't bring myself to say as much, so I stay with her until she falls asleep against my chest.

With gentle fingers, I lay her on the bank, covering her with her dress. I press my lips lightly against her forehead before I adjust my clothes and head back through the trees.

While most of the followers have gone home, a few are still out on my way to the ranch. It's still early enough that the sun has yet to rise, but I know this compound well enough without it. I say a silent prayer of thanks when I arrive home to find no lamp or candlelight in the windows. Taking off my shoes, I open the screen and front doors, cursing the floor when it creaks beneath my feet. I creep to my study and let out a breath when I close the door behind me.

"Zebadiah?"

I jump at the small voice. "Marybeth?" The illumination from a match appears, and she lights a lamp, casting a shadowed glow across the room. I look up to see her standing next to my desk, completely nude. I'm frozen in place, unable to do anything besides watch her walk to me. "What are you doing? You should be in bed."

She reaches out to rub her hand over my trousers, grabbing my dick which was just inside of Laurel Ann.

"I want to give you a child. I'm ready for you to take my body as your wife."

She takes my hand, rubbing my fingers against the slickness of her arousal. Immediately, I yank it back. I wish I could believe my reasons for not wanting to fuck her are because I just committed adultery against her. If I'm being honest with myself, I know regardless of what happened with Laurel Ann, I've been dreading this.

The guilt is suffocating when her face falls. It's my duty as her husband to do exactly this. She is my wife, chosen for me by Zaaron, so why does the idea of touching her, her touching me, make my stomach turn? It was different with Mia. We were bound for years before she came to me. She had hair between her legs, full breasts, and the same blood as Laurel Ann running through her veins. Even though I have no unique feelings for her, the sight of her body would make the blood rush to my cock. Seeing Marybeth naked before me has my eyes searching for a quilt to wrap around her.

Tears fill her eyes when she hugs her arms around her body. "Have I done something wrong? Do you find me ugly?"

Shame weighs heavy in my stomach as I reach out and pull her to me. "My sweet Marybeth. You have done nothing wrong, and you are absolutely not ugly." Her arms squeeze tight around my hips at my words. "If I will be spending half my nights in your bed then we must consult Mia and make a schedule. I have also had an eventful day, and I'm simply exhausted." Reaching down, I lift her chin to make her look up at me. "You understand, don't you?"

She nods and whispers, "Yes, husband."

I bend over to kiss her. "Now get on to bed. We'll discuss this tomorrow."

Her spirits seem momentarily lifted as she leaves the room. Once the door is closed behind her, I collapse into the nearest chair.

I have no idea how I am going to hold her off for very long. It's going to be trying enough to go to bed with Mia, now that I've tainted our binding.

I need to talk to Laurel Ann before I speak with either one of my wives. I stand and groan as the exhaustion settles in my head. It looks like I'll be sleeping in the tabernacle tonight.

Even with my fatigue, sleep evades me. I toss and turn on the bed in the holding room until I can't stay here any longer. Pulling on my trousers, I grab my shirt and head to my office.

The rising sun shines through the windows casting a warm glow across the room. I no sooner sit down when there's a knock on my door.

"Prophet?"

Her voice freezes me in my chair. Last night, we were under the influence of Zaaron, but now, in the light of the morning sun, how will she react to what we've done?

When I open the door, my exhale catches in my throat at the sight of her in the same dress as last night. Memories of her soft skin beneath my fingers and how exquisite she felt around my cock flash through my mind. Her light red hair is wild while she stares at my chest.

I look down to realize my shirt is open. Spinning on my

heel, I quickly fasten the buttons and sit back down.

"Come in and close the door behind you."

Her movements are slow and hesitant, or maybe that's just how it feels watching her. Lowering into the chair, she fidgets with her dress as she holds her hands in her lap.

"Prophet…last night…" Her voice cracks when she continues, "I'm more confused than before."

She looks up at me through her lashes, bringing my cock to life. More than anything, I want to get up, grip her by the arms, and kiss her. Last night did nothing other than increase my desire, so I stay where I am, fighting my erection.

"I don't think it's that confusing. You want me to fuck you, you just don't want to be my wife."

I know the words are unfair and harsh the moment they leave my lips. As her Prophet, I shouldn't let my personal feelings get in the way. She crosses her arms, her face shifting between pain and anger.

"You said last night was separate. I was under the impression that this morning it would be as if it never happened." She sighs, closing her eyes. "I betrayed Zaaron last night. I betrayed my sister." When her eyelashes flutter open and she looks at me, the fearful lust in her eyes has me standing to my feet. "But just looking at you…I can't stop thinking of it. Though you are correct, I can't be your third wife."

I'm aware she said as much last night, but hearing it after what happened between us, with a clear mind, makes me angrier than expected.

"Why?! I was always going to take other wives whether you were first or not. I don't understand the difference." My footsteps are the only sound as I storm around my desk to stand in front of her. Placing my hands on the armrests of her chair, I lean down to her level. Her eyes light up, her plump lips barely parting with a small breath. I lean forward and softly

kiss the freckles on her cheek before I trace my hand slowly down the front of her body over her dress. "I could touch
you every day, whenever I want, if you were my wife." I don't
know what I'm doing when I kiss her neck and move my hand
to rub between her legs. "Do you not want this? Want me?"

Her whisper comes out shaky. "Of course I do, but…"

The 'but' makes my skin hot. 'But' fucking what? I storm
over to the large chest in the corner of the room because it's
the furthest I can get from her right now.

"You seem to forget I am your Prophet. If it is Zaaron's
will for you to be bound to me, I will make it so." Having my
back to her makes my threat come out easier, though I feel
regret once I say it.

The light *tap, tap, tap* of footfalls behind me has my teeth
grinding. Then, her hand touches my arm, and my muscles
instinctively loosen.

"Zeb."

She whispers my name, and I spin around to see her biting
her lip in uncertainty. "What did you expect to happen, Laurel
Ann? You're here, yet you might as well still be bound to my
father if you refuse this."

Her eyes trail over my body and keep landing on my
lips. "I don't know. I just wanted to come home." She meets
my eyes and straightens. "Maybe this was a mistake. Zaaron
turned me away for a reason."

The thought of her leaving me again erupts across my
mind like the ignition of a flame. My hand wraps around
her shoulder to push her over the oak chest. I press my body
against her back before my mind catches up to my actions.
Her ass presses against my cock as I brush the hair away from
her ear with tender fingers.

"A mistake? He doesn't make mistakes." At any moment,
she could stop this. The very thought makes me feverish in

shoving up her dress. She shudders the moment my lips brush across her ear. Reaching around, I pull at the string of her bloomers, clawing my fingers around the waistband to pull them over her ass.

"We can't do this, Zeb," she gasps, with her cheek pressed to the wood of the chest.

As I slip my fingers between her legs they become slippery with her arousal. "Then tell me to stop."

Undoing my trousers causes me to harden from anticipation, and I groan at the relief of stroking myself. She attempts looking at me over her shoulder, her lack of response more of an answer than any words could have been. Bent over like this, the sunlight shines across her freckled body, her beautiful, wet pussy glistening. I line myself up, and she pushes her ass back, begging me to enter her.

She moans, her fingers curling around the edge of the chest. I thrust into her, and she's so tightly wrapped around me I grow larger inside her body. I've never been in this position before. It feels fucking amazing, but the truth is, I don't know what's happening with us. She just refused to be my wife for the second time.

I watch the skin of her cunt holding on tight as I slowly slide out. We both release a moan at the sensation of me pushing back in.

Grabbing her by the arm, I spin her around, picking her up and sitting her on the edge of the chest to face me. I pull her bloomers the rest of the way off, preparing to enter her again, when her hand wraps around the base of my cock. She strokes me slowly at first, speeding up as she builds momentum. I look up at her watching herself masturbate me. Finally, her eyes move to mine, and I press my lips hard against hers.

"This isn't a mistake, Laur. Say you'll be my wife, and we can have this forever."

She shifts her hips beneath me, sliding herself over my body. That little movement says she wants this just as much as I do. I don't understand why she's fighting a binding. My lust, frustrations, and anger have me going faster. She thrusts against me, her arms wrapping around my neck as if letting go would cause her to fall into the abyss. She's not only giving her body to me, she's taking mine with a hunger that has my cock twitching against the pressure of her entrance. She kisses me, and I slide my tongue into her mouth. I've never kissed this way before. I don't know why I do it, and it doesn't matter, because she responds by putting hers in mine. With our bodies connected this way, it feels like we could go on forever in our perfect circle.

This has to stop if we aren't bound, but with her taste in my mouth and my flesh in her flesh, I don't know if I can quit this. Quit her.

Knock, knock.

"Zebadiah?"

My eyes widen at Mia's voice, and I break our kiss. Laurel Ann has a similar expression as she covers her mouth with her hand.

"I'm in the middle of something, Mia." My cock pulses, and I hate myself when I slowly keep moving myself in and out of her.

"You never came to bed last night. I was just checking that you were all right," she calls through the door.

The building pleasure breaks through, and I clench my teeth as my come splashes against the walls of Laurel Ann's pussy. "I'm fine." My voice shakes with my ebbing orgasm. "Begin your duties, I'll be out shortly."

The look on her face makes me feel slightly queasy. There's clear disgust there, I'm just not sure if it's with me or herself.

"Yes, husband," Mia responds, mere feet from me desecrating our binding.

We stare at each other until Mia's footsteps fall silent. As I pull out my semi-erect cock, my come drips out of her, down the chest, and drops onto the floor. She feverishly jumps down and pulls up her bloomers while I re-fasten my trousers. Her breathing becomes heavy, and she wipes her hand over her face to her mouth.

I swallow, despising the shame that I feel. What am I doing? I am her Prophet. I'm supposed to be a holy example to all the children of Zaaron.

I am failing you... I'm failing them all.

She looks at me for guidance, and I respond the only way I know how. "This has to end. I cannot keep being unfaithful to my wives." With her lips in a hard line, she nods. Tucking in my shirt, I grab my jacket and hat. "I'm going to tend to Mia. Go to the placing dorms. I will assign you your duties this afternoon."

Without giving me the courtesy of eye contact, she says, "Yes, Prophet."

"Wait five minutes, and then you may go."

The room has become frigid. While I have to fight my desire to comfort her, she's made her choice, and it isn't me. I'd be lying if I said I didn't feel betrayed and confused. We finally have the opportunity to be together, really be together, and she refuses.

I open the door, smoothing my hair before putting on my hat. I make my way into the meeting hall to find Mia gathering the candle holders from the altar, placing them in her apron.

"Here, let me help you."

Picking up the brass pieces, I walk through the pews to lead her to the bride room in the foyer of the tabernacle. Once safely inside, I close the door and lay the pieces on the table before turning to Mia.

"I'm glad to see you are well," she says with a smile. "Marybeth said you needed to speak with me?"

I rub the back of my neck and sigh. I need to pray. I don't know what the hell I'm doing. "She says she's ready to lay with me, but I just think she's in need of more attention. I would like you two to make a schedule, splitting up nights of the week, giving you four and her three. You need to decide if there are any exceptions, and you must lay down ground rules."

She picks up a cloth, dipping it in polish to begin shining a candle holder. "Of course, Zebadiah."

"I will give you one week, and then we will set whatever you've decided into place. She needs to understand that as my first wife, you have seniority and ultimately, the final word. Don't let her manipulate you."

She tilts her head in amusement. "With all due respect, husband, I do not let her manipulate me. I simply relate well to her. If I'm guilty of anything, it's letting her make her own decisions."

I hold my hand up in surrender because every husband in the Anointed Land knows it's best to let their wives work most things out for themselves.

"About last night, I apologize. The evening got away from me with Zeke and Jacob."

Her eyes flash. "You were with the Counselor and Apostle the entire night?" My tongue swells in my mouth, so I nod my head in deception. Her expression falls neutral as she turns back to her task. "Well, I'm pleased you had a nice time with your brothers."

A sickness rolls in my stomach. She knows something. I step beside her and lift her chin to kiss her. "I'll see you later this afternoon."

I close the bride room door behind me, take off my hat, and drop my head against the wood, allowing air to rush through my lips. Even my guilt is confused. I glance toward my office. I don't regret for a single second what I did with Laurel Ann, yet I hate knowing I betrayed Mia and Marybeth.

Leaving through the front doors, I wave at passing followers on my way to the back of the tabernacle, for the buggy Mia brought.

I ride back to the ranch I share with my family. After my father died, I allowed my mothers and siblings to stay at the ranch until they become bound. I stop the buggy on the pathway in front of the barn, remove my hat, and enter my home to find the dining room full of my mothers, siblings, and wife. They all tell me, "Good morning," before I receive a kiss from my mother and Marybeth. Zeke sits at the table eating his breakfast, nodding at me in greeting.

"May I have a word, Apostle?"

He furrows his brows as he wipes his mouth and follows me outside. Walking next to him, I wait until we get far enough from the house to not risk being heard.

"Did you talk to Mia at all last night?"

His nose scrunches with a look of confusion. "Uh, yeah, just for a minute. She asked me where you were."

Shit, shit, shit.

"What did you say?" I ask, breathless.

Raising his eyebrow, he scratches the scruff on his jaw. "What do you mean? The truth. That I hadn't seen you since the dispersal of Zaaron's gifts."

Fuck.

26

THE BINDING PLAN

Laurel Ann

I CAN'T BREATHE. I CREEP FROM THE TABERNACLE AND MAKE MY way behind the building. As soon as I'm safe from prying eyes, I fall to the dirt and allow myself to cry. I'm covered in sin, and my Prophet can't cleanse me without damning himself. I don't understand how I have such little control over my fleshly desires when it comes to Zeb. Last night felt like a dream, but this morning my thoughts were clear. I knew what we were doing was wrong, and I still opened my legs for him like a whore.

All this time dreaming of being with him, and now I can't do it. His touch is impossible for me to deny, yet knowing he does the same to my sister and eventually Marybeth is suffocating. And there will be more. He will continue taking wives until Zaaron desires him in the Paradise Star. He's right, I have always known he would have many wives, but actually seeing it is incredibly more painful than I was prepared for.

He's all I want. I've never had a single desire for anyone other than him, but I can't share him. I can't live like that for the rest of my life, and I'm furious at myself for it. I cry and rub my chest, my heart physically aching. The reality of my sins crushes me as shame covers me in a thick sheen.

I have to purify.

Keeping my eyes peeled for anyone who may see me, I hurry to Benji's cellar. I reach the wooden door, my heart leaping at the missing lock before I heave it open. Once I'm down the ladder, I find the lantern, lighting it and turning the knob to bring some illumination into the space.

My eyes scan the shelves of boxes. I doubt there's an order to them. Taking down the first one to my right, I sit on the mattress, rummaging for something I can use.

One by one I search them. After eight different boxes, I find a Zippo and a necklace with a small, metal star pendant.

Holding the chain, I dangle the jewelry above the flame until I see a glow. I carefully lay the star on the inside of my elbow, groaning at the contact of heat. I grit my teeth, using his blanket to push it deeper into my skin. I whimper and gasp from the pain, yet I welcome the small weight lifted off my soul.

Tears fall down my face as I peel the pendant from my skin. In an attempt to relieve the burning, I press the blanket against the wound, though it does nothing to diminish the pain.

Returning the items to their boxes, I hear footsteps behind me. "Hey, Laur, whatcha doin'?" I turn to see Benji jumping off the ladder. Because I don't want to tell him about my personal cleansing, I try to think of an excuse when the thought I had last night about Kaila's photo, ping-pongs in my head.

"I'd like you to keep a secret for me."

I reach down and remove my boot for the photo. Benji's eyebrow is arched at my actions until his eyes find the picture, then they widen.

"Is that a photograph?" I nod, presenting it to him. He

reaches for it tenderly, holding it in his palm as if it will turn to ash at any moment. "Who is she?" he whispers.

I don't stop the smile creeping across my lips at not only how gentle he is with it, but also thinking of her. "Her name is Kaila. She was the first person who was genuinely nice to me out there."

His mouth quirks as he runs his fingers over the glossy photo before slowly holding it out to me. "She's very pretty."

I don't take the picture from him. Instead, I trace my hands along the different boxes. "Zebadiah already found it. He warned me he would destroy it if he saw it again." I turn to find him looking at me like I've grown wings. "Can I keep it here?"

He shakes his head. "Wait. Zeb knows you have this?" I nod and he asks, "When did this happen?"

Dropping my gaze to the ground, I tug on my dress with my fingers. It feels suffocating all of a sudden. "Last night."

He whistles and picks the smallest box off the top. It's a wooden box with a bird carved in the grain. He lifts the lid and gently places the photo inside.

"Last night, huh?" He turns to me and grins. "How'd that go?"

I let out a breath and sit on his bed. "Not how it should have."

Sitting next to me, he nudges my shoulder. "Did something else happen between you two?"

I shake my head and laugh because if I don't, I'll cry. "It doesn't matter. He would make me his wife, regardless of Zaaron's wishes, and still...I just can't. I can't spend every day watching the man that I love touching other women. Especially Mia. The fact that she is his wife, his first wife, makes me feel an anger that I shouldn't."

He tilts his head as if torn on my statement. "I guess I

understand that."

"I don't. I should take him however I can, but even thinking about him with them makes me feel ill." I look at him, and the thought lights up my mind like a lightning storm. "You love my brother, don't you?"

His face flushes with his grin. "Sammy is…" He laughs and ruffs up his hair. "Yes, I love him. Very much."

"What if you never had to worry about being bound to someone else? What if you could be with Samuel without fear of getting caught?"

He raises his eyebrows, nodding his head in thought. "That would be amazing, but how do you plan to make that happen?"

I turn to him and take a big breath. I know this is the only way. For everyone.

"Benji, will you be my husband?"

He busts up laughing. "That was cold, freckles. I thought you were serious."

"I am. If you agree, I will inform our Prophet, and he will allow it. I can promise you that."

"You're not joking?" He's gaping at me, though there is clear hope behind his shock.

"No. This is what's best for all of us. You can be with my brother in our home, and I won't have to worry about being placed with someone else."

His thumb slides under his suspenders with his laugh. "Well, I'll be damned. Laurel Ann Johnson."

Climbing the steps to the placing dorms, I open the screen door and consider knocking before deciding to just walk in.

The beds are already made with most of the movement in the back toward the kitchen. I don't even get past the dividers when a much older Evelyn Taub rushes toward me.

"Laurel Ann! Welcome home, child!" She hurries me to the hall behind the kitchen, taking me directly to the washroom. "I'll have some water put on the stove, and then we'll get you some clean clothes and some food in your stomach. I already have a bed saved for you. Number sixteen." Pointing to one of the baskets in the corner, she says, "Put your soiled clothes in there. We'll return them to your bed once they've been cleaned."

"I am grateful for your kindness, Sister Evelyn."

"Of course, dear." She opens a cabinet and gives me a small bag. "This should have all the toiletries you need. Sister Delilah and I will be back with your clothes and water."

She leaves me alone in the washroom as I open the bag. I could squeal when I find a toothbrush and small jar of toothpaste. After I brush my teeth, I use the hair brush to untangle my ends.

Sister Evelyn returns with my clothes, shoes, and a towel. "Go ahead and get undressed. The first pot is almost ready. It's cooling to a comfortable temperature now."

Once again she disappears before I take the soap and shampoo from the bag, placing them next to the tub. As I take off my dress, I can feel the rush of Zebadiah's fingers pushing up my petticoat. I hold back a sob at the odd mix of arousal and heartbreak that consumes me. There's a secret part of me that is selfishly grateful I was able to experience what it's like to lay with someone I love. I wonder when my conscience became so jumbled.

I climb into the tub when Sister Delilah comes in with the hot pot of water. Being careful to hide my fresh cleansing wound, I press my arm close to my side and adjust myself comfortably. She pours the water over my head, the warmth gushing across my skin, making my body hum in relief. The liquid stings against the star burn on my arm, and though it hurts, knowing it's being cleaned helps me ignore it. Saying nothing, she leaves, returning moments later with the next pot. I lather up my hair and body, reveling in the feeling of being clean.

My stomach is full, my skin is clean, and my clothes are fresh when I leave the placing dorms. I pass the schoolhouse, making my way to the tabernacle to talk to Zeb. Climbing the steps, I reach for the handle as the door swings open, putting me face to face with my sister.

She gives me a forced smile and closes the door behind her. "Sister, how convenient. I've been wanting to speak with you." Stepping down the stairs, she gestures ahead of us. "Would you take a walk with me?"

My ears heat up, and my stomach tightens. If I wasn't avoiding her before, I surely am now. The last thing I want to do is be alone with her with the inevitability of Zebadiah being mentioned.

"I apologize, but I must meet with the Prophet about time sensitive matters."

She nods, her bonnet casting a shadow over her eyes. "Certainly. I shall wait until you're finished."

I swallow and nod. "Yes, of course."

Rushing inside the tabernacle, I'm desperate to get free from her gaze. Closing the door behind me, I let out a breath and a prayer that this guilt will wane over time.

"Laurel Ann! What are you doing back here?" I turn

around to see Zebadiah marching over to me. "We can't be alone together. Mia knows, or at least she suspects something."

My body sways at his words. "What? What did she say?"

"Nothing, she just knows I wasn't where I said I was last night. We mustn't be seen together."

While he may be right, his crassness has me crossing my arms. "Then you'll be pleased with what I have come to tell you." His hands slide into his pockets as he quirks an eyebrow in curiosity. "I want to be placed with Benji Johnson."

His face and shoulders fall before a glare crosses his expression. "What is this, Laur?"

"This is me figuring out my place here. My place is with Benji."

"You can't be serious. You would rather be bound to Benji Johnson than me?"

His furious expression mixed with his woeful eyes breaks my heart so deep I yearn to clutch my chest. I don't know how to explain feelings that I can't make sense of myself.

"I'm sorry."

He scoffs and looks at me as if waiting for me to take it back. His features become hardened to the point there is no emotion in them at all.

"Fine. If that's what you wish. I will announce your binding by the end of the week."

Without another word he turns around, walking toward the back of the tabernacle. Tears fall down my cheeks, and I wipe them away because they will fix nothing.

My feet move slowly, knowing Mia is waiting for me outside. I have to eliminate any question she has about me and Zeb. It's over now. Nothing would come of her knowing.

I push open the tabernacle door, and there she stands with a sweet smile on her face. "Is everything in order?"

I nod as I walk down the steps. "Yes, thank you."

She loops her arm through mine, leading me from the tabernacle "I thought it would be nice to converse away from inquisitive ears and eyes." In all the times I fantasized about coming back here, I never dreamed I would be this uncomfortable around her. I can't think of anything to talk about, so I'm grateful when she picks up the conversation. "How bad was it?" she whispers, "The dark, new world?"

I sigh, debating whether to tell her anything. While being friends with a Philistine isn't specified as a sin, it's definitely not something seen to be acceptable.

"It wasn't how I thought it would be. There is evil, but Philistines are all very different. They're all sinners of course, yet some of them never did anything besides be kind to me." Her eyebrow raises in question, though she doesn't voice it. "I became very close to one in particular. Her name is Kaila. She's very…" I laugh remembering all the times she had to 'make an entrance' or how it was nearly impossible to be in a bad mood around her. "Vibrant. Because of her, life became bearable. Even good, sometimes."

She blinks in shock at my words. "You truly care for one of them?" There's judgment there, but it's apparent she's attempting to hide it. In return, I keep my retort to myself. Lightly squeezing my arm, she says, "I'm pleased you were able to find comfort there."

We don't seem to be going in any specific direction when we come up on Job Talbott's place. They do all printing of *The True Testament*, hymnals, school books, and other spiritual text. There are cute little lambs running around in a pen, and I reach down to pet them.

They bleat and all come to me, seeing if I have anything tasty to give them. "I'm sorry, babes, I don't have anything."

"Laurel Ann." Her tone requires me to look at her, and there are tears in her eyes. My skin gets clammy as the sun beats down on me. She's going to confront me about Zeb, I just know it. "Many years ago, you trusted me with an important secret. I didn't keep that secret, and because of my betrayal, you suffered a life without Zaaron, your family, and… Zebadiah. I want you to know I live with the fault of that."

I'm not sure where she's going with this. My tongue rolls around in my mouth as I try to speak. "You did what you knew was obeying spiritual law. There is nothing for you to feel guilty about." There is a part of me that truly believes what I'm saying, however, the part that's been tainted by the outside world is grateful she had to endure some suffering for her actions. "And as for the Prophet, he and I are both grown. We were close a lifetime ago, but we're different people now."

For a split second her eyes darken before she drops her shoulders and sighs, looking toward the Talbott house. Four of Job Talbott's wives come out of the print shop carrying cases of freshly printed books to load into the wagon.

"I understand your hesitancy to be honest with me." My burning face along with the thumping in my chest is about to force the truth from my lips. "You have no reason to trust me. I just knew when I found out you had returned, I had to tell you my secret." Her bonnet strings blow across her neck as she silently cries. Her tears make me nervous, and unsure that I want to know this secret. "And you can do with it whatever you wish."

"Mia, you really don't need to tell me anything."

She nods and takes in air with a shaky breath. "I do." Gripping the sheep's pen, she watches the Talbott women. "I am in love with someone, and it is not the Prophet." Her voice cracks on the statement, and my mouth falls open, but I quickly close it. "I've loved her before I knew what love was."

I follow her gaze. She's not watching the Talbott wives, she's watching one in particular. Squinting my eyes, I realize it's a grown-up Kelsey Garrett, Dawn's little sister.

I do my best to conceal my shock because her telling me this is paramount. Somehow, it relieves some of my guilt about Zebadiah.

"Mia…"

She turns to look at me, her face twisted in disgust. "I know it's repulsive, and you have every right to inform the Prophet of my perversions." I want to tell her I understand. I know better than anyone that love isn't always a choice, but doing so would expose my true feelings toward her husband. "I don't know why the Devil tainted me with this sickness. I don't want to feel this way. Zaaron blessed me with the holiest husband on the compound, yet my desire for her only festers. Please understand, it was never intentional. It just happened." My ears burn with muted anger because she's right. She has everything I've ever wanted and she takes it for granted. When I open my mouth to respond, every word that rises up feels selfish. We stand in silence, watching the sheep when she suddenly says, "Do you remember Serah Johnson? Brother Benji's younger sister?"

She was the third to Kelsey and Mia when they were children. When you saw one, you usually saw the other two.

"Yes," I respond, realizing I haven't seen Serah since being back. Mia's tone and expression make a heaviness drop in my belly.

"A few years after you left, things changed with Serah overnight. She stopped talking to us and ignored everyone. Kelsey and I tried so many times to play with her, but eventually we gave up, figuring she would come to us if she ever wanted to be friends again." She licks her lips and looks back at Kelsey. "Then one day, she was just…gone. She hung herself from the rafters in her barn."

"What?!" I don't know why it bothers me that Benji didn't

tell me. It's not as if it's something that normally comes up in conversation. "Why?"

Mia lets out an instable breath and pushes her bonnet off her head. "I don't know. We never will, either, because for some reason, she didn't trust us. We weren't allowed to mourn her, publicly. Everyone acted as if she was never here, never existed. Kelsey and I were both in pain, and all we had were each other. Our friendship became deeper, and over the years I began feeling things for her...romantic things. It's not gone past kissing, but that is more than enough. I begged Zaaron to take my love for her away. Maybe his refusal to do so is my penance. When I was bound to Zebadiah, I put an end to it." She can barely keep her gaze off Kelsey. Sighing, she says, "Looking at her, watching her every day and not be able to touch her is so much to bear." Wiping her tears, she stands straighter. "I wanted you to know that I'm also unable to be where my heart wants me to be, and I have known loss."

"Mia, I'm terribly sorry. I never wished you any suffering."

When I meet her stare, her eyes narrow, and I have no doubt she knows about me and Zeb. "You have a choice to make. Whether you confess it to me or not, I'm aware there's something between you and my husband."

My body sways, and it's as if every drop of blood has evaporated from my veins. My sins feel greater since coming home then they ever were on the outside, yet here I am continuing in my deception.

"I don't know what you think, but I am to be the wife of Benji Johnson." Surprise flashes across her face. "Your husband is nothing more than my Prophet."

Her face hardens, and she gives one last look toward Kelsey before turning back to the common ground.

"Lie to me if you wish, but he is *my* husband. Do not humiliate me, sister."

27

BENJI JOHNSON'S BRIDE

Laurel Ann

THE NEWS OF MINE AND BENJI'S BINDING SPREADS THROUGH the Anointed Land like wildfire. It's all anyone has spoken of to me for the last two days. Considering recent developments, Zebadiah makes the rational choice of assigning me to work with the Johnson family where I'll eventually learn how to make all the hygiene products used in the compound. I spent the day yesterday in the greenhouse with Benji's sisters learning about the plants and their uses, though little to none of it was retained.

Zeb and I have kept our distance from each other. When he does look at me, I can hardly bear it. There have been moments in the last few days where I've questioned this decision. What more do I want from him? He's done nothing wrong. It's simply easier on my heart to be with a kind man that I don't love than only have part of the man that I do. Maybe I would feel differently had I never left, I do not know. I just know how I feel, now. My jealousy would fester, and I fear I would grow to resent him for choices that weren't even his. That would be no life for any of us.

While my discussion with Mia did alleviate some of my guilt, it doesn't affect my choice on the matter. I take a deep breath, because I can't be seen crying on my binding day. The process of preparation has not been altered since the last time I was bound. The biggest difference is this time I'm not terrified. This time it is my choice.

I wait in the bride room, enjoying being alone as I spin around in my beautiful binding gown. Since I am to be the first wife there are no children or sister-wives with me this time.

My attention is whipped to the door at the sound of it being opened. Ezekiel stands on the threshold, motioning for me to follow him.

"It's time to present yourself."

I take a deep breath, pick up my bridal skirts, and step into the foyer. Hundreds of eyes are on me when I enter the meeting hall. I keep my head held high, finding Benji in a front pew, grinning. I don't take my eyes off of him. Not only for appearances, but also because there's no way I can do this and look at Zeb.

Benji smiles at me as I take my place next to him. "Hello, bride," he whispers.

"Hello, groom."

I don't think I'm imagining Zebadiah's sermon being aimed toward me. He talks about selfishness and greed. About being thankful for the things we are blessed with instead of dwelling on things we are without. It doesn't help that our eyes meet on multiple occasions while he projects across the meeting hall, making my heart stop each time. I wonder how long it will hurt like this. The tears rim my eyes no matter how hard I push them back.

At the end of the sermon he invites everyone to mine and

Benji's binding, instructing them to take a candle on the way out.

Soon the meeting hall is empty other than me, Benji, and Zeb. Benji takes my hand as we turn to our Prophet. Glowering down at us, he makes his way across the stage.

"You two really want to go through with this?"

I squeeze Benji's hand as he says, "Of course, Prophet."

"Yes, Prophet," I respond.

"Fine." He brushes past us, and we turn to follow. "Let's get this over with."

"Yes, lets," Benji says, pulling me behind him. "I can't wait to see under this dress."

He's trying to rile Zeb up, and it's working because Zeb gets more tense with every step. I lightly smack Benji's arm to get him to stop taunting him. I'm not doing this to hurt Zebadiah.

We follow him to the common ground where the followers are waiting in their circles, breaking their clasped hands only to allow us through. The binding pyre is already lit, and as Zeb blesses the flames, he spits out the words like they taste bad on his tongue.

Benji and I begin lighting the first circle before they turn to ignite the candles in the next ring, creating the five circles of fire around us.

Benji ties the ribbon around my wrist, and I around his, vowing our false promises to each other. When he slips on my binding bracelet and Zeb announces us officially husband and wife, the cheers burst around us like Philistine fireworks.

I'm surprised I feel nothing. No fear, no happiness. I am simply going through the motions to survive in this life.

"Are you still happy with your choice, Laurel Ann Johnson?" Benji asks as he glances at our bound wrists.

"I am. Are you, husband?"

He smiles. "There is no other woman on this compound I'd rather be bound to."

The music plays around us while he leads me to the middle of the followers to dance. And dance we do. I've never been much of a dancer, even as a child, but Benji has me jumping around and laughing in no time. He spins me in a circle to see a grinning Samuel. I haven't had the chance to talk about this with him. However, Benji said he was on board, and from the look on his face, he's more than thrilled. He hugs me tight before brushing his fingers over Benji's hand.

Unable to wipe the smile off his face, he signs, *I'm not sure why you did this. Just know it means everything to me.*

You're welcome in our home anytime, brother.

His cheeks pink because he knows what I'm implying. He pats Benji's shoulder, quickly running his fingers across his neck, making Benji grin. *Congratulations on your beautiful bride, Brother Benji.*

"Thank you, Brother Samuel."

Sammy backs away with a wink as the smells from the food hit my nose, making me realize how hungry I am.

We eat and laugh with my old classmates, and even though I've tried to ignore my thoughts of Zebadiah, I find myself searching for him throughout the evening. He stays as far away from us as possible while still participating in the celebration.

It's grown late into the night, and we both know we must make our leave to our binding bed. We haven't had much time to talk the last couple of days and not at all about how we are going to spend our binding night. As I was saying my vows, the fact that children are going to be expected slid into my thoughts and has stayed there all evening.

Leaning over to his ear, I whisper, "I think it's time we announce our leave."

I'm certain his face pales a shade with his nod. "Of course." He stands and speaks loud enough to be heard across the common ground. "Brothers and Sisters, thank you for your kindness toward me and my bride on this joyous night. Please enjoy yourselves as we retire for the evening."

My attention is on Zebadiah with the clapping and rejoicing sounding in my ears. He doesn't do either. He doesn't smile or nod. He just watches my new husband lead me to our home as flowers are thrown around us.

The walk to our house is a short one which we spend on meaningless conversation, recounting the evening's events. Once we approach the old farmhouse however, our mouths fall silent. I follow him up the steps and inside the house where he lights a lamp.

Ruffling his hair, he lets out an awkward chuckle and asks, "Are you tired? Do you want to go to bed?"

"We need to talk, Benji."

He gives me an unamused expression. "Really, woman? We've been bound five minutes and I'm already in trouble?"

I wish I could joke about this, but this is something we really need to figure out. "Take me to our room."

His Adam's apple bobs as we walk to the back of the house and into a hallway. Opening the second door we come to, he places the lantern on the tallboy and stuffs his hands in his pockets. I turn my back to him, lifting the rogue curls off my neck that fell down when I was dancing.

"Will you help me with my buttons?" A moment later, I feel his fingers fumbling with my dress. "We have to talk about it, Benji. While I want you to be able to be with Sammy, people will eventually question why we haven't conceived. I hear what the followers whisper about Zeb and his wives not yet having children."

My binding gown loosens as he sighs. "I know. You're

already doing so much for us. I want to do this for you…if this is what you want."

I nod. "It is."

I'm not sure why I'm lying to him. Pushing off my dress, I let it fall to the floor. When he doesn't move to touch me, I remove my bodice petticoat, baring my breasts to him. I have no idea what I'm doing. Zeb was the one who led things. Taking a big breath, I lower my bloomers, revealing my naked body to my brother's lover, my cousin, and one of my oldest friends. I take slow steps toward him. He looks at me as if I'm about to inflict pain upon him. I reach my hand over his trousers, and feel embarrassed at his lack of arousal. Not wanting to keep eye contact any longer, I focus on unfastening his pants. I lower his long johns enough to release his flaccid cock.

I have no idea how to instill desire in a man that has none. I remember watching him with Samuel in the forest, and I fall to my knees. Wrapping my hand around his base, I open my mouth and lick the tip before inhaling through my nose and putting my lips around the head. Mimicking what I saw him do to my brother, I take him into my mouth, slowly sucking along the way. He quickly hardens against my tongue as a tear falls down my cheek. I feel like I'm betraying Zeb and Samuel. I don't understand how I can feel more guilt being with my husband than I did committing adultery.

He places a hand against my head and thrusts between my lips. This is my duty. I've done a lot of things that defy Zaaron, and this is my penance. Letting a choked moan out from his lips, he grows larger in my mouth. If I bring him to completion this way, then this would have been for nothing. I look up to see he has an arm draped across his eyes. Humiliation makes my ears burn, but I take it in stride as I stand.

I lie on the bed, opening my legs for him. A moment later, he climbs on top of me, and his now hard cock is heavy against my clit. I watch him reach down and attempt to wet the tip with my entrance, eventually opting to lick his hand to lubricate my hole. I thought I could be okay with this.

I'm not.

This feels grimy and wrong. The tip of his cock begins to open me as a sob frees itself from my lips, and the tears break through my lashes.

His eyes shift up to mine. "Oh, Laur." Rolling off of me, he lies on his stomach, resting his head on his crossed arms. "Why are you pushing this? It's clearly not what you want."

Self-conscious about my tears, I wipe them from my face. "I don't understand why I can't accept Zaaron's plan for me. All I can think about is wanting to be with Zebadiah."

He laughs. "I've said that exact same thing so many times." He scrunches his nose and adds, "Except not about Zeb."

I laugh despite being more confused than before. I lean over, kissing his cheek. "Thank you for being such a wonderful husband."

My eyelids are heavy, and still, I can't sleep. Benji, however, is having no problems as he snores next to me. Pushing off the quilt, I slip out of bed. Everyone will long be asleep by now. I button up my bodice petticoat and take the sheer housecoat off the back of the door. I decide against bringing the lantern because it will make me more easily spotted.

I leave my new home quietly, and it's not long until I'm coming upon the common ground where the evidence of our binding celebration is still apparent.

I need some real answers because every decision I've made since stepping foot in the Anointed Land has been the wrong one. I push the large door open as I slide inside the tabernacle. I need to pray alone, and this is where I feel closest to Zaaron.

The meeting hall is dark besides the moonlight shining across the pews. I head for the altar when I see a figure move and hear feverish murmuring.

"Why bring her back to me only to rip her away again?" Zebadiah's angry voice booms in the previously silent meeting hall, making me jump as I slowly climb the steps to the stage. "I don't understand! Talk to me, goddammit!" He slams his fists against the sanctorum before swiping his arms across it with a growl, sending ritual implements clattering to the wooden floor by my feet.

"Prophet?" I whisper.

He whips around to face me, staring at me as his features darken in the moonlight. He moves across the stage so fast, he's suddenly standing in front of me. His cheeks are wet, and his chest is heaving. I've never seen him like this. My heart breaks at the knowledge that he's in pain because of my choice. I reach out, touching his face, and he leans into my hand. Suddenly, he grabs my wrist, yanking me against him. He slams his mouth hard against mine and our teeth clash. He kisses me as if he's desperate for breath. My back arches while he fists my hair and pulls my head back.

"What are you doing here?" he growls.

If he were anyone else I would be frightened by the look in his eyes. "I need guidance."

He forces my housecoat off my shoulders, pressing his forehead to mine. "Then let me guide you." The light fabric falls to the floor, and he grips my waist to pick me up. I wrap my legs around him, dizzy in the moment. Our lips collide, and he lowers us to the floor. He lays me on my back while he remains on his knees, staring down at me. The throbbing between my legs drives me mad when he pulls off his suspenders and rips off his shirt. Shoving my petticoat up my torso, he lifts my arms to pull the clothing over my head, his sigil pendant trailing across my chest. With shocking force, he grabs my wrist and yanks off my binding bracelet, tossing it clattering to the floor. He's violent with his kisses. His lips trail their way down my arms to my chest. His hot tongue laps at my nipple as my wrists fight in his grasp. His forcefulness and desire have me arching against his mouth.

"Nothing happened between you and Benji after your binding," he states it in a lazy way, in between licks.

I stop breathing, and my body stills. I never imagined confessing what transpired between us with anyone, least of all with Zebadiah.

He slowly lifts his head, and it feels like he's looking into my mind, seeing what I've done. His jaw ticks as his body trembles above me.

"We didn't consummate," I choke.

His eyebrows relax ever so slightly though his words come out slowly. "What *did* you do?" I can't bear to speak it aloud. It's perverse, and he will surely be disgusted with me. "Tell me."

I try to calm myself because he technically did the same thing to me at the creek when he kissed me between my thighs. "I...I t-took him in my mouth."

He flies backward, jumping to his feet as if desperate to get away from me. I have the urge to cover my body due to the fury emanating from him. He paces the floor, tugging at his hair. Sitting up, I try to explain, but my attention is at his hands jerking open his pants and pushing them down his hips.

"Get on your knees." There's something hidden in his voice that somehow forces me to obey. He touches his swollen cock with violent strokes, and I can't take my eyes off the action. "Did you swallow his seed?"

I shake my head, immensely grateful I can give him this answer. "No."

"Open your mouth, and show me what you did." I lean forward, a thick vein beneath my lips. I kiss the side of his shaft, and he combs my hair with his fingers. Some Philistine men leave the skin that they were born with around their manhood, but not men in the Anointed Land. It states in *The True Testament* that every boy must have the excess flesh removed at their Anointing ceremony as it inhibits reproduction. Because of that, I can see the smooth tip of his head where wetness is seeping from. I have the intense desire to lick it. Brushing my tongue over the hole, I taste the slightly salty liquid before once again kissing his pulsing flesh.

Unlike Benji, Zeb is solid against my lips. I suck the soft tip into my mouth, and open as wide as I can, wanting more than anything to be what he needs me to be in this moment. I fear I will choke, but I continue until I can't take an inch more.

"Fuck," he groans. His breathing picks up, and he grips the side of my face, bucking his hips and making me gag. "I am a direct descendant of Zaaron!" he bellows. "His blood burns through my veins!" He says it like he thinks I don't believe it. Tears stream down my face as I dig my nails into his thighs. Still, I force myself to keep going. In this moment, my only desire is to please him. "Take my holy come in your belly, and be grateful, for this is the closest you will come to sucking the cock of God."

His blasphemous words shock me, and they don't really sound like something Zeb would say. I debate pulling away to ask him what's going on when thick, warm liquid squirts down my throat. He groans, squeezing my head tighter, and his body jolts with the last of his orgasm. I swallow all that I can. It's odd how it warms me to have these pieces of him inside me.

There's clearly more than my binding bothering him. His grip releases my face as he softly runs his thumb over my lips, smearing his come across them.

When I'm with him this way, I don't feel like myself. I become another person, in another life, one that's free to love. I know this is a sin, but...

I want to sin with him.

Wiping his brow, he nods behind him. "Sit on the altar." The altar? What has gotten into him? His temperament makes my mind unsure, yet my body is on fire, starving for his touch. I scramble to my feet and obey. "Spread your legs as wide as you can."

I climb up on the sanctorum with my heart, mind, body, and soul at war.

I love him.

This is wrong.

I want him.

This is evil.

The clanking of metal sounds loud in the meeting hall as he gathers the ritual implements off the floor. Pushing my butt to the edge, I open my legs for him and dig my heels into the corners of the sanctorum.

I am about to ask him what he's doing when he kneels, as if praying to me, sucking my hardened clit into his mouth. I throw my head back and gasp. My moans are jarring in the otherwise quiet room. His tongue has me writhing against his mouth and the altar.

"Stop moving," he mutters before he spreads me open with his fingers. Something cold slides into my body causing air to rush into my lungs at the intrusion. I look down to see what he's doing to me. His tongue licks me along my entrance, and my eyes widen when I realize what's happening. Slowly, he slides the long, pointed end of the brass Anointed sigil in and out of my body.

"Prophet!" I pull away instantly, though not far enough to get it out of me. The sanctorum altar is bad enough, but to desecrate our holy symbol? What is he thinking? "What are you doing?!"

He doesn't stop. He continues slowly fucking me with the sacred instrument. "Making Him talk to me."

"What?" I breathe.

Does he mean Zaaron?

He stands, leaving the sigil inside me as he kisses me and holds up a jar of blessed oil. His movements are almost jagged when he dips his fingers inside.

"My father took your innocence, your *husband* took your mouth, now I...I'm going to take your ass." He reaches between us and rubs the oil over my tightened hole. While there's a tinge of fear, the idea of him claiming that sacred part of me has my body screaming for it. "I need answers. From you and from Him."

I can't seem to inhale properly as I watch him pump his fist over his erection. Continuing to fuck me with the sigil, he uses his other hand to push himself into a place that has never been touched. Even with hot pain splitting through my body and my screams at the intrusion, I won't ask him to stop. I don't know what he means about Zaaron, and I don't know what I haven't answered for him, I just know I'm going to be what he needs me to be in this moment.

Hot tears flow down my face with my sob as my hands grab onto his solid arms. He presses his cheek against mine, shushing me. "Shhhh, listen to my voice." I take in air through my nose, and my body loosens, alleviating some of the pain. It's still very uncomfortable, but the agony has become much more bearable. The sigil rubs against my clit, and the feeling that I'm about to burst takes over my body again. The marriage of pleasure and pain has me clawing at his back, his old soul cleansing scars raised beneath my fingers. I can't stop the sounds of arousal coming from my lips, and I hold him tighter. More tears roll down my cheeks as pleasure overtakes my body, shredding me beneath him. He thrusts into me in a steady movement, a small smile lifting his lips. "Just tell me this: do you love me, Laur?"

I hate that he has to ask, though with the way this has all gone, I can't blame him for his uncertainty. I steady my breathing after a shock of pain. Reaching for the back of his neck, I put my lips next to his ear. "I've always loved you, Zebadiah Fitch."

His tempo increases, and he leans back, reaching across the altar. The blade of the ceremonial knife glistens in front of my face while he turns it. "You said you didn't consummate your binding with Benji. Did you take one another's blood?"

I want to shake my head because I know what he's thinking. We cannot do this. This is more sacred than intercourse. This is what finalizes spouses being able to be together in the Paradise Star. If we do this without being bound, we may as well rebuke it all.

"No, but Prophet, tell me you aren't suggesting we take each other's blood."

His lip twitches when he draws the blade across his torso; his blood appears black as it drips over the sharp muscles of his abdomen.

"Why not?! I'm the fucking Prophet, and Zaaron refuses to speak to me! I can't hear Him. He has left me to lead this compound, blind and deaf. If He won't guide me, then I must guide myself." He grinds his teeth, and I fear he's going to break down. "If it's too late to have you in this life, then I have to do everything in my power to have you in the next." He presses the palms of his hands against his eyes, still holding the blade. My heart pounds at his words. "I did...sinful things before I became Prophet. They were done to evil men, yet done nonetheless." He drops his hands, and when he looks at me, I see the boy who gave me flowers because he thought they'd look pretty in my hair. "Is this my penance?"

I feel like I've lost him so many times. I don't know if he's right or if we're damning ourselves, but I do know, wherever we go, I want it to be together.

Pressing against his chest, I push him out of me and remove the sigil to slide to my knees. Grabbing his hips, I touch my tongue to the dripping blood and lick up his stomach, feeling his muscles flex at the action. When my lips find the wound, I suck as much of the metallic tasting liquid that I can before kissing his cut.

With the hand not holding the blade, he wraps his arm around my waist and lifts me up until I'm on my tiptoes and our noses are nearly touching.

"I love you, too," he whispers. A whimper falls from my lips as he rips the knife across the top of my breast. "Not even in death will we part."

28

THE HOLY PHILISTINE

Zebadiah

I BRUSH MY FINGERS THROUGH HER SOFT HAIR AS SHE LAYS HER head on my chest and plays with my sigil pendant. "Can I ask you a question?"

"Anything."

I hold her tighter because I know we don't have much time until she'll need to leave. The lamp lays on the bedside table in the holding room, casting shadows across my chest where she traces with her finger.

"You think Zaaron won't speak to you because of something you did, right? Will you tell me what it was?"

This is something I planned to tell her eventually. In my mind, she would understand because she loves Benji and had personally suffered at the hands of my father. But now, with my confession on my lips, I fear that after everything this could be what really makes me lose her. I swallow and hold her hand on my chest as if it will help her understand why I did what I did.

"A few years after you left, I found Benji's father sodomizing him with the handle of a pitchfork."

She grips my chest and pushes herself up to face me. Her mouth is turned down in disgust, her eyes holding heartbreak and confusion.

Shaking her head, she chokes, "Why?"

"He caught him in a situation with a man…a sexual situation."

"Was it Sammy?"

I've often wondered the same thing. I rub my hand down her arm because I don't know if she'll accept my comfort by the end of this story. "I don't know. It's definitely a possibility. Benji would never name him though." She nods, and I continue, "He was in a bad way. He bled for a long time, and Zeke and I had to look after him for days." It's been a while since I've confronted this, and I've never repeated the story aloud. My emotions stir in my chest, and I'm surprised that after all this time, I'm getting choked up. "I found out later that Brother Jameson had tried to force Benji and his little sister Serah to have sexual intercourse in an attempt to purge his unnatural desires. When he couldn't perform, Brother Jameson resorted to the pitchfork."

She covers her mouth and sits next to me, hugging her knees. "Is that why Serah hung herself?"

Pushing myself up to sit next to her, I wrap my arm around her. I'm surprised she's heard about that, considering speaking her name is forbidden. "You know about Serah?"

She's suddenly seems nervous as she chews her lip and nods. "Mia told me."

I definitely want to push this conversation and find out more of what they talked about, but we're running out of time, and now that I've started, I want her to hear my confession.

"I knew she was struggling, and I still said nothing. I had promised Benji I wouldn't tell anyone what happened, and I didn't know what the result would be if I did. Maybe if I had, Serah wouldn't have thought dying was her only escape. She wasn't even able to be properly buried, and now she'll spend her eternity in the pit."

"Zeb, you can't carry that blame, and I don't believe Zaaron would keep His voice from you for that."

I give her a smile and caress her cheek. I wish keeping a secret was my only transgression. "That's not the end of the story. I confronted Brother Jameson." I've never muttered these words to anyone other than Zaaron, and they feel as heavy as a rock coming up my throat. "And I…I killed him." Her eyes widen, and she leans slowly forward. Her chest heaves, so I take her hand. Surprisingly, she squeezes back. "I really didn't mean to. It was never my plan. It just sort of… happened."

As she sits quietly, I allow her to ponder her thoughts. I don't release a breath until she looks at me and whispers, "Maybe that was Zaaron's answer. What if He *is* speaking to you, Zeb? You expected to hear Him audibly, but what if that's not how it works? I felt Him the night of the gathering. He was with me, yet He never spoke to me with words."

I had expected it to be clear, unquestionable, though I can't help wondering if she's right. If that's the case, then my blasphemy last night may have done nothing other than anger Him. I just wanted to push Him so He had to speak to me.

I feel like a child beneath the age of understanding. When a child younger than six breaks spiritual law, they are shunned. Nobody speaks or acknowledges them for however long their punishment ensues. It was a terrifying experience, and that's how this has felt.

"There's more." She swallows and sits up straighter, preparing herself. "I lied to you about my father." She tilts her head in confusion, and I can't believe she's still here with me. I lean forward to kiss her freckles. "Six months ago, I helped

Zeke kill him." At this point, I think it's best to just tear the scab off. Her mouth falls agape, but she doesn't pull away from me. "What if that's why? I ripped the Prophet from his position and stole the spiritual crown."

She tilts her lips in sorrow as she combs my hair back. "I'll admit feeling no loss for Hiram. I know the kind of man your father was, and I'm sure you had your reasons." She climbs onto my lap, wrapping her soft arms around my neck. "I don't know why you aren't hearing Him, but I know you, Zebadiah Fitch. You would never do such things for personal gain or selfish desires. That's not the man you are. Thank you for trusting me."

There's a lightness in my chest that hasn't been present since I became Prophet. Telling Laurel Ann about Zaaron's silence has dislodged a tightness in my throat, and divulging my darkest secrets has me in high spirits. I'm more confused than ever, yet I feel stronger. With her by my side, even in secret, she will give me the strength I'm not getting from my God. She won't turn away from me again. She may have gone through with her sham of a binding, but she gave her soul to me.

I suppose if she must be bound to someone else, Benji is the best option by far. She won't touch him again, that much she promised. I wish I could vow to do the same with my wives. I can't keep spending my evenings here 'praying', and Marybeth is getting angry with me for clearly avoiding to continue our conversation.

Laurel Ann left about an hour ago to go back to Benji, and I need to clean up the mess on the stage before Mia arrives. After I pull on my clothes and make the bed in the last holding room, I walk into the meeting hall, bright with the early morning sun.

The chalice and pestle are on the floor behind the pulpit, and I find the mortar on my way to the altar. Candles are everywhere while the incense censor is open at my feet. The black cloth across the altar is haphazard, so I lift it to straighten it when I see a come stain right in the middle. The sight evokes flashes of the previous night, and my cock twitches at the memory of her body.

Shit. If I'm seen washing it, it will appear suspicious, and even if I'm not, there's no way to get it cleaned and dry before Mia gets here.

I rip it off to flip it over when I notice something on the floor beneath the sanctorum. It's odd because all of the ritual objects are accounted for. I crouch down, wrapping my hands around an oak box. A silver lock on the front keeps me from opening it. When I look beneath the altar, a trap door is hanging open from the bottom.

Tracing my fingers over the carved designs in the wood, I can't help but hope this is a message from Zaaron. I suddenly remember the key I found in the desk the first time I went through the tabernacle office after my father's death.

Maybe I did get Zaaron's attention last night.

I hurry to finish setting up the sanctorum, and as I cross the stage to my office, Mia's voice sounds behind me.

"Zebadiah." Turning to her, I get nervous at her panicky expression. Her bonnet hangs around her neck, strands of hair sticking all over the place. She's out of breath as if she's been running. "There's a Philistine at the gates...he's asking for Hiram."

My stomach drops to the floor of the stage, my mind exploding with questions as to what this man's intentions are.

"Thank you, Mia. Let me get my jacket, and I will meet

him." She wrings her hands and nods.

Rushing to hide the wooden box, I hurry to my office to place it in the bottom drawer of my desk. I pull my jacket off the back of the chair and grab my hat off the chest. My heartbeat is like a drum in my ears as I hurry back to Mia.

"Did he say why he needed him?"

She shakes her head as she tries to keep up with me. "No, he just announced that he was here to speak to Hiram. Brother Joe left him at the gate and came to the ranch to tell you." There's slight spite in her voice, and I know it's from my failure to come home again last night.

"Very well. I want you to go back to the ranch, staying there until I fetch you. Go get Marybeth out of school, and bring her with you."

She grabs my hand as we walk into the foyer. "Are we in danger?"

I've lied so much to her. The truth is, if my heart hadn't been given to Laurel Ann, I may have grown to love her. She's a kind and beautiful woman, and even knowing I will never be able to stay away from Laur, I still hate what I'm doing to her.

Brushing my hand over her cheek, I'm as honest as I can be. "I truly don't know, but it's a definite possibility. Now, go get Marybeth."

We leave the tabernacle, and she picks up her skirt to run to the school house. As I make my way to the gates, the sound of horse's feet behind me has me turning. Benji Johnson rides beside me in his buggy, his delivery for the general store clanging around in back.

"I would say blessed morning, Prophet, though from the look on your face, I'm assuming it's not."

I look up at his lopsided grin. His buggy will get us there quickly, and he's always been way too taken by Philistines. Meeting one in the flesh will surely cure his curiosities.

"Take me to the gates, and you can see for yourself."

"Uh...of course. Get in."

I climb in next to him as he jerks on the rein, and in a couple short minutes, we arrive at the gates. The man waiting looks younger than I am. By his stance, he doesn't appear threatening, but Philistines have many tricks. He's wearing blue jean pants and a short-sleeved shirt with his hands in his pockets.

I step out of the buggy to prepare my interrogation when Benji gasps behind me. "Shayne?"

My head whips around to him. "You know this man?" Benji ignores my question and looks away, giving me my answer. I growl under my breath. I'll deal with him later.

Walking up to the entrance, I look at the man through the wire of the gates. "It appears your name is Shayne?"

His brown hair flops around with his nod. "Yes, sir. I'm here to speak with Hiram Fitch."

I slide my hands in my pockets wondering how this boy could possibly know my father. "So I've heard. I'm saddened to inform you that Hiram has passed on. Now, I must ask you to leave here and not return."

His face crumples as if I crushed him. "He's...dead?"

Curiosity is creeping up my spine. The devastation in his demeanor suggests they were close. I don't deal with Philistines unless it's absolutely necessary for the good of the Anointed Land, yet I find myself asking, "May I inquire as to what your business was with my father?"

His gaze shifts up to my face, staring at me in an unsettling way. "Y-you're his son?"

"Yes, though I did not inherit whatever agreement you two may have had."

He clutches the gate. "No, you don't understand. He was...you're my brother."

The oxygen evaporates from my lungs, and my chest feels as if it's been punched by a fist. What he's saying is impossible. This has to be a scheme. "I don't know what you're trying to get from us because that's absurd. I'm well aware of all my siblings."

He laughs, "Sorry man, but you're not. My mother isn't from...here." He waves his hand gesturing behind me toward the compound. "We live in Hobart."

My mind tilts, and I become dizzy with what he's saying. I shake my head and rub my temples. "Excuse my hesitancy to believe you. My father would barely speak to a Philistine let alone lay with one."

His face falls as he swallows and reaches in his back pocket, slipping a folded-up paper through the gate. Taking the paper, I open it, making my knees turn to slush.

It's a photo of my father with his arm around a very young woman swollen with child.

"I never met him. He gave this to my mother before I was born."

Slowly I straighten the paper, my eyes burning with tears.

Shayne,

You will never know me while you are a child. I am a powerful man, and knowledge of your existence could destroy everything my forefathers have built. Just know that you are my son, and my holy blood runs through you. When you become a man, find me.

Your mother will tell you where, and by then, I will have a way to welcome you into the fold. You are a Fitch, and you have a calling. I will pray every night that when the day comes, you will honor it.

Your holy father,

Hiram Fitch

This was written with a quill and ink in what is clearly my father's penmanship. Crumpling the photo and letter into a ball, I throw it over the fence. "You have no calling and no place here. Apparently, that died with my father. Do not ever return to this compound." I want to fall to my knees and scream. I want to curse my father and Zaaron. I feel like they have both lied and betrayed me.

I march to Benji standing by his buggy. "Do you mind explaining to me how you know that man?"

Licking his lips, he swallows before straightening his shoulders. "I met him as he was sneaking around the edge of the compound. He was trying to see inside and asked me about Hiram. He was a lot younger then...it was about four years ago. I liked him, he was curious, and I can relate to that. We made a deal. I would tell him about life here, and he would...uh, tell me stuff about life out there."

I could reach out and choke him. He could have endangered us all. "You will receive punishment for this. I should think it goes without saying that you are never to talk to him or any other Philistine again."

He's intelligent enough to simply say, "Yes, Prophet."

I scoff at his idiocy and rebellion and storm away from him. My acknowledgements to the comments of passing followers are forced as I return to the tabernacle.

Storming across the empty meeting hall, I go immediately to my office. I need to see what's in that box. I go directly to my desk, yanking open the bottom drawer that contains the wooden case. Carefully, I place it on my desk directly in front of me. I can feel that there are answers in here. Answers I need desperately. Rummaging through the top part of my desk, I hold my breath when my fingers wrap around the skeleton key.

I don't understand why my heart thumps in fear when it slides into the hole so easily. After a large exhale, I finally turn the key. The lock *clicks* open, and my fingers gently lift the lid.

Disappointment consumes me when I find nothing more than a stack of notebooks. Sighing, I pick the one off the top and open it. The date scrawled across the heading of the first page is *July 1907*. When my eyes travel to the inscription on the inside, a blanket made of shadows is laid over me.

Nothing in this world is more powerful than fear. Create terror within them while becoming their only means of escaping it, and you will rule the earth. They will follow blindly, and you will become their God. ~Zaaron Fitch

I'm unable to swallow or breathe as my eyes continue to travel through the words. It takes many pages before I understand what I'm reading. These are plans for the Anointed Land and our entire belief system.

There is power in numbers. Breed within the followers, and we can mold the minds of generations to come.

Page after page of the lies my ancestors told throngs of people. He had planned for the Anointed Land to expand much further than it has. Tears roll down my face as everything I have ever thought to be true is ripped away. This elaborate ruse has been followed by every Prophet for over a hundred years. There are instructions outlined for future Prophets to maintain his plan. I killed my father before he was able to tell me the family secret.

By passing the title of 'Prophet' to the first-born son, and claiming power is in the holy blood, control will remain within the Fitch bloodline.

Five notebooks. Five notebooks that controlled the lives of throngs of people through the ages. It talks about being sure to keep us hidden, locked away from future advances, and to use the fear of the abyss and cleansings to keep our curiosities at bay. In the 1920's, leaving the Anointed Land became highly discouraged. 'Age of consent laws' were changing across America, making sexual intercourse with a child illegal. By terrorizing the followers with stories of the outside, it minimized the risk of being found out. Stories I've heard from the elder followers say that by the 1930's anyone other than religious officials became forbidden from leaving the gates.

Spiritual laws are written as a way to control and deceive. Rituals are for implementing fear. Zaaron, as I know him, doesn't exist. He was nothing more than a failed illusionist from New York City—a trickster. His vanity is apparent in his writing as he speaks of his intelligence being beyond that of the agents who rejected him. He moved to Oklahoma in 1906, convincing the original followers that he was God in a man's body by performing 'miracles'. He has lists of illusions, cons, and how to accomplish them—my father's poisoning stunt among them.

The same words are used throughout the pages.

Fear.

Death.

Torment.

Seclusion.

Suffering.

Control.

Power.

God.

Zaaron was just a man; An arrogant, selfish man who wanted to be worshiped and was able to terrify and convince people of his deceits. A sinking feeling in my chest threatens to swallow me whole when I realize there is no Paradise Star. There is no abyss. Is there a God? Does evil even exist?

I squeeze my eyes shut. In the darkness, I see Jameson Johnson defiling his son before swirls of oranges and reds blur my vision. The colors clear as my father beating my mothers and siblings flashes across my eyelids. Tossing me through the past, my memories run rampant, and I'm in the hall the morning after Laurel Ann was raped by my father. Tracing my tongue across my lips, I can almost taste her kiss. I can see the terror in my father's eyes when I cut out his tongue, the beautiful shapes his blood made in the water. Like it's playing out before me, I watch the light leave Jameson Johnson's eyes as I seared the pitchfork into his chest. It all flashes through my mind on repeat over and over until I scream. Serah Johnson's feet dangling in the barn, Laurel Ann lying unconscious in the tomb.

Yes, evil exists. I've seen it. It was just hidden behind my beliefs.

I'm scared and confused. I've always prayed during

turmoil...now, no one is listening. I weep at the loss of my faith. I have disobeyed, yes, but I never doubted, never questioned if it were true. There was so much more security in that than I realized. Now that it's been stripped away, I have no idea who I am.

The emptiness inside me is washed away with memories of Laurel Ann laughing at me as I got in trouble in class, the beautiful way her cheeks pinked the day I gave her the flowers for her crown. *"I thought they would look pretty in your hair."* The way I was certain my heart would explode when I realized it was her at the butcher's shop. Our kisses, her skin beneath my fingers, her moans, my name among her whispers.

Our stolen vows.

Not even in death will we part.

I gather the notebooks, placing them inside the carved box then back in my desk before I run through the door to the meeting hall. She's the only thing I'm certain of. I've always been certain, and in this moment, I need more than her memory.

Sunlight streaks across the wooden floor from the foyer when Laurel Ann comes rushing into the meeting hall as if she could feel my heart calling for her.

She drops the hem of her dress and breathes, "Is it true? There's talk that a Philistine came to the gates. People are getting scared."

I don't know how to tell her. I don't know how to tell any of them. I rush down the steps to meet her in between the pews. I need something, someone that's real. There's nothing keeping me from her now. No honor, no devotion, no faith.

I grab her hand and pull her back across the tabernacle. "Prophet, what's happening? What's wrong?" Squeezing her hand, I lead her to the back hallway and into the last holding room. Once the door is closed, I shove her bonnet off her head and kiss her as I walk her against the bed. She pulls her lips away and scrunches her brows, giving me an unsure smile. "Are you sure you're okay?"

I untie her bonnet strings and pull her head back, exposing her neck to me. "Right now, the only thing I'm sure of is that I need to be inside you."

Kissing down her neck, I turn her around, and she softly moans as I bend her over the footboard. My cock is straining with the need to release. I unzip my trousers and shove them down just enough to fist my cock. I bundle the layers of her dress on her waist until I can untie her bloomers, pushing them down her thighs.

My fingers fondle her slick pussy before I shove myself inside it. Her body constricts around mine, welcoming my intrusion. I groan and try to get deeper…as deep as I can.

"Zeb!" She tugs on the quilt with her scream.

"If I left, would you come with me?"

Her head turns toward me. "What?" she whimpers.

It makes me anxious that her answer isn't immediate. Slamming into her hard, I ask again. "If I left the Anointed Land, would you stay with me?" She is having a hard time processing the question, so I fuck her harder. "Yes or no, Laur?!"

"Yes!" she cries.

I push her dress higher up her body and lift her hips enough for her feet to raise off the floor. My anger at all the lies mixed with the loss of the life I could have had, and the fear of what will happen next all erupts within me. Harder and harder I thrust. She whimpers, dripping on my cock as the door to the holding room swings open.

"There you a—"

Jacob is standing slack jawed next to Ezekiel, Mia, and Marybeth.

I jump out of her to pull up my pants while Laurel Ann

scrambles up the bed. Marybeth instantly starts crying, but Mia…Mia is angry.

"Okay, listen," I try to form some kind of justification when Jacob flies across the room and pulls Laurel Ann off the bed by her arm.

"Adulterous witch!"

"No, Jacob! Wait!"

Laurel Ann squirms and kicks as he holds her arms behind her back. I lunge for him when Zeke pushes me against the wall, rage burning in his blue eyes.

"Her evil has clearly tainted you, brother! How could you do this?" I try to move forward, and he shoves me back again. "To your wives? To Benji? To all of us?!" Once more, he shoves me so hard my head slams against the wall. "You are our Prophet!"

Behind him, Jacob is dragging Laurel Ann out of the room. Mia glares at me and ushers away a hysterical Marybeth.

"Please, Zeke! You can't let him do this! You don't understand!"

"Then tell me, *Prophet*," he snarls. "What could make any of this better?"

I open my mouth, but no sound comes out. I don't know how to say it. He scoffs and turns around, closing the door behind him. I rush to it too late, banging on the wood.

"It's not real! They've lied to us our whole lives. *He* lied to us our whole lives!" My fists throb as I punch, kick, and do everything to get this fucking door down. "I can prove it!"

Letting out a breath, I drop my hands. I can't let this happen to her. When the lock *clicks* my heart speeds up, and I step back to watch the brass doorknob turn. The door swings open to present Ezekiel standing there with crossed arms.

"You have ten minutes."

29

SEALED WITH THREAD

Laurel Ann

J ACOB'S FINGERS DIG INTO THE FLESH OF MY ARM AS HE DRAGS me from the tabernacle and across the common ground to the medical hall.

"You have poisoned and seduced our Prophet for the last time, you whore!"

I hear Zebadiah's child bride bawling behind us. This whole time I was so concerned with Mia's feelings, I never considered her sister-wife. I half expect Zeb to chase after us and try to stop this, but I understand why he doesn't. I accept that I am the harlot in this scenario because I am just as guilty. I allowed a man, who was not my husband, to take my body. Never mind the fact that we are both bound to other people.

It will not take long for news of this to travel through the Anointed Land. It was destined to come out at some point. The thing that worries me the most is what happens to me and Zeb now. People will always be watching us, suspecting. We will have to fight for every moment, and while I'll fight till I die, asking him to do that seems cruel.

I know what they plan to do to me. I'm not the first

adulteress to walk the grounds of the Anointed Land.

Suddenly, a hard thud of agony rolls up my spine, and my body lurches at the impact. I cry out when I am hit again in the arm. A large stone falls by my feet, and I hear my sister behind me.

"Marybeth, no!" Mia screams grabbing her arm.

"Didn't you see him with her?" Marybeth cries. "He's my husband, yet he would rather lay with that *whore* than with me! She deserves to be stoned to death!"

"You must let the law deal with her now," Mia says, attempting to console her.

People gather around to see what is happening, as Marybeth shouts at the top of her lungs. "She was not eradicated of her evil like we were led to believe! She has seduced our Prophet into her bed!"

Murmurs sound behind me while Jacob drags me into the medical hall. Doc Kilmer has his glasses perched on his nose as he looks up from his medical texts at our entrance.

"She was found fornicating with the Prophet," Jacob announces, forcing my ears to burn from mortification. "She must have her womanly entrance closed."

Doc Kilmer shuts his book and rises, setting his glasses on his desk. Glancing over to the open door leading to the clinic, I see Sister Madeline peeking through.

"Yes, Counselor. Of course."

Jacob shoves me toward Doc Kilmer and opens the door. "The Apostle will be here to read the scriptures since the Prophet is clearly unable at the moment." I don't fight my fate as Doc Kilmer leads me into the clinic.

"What do you need of me, husband?" Sister Madeline asks.

He rubs his temple. "Make sure her vagina is clean. I will prepare the needle and thread."

She nods to him, and when he leaves the clinic, her head

jerks in my direction. "What have you done, child?"

I feel ashamed, but it's not because of what I did with Zeb, it's because everyone now has to know of it.

"I love him, Sister Madeline." Even as I say it, I know she can't understand. It's not about love. It's about duty, faith, and honor.

"Oh, Laurel Ann. I warned you of this. There's nothing I can do to stop it now." Seeming to waver between anger and sadness, she guides me to a black chair next to the bed. "Remove your bloomers, lift your skirts to your waist, and sit." I do as she says while she raises each of my legs into the stirrups attached to the chair. Fastening them to the supports, she elevates them to lean me back. "After the procedure, you must be sure to not open your legs too wide."

My heart beats wildly, and my *yes* gets caught in my throat with my sob. She walks to my side, fastening a belt around my torso and wrists. Opening the cabinet, she removes a dark brown bottle, a clear bottle, a razor, a jar of shaving cream, and a stack of cloths. She places the items on the table and looks down on me.

"Was acting on your love worth this?!" she snaps in a whisper. "Don't you think we've all loved those we cannot be with? It's about obeying Zaaron and making oblations for your place in the Paradise Star. The Prophet was not yours to take."

Tears sting my eyes. I deserve to be scared. She's right. I followed my feelings for Zebadiah into sin, allowing them to come before my duty to Zaaron. I desecrated holy implements in the heat of lust while leading the holiest man in the world toward wickedness. I deserve this penance and more.

She picks up the razor and shaving cream after fetching a bowl of water from the basin. As she removes the hair from between my legs, Doc Kilmer enters carrying a plate. I turn my head to look at it when he sets it down. The suture needle is long and curved making me involuntarily swallow. The thread bundled next to it is white and thick. I think I might be sick. I know this is because of my choices, yet I whimper, trying not to beg. He threads the needle once Sister Madeline wipes me clean. When she applies the iodine over my sensitive skin it's cold, and I gasp as a shiver shoots to my toes.

"Is she prepared?"

Sister Madeline nods, standing to allow Doc Kilmer to take his place in the chair. His spectacles rest on his nose as he straightens the thread. He looks between my legs, and my face heats with embarrassment. I squeeze my eyes shut, holding my breath, when I feel Sister Madeline's hand grasp mine.

His hands are much larger than hers as he runs a finger up my slit and spreads the lips apart. Tears fall in shame when he reaches into my hole, lifting the sensitive skin around my entrance. Gritting my teeth, the needle presses into my flesh, and when he forces it through to puncture the first side, the pain is hot, and my scream comes out loud. He tugs on the tight muscle of the other side, instantly pushing on the needle and pulling the string through the holes. The thread is yanked tighter when he shoves the needle in again, repeating the process, and sealing my lustful opening. My body shakes while I freely let myself sob. Sister Madeline squeezes my hand tight at the sound of a door.

"Since it seems the Apostle is attending other matters at present, I will be reading the scriptures."

I slowly open my eyes to watch Jacob walk next to Doc Kilmer and crouch over to inspect his work. The Doc thrusts the needle through— my humiliation and pain dancing together with each tug of the thread.

The tightness becomes more intense, and I scream with every puncture of the needle. I'm almost grateful when Jacob stands to read the scriptures for something else to focus on.

"Laurel Ann Johnson, you were found participating in obscene acts of a sexual nature with a man who was not your husband. The fact that the man you seduced was none other than the Prophet leads me to believe that your time in the tomb of abolishment was not entirely successful. Do you deny these charges?"

Doc Kilmer stabs the needle in again, causing me to yell out my answer. "No, Counselor!"

"These are serious offenses. To remain in the Anointed Land, you must atone for them. You are to remain closed during your time of questioning as well as for the duration of your cleansing." I nod, and Doc Kilmer yanks me even more tightly shut, causing me to suck in through my teeth. Jacob clears his throat, and opens *The True Testament* to a bookmarked page. "'There is no place for lust in the Anointed Land. Lust is a breeding ground for evil, and it must be snuffed out. While both parties must pay penance, those whose bodies are entered are the seducers and therefore must be prevented from further seduction. The orifice which was used in a sexual manner must be sewn closed with needle and thread until their souls are purified of all prior sin, through a cleansing ritual.'" He turns the page and continues as steady tears flow down my face. I don't know how many more times I can handle the needle piercing my tender skin before I pass out. "'Adultery is among the most selfish of sins. It is the destroyer of our families and an enemy of Zaaron. The cleansing for those committing such acts shall be extreme in nature to ensure the sin is not recommitted. If the seducer exceeds three offenses, the closing shall remain permanent.' -23:10*A* through *C*." He shuts *The True Testament*.

Doc Kilmer ties off the thread, and I nearly die from relief. I cry as he presses a cloth against my freshly sewn entrance, even the simplest touch sending pain through my veins, raising my body temperature. He stands with the blood speckled cloth and pushes his glasses up his nose. He takes the clear bottle bottle from Sister Madeline. As he pours it over my fresh puncture wounds, it burns so badly that I sob and contest my bindings.

"The procedure is finished, Counselor."

Jacob glares at me and snarls, "Leave me with her." Sister Madeline pats my hand, following Doc Kilmer out of the clinic. My breathing is harsh with my attempt to control the pain. Once they are gone, Jacob sits where the Doc had, reaching between my thighs. "Let's see how well of a job the good Doc did." He spreads my lips apart, and his finger pushes on the thread. I cry at the shock as he attempts to stick his finger in between the tight string, pulling on the fresh wounds. "Satisfactory," he states, standing to put his hands on my knees. "You have caused my family and this compound nothing but suffering. You're so fond of opening your legs, why don't you open them for me, bitch?" Pushing down on my thighs, I scream at the threading being pulled to its limit. At the very moment I think he's going to tear me apart, he releases me, and I gasp for air through my tears. He unfastens my legs along with my right wrist. "Get up and cover your whore hole."

Sniffling, I undo my other wrist and the belt around my torso. On shaky legs, I stand to retrieve my bloomers from the bed. Jacob reaches into his pocket, pulling out a rope to bind my hands together.

I want to know what they've done to Zeb. I wish it was Ezekiel here instead of Jacob whom I don't dare ask. He drags me through the medical hall as Sister Madeline gives me a sorrowful look. When he leads me through the front door, I don't see Mia or Marybeth among the crowd of followers yelling.

"Evil!"

"Adulteress!"

"Devil's whore!"

"Seductress!"

They cast stones, hitting my legs and my back until one hits my head causing it to ring. My vision falters, and I lose my footing, falling to the dirt. Jacob yanks me back to my feet when a rock hits him in the face, and he yells, "Enough! You will all be called on shortly. Go back to your duties!"

They obey but do not lower their voices as he pulls me to the tabernacle.

"She must still be possessed to be able to seduce the Prophet."

"Poor Sister Mia. Her own kin!"

"She's always had a rebellious spirit."

I try to keep up with him though it's futile, and I still trip. Upon entering the foyer, I search for Zebadiah. Part of me hopes he disgraced my name because there's no reason we should both suffer.

I'll admit to what they accuse me of, and I'll pay the price. If Zeb confesses to wanting me and loving me, everything will fall apart. I never considered that I was risking the foundation of the entire compound by following my fleshly desires. A Prophet has never been accused of such acts. I don't know what will happen to him if they are aware that he knowingly rebuked Zaaron's will by touching me.

Jacob drags me across the stage and into the back hall. Opening the door to the holding room next to the one we were caught in, he shoves me inside and unties my wrists.

"You will stay here until your cleansing," he informs me before slamming the door.

The room spins around me, making my stomach roll with nausea, I stumble to the bed to lie down. The moment my head hits the pillow, I weep into it.

30

THE PROPHET'S CHOICE

Zebadiah

ZEKE FOLLOWS ME INTO MY OFFICE, STANDING IN FRONT OF MY desk. His arms are crossed, curiosity and rage fighting for his expression. I reach for the box containing the notebooks and become hesitant. If the tables were turned, what would it be like to hear this from Zeke? I'm literally about to tear his world down. My hands shake as I place the box on the desk and lift the lid.

"Enough with the suspense. Just tell me what you're talking about."

"Will you at least sit?"

He huffs and rolls his eyes while doing what I ask. I push the box over to him. "You won't believe me if I tell you. You need to see for yourself."

His eyebrow arches, and he reaches inside to pull out the first notebook. As his eyes scan the words, confusion controls his features. I don't see his chest rise a single time until the realization hits and a sob escapes.

"This is…there has to be an explanation. This is certainly fraudulent…" His voice cracks on the verge of producing tears. "It has to be…"

My chest aches as I shake my head. Everything inside me wishes that could be true. "Keep reading. It's all there. It's no fraud."

I watch him learn of every lie we were born being told. Tears fall from his eyes, and it kills me to see my brother cry. He's tough. He always has been, and it's unsettling to see him break.

"He knew…" His eyes are furious as he meets my eyes. "The bastard knew."

"Father, Grandfather Josiah, their fathers and grandfathers. They all knew."

He throws the last notebook across the desk. "Why?! What was the point of it all?"

I chuckle, but not because it's funny. "Power, control, vanity…the very things they preached against."

"What do we do now?"

Now that I've proven to him what I intended, my urgency returns, and I stand. "We go get Laurel Ann."

He leans forward, ripping off his hat. "Are you mad? You'll make things worse for both of you if you attempt that right now. As far as the followers know, you have been seduced by a whore of the Devil." Hearing Laurel Ann mentioned in that way makes my skin so hot it's nearly numb. "If you get caught, they'll hang you up at the cleansing station. Our best bet is to release the books."

The thought has most certainly crossed my mind, though I know the power of numbers and blind faith.

"There's no telling the direction that would go. We are telling them Zaaron isn't our God, that he isn't a God at all. We are rebuking everything we were taught as truth. You can't expect that to be taken well."

"Then what?"

"We have to end this."

At this point, I have no idea what would be the right or wrong way to deal with this. I have to follow my mind, heart, and instincts because I have nothing else anymore.

"What does that mean?" His hand hits the armrest, clearly exasperated by my vagueness.

I rest my forearms on my desk, wondering if he will try to stop me. "I need you to take me into town."

Frowning, he walks to my office door, rage in his fists and loss in his shoulders. "Let me fetch the buggy."

I gather the notebooks as he leaves, locking them back in the box and placing the key in my pocket. I yank off my sigil pendant, tossing it on the desk before opening the bottom drawer and shoving the bloody piece of Laurel Ann's old garment in my pocket. I look out the back window to see Ezekiel pulling up behind the tabernacle with the horse and buggy.

Running across the meeting hall to the foyer, I take a deep breath and open the door to peer outside. The followers seem to have gone back to their daily duties, so I slip down the steps with urgency, gliding between the tabernacle and schoolhouse. Once I'm out of sight from the common ground, I run to meet Zeke. I jump in the back of the buggy, lying down to be hidden.

Moments later, I hear my cousin who guards the gates. "Apostle, you're leaving now? With everything happening?"

"That is *why* I am leaving, to deal with the Philistine who came here making his ridiculous claims."

Very clever excuse. I'm proud of him for thinking of that.

"Of course, Apostle."

The creaking of the gate opening allows the oxygen to release from my lungs as the buggy moves again.

After a few moments, Zeke calls to me. "You can sit up here now." I climb over the seats when he asks, "Where are we going?"

"To the only Philistine that I halfway trust."

Once I say it, I realize she isn't a Philistine. None of them are. Their ancestors just didn't believe the lies. Although I know this, it's difficult for me to shift my way of thinking. The first encounter I had with this girl was less than friendly. I just hope she loves Laurel Ann as much as she claims to.

We enter Hobart, and if Zeke doubts me, he isn't saying so. I direct him through town to Laurel Ann's old street, pointing at her house when we approach.

"Here."

Zeke tightens the reins, stopping the horses. "Whatever you're planning…are you certain of it?"

I shake my head as I jump from the buggy. "No."

His nostrils flare, but he follows me through the yard and onto the porch. We look at each other, and I raise my fist to knock.

"Ugh! Are you serious?!" We hear who I assume is Kaila, Laurel Ann's friend, from inside the house. After some stomping footsteps the door swings open. "What?" She's glistening with sweat, and her hair has curls escaping around her face. What disturbs me is her state of dress. She's in nothing besides her undergarments which are considerably more revealing than those worn on the compound. While I jerk my head to the side, Zeke's eyes don't stop traveling up and down her body. I hit him in the arm to get him to stop violating her with his stare. "Oh, isn't this a fucktastic surprise. What the hell are you doing here?" She crosses her arms until her eyes narrow in realization. "I swear to God, and not yours, there better not be anything wrong with Laurel Ann."

I try to look at her without actually seeing her outfit. "Would you mind getting dressed for this conversation?"

"These are my workout clothes, Prophet McPrude, and I'll wear whatever the hell I want."

Zeke snorts, and I glare at him. "Fine. May we come in? This is of a sensitive nature."

She glances between us, sighing and gestures into the home. "All right." We walk inside, taking off our hats as she leads us into the main living area. "First things first, is Laurel Ann okay?"

Being closed will be painful and cause her much suffering, though she will heal from it, so I give her the answer that is both somewhat honest and will get her to listen.

"Yes, Laurel Ann will be fine."

She grabs a towel off a table and plops on the couch to dry herself. "What's up then?"

I sit in a chair and glance at her television screen. It has a picture of a woman dressed similarly to Kaila, frozen in mid movement. Zeke sits in the blue chair next to me as I take a deep breath.

"I don't know how much Laurel Ann told you about where we're from. We were raised with a specific belief system and laws to follow." I hand her the box and remove the skeleton key from my pocket. "I recently found this." She takes the box and key with a raised eyebrow. "It's documentation that everything we've been taught were the lies of a vain man. I don't know much about your laws, but girls younger than your 'age of consent' are being bound and impregnated by men many times their age. Our rituals are abusive and extreme."

"I'm waiting for the part I don't already know." Kaila reaches over to a small table, placing the box on top before putting a cigarette stick in her mouth and lighting it with her pocket-sized torch.

She may not necessarily be evil, but she's definitely insolent.

"I thought what we were doing was right, what was asked of us by an all-powerful God. Now that I know what I know, I can't allow what's happening in the compound to continue. If you go to your authorities to tell them about the children, will they stop it?"

Her eyes go wide as she blows out smoke like a demon. "Oh, they'll stop it. They'll raid the place. They'll take the children and probably arrest a bunch of you."

"Zebadiah," Zeke snaps. "What are you doing? They're innocent."

She tilts her head in agreement as she points her cigarette to Zeke. "Sexy suspenders over there is right. Why don't you show them this? Give them a chance to make the right choice."

The truth is, I know what she's saying is the kind thing to do. I also know how stubborn the followers can be. There are passages in *The True Testament* mentioning circumstances where death by stoning is done in place of excommunication for fear of this very thing. This definitely falls in the category of 'Denying the existence of Zaaron.' It hasn't happened in my lifetime, but if that is the choice of the compound, it'll be too late to stop it. Then what would they do to Laurel Ann? Blame would surely be placed on her. I shake my head. I'm done allowing her to be put in harm's way.

"It's time we pay for our sins and the sins of our fathers. Every part of me feels that this is the correct path, and that's all I have to go on now."

Ezekiel's face hardens as he nods. "You may no longer be my Prophet, but you're my brother, and I will always trust you."

I look back to Kaila, who has what I reluctantly admit is a sweet smile on her face. I dig into my pocket, holding out the piece of Laurel Ann's bloomers. "One last thing." Her eyes widen in disgust.

"Holy shit, psycho, is that blood?!"

"This is more of a personal nature. I don't know what will

happen to any of us when all this occurs, and I would like to know this is being kept somewhere safe. Can I trust you to hang on to it for me?"

Her nose scrunches as if smelling something foul. "What is it?"

I unconsciously turn to Zeke, embarrassed to be saying this in front of him. He leans forward, resting his elbows on his knees. Raising his eyebrows, he holds his hand out for me to continue.

I sigh and fondle the fabric in my hand "When Laurel Ann got her first blood, I helped her hide the stained under-garments. We were caught, and our penance was her binding to my father. I snuck into his study and saved this piece of her bloomers. It was all I had of her for years."

Her expression softens into one similar to the one my sisters have every time they see any kind of baby animal. "That's actually sorta sweet in a really creepy, stalkery kind of way." She stands up with her cigarette in her mouth. "There's still no way I'm touching that shit. I'm gonna grab a Ziploc."

She disappears into the kitchen, and when I glance at Zeke, he's staring at her barely covered ass.

"Enjoying the view, brother?"

He chuckles, rubbing his neck and looking around the house. Kaila returns with a clear, slick bag, and tosses it to me. "Put it in there, and I'll keep it for you."

"Thank you." I take a deep breath as I put it inside and hand it back to her.

Sliding her fingers across the top of the bag, she walks to a desk against the wall, opens the top drawer, and places the bag at the bottom beneath a stack of papers.

"So, when am I doing this?"

My heart picks up pace at the reality of her question, and I stand. "Immediately if possible. While Laurel Ann's life is not in any danger, more harm will come to her if you don't hurry."

Her mouth drops open. "You're just now telling me this, you dick?"

I swallow her disrespect because it's not exactly unwarranted. "I needed you to listen."

She spins around to grab the box and key. Storming across the room, she picks up a yellow bag from the floor by the foot rest.

"Well, I listened, now I'm going to get my friend back." She opens her front door, pulling her bag straps over her shoulder. "Whatever you're gonna do, you better do it quick."

I follow Ezekiel out the front door as I nod at Kaila. "Thank you. For this and for always being a friend to Laurel Ann."

She places a hand on my arm, and I fight the natural urge to flinch at her touch. "If you see her before I do, tell her I love her."

As we near the compound, blackbirds fly across a lightning streaked sky. A moment later, thunder cracks around us, and Zeke snaps the horse's reins to move us faster.

"Are we going to talk about the Philistine claiming to be our brother?"

I scoff, "Do you really doubt it now?"

He wipes his hand over his mouth. "I don't know what to doubt or believe at this point." He jerks his head behind him. "We're getting close. You might want to get in the back." I climb over the seat, and just as I lie down, he asks, "I hope you're sure about this."

"I am too." I add, "When we get there, pull back behind

the tabernacle. I want to check on Laurel Ann."

He nods. "Heyah!"

The buggy goes faster as raindrops pelt against the roof. I lie down in the back, and within a few moments, Zeke is let into the gates. When we stop moving, he looks over the seat.

"We're here. The rain has most everyone inside, so we shouldn't be seen."

I climb out, instantly running alongside the tabernacle with Zeke on my heels. The wind picks up, blowing my jacket when I climb the steps. We go inside and walk through the foyer. I sigh in relief at the empty meeting hall. Lighting flashes across the windows when I hurry to the stage. Zeke is right behind me as I sprint down the hall, and head for the first holding room. He swiftly removes a key from his pocket, unlocking the door. The *BOOM* of the thunder sounds the moment I burst inside.

Laurel Ann jumps up from the bed, and her eyes widen at the sight of us. "Prophet..."

She doesn't appear to be in too much pain, just unsure of my purpose. I rush to the side of the bed to wrap my arms around her.

"Are you all right?"

She nods, and her hands cup my face. "What's happening? What will they do to you?"

I know she's referring to the followers; I just don't have time to clarify. "I don't know. I can't explain everything right now, but if I am not able to speak to you again, Kaila will elucidate."

Her head shakes in confusion. "Kaila? You've spoken to her?"

I smile, kissing her before I back up toward the door. "She says she loves you." Laurel Ann leans up on her knees as if contemplating following me. "Stay in this room." I wave at

Zeke to come with me. "I love you, Laur. Stay safe."

Her eyes fill with tears as I close the door.

"What now?" Zeke asks with crossed arms.

"Tie up any loose ends you may have. I don't know enough about Philistine laws to know what they'll do to us, so prepare for the worst. I need to speak with Mia and Marybeth."

He drapes his arm across my shoulder. "May the hol—" he stops himself to shake his head. "Be careful, brother."

I hurry through the tabernacle, rushing outside, and I'm drenched by the time I jump back in the buggy. I flick the reins to speed up the horses when I see the ranch I grew up in. The home I inherited when I killed my father. I might never see it again. I may never see this compound again. Even knowing this place was built on a lie, there's a part of me that is woeful by it coming to an end.

I stop the buggy in front of my home, running through the rain while more lightning brightens the sky. I hurry inside to be greeted by the angry eyes of my wives. I wonder if anything I say will help. It won't change the fact that I betrayed them.

Mia stands up in front of Marybeth like she's shielding her. Thunder explodes around us.

"What are you doing here, Zebadiah?"

Mia's voice is laced with venom as she stares at me with an anger I've never seen present in her before.

"I don't have an excuse for what I did other than I love her. I've always loved her. She didn't seduce me or trick me. She's simply Laurel Ann. I couldn't give you my heart because it hasn't been mine for a long time. Please know that any man would be lucky to have either of you as wives, and you both deserve someone who can return your love. I'm sorry that it can't be me. I'm sorry I hurt the both of you."

Mia storms over to me, shoving me. She screams, "You

humiliated us! You humiliated Laurel Ann! You humiliated *me*!" Her hands press against my chest to push me again. "You're our husband! We trusted you! And more than that, you are our Prophet."

She puts her hands on me again, and I grab her wrists. "I'm not your Prophet. I'm nothing more than a man." I release her and look between them. "I hope someday you'll forgive me."

Mia's anger morphs into misunderstanding. "What do you mean you're not our Prophet?"

"I can't explain. Just promise me that when this is all over, you'll find Laurel Ann or Zeke if you can, and protect yourselves."

Mia steps toward me, grasping onto my arms as I back toward the door. "You're scaring me, Zeb. When what is all over?"

I lean forward to kiss her forehead. "Goodbye, Mia."

Pulling my arm from her, I walk out the door. I leave down the pathway, hearing them call my name until the wind drowns them out.

The buggy does little to stop the rain from pelting me on my ride to Benji and Laurel Ann's home. The horses are barely stopped before I run up the porch steps to bang on the door. A moment later the hinges creak, and Benji gasps through the screen door.

"Oh shit, get in here," he says breathlessly. I enter the house, and he hurries to close us inside as I remove my hat. "What happened? They won't let me see Laurel Ann. They're saying she's still possessed? That she tricked you into sleeping with her?" He crosses his arms. "At least you waited until after our binding night to fuck my wife."

Swallowing the urge to tell him that I actually didn't, I pull out a chair next to the table and fall into it. "Explaining everything would take a lot of time and we don't have it, so don't ask questions. Just sit there and listen."

With raised eyebrows, he lowers into the seat beside to me. "All right, sure, I'm all ears."

"I found proof that everything we've ever been told was a lie. All of it. Zaaron, the Paradise Star, the cleansings…it's all horse shit. What we've believed to be righteous is wrong. We aren't 'Anointed', we're just conditioned. I made the decision to put an end to this compound. People are coming, and I'm sure we'll be made to answer for the crimes we've committed. You do not have any wives below the age of consent, and you've done nothing that you should be penalized for. I need you to promise me that you'll make sure Laurel Ann and my wives are safe. Can you do that?"

His expression is frozen, and I'm about to snap my fingers in front of his face when he says, "I don't believe this. Are you sure?"

Standing to leave, I tell him, "I don't need you to believe it. I need you to promise me, and I need to know they will be watched after."

"Yes, yes, of course."

As I put my hat back on, I walk toward the door. "I must go. Thank you for your friendship through the years, Benji. I didn't always deserve it."

I push open the screen when he asks, "Are you going to be okay?"

"I'll get what I've earned."

Running into the rain, I climb in the buggy to drive back to the common ground. My insides turn at seeing the followers going about their duties. They have no idea what I'm about to do to them. Doubting my choice is pointless. What's done is done.

I leave the buggy in front of the tabernacle to run inside

and retrieve the binding, birth, and death logs. Stuffing the books under my arm, I go back to the entryway and look at the holding room, resisting the urge to go to Laurel Ann.

I love you so much. I hope you understand.

As I run through the meeting hall, shouting and an intrusive alarm sound fills my ears. Shoving open the door, I step outside to find the common ground in chaos. Men with guns and black clothes that say 'POLICE' cover the area in front of me. Women are screaming and their children cry. I squint through the rain, and as the lightning strikes above us, I see many of the Brothers are already on their knees.

The thunder makes my heart thump harder when I hear a *click*. "Down on the ground, now! Hands behind your head."

I turn to see a man in black aiming a gun at my face. I drop the logs and fall to my knees, cupping the back of my head. He rips my arms behind my back, fastening them together in a binding.

Raindrops roll down my face, and I watch them tear apart what has always been my home. I thought I was sure of this, but as I witness the fear and pain I've brought upon the people who trusted me…

I weep.

31

FITCH BROTHER THREE

Laurel Ann

MOVING TOO MUCH IS PAINFUL. SITTING TOO LONG IS painful. And now, my bladder is full. I've been putting off using the washroom because I'm scared to go. At this point, it's going to come out either way, so I carefully sit down on the toilet. I grit my teeth through the burn, though I feel much better having emptied myself. As I pull the chain to flush, I hear an odd sound.

I walk back out to the room, listening closely. Without windows it's difficult to make anything out, but I think there are sirens. When something that resembles screaming hits my ears, my heart triples in speed, and I fall to the floor. I carefully lie flat on my stomach and scoot under the bed, trying to listen for what could be happening outside.

Whether this has anything to do with the Philistine that came to the gates, I don't know, but they went to see Kaila. I'll admit having jealousy at that. They both wore corresponding expressions of woe and anxiety, and the news they brought was no more assuring. My skin is clammy beneath my dress, and I can hear the rapid *thump, thump, thump* of my heart in my ears.

Every scream, yell, and intrusive sound I hear brings me closer to hyperventilating. There are moments when I think whatever chaos is going on outside has dispersed, then I'll hear something again. The minutes have frozen, making time go on forever.

Click.

The noise has me holding my breath, terrified to look toward the door. Footsteps sound in the room, and I brave a glance, peering beneath the bed skirt. Dirt covered boots and trousers are all I can see.

"Laurel Ann?" Jacob's voice calls for me as he walks into the washroom. For some reason, even knowing who it is, I can't move myself from this spot. "Where are you? Zebadiah sent me for you."

My heart leaps at hearing he is safe and well. I pull myself out from under the bed. "He's okay? What's going on? I heard noises." I stand up and turn to see him shutting and locking the door. My guts roll around inside of me when my eyes land on the rope in his hand. He glares down at me with a venomous hatred. "I thought we were going to see the Prophet?"

His jaw ticks, and he stalks toward me, forcing me to step back as if I have somewhere to go. "This is all happening because of you. You have poisoned this land and torn it from beneath our feet."

I shake my head because I'm confused. "I don't know what you mean!"

"I don't need your confession. Lie to me if you wish, you evil whore."

Before I realize he's lunging for me, he shoves my face against the bed and digs his knee into my back. I cry at the sudden pain while he jerks my arms behind my back.

"Counselor, why are you doing this?!"

He hits my head with what I think is his elbow. "Shut your

demonic mouth! All that falls from your tongue is deception."

I gag when he shoves a cloth between my lips, nearly choking me. The *swoosh* of a belt being ripped from its loops has me screaming around the fabric as I fight to get free from beneath him. He wraps the strap of the belt around my head to secure the cloth in my mouth, fastening it so tight, it digs into my cheeks.

I don't understand what he's doing or why. Where the heck are Zeb and Zeke? This can't be sanctioned. He lifts me by my shoulders to pick me up and spins me around to face him.

"I'm going to enjoy watching your eyes burn in pain just as your soul will burn in the pit."

He throws me on my back moments before crushing me with his weight. He's heavy and impossible to shove off. Grabbing my wrists, he wraps them in the rope and secures them to the headboard. Tears fall from frustration and fear at losing the use of my arms. My ability to protect myself has been significantly reduced, allowing me the power to do nothing more than kick and writhe beneath him.

He simply chuckles, "Fight all you want. I enjoy the struggle."

The belt itches my cheeks with the wet skin trapped beneath it. When he pushes up my dress and his fingers rip at my bloomers, panic overtakes all else. I shake my head, pleading with my eyes for him to not do this.

"This seems to be the Fitch family pussy. I'm dying to fuck the cunt that fucked us all."

Though he's never been kind to me, this is something else entirely. I know what he's planning to do, but it's as if it's behind a wall and my mind refuses to access or believe it. Every time I've been with a man it's either been my calling or my desire...but this... I squeeze my eyes shut, praying that Zaaron will save me.

My wrists scream in their bindings while I flail my body like a woman possessed. I just need to deter him long enough for someone to come help me. I can't scream, I can barely breathe, my arms burn, and my chest aches from the rapid pounding of my heart.

More tears fall once he succeeds in removing my bloomers. His hands clutch at my thighs and forces them open, shooting a hot pain through the middle of my body. My wails are caught behind the cloth as I watch him unfasten his trousers.

I know how this will go. Nobody will believe that the Counselor is doing this. They will say I seduced him. I look at the door, praying, hoping, wishing, pleading, that Zeb will walk through it.

An agony so hot, my vision turns white consumes every part of my mind, body, and soul. My focus clears, and my eyes fall to the source of my pain. His erect cock pounds against the string while he attempts to push inside me. With every thrust, the torture multiplies tenfold as he rips, tears, and shreds the thread from my flesh. My mind graces me with seconds of reprieve and blocks of time get taken away. I shouldn't watch, yet my eyes still travel to the intrusion. Blood is smeared on his abdomen and trousers as well as across my thighs. Tremors overtake my body when the thread gives way, and he forces himself all the way inside me.

He laughs. "There it is." His body pumps in and out hard, but all I feel is anguish. "What's wrong? I thought you liked fucking us Fitch men?" His fists wrap around my throat, and he forces my body down to meet his violent thrust. "Look how wet you are..." He grins, and my stomach rolls, threatening to be sick. "Well, I suppose that could be the blood."

Again, I fade, hearing nothing other than his grunts and

obscenities. My screams sound only in my own head, making me dizzy.

He's going to kill me.

Black.

I can't breathe.

Black.

I'm going to die.

Black.

He releases his grasp around me to remove his body from mine. The mix of relief and excruciating pain momentarily stops my heart.

"You aren't worth my righteous come." Warm liquid spurts across my mutilated body, mixing with the blood and burning where my skin has ripped. He groans, releasing the last of his semen and climbing off the bed to pull up his trousers. I can barely keep my eyes open as he leans down by my ear. "Burn in the abyss, Philistine bitch."

He keeps my arms bound and leaves the room, locking the door with a *click*. With the sudden stillness and silence in the room, the pain burns so bright that the blackness is finally victorious in taking me away.

BANG

"Back away from the door!"

BANG

CRASH

I need to get up. I know these are dangerous sounds, yet I still can't lift my eyelids.

"Oh, fucking Jesus Christ! We need a medic!" A man yells, pounding in my head.

"Gomez!" A woman's voice, much softer whispers, "A little respect and decorum won't kill you." The heavy weight of my dress is moved down my body to below my knees. Soft fingers caress my wrists as they are freed from the confines of the rope. Gently lowering my arms to my sides, the owner of the kind voice says, "We're going to take care of you, sweetheart. You're safe now."

With immense effort I open my eyes to see a woman in a black helmet, and look down to see that she's a police officer. I remember the noises from earlier. The only reason they would be here is to raid the compound. My thoughts won't stay organized, and the only thing I can think of is knowing Zebadiah is safe. The rawness in my throat makes the words painful so I say the most important one:

"Zebadiah."

"We'll get him, I promise. He won't ever hurt you again."

Before I can tell her that she misunderstands, my mind slips away.

Kaila's crossed arms and tapping foot aren't going to change my mind. I've told them it wasn't Zeb, and that's all I'm saying on the matter.

"Not pressing charges leaves whoever this was, free to do it again," the police officer says.

I know he thinks he's helping, but by forcing me to think about something that I've been trying to forget, he's doing the opposite.

I can't look anyone in the eye when I speak of this, and it mortifies me that anyone knows it happened.

"This was not an act of random violence. It was revenge…

it was personal."

He huffs as he puts away his notepad. "And the next time it gets 'personal'?"

I don't know how many times I have to repeat myself. My entire world has erupted, and they are keeping the wound fresh.

"I'm not naming him! Now, unless you have something else to speak to me about, I would really like to rest."

The officer takes in a deep breath and backs toward the door of my hospital room. "If you can think of anything else you'd like to share, you know how to get ahold of us."

I nod as Kaila thanks him, closing the door.

She sighs with her personal brand of drama and sits on the bed. "Will you at least tell me why? Why you won't say who it was?"

This wasn't something she could understand before it became so convoluted. And now, I'm confused too. "It happened because of my actions. I caused pain for this person, and they caused it back. Penance is paid."

Her eyes widen as she smacks her hands against her cheeks—an odd thing she does when she tries to calm herself down. "Laur. I need you to listen to me very fucking closely. What happened to you wasn't warranted, deserved, or some sick equalizer. It wasn't goddamn penance. It was rape, okay?!"

What I don't say is that speaking it aloud would make the shame real. The humiliation. If Zebadiah were to know I had his brother in my body, I don't know how he would feel or react. My beliefs have always made things much clearer than I'd realized. Now, I'm struggling to accept the falsehood of everything I've held sacred. When you sin, you pay the price for it with suffering, but what happens when the sin isn't real and the punishment does nothing for your soul? What's the point in all of this? What are we fighting for? Living for? Dying for?

I haven't read the notebooks that prove my life is a lie, though I know what was in them, and that Zebadiah was the one who chose to bring this all out in the open. In a rational part of my mind, I know he did what he thought was best for me and everyone, but the angry and scared part wishes he would have kept it within the compound. Now he, along with many of the other men, have been arrested and are awaiting trial.

For the third time in my life, my future as I know it has been wiped clean, leaving me disoriented and lost. It feels like my entire life was pointless.

My need to sleep and escape the thoughts in my mind is all I want in this moment. "I'm really tired, Kaila."

Her shoulders fall, and she gets off the bed to pick up her purse. "I know you feel alone, but you're not. I'm here for you just like I've always been." She gives me a tender hug. "I love you, Laur."

Everything she's ever done has been to try to be a good friend, and I know she feels she did the right thing. I'm confused at what exactly I'm angry at, and I can't think straight. Still, none of this changes my real feelings for her.

"I love you, too, Kaila."

32

TRIALS AND TRIBULATIONS

Zebadiah

"WERE YOU EVER TOUCHED IN A SEXUAL WAY BY THE MAN you call your husband?"

Marybeth shakes her head. "No, ma'am. He wouldn't. He had no desire for me."

"Was he unkind to you in any way?"

She nods, her blonde curls bouncing. "Yes." My heart tightens because I never was cruel to her. "He was unfaithful to me."

"Did he ever physically abuse you? Lay his hands on you in any way?"

The woman asking the questions is wearing a skirt, yet it's very masculine. Her voice is loud, and her hair is cut short like a man's. The 'jury', the group of people deciding our fates, watches her every move as an old woman in the corner types everything we say into her contraption.

Marybeth's head shakes. "No ma'am. Not me."

The woman tilts her head. "You say 'not you'. Was he abusive to others?"

"Abusive? No. He punished those who deserved it by

breaking spiritual law. It was his duty."

The woman looks at the man in the black robe called the 'judge'.

"You still believe this, even after the release of Zaaron Fitch's notebooks?"

Next to me, Mr. Dressler, a man who they call our 'court appointed lawyer', stands. "Objection: relevance."

He's apparently here to defend us, though I don't understand what stake he has in our futures.

The judge says, "Sustained."

My mind hurts trying to follow what's happening. I don't understand half the words they speak.

"No further questions, Your Honor," the woman states, with a nod.

They release Marybeth from her seat to call their next witness. A woman walks out who I don't recognize. She appears to be in her late thirties to early forties with straight, red hair cut to her shoulders. Her white dress is sleeveless with yellow flowers on it. She sits, looking out across the courtroom.

I turn my head to all the men sitting next to me. Laurel Ann's father, Benji's brother, Doc Kilmer...all the men who had wives younger than the 'age of consent'. I feel their hatred rolling off of them. They glare and threaten every chance they get. They keep us separate in the holding room they call a 'jail', so I have only seen them during the trial.

Apparently, this story is big news because large crowds are always gathered as we come and go from the courthouse building. They are desperate to talk to us, asking multiple questions that all seem to start with 'People want to know,' or 'Is it true?".

This world is loud and obnoxious. The men in the jail are brutes and imbeciles. The thought of having to remain there for any significant length of time has me thinking dark thoughts. I turn my head to Laurel Ann, and her eyes are already on me. She gives a sad smile and signs, *I love you.*

My stomach flips, bringing my own smile to my lips. I nod to her though I don't dare return the gesture.

Turning back to the front of the courtroom, I watch Mr. Dressler stand to approach the unknown witness. She places her hand on their religious text, swearing to their God that she will not lie.

He asks, "Will you please state your name for the court?"

She nods slightly and looks past me into the spectator area. "Celeste Johnson."

My jaw drops, and I, along with half the courtroom, turn our heads to Benji. He tenses, his eyes stuck on the witness. When I turn back to his mother, she's staring at him as well, with tears in her eyes.

Mr. Dressler continues his questions. "You were a member of the group called 'The Anointed' for the first portion of your life. Is that correct?"

"Yes, that's correct."

"What were the circumstances under which you left?"

She shifts in her seat, her eyes scanning along the row of men accompanying me. "My husband at the time was very cruel and abusive. I suffered years of rape, ordained by our Prophet, bearing three children during my time there. There was one night that had me so terrified, I thought my husband might take my life. I was young, selfish, and scared. I ran, but I was gone no longer than six hours before I longed for my children. I feared for their safety, forcing me to return." Tears pour down her face as the judge hands her a box with napkins in it. She thanks him, drying her eyes to continue. "I was deemed possessed by the Devil. The Prophet ordered that I have the demons abolished with a ritual that involved being buried alive. I refused. I didn't want to be there, anyway."

She sniffles and wipes her nose. "They cast me out without my children, without food, or money. I was alone in a world I didn't know."

Mr. Dressler paces the floor, glancing at the jury. "You say you were raped by your husband..." He pushes his spectacles up his nose as he stops in front of Celeste. "How old were you the first time this occurred?"

"I was twelve."

Murmurs and gasps ripple across the courtroom.

"And the age of your former husband at the time of the first alleged rape?"

She sighs, looking down at her feet. "I don't remember exactly. Forty-two? Forty-three?"

"Is that man in this room?"

Glancing across the row of us again, as if needing to be certain, she says, "No, sir."

Mr. Dressler begins pacing in front of the witness stand. "And was it common for girls of such a young age to be married to a man that much older?"

She bites her lip. "Yes, it was the will of Zaaron. We called it being bound, but yes, it was a frequent occurrence. Once a girl began her period she was ready to have children."

He looks at the jury to make his next statement. "Did any of the other girls admit to being raped? Or were they happy to be following what they believed to be their righteous path?"

She rings her hands at her chest. "Y-yes, I mean, there were those who seemed content in their bindings, but there were many cases of sexual abuse on the compound. Not just of young wives. One situation still eats at my mind to this day. A friend of mine was bound to Josiah Fitch, the Prophet. She was distraught after finding him molesting one of his grandsons, who at the time was very young...around six or seven, I think. She was sick about it."

My blood goes cold as if thrust into a winter storm. I whip my head around to Zeke to find him looking at me with horrified eyes. It had to have been one of us. While my grandfather wasn't any kinder than my father, I don't remember anything like that. I swallow hard, turning back to Celeste.

"Was anyone else aware of this?"

"Not that I know of, sir. Just myself, my friend, and the Prophet."

Mr. Dressler's lips press in a hard line when he turns his back to her. "Is Josiah Fitch or your friend in this room?"

She gives the slightest shake of the head. "No, sir."

"Is there anyone who can back up these accusations? You said that they would not let you take your children. Are you not simply saying these things as a way to get back at your former family and church?

"N-no!" Her hands slam against the witness stand. "She wouldn't have lied about this! And neither would I."

Mr. Dressler raises his eyebrows at the jury before walking back to his seat. "No further questions, Your Honor."

The female lawyer stands and approaches Benji's mother. "Ms. Johnson, is it true that Josiah Fitch has multiple grandsons who are very close in age?"

"Yes, that's true."

"And do you know which of these boys was the victim of this sexual abuse?" Celeste looks to her hands, nodding. I think I'm going to be sick all over these ill-fitting trousers. "Can you tell the court his name?" the manly woman asks.

"Objection!" Mr. Dressler calls. "Hearsay."

The judge waves his hand. "Overruled." Turning to Celeste, he nods, "Answer the question, Ms. Johnson."

She closes her eyes for a moment before opening them again and looking out into the spectator area.

"Ezekiel Fitch."

2 months later...

I don't know how I'm going to survive in this place another eight months. It's been impossible to stop thinking of these people as heathens and Philistines. They are corrupt, vile, and uncivilized. Violence is in every dark corner of this place. The only thing that's kept me out of harm's way this far is keeping my head down and only speaking when spoken to. I obey the rules and blend into the background.

I've done my best to be compliant and cooperative with the authorities resulting in a deal of nine months. If I'm honest with myself, I got off easy. Over sixty children were taken away and put into the same child care system Laurel Ann was in. According to Zeke, most of the followers have fled, though there are those who returned to the compound after the investigation to be led by their 'Prophet', Jacob. I can't say I'm surprised. I know he was jealous that I was the first born. I always thought that odd. If anyone had a right to be jealous, it's Zeke. I beat him for first born son by only three months, where Jacob is two years behind us.

Any man with a bride younger than the age of sixteen got time in prison. By the end of the six-week trial, there were dozens of abuse charges. I was personally found guilty of child endangerment with assault and battery.

Since we so publicly found out about Zeke's history with my grandfather, he and I haven't had the chance to have a real conversation about it. I've talked to him on the phone, and he's visited once since then. While he seems a little different, it's not necessarily bad. He's clearly taken with Kaila as she seems to be all he talks about when we do get the chance.

Laurel Ann says her old house has been turned upside down. There was nowhere anyone knew to go, so Zeke, Benji, Samuel, Mia, and Kelsey Garret are all staying in their three-bedroom house until they all find other arrangements.

Marybeth was taken, along with the other children. I still feel guilty with how things happened with her and often hope she can find happiness.

I lie in my bunk, reading a book by someone named Edgar. It's about a man trapped in a cell and the torture he endures there. I can't help but relate to the man trying not to fall in the pit.

"Inmate!" I look up because my cell mate is in medical. "You have a visitor."

I put the book down, and stand. There was a large part of me hoping he wouldn't come. When he requested visitation, I was surprised. The last time we spoke, I made it clear I wanted nothing to do with him. He's clearly stubborn and doesn't give up easily. Zeke has met with him a few times and asked me to give him a chance, so I approved his visitation.

I follow the guard from my cell into a long hall. I look at the gun on his belt and wish that I could have one as a form of protection in this place. We had one rifle on the compound that the gate guard would use. When we were kids, one of my uncles was the guard on duty, and he shot the gun off once for me and Zeb. It was extremely loud. The bullet hit the ground several yards away, tossing up dirt and bits of grass. We were equally mesmerized and terrified by it. We both stood there staring where the bullet had hit, simultaneously saying, "Whoa."

The guard leads me into a room to search me. The first time this happened, I was not aware of how incredibly intricate their searches were. Luckily, the guard was ready for my reaction when his hand went to the last place I expected.

He stopped me before I hit him and added more time to my sentence.

Once I'm cleared, the guard leads me back down the hall and into another. I see Shayne through the glass while I'm led past the visitation room. Now that I've accepted the fact that it's not his fault who his father was, just as it isn't mine, I realize he looks strikingly like Ezekiel.

He stands to greet me, holding his hand out as I approach the table. "It means a lot that you agreed to see me."

I take his hand, not sure how to act around my illegitimate half-brother. "Well, Zeke has spoken highly of you, Mr. Hiland."

The air blows through his lips. "Come on, don't call me that. My professors call me that. Shayne is fine."

"Professors? You're still in school?"

I'll admit this interests me. In the Anointed Land, eighteen was the latest anyone studied their lessons, besides me, when I studied for sermons. Since being in here, I've heard about school for adults called 'college'. You can study to specialize in any field, much like the families in the Anointed Land, but instead, you get to choose.

"Yeah, I'm studying Psychology." I've never felt stupid before. My lack of knowledge about this world was never an issue until now. He must read my confusion because he says, "A doctor of the mind." He taps his temple. Leaning forward, he rests his forearms on the table. "That's actually one of the things I wanted to discuss with you." I feel guilt at the way his eyes turn downcast. I intimidate him, and there's no purpose for that anymore. "I don't have any other siblings, and as you know, I never knew my father. I want to get to know you, Ezekiel, and your friends. Many of them have expressed interest in furthering their education, and I would like to help anyway I can. There are programs…" Shaking his head to himself, he looks up at me, directly in the eyes. "I know what you said last time we met. I just didn't want to step on any toes or anything."

As he awaits my response, he shocks me when he quickly tugs on his ear lobe before he rubs his lower lip. It's a gesture my father often made.

While it may not be holy, we share the same blood. He's offering to help us navigate a place we were taught nothing of. Everything I've ever known was a lie, and he's showing the most kindness I've seen in this world. It would be foolish to turn away his olive branch.

"I must apologize for my reaction to your visit. I was going through a lot at that particular time and was still blind to reality." His lip quirks, making me realize how young he really is. There's an eagerness and innocence he possesses that suggests this life has yet to devastate him. "It would be an honor to get to know you, Shayne."

His smirk grows into a big grin as he lays his hands flat against the table. "Seriously?"

I laugh at his shock because he's definitely entitled to it.

"Of course. We're brothers."

33

OUR OWN WINGS

Laurel Ann

8 months later...

MY PALMS WON'T STOP SWEATING AS I LOOK AT THE PRISON gates. It's been over three months since I've seen Zebadiah. The drive from Hobart to McAlister is a long one, and it's hard to match up my work schedule with his visitations.

I tug on my shorts because I still feel so exposed. Kaila has been more than thrilled with my willingness to expand on my style preferences. I still struggle with changing my way of thinking and my anger at it all. Although I write and talk to Zeb on the phone all the time, I've needed him beside me. Kaila doesn't understand what it's like to get your faith stolen. Benji and Sammy seem to be more than thrilled with their freedom and have been wrapped up in their new handmade furniture business. I still don't really know how Zeke feels about it.

Kaila pushed me to name Jacob as my attacker, even crossing the line of telling Zeke. That made me furious. She had no right to do that. Fortunately, Zeke knows how to keep a secret and has kept his word to not tell Zeb.

At first, I never planned to tell Zebadiah, then I realized how unfair that was when he was honest with me about his own demons. I decided it was unfair to worry him while he was trapped in that place, and I convinced myself I'd wait. Now he's getting out, and I know I need to tell him.

"He'll think you look beautiful," Benji says as he leans against the hood of his car. "Stop being so nervous."

Rubbing my hand down my exposed arm, I admit, "I never dressed like this when I visited him. He's never seen me this way."

He grins. "After nine months away from you, I bet he'll be more than ready to get into those shorts."

I know he's playing around, but the fear that Zeb won't be able to touch me once he finds out burrows into my thoughts.

Sammy hits his arm and grimaces. *Gross, that's my sister.*

Benji snickers as he pushes his sunglasses up on his head and points behind us. "Finally, they're back. I'm parched."

Kaila and Zeke pull up behind us in Kaila's car. She gets out and skips over to me while Ezekiel has his hands full with sodas and burgers from Jay Henry's Barbeque.

"God! It's fucking hot! I really hoped he'd be out by the time we got back," she complains.

Benji and Samuel attack Ezekiel for their food, making quick work of the wrappers once they get back to the hood of Benji's car. Learning to drive was one of the first things Benji did after the raid.

Kaila wraps her arm around my shoulder. "What's wrong? You're finally getting to see your knight in an orange jumpsuit."

I roll my eyes. "That's not what he wore." She nudges

my shoulder as I look down at my clothes. "What if he hates them?"

Looping her arm through mine, she leads me to where Zeke has joined the other boys, inhaling their food.

"Then he's blind and stupid. Not only do I have impeccable fashion sense, but your legs are rockin' out those shorts."

She reaches out to stick a fry in her mouth as Zeke leans over, biting half of it off. Ezekiel has really changed since leaving the Anointed Land. At first, he really struggled. We were never close enough for him to feel comfortable talking to me, but Benji was the friend he needed when his brother couldn't be there. He hit it off with Kaila right away. They flirted shamelessly, though it wasn't until Kaila broke up with Brently, when he took the job in Houston that they acted upon it.

I try to eat a fry, and my stomach flips like the pages in a book. I still don't like this food.

Every time I've seen Zeb, it's been formal. We can't touch or kiss, and I spend the whole time catching him up on what everyone's doing while he assures me he's fine in that place. I hear all these scary stories about prison; I often wake up from nightmares, drenched in sweat.

I was a little upset with him when he chose to take the deal he did. He could have had three months with a year's probation. Ultimately, I understand why he wants to put this all behind him as quickly as possible.

Benji dips his fry in the sauce on Sammy's burger, which earns him a flirty glare. "I was thinking we could all get matching shirts for when we go to Disney World. That way if we get split up, we can easily find each other."

Kaila pokes a fry at his face. "Yeah, that's not happening. Stop reading mommy blogs."

She got both Benji and Samuel addicted to Disney movies, and when Benji found that there was a place dedicated to them, he shoved the laptop in all of our faces, telling us we had no choice in going. We just had to wait for Zeb to get released.

Sucking my soda through a straw, I look up to Ezekiel. His eyes widen, and he jumps off Benji's car. "Zeb!"

I spin around to see Zebadiah grinning at us through the gates. There is a beeping noise when the wire door slides open, allowing him to walk through. Once his feet hit the pavement of the street, mine break into a run, as if leading me to him before my mind can catch up.

Our bodies crash together and our mouths meet. He drops his bag as his hands slide over the denim on my butt, picking me up to wrap my legs around him. He breaks our kiss to move his eyes down my body.

"You look…"

I bite my lip, feeling my ears get hot. "I know it's revealing, but I promise it's what's normal here. Kaila says that—"

"You look fucking beautiful, Laur."

He kisses me again, keeping his lips against mine as he carries me to the others. They are all brimming, even Kaila.

"Brother," Zeke says. He makes his way toward us, and Zeb puts me down to embrace him in a hug.

"So, what now?" Zeb asks.

"Now, we party," Kaila answers, holding up her soda.

Zeb's left eyebrow raises in a mix of humor and horror as he listens to Kaila and Zeke sing their tone-deaf duet.

Keeping his bewildered expression on them, he leans over to whisper in my ear, "What on earth are they singing?"

His hand grips my thigh at the sensation of the car rolling to stop at a light. I know the bus that took him to prison freaked him out a bit, and this is the first time he's been in a vehicle since then.

"Cardi B."

"I don't think I like Cardaby music."

I laugh and kiss his cheek. "I don't either."

The drive back is long, so to get his mind off the car, I suggest, "Hey, let's play the alphabet game."

Zeke turns down the music. "Okay." He points to a highway sign. "Aydelotte, 210 miles, *A*."

The game seems to do the trick because by the time we get to *L*, Zeb's hand subtly begins to creep up my leg. Goosebumps rise along my skin while he traces his fingers over my thigh. My heart knows he's touching me because it beats twice as hard.

There have been nights when the thought of his kiss, the desire for his touch, and the need to have him with me have been too much. The ache between my legs would become so maddening, I would find my fingers roaming, rubbing my most sacred place. I would close my eyes and will my memory to hurl me back into his arms. My fingers would become his, then when the pleasure came to its peak and shattered every cell of my body, I would cry because he was never there when I opened my eyes.

His fingertips caress the hem of my shorts before sliding beneath them. I look up at him, and he's already watching me. His blue eyes blaze as they explore my exposed body. He licks his lips, his nostrils flaring the moment he lightly touches the fabric of my panties. I find my gaze traveling to his lap where his erection is evident in his trousers. I fight my nearly twitching hand to reach out and touch it. I will tell him about Jacob, but I want it to be when we're alone. For the moment, I'm just going to revel in being able to be next to him again.

My breath comes out shaky as Kaila says, "Weatherford,

40 miles, *W*. We're kicking yawl's asses." I suddenly realize that we're in the car with other people. She looks in the rear-view mirror. "Are you okay, Laur? You look flushed."

My ears burn and my laugh is awkward. "Oh yes." Embarrassed that I let him touch me this close to them has me taking his hand from my shorts and lacing my fingers between his. "I'm just ready to be home." I look at him, moving my eyes to the front seat to convey why I stopped him. His smirk has me pushing my legs together.

The last thirty minutes are painful, and the bulge in Zebadiah's pants has yet to go down. When we pass the Hobart city sign, he sighs a relieved breath and tightens his hold on my hand. The car has barely stopped in our driveway when he pushes open the door, pulling me from the seat hard enough to snap my head back. Zeke and Kaila open the trunk as Zeb leads me to the door.

"Uh, you gonna help with the luggage?" Zeke calls after us.

I pull out my house key and Zeb calls over his shoulder, "Just leave it in the living room. I'll get it later."

Zeke scoffs as I unlock the door. "I'm not your Apostle anymore, so you better get used to doing stuff for yourself."

Ignoring him, he leads me into the house, seemingly on a mission until he stops at the staircase.

"Where's your room?" he asks in an almost exasperated tone.

While I'm eager, too, his desperation to get me alone has me nervous. I bite my lip and take him up the loudly creaking stairs to my room at the end of the hall. I turn on the light, shutting the door behind us. Taking a deep breath, I turn around, and he instantly brings his arms around me, hugging me tight until he picks me up, allowing my legs to wrap around him.

"I missed you terribly," I whisper.

His lips trail kisses up my neck as he carries me to my bed. Laying me down, he digs his nose in my hair, inhaling before he murmurs, "You were how I made it through in there, Laur. I would count down the hours to lights out so I could finally close my eyes and be with you."

I hold his face in my hands and trace my fingers over his shut lids. "You don't have to close your eyes anymore."

Wrapping my arms around his neck, I put my lips softly to his. Now that I have him alone, I should tell him. I know I should, but as I try to force out the words, they get stuck before they can fall off my tongue. I want him to be the last person to fill my body, and if I tell him, it may not happen. I've dreamed and ached for this. I need to feel him one more time.

He devours my kiss, pushing up my shirt, and I let out a harsh breath when he lifts it over my head. His Adam's apple bobs with his swallow as he looks at me in my tan, lace bra.

"Wow…" He lightly touches over the fabric, running his fingers beneath the strap. "I like this."

Soft kisses are placed along the faint scar from the night we exchanged our blood. Inhaling deeply, my chest rises when his thumb slides beneath the lace of my bra, rubbing over my hardened nipple. Not bothering to remove the lingerie, he tugs the cups down, baring my breasts to him. I want his mouth on me so badly, I find myself arching my back to get closer to his lips.

He's wearing an amused expression as his tongue darts out and traces around my nipple. When he sucks the nub in between his lips, I whimper, grasping at the back of his neck. I need to feel his skin against mine. Moving my hands down his back, I push up his shirt. He leans back to pull it off, and I lick my lips watching the cluster of muscles on his stomach flex. His arms are large as they rise above his head. I undo my bra, leaving nothing between us when he kisses me hard.

Trailing down my ribs, his fingers find the button on my shorts, undoing them before he pushes them down and off my legs. He touches over the fabric of my panties as a shaky breath releases from his lips. I have a pang of fear that this will hurt. I've felt nothing more than my finger since what happened between me and Jacob. It doesn't matter. The pain will be worth it, to feel that close to him again.

"Your pretty undergarments are wet."

Flushing from embarrassment, I push my palms against his shoulders to roll him on his back, and he allows me. I lift my leg over his hip, feeling his hardness beneath his pants. I kiss his stomach, placing my mouth to his scar like he did mine. His muscles rise beneath my lips as I make my way back up to his mouth, rocking against him.

I want to show him how much I desire him and love him. My heart tells me to not be scared. He will love me regardless of what happened. Yet my mind wonders how he could ever see me the same way.

He looks between my open legs and grabs my hips, moving me up his torso. I let out a squeal when he puts his arms beneath my thighs, scooting himself beneath me until the lace of my panties touches his lips. As far as I know, the rips and tears are all healed, so I try to slow my heart with the knowledge he shouldn't be able to tell.

My pulse pounds at his close proximity, and I moan when he tugs the fabric to the side. I look down at him as his tongue traces my wet entrance.

"If anything is Godly, it's this." Even with knowing it's not blasphemous, his comment is still shocking, turning my ears red. I'm embarrassed by the giggle that falls from my mouth. He lifts me by pushing up my ass, allowing his fingers to make their way inside me. He moans against me, the vibrations of his lips pushing a whimper from mine. I lift my body on and off his fingers while his tongue licks around them. "Does it still hurt?" My stomach drops until he adds, "Where they closed you?"

He gently touches over the area that was damaged, and I shake my head. "No."

"I'm sorry, Laur. I can't believe I let that happen," he whispers between licks. He softly presses his lips to my clit, kissing it gently. "I should have never left you. Do you forgive me?"

His tongue has perfect pressure as he pushes it against my clit in fast pulses, his fingers pumping in and out of me so fast I hear the evidence of my wetness.

"Forgiveness is…" I moan out my response and reach down to grip his hair. "Unnecessary. I never blamed you for that."

Gasping, I hang on to the headboard as I thrust against his mouth and tingles overtake my body. The tightness builds until it can no longer hold it, and still, he goes faster.

"Zeb! Oh, yes, keep going." Tears fall down my face from the elation of finally being with him again. I burn with euphoria, murmuring his name, bursting from the inside out. It feels like it lasts forever until slowly, I lower from my high. I sigh as I move myself down his body to sit on his stomach and kiss his wet, grinning mouth.

He fists my hair while his other hand goes behind my ass to undo his trousers. I'm nearly panting with the need for him to be inside me. Our mouths refuse to separate as I pull off my modern undergarment and he kicks off his.

His hands spread my ass cheeks to lift me, and I feel the tip of his cock poking against my sensitive entrance.

He smiles and his body jerks. I'm instantly stretched full, and I moan, digging my nails into his shoulders as I rock myself to adjust. It doesn't hurt, but I'm stretched so tight, he has to thrust a few times to get all the way in.

Having a man inside my body again flips a switch in my mind. Memories of Jacob flash behind my eyes, and my chest constricts in fear, my body reminiscing the pain. The hate on his face, the excruciating desire to die…

Burn in the abyss, Philistine bitch.

Terror overtakes me, bringing me back to the moment when I knew nobody was going to save me.

I can't scream.

I can't breathe.

I'm sobbing before I realize the tears are falling.

"Laurel Ann…" He wipes his hands across my cheeks, and when I open my eyes, his bright, baby blues bring me back to him. "What's wrong?"

He's not thrusting hard, just little pumps, and I caress his cheek. I can't wait. I have to tell him. He deserves to know.

"Zeb…" This is so hard to say. I've never had to repeat this before, and telling him puts my heart at stake. "I have to tell you something."

He stops moving while I slowly rock on top of him. I wish I could feel this with him forever. The pleasure mixed with my fear and anxiety forces tears to trace down my cheeks.

"You can tell me anything, Laur."

I can't stop my sob. "I hope so."

He sits up to hold my face, brushing my hair back. "What's going on?"

Sliding my body up and down his, I don't look at him. "D-during the raid…" I ride him faster, and I don't know if it's to make this easier on him or me. "Jacob came into the holding room." Rolling my hips, I squeeze his hard biceps and finally raise my eyes to the fury already burning in his. He lies still, aside from his chest rising and falling at a rapid pace. I don't need to say it. I'm sure he already knows from the ticking in his jaw, and I break. "I'm so, sorry." I fall against his chest, crying harder when he wraps his arms around me. "I tried to stop him, I swear."

Since I'm shaking with my sobs, it takes me a minute to realize he's shaking, too. His arms are squeezing me tight, and another flood gushes from my eyes. Now that I've said it, I can't seem to stop crying.

He doesn't say a word. He just holds me as our bodies remain connected. Finally, I lift my head to look at him. His cheeks and eyes are wet with tears, but his jaw is clenched, and a vein is straining in his neck. "I'm going to kill him," he whispers. "I'm going to cut him open, throat to stomach and leave his intestines to fertilize the earth." His face goes blank for a second before the blue in his eyes goes dark. "You were still closed during the raid."

I can't seem to get enough air to speak, so I nod. He grabs my arms to lift me off of him, making what he just said really sink in.

"No!" I scream as I use all my strength to push him back down. "Don't leave me. Don't ever leave me again."

He pulls me to his chest, wrapping his arms around me and rubbing the healed soul cleansing scars on my back. "Shhh. I won't leave, I promise."

His words calm me as I murmur against his chest. "I don't want you to kill him. There are eyes on the compound, and if you got caught, I'd never see you again." I take a deep breath and press my hands against his chest to push myself up. Rolling my hips again, I push him deeper into me. "Don't let him or that place take anymore from us, please. I want to move on with you and Kaila, Sammy, Benji, and Zeke. I want to start fresh. Promise me."

His expression sways between fury and contemplation until finally he leans forward to kiss me. "I promise," he says against my lips. His body moves inside mine before he flips me over to my back, pushing in hard.

As my fingers trace over his eyes and cheeks, he smiles a sad smile. For the first time, we can truly be together. "I love you, Zebadiah Fitch."

He presses his forehead to mine. "I love you, Laurel Ann Henderson. And I always will."

"Quit being a baby, let us see. We have a plane to catch," Kaila spouts as she smokes her cigarette.

Ezekiel laughs when Zeb walks down the stairs, yet my breath gets caught in my throat at his reveal.

"I look ridiculous," he grimaces.

I have to disagree. Those jeans are hanging low on his hips, and that tee shirt is hugging him everywhere it needs to be.

"Uh, no. You look hot," Kaila says, and Zeke gives her a shocked look that makes me giggle.

"Do you have anything else?" Zeb says as he tugs on the waistband of his jeans. "They're heavy."

I walk up to him and hug his waist. Our bodies never separated once last night. We tasted every inch of each other and drank one another's tears. Whispers of 'I love you' and 'I'll always stay' filled the moments of silence. I feel ashamed that I ever doubted him.

I lick my lips as I stand on the tips of my toes to kiss him. Seeing him like this is making me tingly all over.

"Kaila's right." My cheeks burn, and I can't make myself look at him when I say, "you look hot."

He smiles so big I think he's going to laugh. Benji comes

out of the kitchen and whistles. "Look at you, Zeb." He claps his hands and pulls on his backpack. "Mia and Kelsey are meeting us at the airport in an hour and a half." He leans over and kisses Sammy who's checking boarding times on his phone. "You got the salt and vinegar chips, right?"

Samuel deadpans and signs, *And the Monsters, beef jerky, and pork rinds.*

"Nice." Benji pulls out his phone and taps on the screen. "Okay, the airport is an hour away. Make sure you go to the bathroom now." Grabbing Sammy's hand, he pulls him to his feet as he nods to me and Zeb. "You guys are riding with Zeke and Kaila. The luggage is packed in my car."

As we double check that we have everything, Zeb anxiously zips up the backpack I got for him.

I lean my head against his arm. "What's wrong?"

"I'm just kind of scared to get on the plane." He gives me a nervous chuckle to lighten his statement.

"For the most part, it almost feels like you're standing still." I grab his hand. "I was scared the first time too."

"If we were meant to fly, we'd have wings."

He says it almost to himself, making my chest ache. I know he's still struggling with his faith. Kissing the side of his mouth, I whisper against his skin, "Now, we have the power to give wings to ourselves."

"Laurel Ann!" Mia calls across the terminal. She runs up to us with Kelsey hurrying behind her. She slams into me, squeezing my neck.

"You look amazing!"

She's nearly about to combust with joy, and seeing her

happy like this makes me laugh. I hold her at arm's length. She's wearing a sleeveless, blue sundress that goes to her thighs, with copper jeweled sandals. I haven't seen her in months because she and Kelsey moved to Oklahoma City to go to school.

Things weren't easy with us at first. She stayed with me, but was still angry with me about Zeb, and as a continuation, put the blame on me for Marybeth getting taken away. Eventually, she and Kelsey were able to really explore their relationship, and Zebadiah no longer seemed that important to her. She found Marybeth and keeps in touch. She apologized for blaming me and admitted her struggle with learning of the notebooks as well.

"You are beautiful, Mia."

Everyone hugs them, excited in their greeting, though Zeb and Mia are a little awkward and settle on a handshake.

We board the plane, sliding between the aisles to our seats. Zeb is fine until we start moving down the runway. As we lift in the air, he squeezes my hand and holds his breath.

"I promise, it'll be fine. Just let it get in the air."

Even though he nods, my fingers feel close to breaking with how hard he's grasping them.

Benji however, looks like he's having the ride of his life.

Once we get in the air and straightened, Zeb finally relaxes, looking through the magazine on the back of the chair in front of him. His jaw drops as he flips through the pages.

"I have no idea what any of this is."

"I know. You'll get there. It took all of us some time to feel acclimated."

Instead of the magazine, we look out the window, reveling in the majesty of being in the clouds.

"Zeb?" He pulls his gaze from the window with a raised brow. "Are you scared to live without a God?"

He sighs as he leans back in his chair. "My cellmate was a religious man. He believed in a very different God than Zaaron. He told me that there are many ways to have faith. I don't know if there's a God, Laur, but I'd like to think there's something."

His words comfort me as I lean over to kiss him. "Maybe we'll find the answers in this life, maybe we won't. I just know I want to do it with you."

He laces his fingers with mine, looking at me while he rests his head against the airplane seat.

"Maybe faith in each other is all we need."

Five hours later we get off of the plane in Florida. We take a bus to the hotel to drop off our things. I barely get to explore mine and Zeb's room before Kaila starts pounding on the door.

"Laur! Come on! We're taking a detour with Mia and Kelsey. I need my girl time. These boys are driving me nuts."

Zeb kisses me, laughing against my lips. "Have fun, we'll meet up later."

I open the door only to get pulled into the hallway by Kaila. She's skips to the elevator, swinging a large purse in her hand. We walk out to the lobby to be waved over by Mia and Kelsey. I follow them all out to the taxi cab waiting at the front of the hotel.

"Where are we going?" I ask Kaila once we get outside.

"Surprise."

I roll my eyes and climb into the cab after her. I'm finally accustomed to riding in a car, though it took me a while. As we pull onto a highway, Kaila asks Mia about life in Oklahoma

City. That's all it takes for her and Kelsey to ramble on about school, work, and their friends.

We stop for froyo, and soon we're pulling in front of a building that almost looks like a house. We walk inside to find a woman in a suit smiling at us.

"Welcome!" She holds out her arms and gestures for us to follow her. "Right this way. My name is Riley Orchid." We walk behind rows of chairs lined up facing a stage, and she leads us to a room with an open door. "I'll be outside, in back, if you need me."

"Thanks, Riley." Kaila hands her a piece of paper before placing her bag on the table. Digging inside, she pulls out a white, folded stack of lace. When she drops it open, my skin burns hot.

It's a dress.

"Put it on," she urges.

My stomach flips as a thought flutters across my mind that I can't allow myself to think, much less hope for. I unbutton my romper and drop it to the floor before sliding the white dress over my head. While there are no sleeves, the straps are thick and the neckline is modest. The fabric beneath lands at my thighs, and the top layer of lace falls to my shin. I look up to see Mia grinning at me, holding out a crown made of white and yellow flowers. Mia sets a pair of white heels on the ground, and I slip my feet inside. I still can't make myself say anything.

"Time to go." Kaila opens the door.

I follow them back into the main room. We walk along the side of the chairs to another door, and when Kaila opens it, the sun shines bright as we go outside. There are chairs set up out here too, and once my eyes reach the front, a laugh escapes, and my eyes fill with tears.

Zebadiah stands inside of a gazebo, wearing a suit and

looking more handsome than I've ever seen him. Zeke, Benji, Sammy, and Riley are all standing with him, grinning at me. Music plays while we walk to them. I notice a man sitting in the chairs, but I'm simply too overwhelmed to focus on him. When we arrive at the gazebo, Kaila, Mia, and Kelsey move to the side.

I laugh again, and Zeb takes my hands with a smirk. "Hi."

"Hi," I choke out.

He presses his forehead against mine and whispers, "Will you be my one and only wife?"

The tears freely pour down my cheeks. I hug him tightly against me. I can't speak, so I nod profusely against his shoulder.

We stand in front of Riley as she says, "I understand you have your own vows?"

Zeb nods, and I panic. I am in no way prepared for this. Riley gestures behind us to the man sitting in the chairs. He steps into the gazebo, reaching for what looks like a pen, but it's plugged into an outlet. When he gets closer, I recognize it as a wood burner from taking woodshop in high school. Zebadiah holds out his hand, and the man takes the finger next to his pinky. He grits his teeth while the man puts the contraption against his finger, groaning as his skin sizzles. The man burns a line all the way around, making a complete circle.

I feel light at the symbolism this represents. We don't know what we believe anymore, and until we figure it out, we are going to do what feels right. Burning our earthly bodies with the sigil of our love...that definitely feels right.

"I can't promise wealth or that things won't ever be hard, but I vow that I will always love you. I will always be faithful to you and will stand by you no matter what struggles we endure. I will do everything I can to make you happy for the rest of this life and the next." He smiles at me, and his voice is a shaky. "Not even in death will we part."

Laughing with my cry, I hold out my hand. The man burns my promise into my finger while I look at the only boy I've ever loved. I say what feels important to promise to him.

"I will always be honest, and I will always support you. I vow to be an honorable wife, and I will never stop loving you...only you. I long to spend the rest of my life with you and whatever comes after." I take in my friends, our freedom, and smile as my heart patters in my chest. "Not even in death will we part."

The End

Anointed
PLAYLIST

1. Miracle—The Score
2. Way Down We Go—Kaleo
3. Glitter & Gold—Barns Courtney
4. Blackbird Song—Lee DeWyze
5. Heaven—Troye Sivan feat. Betty Who
6. Bartholomew—The Silent Comedy
7. Lovely—Billie Eilish
8. Blood//Water—Grandson
9. Hellfire—Barns Courtney
10. Lead Me Home—Jamie N. Commons
11. I Walk the Line—Halsey
12. Hurt—Johnny Cash
13. Demons—Imagine Dragons
14. Losing My Religion—R.E.M.
15. Human—Rag 'n' Bone Man
16. Broken Bones—Kaleo
17. Believe—Mumford & Sons
18. Burn Fast—Bryce Fox

HELP LINES AND WEBSITES

www.encourage-cult-survivors.org

www.cult-escape.com/help

www.catalystcounselling.org.uk/about-catalyst.html

www.familiesagainstcultteachings.org/Support

Acknowledgements

I want thank my readers and fans in the *Broken Babydolls*. You guys always put a smile on my face and have accepted my weirdness with open arms. You support me on a daily basis. Those of you who have shared my books and posted your reviews have helped me in my success so much more than you realize. This is a hard business sometimes, but you guys are always there to remind me why I do this.

Kim BookJunkie, I am beyond grateful for everything you have done for me and this book. It would not be what it is without you. Your touch made it the best it could be. You were such an important part of this project and your enthusiasm just added to my excitement. You have really helped me with my confidence, and I am lucky to call you a friend. I am so happy that we have come into each other's lives.

Maureen and Kathi from the *Maureen and Kathi Read Blog* and *The Dark Angels*. You guys have not only been an amazing support system and a huge help when I was completely lost, but you have also been incredible friends. You have been there for me, promoted me, given me the honesty I needed to make this book the best it could be, and so much more. I would not be where I am without you guys. Thank you for everything you have done for me.

Synclare Moss at *Wickedly Sweet and Synful Book Blog*. You were one of my first fans and have made me laugh and smile every step of the way. You have been not only an incredible support but an amazing friend. You are such a wonderful person and I grateful to have you in my life.

Ann R. Jones, Anja Scheidhauer, and Tricia Buttram at *Dirty Little Secret Book Blog*. Oh my gosh, talk about a hilarious group of women! It's impossible not to be laughing when you guys are involved. You have not only supported me and my books every step of the way, but you have been great friends. I am so grateful that I met you!

My PA Elaine Kelly. Thank you for giving me a chance and sticking by me when I had no idea what I was doing. Thank you for reading for me, promoting for me, and being there for me. I truly appreciate all that you do.

To my Beta readers, Kim BookJunkie, Robin Craig, Kween Corie, Katrina Rains, and T.L. Martin. You guys do not have an easy job, but I appreciate all your help. You guys are an incredible support system and amazing friends. This story wouldn't be what it is without you.

All the authors that have given me support, done guest spots, allowed me in their groups, and promoted me. I am so lucky to have incredible women like you in my corner. I love that we can bring each other up instead of compete against each other—there is something amazing in that. The only reason I don't list you by name is the fear of leaving someone out. There are just so many of you, and you know who you are.

To my editor, Joanne La Re Thompson. Thank you for all your help in everything, not just edits. You were one of the first people to really help me out, and I will never forget that. You not only help my stories look pretty, but you give me guidance and are a huge support for me. These books are possible in part, because of you.

Jay Aheer from Simply Defined Art. Thank you for your unicorn magic and making this cover more stunning and perfect than I could have ever dreamed.

Stacey Blake from Champagne formats. Your work never ceases to amaze me. It is truly beautiful, and I am so grateful to you for making my books so beautiful!

Megan Gunter from Mischievous Designs, your teasers are incredible. Thank you for all the help you've given me and the impeccable work you've done.

All the blogs that have shared my books, reviewed, or promoted me. I know there are a lot of books out there, so it means a lot when you choose mine. Thank you.

Last, but not least, thank you to my husband for supporting me in following my dream. None of this would have happened without you.

Books by
CHARITY B.

Anointed

The Sweet Treats Trilogy

Candy Coated Chaos

Sweetened Suffering

Cupcakes and Crooked Spoons

About the Author

Charity B. lives in Wichita Kansas with her husband and ornery little boy. The Sweet Treats Trilogy was her debut series and she is constantly preparing for her next release. She has always loved to read and write, but began her love affair with dark romance when she read C.J. Robert's The Dark Duet. She has a passion for the disturbing and sexy and wants nothing more than to give her readers the ultimate book hangover. In her spare time when she's not chasing her son, she enjoys reading, the occasional TV show binge, and is deeply inspired by music.